A Djinn and Tonic

A Novel of the Magical Underground

Book Two

Nan Sampson

Many thanks to my family, my dear friends in the Hive, the amazing folks of the ATA, and most especially, Conscious Cup Coffee Roasters in Crystal Lake for enormous support and many cups of excellent tea and coffee. Without all of these, this book would never have been finished. Oh, and also a huge debt of gratitude to "his nibs", who has been and always will be, my Muse.

ONE

31 December 1922
Rue de Belleville, 19th Arrondissement, Paris

C eleste Marie Bérenger, witch and troublemaker at large, stood in the small kitchen of the apartment behind the apothecary shop she and her life partner Tolly ran and wished ovens came with windows. Most of the New Year's Eve guests had arrived, and the canapés weren't ready. Or rather, they still had three more minutes to go on her egg timer. Whether they were done remained to be seen, since ovens did not come with windows.

She bit her lip, hand on the door handle, and recalled the first rule of baking was not to open the oven to peek inside. Well, no, the first rule was to measure your ingredients precisely, but not peeking and letting the heat out had to be right up there.

She peeked. She'd never been good at following rules.

"Celie, people are hungry." Celeste's partner in business, magic, and life, Astrid Tollefsen, breezed in, a frown marring her elegant, Nordic features.

Celeste straightened, grabbed an oven mitt, and pulled a tray of puff pastry salmon pinwheels from the oven just in time. Golden brown, but another minute and they'd have over-baked.

"Perfect." She handed the love of her life a spatula and pointed to a doily-covered plate. "First batch is done and ready to be served. Oh, and the pâté de foie gras is on the table with the sliced baguette."

Tolly, a nickname Celeste had used for her partner since their second date, arched a thin, sculpted eyebrow. Celeste batted her eyelashes. "That is, if you wouldn't mind taking them out to the guests. You're a lovelier hostess than I could ever be."

"You are an appalling bootlicker, my dove. You have no skill at it." Although Tolly huffed a breath, the drama was all show. "Fine. I will serve our guests the pinwheels." She plated the hors d'oeuvres with a garnish of parsley and carried the platter out with a swish of lilac satin skirts.

Celeste pulled the tray of shrimp from the icebox, whisked the cocktail sauce a final time, and after popping a batch of cheese puffs into the oven, followed Tolly into their living quarters.

Located on the street that divided the Magical Quarter from the mundane world, the shop received traffic from both sides. The mundanes, of course, didn't realize the Magical Quarter even existed. Mortals saw another run-down neighborhood, where gas lamps still lit the streets and automobiles were as rare as unicorns. Not that ordinary humans could properly see a unicorn, since their natural camouflage made them look like ordinary horses.

The crowd, if five guests constituted one, sat chatting in the cozy sitting room. Alistair, Tolly's son and high priest of the coven to which she and Tolly belonged, sat next to his wife on the settee. A month past, he'd received a promotion from the Witch's Council and had been elected as leader of all the covens in Paris, a heavy and contentious job in itself, but more, he now sat on the Conseil d'arrondissment for the 19th, and therefore de facto representative for the neighborhood the Magic Quarter comprised. Heady responsibilities, but she liked and respected the man, despite him being a 'person of authority,' and had faith in his ability to speak for the entire magical community.

His wife, Isabeau, however, was a supercilious, frigid busybody. She sat with hands folded in her lap, speaking to no one but her husband. She'd even refused a cocktail. Her high-collared dress, fashionable perhaps fifty years ago, probably prevented her from swallowing, and Celeste wondered how often poor Alistair got any.

In her head, she heard Tolly's voice through the mental link they shared. *Celie! You've not the slightest clue what goes on in their bed. Nor have you the right to wonder.*

Bah. Isabeau never offered Celeste a gram of respect. She would not feel guilty about withholding hers, though, in fairness, the woman grew up mundane and Catholic. She'd come to her powers later in life. As a result, she vehemently disapproved of Celeste and Tolly's relationship, an arrangement quite common in the magical world, and although she kept her opinions to herself, the sentiment frequently writ itself large on her naturally sour face and in her behavior toward Celeste. To Tolly, of course, Isabeau remained fastidiously polite—Tolly was her mother-in-law, after all—but she did little to disguise her disapproval of Celeste.

Celeste set the tray of shrimp on their tea cart and made her way to the 'bar,' a narrow table usually used to hold decanters of cognac and port. Eddie, one of their two gargoyle friends, had agreed to act as bartender. He leered, grinning, as she approached.

"Lookin' good tonight, doll. Nice gams." He directed his gaze at her exposed knees. She wore a new party dress designed by Coco Chanel; likely the most daring outfit Celeste had ever worn. It was part of a collection the couturiere created for her in exchange for a potion Tolly provided to prevent conception.

Celeste blushed at the gargoyle's compliment but enjoyed it, nonetheless. Eddie acted like a womanizer and reveled in smoking and gambling, but he had an enormous heart. A heart that currently belonged to the young mortal woman named Eugenie, who stood near the fire in animated conversation with Byron and Martin. "What can I make you?"

"I'd kiss you for a Sidecar."

Eddie's grin broadened. "I'll hold you to that. You really shouldn't make deals with one of the Fallen. We always collect."

He mixed her drink, and when he handed it to her, she bussed his cheek. "And I always pay my debts."

A voice in her ear startled her, soft and seductive. "Speaking of debts, I'm still waiting to collect on mine, my sweet." Hands went round her waist, icy despite him having warmed them by the fire for the last twenty minutes.

She divested herself of those cold hands and turned to face her best friend in the world besides Tolly. "You'll get yours, George."

Lord George Gordon Byron, sixth baron of his line, and the best poet of this or any other century, plucked up her hand and smelled her wrist as though it was a fine bottle of Pouilly-fuisee. His breath tickled her skin. "I'd better," he purred.

If he'd been another vampire, the action might have felt threatening, but she'd known Byron since she'd tutored him as a ten-year-old mortal boy. While it was never safe to forget what he now was, she also knew who he had been, and he'd proved himself trustworthy several times over during the last few months. He posed no danger to her.

She felt Tolly prickle. Celeste trusted her oldest, dearest, and now undead friend, but Tolly didn't. That her partner had allowed the vampire in her home indicated she might be softening, but if Byron continued to behave in a predatory fashion, Tolly wouldn't tolerate him for long, act or no.

"Better watch yourself. Martin will get jealous." She glanced toward the other gargoyle present, who regarded her with deep blue-eyed disdain. Like Isabeau, he was not one of her admirers.

"I can handle him. Besides, you are such a delectable morsel."

She gave him a playful punch on the arm. "Bah. You know you have eyes for no one these days except your fallen angel."

Byron's gaze softened when Martin, realizing the vampire was looking his way, flashed him a devastating smile. "How could I? Just look at him."

Eddie, still standing nearby, groaned. "Keep that up and he'll be even more impossible to live with."

Celeste nodded. "You're so smitten, it's revolting."

"Indeed." He exchanged another smoldering gaze with Martin. "Meanwhile, we were talking about payment for the Christmas gift that I finagled for old Pinch Face. Acquiring those seats required a degree of..." He searched for a word. "Infernal influence."

She put her hands over her ears. "I don't want to know." Tolly had been thrilled. Saint-Saëns was her one of her favorite performers and there was no way Celeste could have afforded the tickets her own.

"Then I shan't tell you. The point, my sweet, is the debt you still owe. I have business in town tomorrow. Business best handled during daylight hours. May I suggest we retire to the kitchen for a few moments? I'll have my little taste, then we can return to the party."

Witch's blood gave vampires special abilities, like being able to tolerate sunlight, one reason the Council of Witches forbade bloodsuckers to partake of it. But Byron was her friend first. She knew how much the feel of the sun's warmth on his skin meant to him. So, they had an arrangement.

She glanced at the clock. Three hours to midnight. Time to examine the next batch of cheese puffs. "Fine. Come along then but be quick. Tolly can't know. And afterwards, I'm putting you to work in the kitchen."

"I am not a scullery maid."

"If you want your little cocktail, you are."

Turning her back on the poet, knowing he would follow, she hurried to rescue her hors d'oeuvres.

The ormolu clock on the mantle chimed ten, the hors d'oeuvres had been a hit, the shrimp gobbled up, and Martin had just opened one of the bottles of expensive champagne he'd brought. Celeste sat on the floor at Tolly's feet, laughing as Eddie entertained the crowd with a routine that should have played on the vaudeville circuit. Over the sounds of whoops and appreciative groans, Celeste barely heard the knocking on the door.

Byron had sharper ears. He jerked a thumb toward the hall and raised his eyebrows, silently asking, "Expecting someone?"

She scrambled to her feet, careful to make sure she didn't flash anyone in her shorter-than-usual skirt, and hurried to the entryway, sensing Father Dom on the other side of the door. "Father! So good of you to come!" She gestured him inside and was just about to close the door when another figure pushed his way across the threshold.

Before she could react, Magister Corverus gripped her by the shoulders and kissed her on both cheeks. "My dearest Celeste. Allow me to wish you season's greetings. Father Dominick and I walked over from the rectory together. I was telling him that my invitation to tonight's festivities must have been misplaced by the Bureau de Poste. Since the war, the government has become quite lax about such services."

Corverus, the blackmailing bastard. The sight of him soured her mood and a jittery panic arose in her stomach. Earlier in the fall, while she'd been investigating Eddie's kidnapping, he'd discovered that she'd violated a creature's free will, one of the Council of Witch's most important strictures. The creature in question had been his beady-eyed crow familiar, Crowley.

He'd given her an ultimatum. Either she joined with him during the Great Rite at Beltane, the celebration of the mating of the God and Goddess, and the occasion during which the Council arranged the merging of promising witching bloodlines, or he'd report her to the powers that be. Usually, the matings were consensual, but sometimes leaders stepped in. She was already on shaky ground with the witching community's ruling body. Another strike against her could mean a death sentence, and he knew it.

He took in her bare legs and the way her satin dress hugged her curves the way Celeste salivated over one of Madame Zofia's cream-filled profiteroles. "You look ravishing tonight."

The gall of the man. His appearance at her door and his lewd behavior left her unusually speechless. Father Dominick, bless his Irish heart, came to her rescue. "I hope I'm not too late. I had to wait until after Mass." The plump, tonsured, cassock-garbed fellow gave her an apologetic smile. Whether he apologized for his lateness or for the unwelcome guest that had turned up with him, she was unsure.

"It's quite all right, Father, we're just getting started."

His blue eyes twinkled. As the parish priest at Saint-Denys, it was his unofficial job to look after Eddie and Martin, who decorated the church in their stone gargoyle form during the daylight hours. Despite having spent over a quarter of a century in Paris, he still spoke French with a soft brogue. "I brought this to enliven the festivities." He handed her a bottle of something that bore no label. "It's an old family recipe for heather wine. A bit on the potent side but guaranteed to warm the cockles of your heart on a night like this, if you take my meaning."

Studiously ignoring Corverus, she took the priest's overcoat, covered with a smattering of snowflakes, and hung it on the hall tree. "Thank you, Father. Go on in and make sure you nab some cheese puffs before Eddie eats them all. I'll join you in a moment and we can toast the season with your gift."

He left her quickly, probably just as eager as she was to get away from Corverus.

The moment the priest passed through into the sitting room,

Corverus caught her in an embrace. This time, the kiss was on the lips and involved a disgusting amount of spit and tongue.

She kneed him in the crotch.

With an oof, he staggered back and bent over, wheezing.

"Celie? Who—" Tolly entered the front hall and abruptly halted. "You." Her tone should have caused the melting snow on Father Dom's coat to freeze again. "I'm sorry, Magister, but this is a private gathering."

He straightened, wheezing. "But surely I am invited, given my relationship to Celeste."

Tolly brushed past Celeste and opened the door, letting in a flurry of snowflakes. "You are not. We wish you a bonne année, monsieur."

Celeste's lips curled in a fierce smile. Tolly to the rescue. Goddess, what a woman she had chosen to share her life with. Even Corverus should know better than to go toe to toe with her.

He didn't. He sneered at Tolly before shifting his gaze to the figure who had just joined them. Celeste didn't need to look to know Byron had slipped into the foyer in that silent way of his kind.

"But *he* is welcome here? A vampire? Does the Council know you are entertaining excrement like this in your home?"

Byron stepped forward. "As you well know, I have special standing with this coven. Now I believe the ladies have asked you, much more politely than I would have, to leave."

Corverus' face grew florid in either anger, pain, or both, but his expression remained stonily polite. "We shall see about that."

He grasped Celeste's hand and bowed over it. "We will meet again soon. À bientôt." Straightening with stiff dignity and, Celeste hoped, in considerable discomfort, he backed out the door.

Tolly slammed it behind him, rattling the windows in the frame. "*Dra til helvete, faen.*"

Celeste didn't know precisely what that Norwegian phrase

meant, but she knew it was an epithet and helvete had something to do with hell.

Turning, Tolly scowled at Byron. "I didn't need your interference. Now you've gone and made things even more untenable for us, and Alistair too. I never should have let you and your fellow miscreants in here."

Celeste did not say, "then we'd have had no one to invite." Tolly stalked back into the sitting room to resume her seat next to Isabeau.

Byron shrugged apologetically. "Sorry, my sweet. I didn't mean to start trouble."

"You and I excel at that, don't we?" She wiped Corverus' sloppy kisses from her cheek and lips. "It's not your fault; you were only trying to help."

"Should I speak with her?"

"Gods, no, you'll only make it worse. Just leave her alone, let her calm down. Another glass or two of champagne and a little, er, TLC later, and she'll be fine."

"Well, I believe you need another glass of something yourself. Something to wash the taste of that man's tongue out of your mouth." He pointed to the bottle of homebrewed hooch Father Dom had brought. "Perhaps some of that, eh?"

She chuckled. "Probably take the varnish off the drinks cart, but yeah."

He crooked his arm in invitation. "Come, let us warm our cockles. I believe Eugenie is about to sing. You won't want to miss that. She has the voice of a nightingale."

Taking his arm, she let him lead her back to the party. A brand-new year prepared to dawn, full of possibilities. She was with the people dearest to her heart and the woman she loved beyond anything she'd ever imagined. She would not let anything, even the spectre of Corverus, ruin this night.

Two

The cork of the fancy champagne Martin had left with them shot up, bounced off the high ceiling of the sitting room and dropped onto the oriental carpet, now littered with confetti from poppers. Celeste filled their glasses with pricey, bubbling golden liquid.

"Bonne année, cherie." She clinked glasses with Tolly.

"*Godt nytt ar, elskling.*"

The guests had gone, and it was nearly two in the morning. Replete with both laughter and bottled cheer, they sipped the bubbly in a final tribute of welcome to a new year. Celeste kissed Tolly on the cheek, then sat on the floor next to where Tolly lounged on the couch and tucked her feet up under her. Resting her head on Tolly's knee, she soaked up the warmth of the crackling fire in the grate. "Are you almost packed?" They left in a few days for a holiday to the Cote d'Azur, away from the chill and the ice and the snow. It would be glorious.

Tolly ran her fingers through Celeste's dark curls. "I am. I couldn't find my straw boater, though. Have you seen it?"

Celeste basked in the soothing sensation. She loved it when Tolly played with her hair. "You have at least a hundred hats. I'm not even sure I know what a boater is. Do we really need to take all of them to Collioure? We'll be on the beach. They'll get covered in sand." Not to mention the fortune it would cost to hire porters to carry all the damn hat boxes.

Tolly removed her hand. "I am not taking all of them. Only five or six." She straightened, swinging her feet to the floor. "We will have time at the shore, of course, but there are many other things to do, Celie. And I cannot wear my beach costume to dinner or the theatre. Or whilst shopping."

"For more bloody hats."

Tolly relaxed back against the couch. Her fits of pique never lasted long, and the champagne and the night's entertainment had mellowed her earlier anger. "You are baiting me."

"Not on purpose. Although fights lead to making up." She met Tolly's changeable blue eyes, which were a soft, warm azure now. "And you know how I love making up."

Tolly smiled and resumed stroking her hair. "We don't have to fight to do that. But right now, I just want to sit and enjoy the fire. By all the gods, it's been a long year. I am so happy to say goodbye to 1922."

It *had* been a hell of a year. Celeste rested her head on her partner's knee again. "Next year will be better."

Someone rapped loudly on the door to the shop.

"Good Lord and Lady, now what?"

Tolly frowned. "Perhaps a customer? If it is, it must be an emergency. Madame Giraud is the only pregnant woman we have right now, and she is not due to give birth for at least three weeks."

Since their shop straddled the mortal neighborhood and the Magical Quarter, they counted both mundane and magical folk in their clientèle. To the mortals, they sold poultices, herbal sachets, and tinctures. To those who made their home in the Quarter, they provided potions, spells, and charms. Midwifery and other basic first aid services could be had by any who needed it, so late-night visitors formed a fairly common part of their custom.

Celeste headed into the front hall and peered through the door. A slim, short figure stood limned in the light from the gas streetlamp, wearing a little red cap. Sending her magical senses through the door gave her a hint as to what sort of creature she might be letting in. "Fae," she murmured to Tolly. At least Corverus hadn't made another surprise visit.

"Telegram," Tolly replied, also clearly having sensed who and what stood outside. She pushed Celeste aside to open the door. "Hello, young Pyp. Bonne année."

The young man, a changeling youth barely past twenty-five years and still in the throes of fae adolescence, touched his hat and ducked his head in a respectful greeting to Tolly. He'd become a fixture in their circles since Celeste had first met him a few months ago. Tolly had taken a liking to him, and Byron doted on the boy. "And to you, Madame. Telegram for you." He gave Celeste a grin and a saucy wink that reminded her of Byron. She'd introduced the two some weeks back and clearly the poet was already having a bad influence on the lad.

Pyp handed the pink telegram to Tolly. Sealed with wax and a privacy spell, it hadn't come through the regular telegraph wires, but a line that went directly to the office in the Magical Quarter. No ordinary mortal had sent it, nor had the sender wanted a mortal to read it. Tolly exchanged a look with Celeste.

Celeste shrugged. "No idea."

"Please tell me when I open this you won't be saying 'I'm sorry' for something. Again."

Celeste shook her head. "Nope. I've done nothing." Lately.

Tolly grabbed her handbag from underneath her coat on the hall tree and dropped a few centimes into Pyp's hands before they bid him goodnight. When they returned to the sitting room, Celeste stood on tiptoe behind Tolly and peered over the woman's shoulder as Tolly stood before the fire, unspelled the magical closure and read the brief missive.

"Come at once. Carter's unleashed hell in Egypt. Two dead already. No idea how to stop it. Aubrey."

Tolly's hands trembled, then dropped the one holding the telegram to her side.

"Tolly?"

Her partner stared into the fire, silent.

"Tolly, who's Aubrey? And what does he mean when he says Carter's unleashed hell?"

Tolly clutched the telegram, crumpling it before moving to the side table next to the settee. She sloshed more champagne into her glass and drained it dry. When she met Celeste's gaze again, her eyes had turned a cloudy grey-blue. "Aubrey is, or rather was, my husband. I'm sure you've gathered that he's one of us. A witch. We met after I was released from my period of probation. After...the incident."

Tolly never talked about the circumstances for which the Council had bound her powers for one hundred and fifty years.

Tolly grimaced and continued. "The Council made us a match, and we were hand-fasted at Beltane." She dropped onto the couch, held out her glass.

Celeste filled it again, waited.

"He's Alistair's father."

Champagne sloshed out of the overfilled glass, onto Celeste's stockinged feet and the new oriental rug. She jerked the bottle upright. "He's what?"

"He's Alistair's father." Tolly sighed. "And the father of Dagmar as well. You've never met her. She..." Tolly sighed out a breath. "Let's just say she and I parted ways a long, long time ago. Alistair keeps in touch with her, but she'll have nothing to do with me. Not since Aubrey and I dissolved our union when she was 20."

It was a lot to take in. Tolly also never talked about her Council-arranged pairing with Alistair's father. In fact, it wasn't until a month ago that Celeste had learned that Alistair was Tolly's son. She supposed the reticence might be considered odd to a mortal, given all the time they had been together, but most of the witches she knew had pasts and a resultant streak of protective stubbornness about sharing those pasts. When you could share thoughts and feelings with your nearest and dearest, life together created a certain necessity to not invade private mental spaces.

Joining her on the couch, Celeste squeezed her hand. "All right. I've about a hundred questions, but the history lesson can wait. Let's focus on the telegram."

Tolly looked at the crushed piece of paper as if it were a noxious insect. She handed Celeste her glass, squeezed her eyes shut, and pinched the bridge of her nose. "Why do I always forget that champagne gives me a headache?"

"Because you don't let us have it very often." Draining the dregs from Tolly's glass—there was no point in wasting good champagne —she set the glass on the table and rubbed the back of Tolly's neck with gentle soothing strokes until some of the tension eased. "Now, tell me what Aubrey is doing in Egypt of all places, and why he wants you to come bail him out?"

"I wish to hell I knew. The last I heard he was in Palestine. But that was, oh, fifteen years ago?" She glanced down at the telegram, tossed it aside. "He's a historian. Fascinated by the past the way I am fascinated by—"

"Hats?"

"I was going to say art." But she laughed. "You are incorrigible."

"And it's a lot of work. Back to Aubrey."

"I suppose he's in Egypt because that's where every historian or antiquarian or archaeologist wants to be right now. You've surely been reading about Lord Carnarvon and his discovery in the Valley of the Kings."

"I don't even know who this Lord What's-It is. The only things I know about Egypt are that it has pyramids, is hideously hot, and that the men treat their women like cattle."

"Chattel, Celie. The word is chattel."

"Heh, no, I meant what I said. They treat them like farm animals, good only for breeding and the amount of money the young ones can be sold for. I've read that they perform horrible mutilations to some women to remove their—"

Tolly held up her hand. "I know, you don't need to say it and it's unspeakable." She rubbed her temples. "But please, stop shouting."

"I'm not shouting!" Scowling, Celeste lowered her voice. "Sorry. Do you want me to get you a lavender sachet? Or maybe some chamomile tea?"

"No." She waved off the offer. "What I'd like is for you to keep abreast of current events."

At this Celeste bristled. "I do keep up on current events. King Fuad is now the leader of Egypt. Byron says—"

"Byron," Tolly spat.

Celeste continued. "Byron says he's a useless twit with no backbone and a tendency to curry favor with whichever faction invites him for tea. And that it will take a war to get Britain out of the mess they've gotten themselves into there."

Tolly's jaw clenched, and Celeste began rubbing her partner's neck again. "Be that as it may, I was talking about news with a less militant bent. A focus on political affairs will only lead you into trouble, *elskling*. You know that." She shook her head, tendrils of honey-blonde hair coming unpinned. "The telegram refers to a recent excavation led by a young archaeologist named Howard Carter, and funded by George Herbert, the Earl of Carnarvon. Natalie's people were friendly with Carnarvon's lot."

Natalie Westmont had been their coven leader when Celeste had been in England in the 1870s, not to mention a former lover. In fact, it had been Natalie who had introduced Celeste to Tolly. "I still owe her," Celeste said softly.

Tolly sagged back against the couch. "I met the current earl's father, Henry, a time or two." She pulled the rest of the pins from her hair and rested her head on Celeste's shoulder. "This was a decade or so before I officially joined Natalie's coven. Before I met you."

"While you were still..."

Tolly nodded. "Yes, while I was persona non grata and my powers were still bound. It's not a time I like to remember. But Natalie was always a joy and the weekends I spent at Carnarvon's country house were some of the happiest during those benighted days." She reached for Celeste's hand, intertwined their fingers. "In any case, this Carter fellow finally discovered Egyptological gold in November. Literally. An undisturbed royal tomb. He sent word to Carnarvon, and the old earl caught the first boat out. The papers were full of it. Gold everywhere inside. I cannot believe you didn't read about it."

"I've...seen the headlines."

Tolly shifted, gave Celeste a skeptical look, and sighed. "I admit, we've been so busy preparing for this trip, I haven't paid much attention to the news since. Clearly something's happened. You know all of those tombs have curses associated with them."

"As you would say, stuff and nonsense."

"And as you know perfectly well, not all curses are simply mortal superstition. No, if Aubrey says Carter's unleashed hell, then something serious—something magical—is going on."

"And he thinks you can fix it? Why can't he?"

"That's the crux of it, my dove. Aubrey is a powerful witch. If he can't handle this, I don't know why he thinks I can. But whatever our differences, he is a good man, and if he needs my help..." The look of resignation she gave Celeste finished the sentence for her.

Celeste said a mental goodbye to a holiday on the coast. "I guess we're going to Egypt instead of the seaside." She kissed Tolly's forehead, wishing she could take away the throbbing pain she sensed there. "At least there'll be sand."

THREE

Celeste reclined on the blue velvet chaise longue in the suite of borrowed rooms Byron occupied. The house, a three-story monstrosity on the Rive Gauche, was owned by Desmond Harrington-Smythe, Byron's new vampiric best friend, and served as Byron's temporary residence after arson had destroyed his own home. After the destruction of their Family, the two vampires had joined forces to create a new Family, which would have been fine if Desmond wasn't a psychopath who embraced his undead life with unbridled glee.

Byron paced the room in his silk dressing gown, picking up sheaves of papers on which he'd been scribbling a new canto for *Don Juan* and setting them down somewhere else, only to pick them up again to wave in the air as he ranted. He was in high dudgeon this evening since she'd told him about her and Tolly's altered travel plans and had been stomping around his rooms in a fit of pique. Two crystal port glasses lay in shards in front of the cold fireplace, and he'd swept most of the contents of his desk across the floor like New Year's confetti. It was a sign of his utter agitation that he paced, as he disliked anyone seeing him limp.

"I cannot believe you're going to Egypt," he said, throwing his hands in the air. "I had planned to join you in Collioure, an easy trip for me. But Egypt? A week by boat? It is completely untenable. I can't be expected to make arrangements in just two days. The logistics are impossible."

She'd grown tired of apologizing about an hour ago. "I can hardly refuse, George. Tolly's former husband needs her."

"My name is Byron," he growled. "She could go alone."

Celeste tipped her head back and stared up at the ornate ceiling medallion. "You're being childish. And your mother named you George."

"Don't bring that harridan into this." He slapped the paper down on a leather armchair and whirled to face her. "What am I going to do for weeks on end? I'm trapped here since my own home is still being rebuilt. Desmond is busy with his growing harem and is difficult company at the best of times. And Martin..."

She returned her gaze to him. He had paused his pacing diatribe and stared into the fireplace as though flames danced there. "Trouble in paradise?" she asked.

He sighed. "As I understand it, Paradise is highly over-rated."

Celeste swung her feet to the floor and went to stand beside him. "Is he upset about Desmond?"

"He thinks I am making a mistake by throwing my lot in with him."

"Well, Desmond's not exactly trustworthy, nor will your interests ever be important to him if they differ from his own."

Byron shook his head. "I've thought it through a hundred times. There is no other family I would choose to align with, and a vampire cannot operate entirely outside the pale. I'd become a target. Besides. We're related by...blood."

Yes, Celeste thought. However unlikely, Byron and Desmond shared a vampiric sire. "And when Desmond decides he no longer needs you? You've said yourself he wants to create progeny, once your charter is accepted by the Elders."

He leaned on the mantle with one forearm and stirred the cold ashes in the grate with a poker. "I suspect he's already done so, though where he's keeping him or her—"

"Her. Bound to be a woman."

"—I haven't a clue."

"So, Martin is pissed off."

The scrape of metal against the stone hearth grated on her nerves, but she waited. He wouldn't stay silent for long.

"He's also dealing with some issues with Eddie."

She grew alert. "What's wrong with Eddie?" Gods be damned, she'd nearly lost everything saving him not so long ago. If he were in trouble again, she'd kill him.

"Nothing from my perspective. He's happily in love."

Well, that was obvious to just about everyone who knew the rotund little imp. In love. Smitten. Utterly infatuated. "Martin doesn't like Eugenie?"

"That's just it. He adores her. But he's concerned for her soul. He's afraid that associating with Eddie is going to imperil her since the little imp is one of the Fallen."

So was Martin. She'd stumbled across his journals and suspected a sexual liaison with a Greek sculptor had instigated both former angels' fall from grace. She wasn't sure how Eddie had been complicit in that sin, but he'd taken to being on the wrong side of Heaven like a duck to water, while Martin could not make peace with who and what he'd become.

"Seems to me like Martin should be the last person to cast stones."

Byron straightened and faced her. "Martin cares deeply. You cannot fault him for that."

"I understand that, but Martin needs to butt out. Eugenie is well aware of what Eddie is. And you are in a position to know she is no innocent ingénue. You rescued her from a brothel where she'd been deliberately addicted to heroin. At this point, Eugenie can and should take care of her own soul. She doesn't need Martin dictating her life."

Byron cast the poker across the room and collapsed into his chair, one leg over the arm. "It's all a mess. And you're going to disappear for weeks on end, and I'll be left here with no one."

"Why don't you go stay with Martin while I'm gone?"

"Faulkner doesn't like me."

Faulkner was Martin's valet, and although Celeste still hadn't figured out what sort of magical creature he was, he was as devoted to the gargoyle as a vampire's familiar was to its master. Except without the addiction to blood and other nasty side effects. "Faulkner can go pound sand. You'll kill multiple birds with one stone if you do. Martin will like that you're not hanging around Desmond, you can encourage him to help you with the renovation of your house, and if he's occupied with you, maybe he'll cut Eddie a little slack."

Byron flung out his hands to encompass the pages of his manuscript that now littered the floor. "But my work."

"Take it with you. You can bounce new stanzas off Martin. He must be excited that you're writing again. Hell, even Alistair is excited. He keeps asking me how it's coming and when you'll have it ready." She knelt next to his chair and put her hand on his knee, the way she'd done all those decades ago when he'd have a temper tantrum during language lessons. "Go stay with Martin."

He studied his fingernails. "I'll miss you."

"Then write me letters. And I'll write you."

"They'll take forever to get there and back."

"You sound like a twelve-year-old."

"Hmph." He squeezed his eyes shut and let his head loll back against the wing of the armchair.

And startled the hell out of her when he suddenly leapt to his feet. Beaming at her, he grabbed her hands and pulled her to her feet.

"I've got it! I'll get Pyp to bring you messages. He's fae, despite the fact that he's been dumped here. He runs messages all the time for his fae betters through the Betwixt."

The Betwixt was a sort of wormhole that led not only to Tir Na Nog, the Land of the Fae, but to other places on this plane. A fae could enter the netherspace in Paris and come out halfway around the world in the blink of an eye. "Won't he get in trouble for using the Betwixt for non-fae business?"

Byron considered this and shrugged. "I can ask. But like us, he's not much for rules."

She liked Pyp, and she didn't want him to risk upsetting his fae masters. On the other hand, if she naysaid this idea, wasn't she being like Martin and making decisions for someone else? "Just make sure we're not putting him in the way of problems. The kid deserves better."

"Don't worry. I won't let him come to harm." He was all sunny smiles now, the anger and frustration burning away in light of his bright idea. He scrabbled through the pages on the floor and plucked up a few sheets. "Have I read you the latest verse? Don Juan has just been turned after his dangerous encounter with Alexander near the Temple of Hercules Victor in Rome and is considering his choices for a first meal."

With the crisis safely past, she sat again on the chaise longue and listened as he read, happy to see him creative again. She'd miss him too, but Tolly came first. All she could hope was that things in Egypt could be resolved quickly and there would still be time and budget for them to have that holiday on the Cote d'Azur as well.

FOUR

January 1923
Alexandria, Egypt

"Stars above, I hate boats." Celeste stumbled into their room at the Hotel Cecil in Alexandria, flung off her cloche and fell limply into a chair the minute the porter had closed the door behind him. Their suite included a spacious sitting area and a separate bedroom, and the tall open windows that overlooked the hotel gardens let in the bright Egyptian sunlight along with a much-needed breeze. The room spun around her, and her stomach heaved as though they were still at sea.

Tolly stood arms akimbo and surveyed their rooms. "I told you to wear your flannel."

Celeste groused a response. "It has been scientifically proven that wearing a flannel does not prevent one from getting a catarrh, Tolly. Besides. I don't have a cold, I've been seasick."

Tolly removed the pins from her hat and settled onto the sofa. "I also told you to take ginger, but you didn't listen to that advice either."

Celeste dragged herself into the bedroom and flopped backwards onto the bed, which to her delight was actually comfortable. The berths on the ship they'd taken from Marseille had been little better than the straw pallet she'd slept on as a child. And the constant rolling of the boat—dear Brigid! They'd been off the ship for more than two hours now, and she still felt as though the ground were moving beneath her feet.

Her smart new ensemble, navy blue silk pajama trousers and a matching white and blue-trimmed sleeveless sailor blouse courtesy of Coco Chanel, was damp with sweat and probably so stained under the arms she despaired of ever getting it clean. As she lay there, gasping like a dying guppy, a hot breeze blew an exotic floral scent through the open window, helping to dry the dark curls plastered to her forehead. How did the locals live like this? She closed her eyes, felt the bed depress next to her, heard a small tin being opened.

"Here, my dove. Take a piece of ginger candy and rest until teatime."

"Tea." Celeste groaned and popped the chewy piece of ginger in her mouth, eyes still closed. Either the relative darkness or the candy helped the room stop spinning. "How can you even think about drinking something hot when it's already a thousand degrees in here?"

Tolly bustled about, the skirt of her voile dress swishing, then placed something wet and delightfully cool on Celeste's forehead. It smelled of mint, lavender, and camphor. "Next time, you will listen to me, won't you?"

"Maybe."

Tolly laughed. "We'll see. Fifty years and I'm still waiting for that day. Rest now. I need to use the house phone in the lobby to call Aubrey in Cairo to tell him we'll be taking the train down day after tomorrow. Hopefully you'll have your land legs back by then."

Even if she didn't, she'd never admit it. She knew how important the appointment with Aubrey was. They needed to get a handle on whatever had disturbed him to such a degree. Best case scenario? He'd overreacted. If so, she'd convince Tolly to see the pyramids and get the hell home.

Bah. Best case scenarios were like the animals one saw in the clouds, illusory images that delighted the mind then quickly disappeared.

Moments later, she heard the door to their room snick shut behind Tolly. Reveling in the coolness of the compress on her face, she let herself drift, like those fantastical creatures in the sky, hoping for sleep.

She wasn't sure how much time had passed when she heard a series of noises coming from the other room, as though Tolly were rummaging through their luggage. It couldn't have been long; she felt like she'd only just started to drift off, the wisp of a dream where she and Tolly splashed happily under a waterfall while tropical birds chattered around them had only just begun to feel real. With the compress still over her eyes, she lay there, hoping Tolly had reconsidered the wisdom of going down for tea. Maybe if she pretended to be sleeping, the time to dress and arrive downstairs would pass and they could spend the rest of the afternoon doing something more interesting. If being sweaty was going to be a constant state of affairs, she could think of more entertaining activities that would result in that condition than sipping tea on the hotel terrace.

Soft feet padded into the bedroom, halted.

The bracelet she wore around her wrist, the one Tolly had charmed and given her to warn of danger, grew hot against her skin and made her whole arm tingle, like she'd touched a live wire.

Tossing off the compress, she bolted upright. The sour smell of the man who stood in the bedroom doorway hit her. She flashed back to the streets of London in the year of the plague; the stench of rotting bodies and the unwashed masses shuffling through narrow alleys, half-starved, looking for a place to lie down and die flooded her thoughts.

She blinked the past from her eyes. The grimy man standing in the doorway could have stepped out of that past, but his long, gray galabeya and the sweat-grimed turban around his head was a product of Egypt, not England. He raised his arm with a snarl and whipped a dagger toward her.

The blade missed, and thunked into the wall behind the bed.

A crash sounded from the other room. The knifeman shouted harshly in Arabic, spun, and ran.

Stunned as she was, and still trying to pull her drowsy wits together, it took her a few seconds to react and follow. By the time she reached the sitting room, the two intruders had clambered out the window. When she reached the aperture, she saw two men descending from the third-floor room like monkeys, jumping from balcony to balcony. They hit the street running and quickly disappeared into the throng of tourists and peddlers in front of the hotel, becoming two among many dressed in galabeyas and turbans.

Turning, she groaned as she viewed their room. Every one of their trunks and cases lay open, the contents strewn all over the floor. One of Tolly's new couture dresses had grubby handprints on the pale, yellow fabric. As she stepped gingerly through the mess, she saw something that dismayed her even more. There on the side table, sitting in a puddle of gore next to a vase of fresh flowers, lay a gruesome lump. She was loathe to get close, but from where she stood, it resembled a human heart. Which was utterly unlikely, so therefore probably the heart of a cow or a sheep or whatever sort of domestic animal inhabited Egypt.

Even more bizarre, a little carved figurine of a man, arms folded in front of him like a mummy leaned up against the bloody organ. She'd seen pictures of such figurines in the books Tolly had foisted upon her during their journey. They were called ushabtis, and they littered ancient Egyptian tombs. Representing servants, they were supposed to assist the dead in menial chores in the afterlife, a tiny faience army of housemaids and butlers and cooks and whatever else the wealthy ancient dead might require.

The door to their room swung open, and Tolly waltzed in, humming. Both sound and movement stopped abruptly. "Dear Lord and Lady! What on earth have you done?"

"It wasn't me. Two men crept in while I slept and ransacked our room. One of them threw a knife at me."

Tolly hurried to her. "Are you alright?"

"I'm fine. He missed, hit the wall. But that isn't the worst of it." She pointed to the side table and its grisly occupants. "They left us that as well."

By dinner, the hotel staff had cleaned the mess in the room and their belongings had been restored to their luggage, except for the clothing they'd need tonight and tomorrow.

Celeste turned the conversation back to the topic they'd been rehashing since the afternoon. "It has to be related, Tolly. Why would some local miscreants leave a pig's heart in our room? That is not the act of a couple of thieves, as the hotel manager suggested."

Tolly finished putting on her earrings and shrugged those slim, pale shoulders Celeste loved to touch. "Perhaps it is some local custom we don't understand."

"No, it has to be related to why we're here."

"Well, I don't see how. Who would even know we were coming?"

"Aubrey must have told someone."

"Who would he tell? If he told someone on the Council, one of their operatives would be here instead of us. And if he'd telegrammed Alistair, Alistair would have mentioned it to me."

"Did you mention our trip to him?" Celeste crossed her arms, the back of her unzipped dress gaping open.

Tolly moved behind her. "No."

"Why not?"

"Because Alistair is tied to the Council. And Aubrey contacted me, not them. I'm done discussing this, at least for tonight. We will talk with Aubrey about it when we get to Cairo. Hold up your hair."

Celeste let the subject drop, knowing from experience that continuing would be pointless. Tolly's stubborn streak ran even deeper than Celeste's. Still, she grumbled as Tolly zipped up the back of her pale green dinner gown. "Why can't we just dine in our room? They have room service."

"Stop fretting. We now have a young man in the hallway, a suffragi, watching our rooms. His name is Mahmud. No one will come back."

Celeste shivered. The sense of being watched had been tormenting her since the incident. "He could be in cahoots with them," she said of the pretty, brown-eyed, youth the hotel manager had arranged to stand guard the next two nights.

"He is not one of them. There is no 'them'." Tolly forced her onto the stool in front of the dressing table and started fussing with Celeste's new, short haircut, arranging her curls with her fingers. "Coco was right, this modern style suits you wonderfully." She pinned a marcasite barrette into Celeste's hair and then kissed the back of her neck. "You'll turn the heads of all the bright young things tonight."

Celeste grabbed Tolly's hand, kissed the palm. "I don't care about bright young things. If we have dinner in, we can dance together. In the moonlight." She pointed out the window at the twinkling stars beyond the gently billowing curtains.

"We are going down for dinner, Celie. Put on your shoes. Now. And leave that gruesome little trinket here. I don't know why you're carrying it around."

Celeste studied the statuette. She felt drawn to it. Several times during the afternoon she'd attempted to probe the thing with magical senses. It felt completely inert. No emanations from it at all.

Yet she couldn't stop touching the turquoise-colored figurine. Reluctantly, she set the ushabti on the dressing table and dabbed on some eau de parfum. Standing, she turned to Tolly. "Acceptable?"

"Lovely."

At dinner, Celeste became conscious of a number of young men watching her, trying to catch her eye. In Paris, in the company they usually kept, and certainly in the Magical Quarter, she received very little of that kind of attention. People knew her, understood she and Tolly were a couple, and for the most part, were accepting or didn't care. They never flaunted their relationship in public, so those not on the *qui vive* had no cause to suspect. Here, though, there was no Magical Quarter, no safe place. She felt like a prized pooch at the dog show and wished fervently she hadn't allowed Tolly to doll her up.

As the meal wore on and people retired to the ballroom for after-dinner dancing, she leaned toward Tolly. "Please tell me you don't want to stay down here for dessert."

"Are you that uncomfortable? I would think you'd be flattered."

Celeste shrugged. "It's just different here."

"We can have coffee served upstairs if it makes you feel better. Or perhaps outside on the veranda?"

Celeste shook her head. Ordinarily she would have been happy to indulge her partner. Tolly loved social occasions, and the more frippery and primping required, the fancier the affair, the happier her peacock of a partner was. While Celeste liked to see the tall, elegant Norwegian all dressed up and catching the eyes of both men *and* women, tonight felt different. Dangerous. "No. Please. It's like I'm under a magnifying glass."

"Of course, *elskling*." They stood and made their way out of the dining room and up the broad staircase to their room. Mahmud sat cross-legged on the floor across from their door and beamed wordlessly as they entered. He likely spoke little English or French, but since she'd not heard him utter a sound since he'd been introduced, he could be mute.

Once inside, Tolly pressed her lips to Celeste's forehead. "You're not coming down with something, are you? Hm. You're not hot."

Celeste pulled away and dropped onto the sofa. It was like sinking into burning sand at the beach. Her head throbbed and her eyes burned. "I'm abominably hot. It's nine thousand degrees here. We might as well be in the Ninth Circle of Hell."

The expected scourging comment didn't come. Tolly sat next to her and pulled her head into her lap, where she massaged Celeste's temples with cool hands. "I forgot how much you despise the heat. No wonder you kept going back to live in London time and again. Miserable rain, chilly temperatures. While I'm not overly fond of the humidity in Alexandria, I absolutely cannot wait to feel the heat of the desert."

Just the thought of it made Celeste's stomach churn.

Tolly stroked Celeste's forehead. "My poor dove."

She still couldn't shake the sense of being watched, but after a time, under Tolly's ministrations, she began to relax. "Did you still want coffee and dessert?"

"Probably best not to indulge. We can have a lovely breakfast in the morning."

"Okay." Tolly's fingers soothed her, making her drowsy. "This was not the way I had planned to spend tonight."

"The best laid plans. I think a cool bath and an early bedtime might be just the ticket."

Soaking in a bathtub of cool water sounded like heaven. "I agree. But I took a bath before I dressed for dinner."

Tolly shook her head, gave Celeste just enough of a push to force her to get up. "That was to scrape off the dirt. This is to bring your temperature down. Go on, sponge off and then crawl into bed. I'll join you shortly."

Celeste did as she was bid. The tepid water did feel wonderful. With the window open in the bedroom and the ceiling fan circling lazily over the bed, by the time she'd donned her new, satin night-gown, her arms had goosebumps.

She brushed out her short damp curls at the dressing table and padded out to the sitting area where Tolly sat, curled up reading yet another treatise on Egypt, a volume entitled *A Thousand Miles up the Nile* by Amelia Edwards, one of the first women Egyptologists. She gave Tolly a quick peck, received a mumbled and distracted response about coming to bed in a few minutes, then went back to the bedroom and slipped between clean, cool sheets.

She awoke late in the night, with Tolly snuggled up behind her, not quite snoring in her ear, and realized she hadn't seen the little ushabti on the dressing table before bed. Had she just missed it? Maybe the figurine had just been knocked to the floor. It's not like it could get up and walk away.

Right?

Too exhausted to get up to check, she convinced herself of that and drifted back into a fitful sleep as the stars faded into a sky of inky blue.

In the misty time between dawn and sunrise, they were both awakened by the ululations of the muezzins, the men at the mosques who called the faithful to prayer. They cuddled under the sheets for a while, but as soft rays of morning sun lit the room, Tolly slipped out of bed and started to ready herself for the day. She rummaged through the top drawer of the bureau, then turned to face Celeste.

"Where are my underthings?"

Celeste shrugged. "In the drawer, last I saw. You can't have lost them, almost everything we own is packed."

"I put them right here last night. Did you move them before you went to bed?"

"No," Celeste grumped, annoyed at being accused.

Tolly opened the next drawer down, muttered something in her native Norwegian that Celeste knew was rude. "I did *not* put these in this drawer." She pulled out her underclothes, as well as Celeste's, and flung them at her. "You must have moved them."

Celeste bit back a sharp response. It was too early to start an argument. "I didn't move anything. Perhaps one of the hotel staff moved things around. They turned down the bed clothes, so they were in here."

Tolly dressed quickly and sat down at the dressing table. "I will talk with the manager before we leave. I do not care to have anyone grubbing about through my small clothes. It's just not done."

Celeste agreed, but the incident nagged at her. What if it hadn't been the hotel staff? Had someone searched their room again while they slept? And if so, why?

Tolly reached for her face powder, her expression turning from frustration to appreciation as she watched Celeste dress through the mirror. First the nightgown came off, then she pulled on the silk knickers that had come with her new wardrobe. With a smile in her voice, Tolly said, "Celie, where's the little blue ushabti? Didn't you set it here last night?"

Celeste turned, her gaze scouring the dressing table and the floor around it, but the figurine had disappeared. "I did. I remember realizing in the middle of the night I hadn't seen it when I brushed my hair, but I thought it must have fallen."

"Then whoever rummaged through our things must have stolen it. Good riddance, I say. I don't know why you wanted to keep it in the first place. Should have gone out with the other unpleasant gift."

Celeste's scalp rippled and the sensation of being watched returned. She scanned the room, looked out the window into the gardens below, and peered into the sitting room, but saw no one.

"What are you doing?"

Celeste shook her head. "Nothing." She plunked down on the bed to dress, still scanning the corners of the room, not only for the source of the watcher whom she still felt, but also for the ushabti.

Somehow the two things were connected, she just didn't know how. But she kept her mouth shut. Tolly would only accuse her of imagining it all, so she'd say nothing until she figured it out.

FIVE

They breakfasted on the terrace. Tolly wanted sunshine and Celeste refused to luncheon on the terrace in the heat of the day, so they compromised. Afterwards Tolly proposed a visit to the Suk, no doubt to shop for Egyptian lady's hats.

"Please, please, please don't make me go with you. You know I hate shopping."

"But it will be so interesting. You can learn so much about a country by shopping the local markets. And we need to bring back at least a few souvenirs for gifts."

"You say that every time we go anywhere. I didn't like shopping in Shanghai, I didn't like shopping in Athens, I didn't like shopping in St. Petersburg. I don't even like shopping in Paris."

"You like shopping if there is a bakery."

She hated when Tolly was right. She tossed her napkin onto the table. "That's different. Look, hire one of the men to escort you, and carry your packages. Have a lovely morning wandering around looking for treasures. I'll be here waiting for you at lunchtime."

"I hate to leave you all alone. What will you do with yourself?"

"Play Patience?"

"You hate card games."

She rested her hand on Tolly's. "I'll be fine. I may just take some time to relax. Somewhere cool. With a lemonade."

Tolly frowned. "You'll find trouble, is what you'll do."

"I won't. Promise. I won't even leave the hotel. Now go." She made a shooing gesture at the street below the terrace. "Have fun. You can show me all your finds when you get back."

"Very well. Just don't do anything I wouldn't do."

Ten minutes later, Tolly was on her way with her new guide and Celeste had retired to their rooms. She'd ordered a pitcher of lemonade, and once it was delivered, she stripped off her clothes and splashed tepid water onto her flushed skin to combat the relentless heat. Turning on the table fan in the sitting room, she sat naked on the divan and sipped lemonade while the breeze cooled her skin.

Gods, how did people live like this, day in and day out?

She had just closed her eyes, enjoying the relief from the heat, when her scalp tingled, and she felt a buzzing in her molars. What on earth?

With an audible pop, a figure appeared in the room. Short, thin, dressed in a red jacket and cap, and grinning lewdly at her.

She flew off the divan and raced into the bedroom, grabbing up her robe and hurriedly belting it around her before returning, red-faced and seething, to the sitting room. "Pyp, you little idiot! What are you doing here?"

The young changeling's grin widened, not one iota ashamed or embarrassed. "Nice gams, doll. And other bits."

"By the stars!" She paused to collect herself. "Gams? Doll? Have you been spending time with Eddie?"

"A bit. I run errands for him, like I do for Byron and Martin. Hey, a fella's gotta make a living."

She'd need to speak to Byron about this. She wanted to give Pyp an opportunity to earn some money, not an education in the seamier side of the Magical Quarter. "What are you doing here?"

"His lordship sent me. He hadn't heard from you since you left and wanted to know how things were going." He held up a creamy white piece of stationery. "Also wanted to know 'what sort of trouble you've gotten yourself into.'" Pyp delivered the last in a voice so like Byron's, replete with a scathing but humorous tone, that Byron might as well have been standing in front of her. It was unnerving, considering her state of undress.

"We are in no trouble, thank you very much. Just intolerably hot. The sun beats down relentlessly. Tell George that he would not care for Egypt at all."

Pyp tried to hide another grin. He failed miserably. He referred to his paper, clearly a letter of some length. "He says, 'You'll be complaining about the heat, and likely the number of hats La Tollefsen has purchased along the way. But—"

Celeste raised her hand imperiously. "It might be best if you just read his missive start to finish." She settled herself on the divan, careful to keep the robe from gaping open.

"Of course, mademoiselle." He snapped open the letter and cleared his throat. When he spoke again, his imitation of Byron, both in voice and in body language was startling. Had to be some kind of fae glamour magic.

"My sweet Celeste,

I hope this letter finds you well. I imagine you had quite a time aboard ship suffering from le mal de mer. I still remember your reticence to go back across the Channel from London to the continent, once you settled in 'England's green and pleasant lands."

She groaned. "Dear Goddess, he's quoting Blake now? A pox on all poets."

Pyp continued in Byron's voice.

"I can hear you groaning now, knowing how much you dislike Blake. But it was so appropriate!

"In any case, by my reckoning you've been in Egypt for a fair few days. You'll be complaining about the heat, and likely the number of

hats La Tollefsen has purchased along the way. But despite all the ills of travel, surely you have a spare moment to send for Pyp to bring me news of your journey.

"You've been quite neglectful and, dare I say, selfish. I'm pining for your company and have resorted to spending my evenings at the Red Belle just to relieve the ennui. It is dreadfully dull here without you and Martin is being, well, Martin.

"I'm dying (hah!) to hear about what you've experienced so far and what sort of trouble you've gotten yourself into. Please scribble—we both know your handwriting is atrocious, so you cannot possibly quibble about the word scribble (and I say Hah! again!) an account of your days since our parting, posthaste, and give it to Pyp to bring to me.

"I beg of you, do not let me languish here in desolation much longer or I shall perish from sheer boredom.

"Your devoted et cetera et cetera,

"B.

"P.S. I met a gentleman—or warlock, to be precise—at the Red Belle the other evening who is from your homeland. Tangi something or other, I admit I lost interest when he had no idea who I was. Don't suppose you know him?"

Finished, Pyp relaxed and folded the piece of stationery. "I was told by his lordship to wait for a reply."

"Is he making you call him that? He's no longer the lord of anything, you know."

"He isn't. Just tryin' to be respectful. Not sure how it works here in the mortal world, but in Tir na Nog, once a toff, always a toff, and you best not forget it. There will be," he intoned in a sober imitation of his fae betters, "consequences."

"Well, there'll be none from Byron, I assure you. Or *he* will be the one receiving consequences."

Pyp laughed, his relative youth in fae terms showing. "Much appreciated. But he's fine. I actually like working for him. He pays good and he's a lot of fun."

"Pays well. Just don't let him lead you into anything dangerous."

"I won't." He laid Byron's letter on the other end of the divan and stood with his hands clasped before him. "Do you need stationery, miss? His lordship gave me some to bring along. Just in case."

Of course he had. She stood, still clutching her robe closed. "Thanks, I'm good. Give me a minute to dress." She pointed to the pitcher of lemonade. "In the meantime, help yourself."

Since she'd be going down for luncheon in the dining room when Tolly got back, she chose a pale blue skirt and white blouse, leaving a drop waist, spangled evening dress in a midnight blue with a daring draped back for dinner.

When she re-entered the sitting room, Pyp was reclining on the divan, his feet on the cushion, hands clasped behind his head, eyes closed. He'd adjusted the fan so it blew full on him, ruffling his red-gold curls. "Bloody hot in here."

"Welcome to Egypt." She knocked his feet off the couch and moved the fan so it would blow on her while she sat at the little secretary to compose her reply.

Unperturbed, he sat up. "I liked your original outfit better."

She ignored him.

Dear Georgie,

she wrote, knowing the childhood name would automatically irritate him.

I cannot possibly know a random man from Brittany named Tangi, it is a common male name, at least in times past.

Did she need to mention Tangi had been a Breton saint? Or that even her youngest brother had been given the name? Or that it meant fire dog? She scribbled it all down (damn him, her handwriting was not that bad) anyway. Let him be on the receiving end of a history lesson for a change.

The trip has been fairly uneventful. Yes, I got seasick. Yes, the heat is like being in Dante's ninth circle of hell, although Tolly is perfectly fine with it. We are in Alexandria at present but will be taking a train to Cairo in the morning, where we'll be staying at Shepheard's. Although it is peak tourist season, Tolly apparently knows someone who has an in with the hotelier, so we were able to get a nice suite. Outside of that, nothing of note has happened.

She almost wrote 'yet'.

So, to answer your other question, I haven't gotten myself in any trouble whatsoever.

She paused, having gripped the fountain pen so hard her hand cramped. Putting aside the instrument, she wiggled her fingers, then got up to fetch her glass of lemonade. What she wanted was *cool* lemonade. Tepid lemonade, even with the sprig of mint someone had added, did nothing to help.

Pyp still sat on the divan, feet now on the floor, and was writing on a piece of Byron's stationery that he balanced on his knees. She watched as he studied the page, then looked pensively into the distance. Was he reporting back to Byron? She had no idea he even knew his letters.

Glass in hand, she walked behind the couch to peer over his shoulder, causing him to hunch protectively over the page.

"What are you writing?" She tried to keep her tone innocuous.

"None of yer business." Then added, "Miss."

"It better not be some snide note to Byron."

He folded the piece of paper and straightened, his chin jutting, his eyes gone cold. "It's just stuff for me."

She let it go. She hadn't meant to make him angry or defensive, and it appeared her curiosity would go unsatisfied. Feeling both guilty and curious, she returned to the desk to finish the note.

Sadly, that is all I have to satisfy your rampageous inquisitiveness. Tell me truly, how are things with Martin? Did you move back in with him or are you still at Desmond's place? Far be it for me to interfere in your romantic liaisons, but I know how much you care for each other. Might be good for you to try to work it out with him.

I promise to write as soon as anything interesting happens.
With deepest regards,
Celeste

She folded the letter, stuck it in an envelope and sealed it before handing it to Pyp. "There. My response, as requested."

"Kinda short, isn't it? He likes long ones."

"He likes long everything," she said, thinking of his epic poem Don Juan, an adventure tale that never seemed to end.

Pyp sniggered. "Yeah, I've noticed that. Even his friends."

If the changeling was making a salacious reference, she didn't want to know how he'd acquired that knowledge. But she *would* be talking to Byron about the lad when she got home. "That's quite enough of that." She crossed her arms, indicating her desire to end their business.

He looked her up and down. "What, no tip?"

"Byron is paying you plenty." In truth, she had no ready cash in small enough denominations. Tolly never left her with much in the way of walking around money, knowing it would just end up in the hands of the nearest pâtisserie.

Pyp shrugged before saluting her. "Very good then, miss. See you again soon!"

And with another audible and entirely unnecessary pop, he vanished back into the Betwixt.

Wary of any additional intrusions, she kept on her luncheon attire even though she was sweating again. Curling up on the divan with one of Tolly's books on Egypt, she whiled away the hours educating herself until her partner's return.

After an uneventful evening, they boarded the train the next morning for Cairo. Arriving sweaty and rumpled, they took a taxi to Shepheard's Hotel, *the* place to stay, according to Tolly, crawling through the overcrowded streets while the lunatic behind the wheel jerked and jolted his way through traffic like a typical Parisan cab driver.

The second largest city in Egypt, Cairo felt both familiar and unfamiliar at the same time. Like other big cities, it bustled. It teemed. It swarmed. And like all the rest, it overwhelmed. The minute they stepped off the train, the sounds and scents threatened to swamp Celeste's senses.

A wild mix of both modern and antique mashed together in a discordant harmony. Mudbrick apartments and store fronts sat side by side with colonial looking British facades. Electric streetlamps had been planted haphazardly along the main routes in the touristy areas, and cars fought for space on the roads, paved and unpaved, with donkey carts and masses of people in both local robes and European clothing.

It felt like ancient Cairo phased in and out of existence. Or maybe that was modern Cairo that did the phasing. One moment, they were passing a chic European clothing boutique, and the next the cab jockeyed around a little vegetable cart that might have been there since the 1800s. Or maybe even the 800s. The locals looked as though they'd stepped out of a painting from the days of the crusades, and any moment she expected to see a Knight Templar in a doorway.

Then they'd drive past a French cabaret, with signage featuring a modern young woman wearing a cloche and puffing on a cigarette, and Celeste experienced a sort of temporal whiplash.

She loved cities. Loved the hustle and energy. Yet she had to admit to a certain amount of relief when they'd been admitted to their rooms and shut the door for a few moments on the overstimulating and confusing onslaught.

It took her a short rest and a change of clothes to acclimate a bit.

By the time Tolly had phoned her ex-husband Aubrey to set up a meeting, and they descended the grand staircase from their suite of rooms, the late afternoon sun cast long shadows over the throngs of

European tourists crowded around the tables on the broad terrace of the hotel.

Celeste sipped her lemonade and fanned herself, watching Tolly twitch in her chair like an anxious cat every time a taxicab pulled up in front of the place. Not even a breeze stirred the broiling afternoon sun while they waited for Tolly's former husband to arrive.

Celeste adjusted her hat to better shade her nose, which already felt burnt, and leaned forward. "Are you sure he said he was coming now?"

"Yes."

"It's been half an hour."

"I *know*, Celeste." Tolly tensed as another taxi pulled up in front of the hotel. When it disgorged an elegantly dressed couple with loud voices and nasal American accents, she sagged back.

"Do you know where he's staying?"

"For the love of Freya, stop badgering me."

Celeste pressed her lips shut to keep from snapping back.

Almost at once, Tolly laid a hand on Celeste's knee under the table. "I am so sorry. I'm just so worried." Her changeable blue eyes, now of a hue to match the cloudless Egyptian sky, filled with tears. "I'm being beastly. Forgive me?"

"There's nothing to forgive." She patted Tolly's hand then let it go. This was not the place to create a public spectacle. "But *do* you know where he's staying?"

"No. I don't."

"Well, someone in Cairo must. What does he do here? What's his cover?"

"I'm afraid I don't know that either. Frankly, I have no information other than what he wrote in his second telegram. We're to contact him on arrival."

Celeste allowed herself a small smile. "What? The great Astrid Tollefsen left home without a battle plan? Is that what I'm hearing?"

Tolly's brows knit together. "Do not be snide, little miss fly-by-the-seat-of-her-pajama-pants."

"Okay." Every country had a different method for communicating with others in the magical underground. Celeste had no clue how to access the witching community here. "Do you know how to contact a representative of the Council here? Surely, they would at least know where he's living. We could say we're sightseeing and wanted to say hello."

"I'm afraid to do that."

"You think he's in trouble with the Council."

"He might be." Tolly finally relaxed enough to smile. "I seem to attract that sort."

"Must be that fancy Parisian perfume you like to wear. We troublemakers can't resist Chanel No. 5." When Tolly's smile reached her eyes, Celeste also relaxed. She'd never seen Tolly so temperamental, and it eased her heart to see her break free, at least momentarily, of her fear and frustration. "What else can we do? You said he keeps in touch with Alistair. Maybe you could send him a telegram? See if he at least knows what Aubrey's cover is here?"

The moment of calm dissipated and Tolly pinched the bridge of her nose. "You're like a dog with a bone."

"Well, do *you* have a better suggestion? We can't sit out here indefinitely. For a start, you left your hat with the bellhop, and your nose is turning as red as mine feels." She removed her own hat and handed it to her partner. "Put this on. I imagine your scalp is getting pink too."

Tolly made a moue of distaste. She did not care for Celeste's less ostentatious headgear. As she adjusted the hat at a rakish angle, a tall, lithe Egyptian boy came running up to the table. Dark curls, dark eyes, and long eyelashes, he looked like every other local boy until he smiled, an impish grin that lit his whole face and twinkled in his eyes. He seemed half angel and half demon.

"Baksheesh?" He held out his hand as they all did, begging for coins from the tourists, while with his other, he slipped a piece of paper underneath the table and into Celeste's lap.

Tolly frowned. "If you give him anything, we'll be swarmed, Celeste. You cannot give money to every child in the country."

Celeste clutched the note in one hand lest it fall to the ground. "Of course not." She winked at the boy and subtly slipped a coin from her purse into his hand.

"Celie!"

The boy bowed, blew Celeste a cheeky kiss, and ran off just as a waiter hurried over to their table. "Scoundrels. My apologies, ladies, I hope that child wasn't begging. They know they are not supposed to come onto the terrace."

Celeste gave the man her most charming smile. "Not at all." She stood. "Thank you so much. With your wonderful service, I know we're going to enjoy our stay. Now, Tolly, we must get you out of the sun. Come along inside."

"But Celie, what if—"

Celeste took Tolly's arm firmly and drew her to her feet, nearly upsetting the table. "Now, dear. We need to refresh ourselves and get changed for tea with the Arsenaults."

"The...the Arsenaults? Has the heat finally gotten—"

"Shush," she whispered. "Just follow my lead." She tugged at Tolly, pulling her along through the doors, into the lobby, and up the stairs. When they reached their rooms, Celeste locked the door behind them and searched to make sure no lurked either in the bedroom or out on the balcony. Assured they were alone, she revealed the slip of paper the boy had dropped in her lap.

Tolly's eyes widened. "I thought you had suddenly lost your mind. We haven't seen Guy Arsenault and his wife in thirty-five years. What is that?"

"The little boy brought it. It's a message." She glanced at the paper, which had been folded in two. "There's an A on the outside.

My guess is that it's from Aubrey." She handed it to Tolly. "Which means it's for you."

Tolly took the paper, then passed it back. "I cannot. You read it."

She'd never seen Tolly so shaken, so fearful, not in all the years they'd been together. She turned on the fan, which did nothing but blow hot air around, and unfolded the note. It had been written in code; a magical alphabet called Futhark, based on Nordic runes.

She remembered learning several magical alphabets under the tutelage of Marguerite. Huddling by the fire in the little cottage in the woods, while the winter winds blew gusts down the chimney and scattered sparks and ashes, she had gripped a piece of charcoal with cramped, cold fingers and, under her mentor's critical supervision, scratched marks onto a piece of slate.

"Leave it to Aubrey to be obstinately arcane." It took her a several minutes to decipher the stick-like lines and cross bars. She'd been better at Ogham, the ancient script of the Celts.

Transcribing the message onto a piece of hotel stationery in French, she showed Tolly both the original and the translation. "It says we're to meet him in the Ezbekieh Garden at 9 pm. By the bandstand." She frowned. "Could it be a trick? A trap?"

Tolly examined the paper the boy had given them and put her finger on a symbol at the bottom of the page that Celeste hadn't recognized. "That's Aubrey's mark. He signs all his artwork with it. No one knows about it but his family and close friends. It has to be from him."

"He's an artist?"

That evoked a sad smile. "A brilliant one. He's thinks he's a poet too, but that's best not encouraged." She sat down on the couch, tossed off Celeste's hat. "Not all those days were painful. We had happy times too, especially when the children were small." Tolly must have seen the flash of jealousy Celeste couldn't quite hide. "Not like us, of course. But it wasn't awful."

Celeste managed a neutral sound.

Tolly glanced at her watch. "Nine o'clock. That's hours from now."

"Good. We both need a bath after that horrible train ride, and you've had far too much sun. I prescribe a nap and then a light supper here in our room."

"What is it with you and your proclivity for room service?"

So, her beautiful Norwegian grew feisty, eh? Good. "Bath first. Cool down, scrape off the grime from that dreadful train. I smell like chickens and sweat. Afterward, we can argue about dinner."

Tolly glared at her for a moment, but she couldn't maintain the pretense. "Fine. A bath." She headed towards the lovely, modern bathroom but paused at the door. "Are you joining me?"

"I thought you'd never ask."

Tolly smirked. "Then bring the lavender bath salts and my terry robe. And hurry up or I may change my mind."

Celeste waggled her eyebrows. "About room service?"

"And several other things as well." She clapped her hands imperiously, her grin sly. "Chop chop, my dove. You know how mercurial I can be."

Six

Moonlight silvered the dew on the manicured lawn surrounding the bandstand, while the lack of lights on the pathways cast everything else in deep shadow. Celeste stood, a thin, fringed wrap around her shoulders, shivering. She had the sense of being watched again, although her bracelet remained quiescent. Tolly paced the wooden floorboards of the gazebo-like structure, quiet as a cat, agitated as a caged tiger.

Though she watched for it, Celeste stifled a gasp when a slim black shadow peeled itself away from the flowering shrubs and bounded silently across the lawn. Tolly spun without hesitation and flung herself at the figure.

The man wore a rumpled tweed Norfolk jacket and matching knickerbockers. His fair hair reflected the moonlight, his face a pale, angular oval, with sunken eyes Celeste would have bet were a pale blue.

"Aubrey!" A flurry of rapid-fire Norwegian followed.

The man embraced Tolly, then quickly pulled back, hands on her shoulders. "You know I can't follow when you speak that quickly."

"I'm sorry. I've been so worried." She held his gaunt face in her hands, a face Celeste could barely see in the darkness. "Are you alright?"

"No." He glanced at Celeste, then all around. "There's someone here. We're being watched." He jutted his chin toward Celeste. "Who is she?"

"This is Celeste Berenger. My partner."

He gave her a curious look. "Ah. The troublemaker. The boy has mentioned her."

The boy? Did he mean Alistair? How...dismissive.

Aubrey raised his hand, waving away Celeste's existence. "No time for this. We need to go someplace safe."

"Aubrey, you're frightening me."

"Good. You should be frightened." The thin, blond-haired man's round spectacles glinted as his head swiveled right to left, scanning the park.

Celeste stepped closer, the better to see him. His narrow features, set in sharp contrast by the moon and the shadows, bore a striking resemblance to Alistair Finlayson, the son he and Tolly had together. Except that Aubrey's scarecrow frame was narrower, his stature smaller.

Tolly echoed her thoughts. "You've lost weight. You're positively skeletal."

Aubrey shook his head. "Not now. Come with me."

"Come where? Aubrey, let's go back to the hotel. We can have sandwiches sent up to our room for you. And some good strong coffee."

"No, there's no time for that." He grasped Tolly's hand. "You must trust me, Astrid. We're in danger out here in the open, but I had to make sure you weren't followed."

Tolly's tone remained calm, but Celeste could hear the strain beneath. "Very well. Shall we get a taxi then?"

"No, no, I have a car. Quickly, now, come with me. You and what's-her-name."

"Celeste," Celeste reminded him. Then muttered, "The troublemaker."

"Whatever." He scanned the dark again, licked his lips. "I'll cast a glamour. Whoever is out there will think we're still standing here. It should buy us a little time."

"Aubrey—"

He raised a hand, closed his eyes, and in the stillness that followed Celeste heard the sound of nightjars calling from the trees. Then she felt it, a veil constructed of pure magic, pulled not from the elements but from some more arcane source. It fell around them like mosquito netting.

After a moment, Aubrey grabbed them both by the hand. Celeste stole a glance at Tolly, who nodded, then allowed herself to be led from the bandstand and across the greensward, silent as if she'd been floating instead of hurrying, towards one of the exits to the gardens, while magical facsimiles of the three of them still stood, murmuring quietly, behind them.

Even by the standards of a Parisian taxi driver, Aubrey's driving made this morning's Egyptian cabbie's efforts look cautious and sedate. European tourists crowded the streets, heading for dinner and other forms of entertainment. Aubrey wove in and out of traffic down the wide boulevard, then veered into an alley. His speed and abrupt swerves made Celeste want to close her eyes. He was, if possible, a worse driver even than Tolly.

They turned a dozen times, into ever-dingier passages, until she lost track of which direction they traveled, or how far they had gone. After an interminable time, he pulled underneath a large, plastered archway and slammed the saloon car's gearshift into park. "Quickly. Follow me."

Plunging through a wooden door that hung from rusted hinges, he hustled them up a flight of stairs and into a corridor so narrow

Tolly's shoulders brushed either wall. At the end of that, they climbed a second flight of stairs and along another tight hallway to a door at the end. Through this, Aubrey dove, as though the devil himself chased him. She and Tolly barely cleared the threshold when the man slammed the door and braced a chair against it.

Brushing past, he collapsed onto a wobbly stool in front of a table and clutched his head in his hands. In the glow from a single candle sputtering on the tabletop, he looked even more gaunt and haunted.

Tolly gave Celeste a worried look, then knelt in front of her former husband. "Aubrey, please. Tell us what is going on. And you need to eat, drink something. Celie, can you...?" She waved a hand at the cupboard next to a stained sink.

Irritated at being relegated to serving wench, Celeste rummaged through the cabinet, a simple task as it held little except a chipped bowl and a ceramic cup. On the shelf above the sink, she found crackers, a tin of sardines, and six or seven bottles of beer. While she gathered the meager repast, she listened while trying to give them a semblance of privacy, a harder chore since the room measured a scant three meters square.

In a low, soothing voice, Tolly urged Aubrey to calm himself. "Tell me the story. From the start, please."

Celeste dumped the sardines into the bowl, arranged some crackers around the little fish, and filled the ceramic cup with sour smelling beer. These she set on the table, then stood back. She felt like an intruder. A voyeur to a meeting between two estranged lovers. As Tolly stroked Aubrey's hand in the same soothing manner that she might have stroked Celeste's, irrational anger and jealousy heated her face. She knew Tolly loved her. They'd been together for decades. Yet seeing Tolly touch someone else with such affection—a man she'd been intimate with, no less—made her teeth clench. Stupid. But there it was.

"Here. Drink this." Tolly pushed the cup into Aubrey's hands.

His hollow cheeks, cracked lips, and shaking, almost palsied hands aged him decades. Even the signet ring he wore on the little finger of his right hand spun loosely, as though he'd lost weight. Perhaps he was far older than Tolly, centuries older, but Celeste didn't think so. Something had worn him down.

The male witch drank a bit, set the cup on the rickety wood table, and after a moment straightened himself. "I'm sorry. Forgive me. But you cannot know the pressure I've been under."

Tolly shot a grateful smile at Celeste, then perched gingerly on the other stool, leaving Celeste to prop herself against the wall like a piece of discarded furniture.

"Aubrey, you need to trust us," Tolly urged. "You mentioned Carter in your telegram. I assume this has to do with the opening of King Tut's tomb?"

The man nodded, scrubbed at his sandy hair, a gesture he shared with his son Alistair. "He released something. Maybe more than one something." The man's watery blue eyes lit with a kind of madness. "I don't know exactly what. I've been reading, researching, trying to figure it out, but to no avail. And of course, I cast a circle, tried to probe the entity. Big mistake.

"Whatever it is, it's evil, Astrid. And it's responsible for several deaths."

"What did you sense when you probed it?"

"At first, nothing. Then..." He shuddered, buried his face in his hands again. "It came after me. It chased me on the astral, tried to follow me back to my home. I cut the connection just in time, but it was a close thing."

"What did you sense?"

He tried to pull himself together. He shoved his hand in his pocket, toying with a worry stone, perhaps. "Goddess help me. I haven't slept in days. What did I sense?" Another shaky breath. "Old. So old. That spirit, being, whatever, has been trapped in that tomb since the priests sealed it and now it's loose."

"Surely you aren't telling me it is the spirit of the dead pharaoh."

"Don't be ridiculous. I know a phantom when I encounter one. No, the best I can determine is that it's some sort of local spirit or creature. The workers on the dig site are always talking about ifrits. I checked around, but other than bogeymen and fairy tales, I can't get anyone to give me concrete information on them."

"Alright. When were you first aware of the ifrit? And who have you consulted about them? Surely someone knows something."

Celeste interrupted. "Doesn't the local Council library have any information?"

"*Elskling*, you know Muslims do not share their magical knowledge with the Christian world." She pushed the cup toward him. "Drink."

He sipped grudgingly. "There are local legends." He snorted. "But you can't trust mortals to get the details right. It's all fables and mythology to them and they conflate entities and build silly stories out of ancient memories. Utterly unreliable." He lost some of his haggard look.

Tolly patted his shoulder, the way she would a child. "Keep going. And eat some crackers."

"I cannot do both at once, woman." His snarl had Celeste clenching her fists. No one treated Tolly like that. But she knew Tolly would chide her for interfering.

Aubrey continued, rubbing red-rimmed eyes. "It started in Luxor, the day after Carter opened the tomb. I was at the dig site, watching with everyone else. The Council wants people on the spot for these events."

"You're working for the Council now." Those who did not know Tolly well would not have seen the shift in her demeanor. The slight downturn of her lips, a tightening around mouth, the change in her eyes from warm blue to steel. Celeste saw it. She also knew that, as a rule, Tolly had no quibbles with the Council despite having suffered at its hands and Celeste presumed her annoyance had more to do with the kind of work Aubrey did for them, rather than the Council's interest in matters archaeological.

Aubrey, to his discredit, didn't notice the subtle change in his former wife's attitude. "Yes. For many years now." His tone implied Tolly should have known this and was just condescending enough to raise Celeste's hackles. She must have telegraphed her thoughts because before Celeste could speak, Tolly raised a hand, forestalling her.

"So. You said you were at the site..."

Aubrey drained the beer in his cup. "It was late in the day. Tourists had swarmed the dig site all day, along with the damnable so-called journalists, but by three o'clock, most of the huggermuggers had already gone back across the river to their hotels. The western cliffs cast long shadows over the valley, and those of us still swimming in our own sweat were grateful for the shade."

Tolly made a rolling gesture. "Enough with the poetics, Aubrey. Get to the point."

His expression grew cutting too. Celeste watched him slide his hand into his trouser pocket again, a gesture that seemed to calm him. "The men started coming up the steps, and I saw Carter and one of his staff, Harry Burton the photographer, I think, come out. They walked away furtively, heads bent together, clearly having a conversation they wanted no one else to hear. Naturally, I started to set up a listening spell."

"What did they say?"

Aubrey pushed the crackers around the plate. "I have no idea. Before I could trigger it, I noticed one of the workers exiting the tomb. He had something in his hand, staring at it with what I can only describe as maniacal glee."

Tolly pursed her lips in annoyance. "Really, Aubrey. I know you fancy yourself a storyteller, but can we please just get to the point?"

"You have no romance in your soul, Astrid."

Celeste couldn't keep her mouth shut. "You don't know her very well."

Tolly held up her hand again. "Let's stay focused. Who was this man and what did he carry in his hand?"

"It was a ring."

Tolly rolled her shoulders, a sign of growing impatience. "Then what happened?"

"Well, then the deaths started. And the visitations." He shoved his beer cup at Celeste. "More."

She complied, gritting her teeth. Pompous, entitled, condescending bastard.

He took another swig and continued. "First there was Feisal. Then Sallah, the father of the boy who found the steps, keeled over. At first, I thought it coincidence. The natives are always dying of something. Then, on the 2nd of December, I was in the market, looking through old scrolls in a stall, when someone rushed me, knocked me to the ground, and tried to drive a knife through my heart." His eyes widened, wild again. "It was the man who had stolen the ring from Tut's tomb. The keeper of the stall pulled the fellow off me, started to shake him. The thief laughed. Hysteria. He kept repeating something in an Arabic dialect I didn't understand. Something about an ifrit. Then he pulled a ring—*the* ring—from his finger and hurled it at me."

Aubrey's hands shook, and he sloshed beer down his shirt front as he gulped down more of the pungent beverage. "The mangy cur was a small, wiry fellow. He squirmed free of the stall owner and ran away, but someone must have called the authorities. They arrived in moments, and the stall owner told them the man had attacked the *howaji*, and they gave chase. As I struggled to my feet, I heard a shot." He sagged on his stool, depleted from the telling of his tale.

"The police killed him?"

"He attacked a white man. He might have died a far worse death if they'd taken him in for questioning. The government does not tolerate attacks on Europeans."

The callous remark made Celeste's blood boil. "He was a human being. And clearly either mad or ill."

Tolly regarded Celeste with that familiar mix of understanding and frustration with her partner's compassion. Then she turned back to Aubrey. "Or possessed." She paused. "That is what you are thinking, isn't it?"

He nodded. "By an ifrit. The spirit of a murdered man. The locals say that such an entity will try to hunt down his killer, that it won't stop until it succeeds. A few claim it might be able to possess a person of weak will. But if this poor soul has been in the tomb since the ancient priests sealed it, he could never gain his revenge. The murderer has been dead for millennia."

"And you believe the thief, having been possessed, was killing people to avenge its own death? Killing randomly?"

"Not entirely. Everyone who has died was there that day. The day Carter entered the tomb for the first time."

Tolly pursed her lips. "Well, if the police shot and killed the thief, shouldn't the killings have stopped?"

Aubrey stuck his hand in his pocket, again fingering something. "Maybe. Maybe not. In any case, I believe the ifrit is now in the ring."

Celeste cleared her throat. "What happened to the ring?"

Aubrey sat quietly, staring into his cup.

"Aubrey?"

He glared at Celeste. "Who does this young woman think she is?"

Tolly scowled. "Just answer the question."

He reached into his pocket and pulled out something wrapped in a torn piece of black silk and set it on the table. With delicate, trembling fingers, he unfolded the fabric, revealing a small gold scarab ring, decorated with inlaid blue lapis and rich, orange carnelian. No faience trinket, this. When Tolly reached for it, he slapped her hand away with a hiss. "Don't touch it." His blue eyes darkened and something unhinged and possessive flickered behind them. Celeste stepped between Aubrey and Tolly.

The man re-wrapped the ring again and stuffed it into his pocket, mumbling, almost cooing over it. "I'm trying to keep whatever is inside it contained." Beads of perspiration appeared on his face. "If I keep the ring wrapped in the silk and maintain the wards, it can't escape again."

He meant the alleged ifrit, not the ring. Celeste didn't buy that theory. She thought the spirit had already found a new host. "Tolly, we should get back to the hotel. It's late. I'm sure Aubrey needs his rest, too."

Aubrey's lips stretched into a macabre smile. "You'll help me, won't you, old thing? We've got to transfer the ring into a ward box and seal it away somewhere, until I can get back home, do proper research on it."

Tolly bit her lip but nodded. "Of course, Aubrey. Of course, we'll help. But you're so tired. Why don't you let me take the ring to the local Council representative? Let someone more powerful than we are take charge of the thing."

Aubrey flung himself backward off the stool. "No!" He pressed his hand against the inside pocket of his jacket, where he'd stashed the ring. "No, it's mine." He shook his head, and the madness behind his eyes ebbed a little. "What I mean to say is that I have to maintain constant attention on the wards. You are not a mage, Tolly. You can't handle this."

Celeste once more placed herself between the two and motioned Tolly toward the door. She triggered a spell she'd hung on a charm on her bracelet, felt the bubble of protection go up around the two of them. "We need to go now, Aubrey."

Tolly stood and took a step back. "Why don't we meet in the morning? We can go to the Council together. How does that sound?"

"The Council will do nothing. Don't you think I've tried? Why do you think I'm here in Cairo? They think I'm crazy. You haven't even heard the rest. There have been two more deaths. And as I've told you, someone's been following me. Ransacked my house. Somebody is looking for this thing. It could be the Council, someone there, someone evil. They want the thing's power. Maybe even Carter himself." He shook his head, the mania glowing in his eyes again. "No. No Council. I'll keep it safe for now. You need to find out who else wants the ring and why." He smoothed his wrinkled jacket, cracked his neck. "Please, Astrid. You must help me."

Celeste took Tolly's hand, tugged. "Tolly, it's very late, and I'm exhausted."

Tolly licked dry lips, but the smile stayed in place and her voice remained steady. "Of course. Come to the hotel in the morning. Say ten o'clock? We can have lemonade on the terrace and determine a plan of action."

His eyes flicked toward Celeste, and he backed away until he bumped into the sink. Had he finally sensed the shield she'd put up? He should have noticed the minute she triggered her spell, but he hadn't. "Excellent idea. Ten o'clock." His grimacing attempt at a smile made the hairs on Celeste's neck stand on end. "Thank you, Astrid. I knew I could count on you."

Celeste waited no longer. She pulled open the door and hurried Tolly outside, scurrying like a mouse in a midnight kitchen until they reached the street. It was pitch black, but at least the pervasive sense of madness faded with distance.

Tolly shivered in the chill air. "We need to get back to the hotel. These streets are not safe for the likes of us at night." She cast a spell of her own and a small blue light appeared before them. A guide spell.

Celeste glanced upward toward Aubrey's apartment. "He's not sane, Tolly. I think he's the one possessed."

Tolly shook her head. "No, I would have sensed that. I scanned him on the astral. He's mad, yes. But it seems he has indeed contained something in the ring."

Celeste would have bet against that, but saw no point in arguing here, now. The guide spell bobbed in front of them, inviting them, providing just enough light that they didn't trip over a drunk or a dead...something in their path. "I guess we'll see in the morning." She worried over the deep sadness in Tolly's lovely eyes. "I'm sorry about Aubrey, Tolly. Hopefully, once the ring is somewhere safe, he can recover."

Tolly squeezed her hand. "I love you, Celie."

Her earlier jealousy evaporated at the warmth in those words. "I love you too."

SEVEN

A t eleven the next morning, on the scorching hot terrace of Shepheard's Hotel waiting for Aubrey, the sun burned Celeste's bare skin like a hot iron. She sipped her third glass of lemonade and rolled her shoulders. Just sitting with Tolly, who sat coiled tighter than a clock spring, made her muscles ache with tension. Neither of them slept well. The night had been pleasantly cool, but Celeste had gotten tangled in the mosquito netting surrounding their bed twice, which had entailed turning on lights, and prompted a great deal of cursing. Given how tired she was, she took pride that she'd remembered to hang protective spells—spells one could trigger with just a word—on her charm bracelet that morning. A good thing too, given the odd portents of danger she'd spied in the grounds of her morning coffee.

"I hate Egypt."

"You hate every place that isn't Paris."

"No, that's not true. I like London."

Tolly grimaced.

"And I enjoy Vienna."

"You like the pastry in Vienna."

"Pastry is important. A very good measure of a place."

Tolly checked her watch again, frowned. "I'm worried."

Celeste reached across the table, rubbed Tolly's arm in what she hoped to outside observers seemed only a sisterly gesture. "I know. Is he normally forgetful?"

"Well, if he had his nose in a book, doing some kind of arcane research, he could be. Most scholars are." She rubbed the back of her neck, winced at the blooming sunburn. "I can't imagine what the Council was thinking, sending him out to do fieldwork. He's a book-worm, not a man of action."

That made Celeste chuckle. "Is that what we are, then? Women of action?" She removed her hand, lest it remain too long for respectability's sake. "I think you've been reading too many books by H. Rider Haggard."

Tolly must have left her sense of humor at home in Paris, along with innumerable hats. "Can you be serious for once? Honestly, Celie, you grow more immature by the day."

A slow count to ten. Try not to say anything you'll regret later, she counseled herself. Tolly was under enormous strain. Still, the flare of jealousy from the night before ignited again, and her next words held a bite of venom. "You must love him a great deal."

Those changeable blue eyes flicked her way, then back to the street beyond the terrace. When Tolly spoke, her voice held sadness. "Love didn't play a part. You know my preferences in such matters. The Council matched us for bloodlines. We had no choice but to make the best of it. We did what was necessary, and I produced two wonderful children. Once they came of age, we went our separate ways."

"And yet you're worried about him." She dipped her finger in the wet rings on the table made by the sweating glass of lemonade. "I can feel what you feel, you know." She couldn't meet Tolly's eyes. Didn't want to see what was in them, didn't want confirmation of her jealousy.

"Oh, Celie, don't be ridiculous. I didn't love him then, and I certainly don't love him now. But you cannot spend that many years with a man and not come to care about his well-being."

"If I had to spend years with Corverus, I wouldn't care if he got eaten by crocodiles." She shivered at the thought of the mage who was blackmailing her to join their lineages in the Great Rite in May.

"That is because he is a despicable and dangerous man. Aubrey is neither of those things." Tolly shook her head. "And we will solve that particular problem. I told you, I have an idea."

"An idea you haven't seen fit to share."

"Because I have to think it through, and there's been very little time to do so."

Celeste took her damp fingers and placed them on the back of her burning neck. She pushed Corverus from her mind and refocused. "Tolly, he's not coming." She watched as her partner clenched her jaw, blinking away burgeoning tears. Her long, slender fingers brushed at the crumbs from their breakfast toast.

"I don't know what to do." Misty blue eyes sought Celeste's. "Celie, what do I do?"

"We're women of action." She stood and grabbed her purse from the table. "Come on. Let's go."

"Go where?"

"Back to that squalid apartment. If he's there, we'll beat some sense into him, and barring a return to sanity, we'll beat him until he's unconscious and them take him to the Council."

"And if he's not there?" She paled. "Oh, by the stars, what if he's not?"

"Then we go to the authorities and report him as missing."

"You mean the Council."

"No, I mean the police. We report that a British citizen, who was recently attacked in the Suq, is now missing." She grabbed Tolly's sleeve and tugged her down the steps towards one of the many, waiting taxis. "Then we go to the Council." She urged Tolly into the vehicle. "You do know who's in charge here in Cairo, right?"

"No, no idea at all."

"But you know how to find them."

Her partner pinched the bridge of her nose, a sure sign of frustration. "I don't. But we'll figure something out. We always do."

Celeste could not fathom how the postal service found addresses in the tangled maze of alleys and twisted narrow passageways in this part of the city. There were no street signs or house numbers. It reminded her of the warrens of Spitalfields in London, a place she'd spent considerable time.

The taxi driver dropped them off at the nearest large intersection, saying it was as far as he would go, and wouldn't the ladies prefer to go to the suq instead?

She and Tolly walked the rest of the way. The neighborhood felt as dicey during the day as it had last evening. Tolly put up a spell to help other people's gazes slide off them, while Celeste used her sensing abilities to follow the trail they'd left the previous night.

All magical creatures left behind a trace, a scent or taste or sound, that others could learn to identify, as a hunter learned to recognize animal tracks. Celeste had discovered that her ability to sense those, even from a distance or after a long time, wasn't shared by her fellow magic workers. It was special. Potent. So far, Alistair had kept the knowledge under wraps, but sooner or later, the Council would get wind of it. When that happened, they'd drag her in and dissect her mind like a medical student sliced up cadavers. She'd have the option of running, or allowing them to rummage around inside her head, and running would have been her preferred option before she'd met Tolly. Now, she didn't know what she'd do. The thought of leaving Tolly felt like losing a limb.

After a handful of wrong turns, they found the tenement,

climbed the stairs, and after a sound-dampening spell from Tolly's own charm bracelet, Celeste rapped on the door.

Silence.

Celeste cast her awareness into the apartment, seeking Aubrey's magical aura. She felt a trickle of something, a whiff of unfamiliar magic like an animal spoor, but one she couldn't recognize. This scent had an exotic quality.

She gestured at the door. "Do you smell that?"

Tolly sniffed the air. "I smell several things, all of them unpleasant. To which do you refer?"

"No, not here. On the astral. Something unfamiliar. Like, I don't know, clover or chamomile or something."

Tolly cocked her head. "Well. That is unusual." She frowned. "But it's not Aubrey. He's not in there."

"You're right. Unless he's..." Dead? She pressed her lips closed, not wanting to voice the thought. She turned the handle, surprised to find the door unlocked. It swung open without a creak.

Someone had been here before them. The ceramic mug Aubrey drank from the previous evening lay in shards on the floor. In fact, the vandals had pulled everything from the cupboard and shelves and tossed it to the ground. Not that there had been much. Before Tolly broke free of her shock, Celeste hurried through the curtained doorway into what had to be the bedroom.

She'd been expecting a body but found only more mess. Sheets from the bed lay in piles, the thin excuse for a pillow slashed. Feathers lay scattered everywhere.

She stepped over clothes strewn from a small chest, around a couple of books tossed from a crude shelf and approached the spot from which the strange magical smell, like a cross between heady Frankincense and the fug of old socks, emanated.

Aware that Tolly had entered, Celeste bent down and picked up a torn strip of black silk from the handkerchief she'd last seen wrapped around the ring Aubrey showed them. A red smear decorated the wall next to it. No bigger than an egg, and about knee height. Right under the only window.

Tolly stood beside her, her jaw clenched in strain. "That's blood."

It didn't take a witch to know that. "Yes."

Tolly turned to face her. "Is it Aubrey's?"

Celeste's eyes widened. "How should I know?"

"You can sense people's auras. Surely you'd be able to read his from his own blood."

That application of her ability had not dawned on her. She crouched down, not wanting to touch it, but knowing she had to. Not completely dry, the sticky red stuff clung to her fingers. Like Lady Macbeth, she wasn't sure she'd ever be able to scrub it off. She focused on it, nodded. "It's Aubrey's."

Tolly sagged. "He's dead."

"You don't know that. For one thing, there's not much of it. And it's under the window. He could have cut himself escaping." She looked out the open aperture down a barren wall devoid of footholds or little balconies, the way there'd have been in a bad adventure novel. If he'd jumped, she didn't see how he would have avoided breaking a leg. Still, Aubrey was a powerful witch. He could have had a spell prepared for just such an emergency.

Tolly allowed herself to be convinced. At least for now. "Can you follow him? Using the blood?"

"I can try." She took her partner by the elbow, led her back through the building and out into the street. "But we should visit the authorities first. Both authorities. This is far bigger than us."

Tolly arched her eyebrows in that familiar, supercilious way. "You're recommending we seek help? What happened to Miss I-Can-Handle-Anything?"

"She retired after the whole 'you got kidnapped and nearly tossed off the Eiffel Tower' fiasco in November."

Tolly relaxed. No, not relaxed. But the tension ebbed, and she drooped in physical and emotional exhaustion. "Well, at least you learned something." She rolled her shoulders. "Very well. The mortal authorities first. They'll take time, but not anywhere near as much time as a visit to the Council."

When they reached the first major intersection, they hailed another cab. Celeste stared out the window as the city swept past, hoping that she wasn't making a mistake.

EIGHT

An hour later, after being passed up and down the law enforcement food chain like a Christmas fruitcake, they found themselves in the small, but well-organized office of Detective Sergeant Ibrahim. He was a tall man with a shrewd gaze and a wide smile. His face held just the right touch of mild, well-mannered curiosity. Given the extraordinary things going on in Egyptian governance, and the imminent independence of Egypt from decades of British rule, it was smart for a man like Ibrahim to be cautious of foreign women seeking help.

He stood to greet them, then bid them take the chairs opposite his battered wooden desk. Still, his pressed uniform, clean-shaven face and pomaded hair did him the credit his tawdry office could not. Despite her natural wariness, Celeste found she liked the keenness behind his polite smile.

"Welcome, mesdames. My Sergeant informs me you have a friend who has gone missing?"

His accent rang of long years spent in England, where he'd likely gone to school. The ring he wore on his right hand also spoke of wealth and privilege, indicating he might be the son of a local pasha or other notable bigwig. Celeste paused, used to Tolly taking the lead, but her partner stared out the tiny window, distracted and deep inside herself.

Celeste leaned forward. "Yes. A friend of ours, Aubrey Finlayson. We saw him last night, and he was supposed to meet us for breakfast this morning at Shepheard's, but didn't show up. When we went round to the place where he'd been staying, we found it ransacked. There was blood on the wall by the window and now we're afraid something's happened to him."

Ibrahim nodded in the manner of all police officials everywhere and scribbled something on a piece of paper. "And you know this gentleman well?"

"Well enough." Should she say he was Tolly's former husband? The locals probably took a dim view of the dissolution of marriages.

"Ah. I see. I assume your friend is a bachelor? Perhaps a handsome one?"

Celeste bristled at the assumption that Tolly had been taken in by a charming womanizer. "Frankly, I've no idea what Tolly ever saw in him, to be honest. Not to mention the fact that he hasn't aged well."

Those dark eyebrows rose. "So a former, erm, acquaintance. And you are here in Cairo to visit him?"

"Yes. Sort of. We're here on holiday, but..." She looked at Tolly, whose gaze appeared fixed on a calendar on the wall. "But we decided to look him up while we were in town."

"I see." He made a note on a tablet in front of him. "Are you sure he's missing? Perhaps he's gone on holiday. Or simply doesn't want to be found. People change, you know. I find especially that Egypt changes men. It is also true that it is often beyond many men's abilities to maintain a flat in a way that most women would find acceptable."

Not only had he been educated in England, but he'd also learned the Englishman's innate sexism as well. Disappointed in him, she scooted forward in her chair and met his gaze. "As I mentioned, we were there last evening to discuss the goings on at Howard Carter's excavation, and it was neat as a pin. Even if he had decided, in some sort of masculine-inspired fit of slovenliness, to toss around his belongings and strip the sheets off his bed and throw everything he owned onto the floor, that doesn't explain the blood under the window. And, I'll have you know, we were not there to resume a former relationship, as you imply."

Tolly finally woke up. "Celeste! That was most impertinent. Apologize at once."

Ibrahim didn't quite smile, but mirth glittered in his eyes. He raised a hand. "No, no, it is I who should make an apology. Please forgive my mistake about your interest in this..." He looked down at the paper. "Mr. Finlayson."

Tolly placed her hand on the desk. "He is an old friend, nothing more. Nevertheless, we fear something terrible has befallen him. He mentioned being attacked in the Khan el Khalili the other day. I believe the police were called, and some person arrested."

Ibrahim's eyes widened and his whole body went stiff. "Excuse me a moment." He stood abruptly, went to the door, and spoke in hushed but urgent Arabic to someone outside who hurried away. After a few moments, the fellow returned, and more rapid-fire Arabic ensued. Celeste reached over and squeezed Tolly's hand. When Ibrahim came back in, he carried a file folder that he leafed through.

"We did not have a name for the victim, he vanished before my officers got back to the market stall where the assault occurred. We take every attack like this seriously, but given the current situation, a crime like this against an Englishman can set off a dangerous chain of events." He closed the file before Celeste could peek inside. Not that she could read Arabic. "So the victim was your friend."

"Yes." Celeste leaned forward again. "And now he's missing, and blood found at the scene of his disappearance."

He nodded. "How long had Mr. Finlayson been in Cairo?"

Celeste looked at Tolly, who shrugged. "We're not sure. Not long. I believe he was in Luxor until a few weeks ago."

"I see. And his business here?"

Celeste could hardly tell him he was on a mission from the Council. "He was a historian, wasn't he, Tolly? I assume it has something to do with his research."

"I see." Ibrahim scribbled something on his notepad and, setting down his pen, placed his well-manicured hands on the desk. "Very well then. I will send some officers to investigate." He smiled, raised a finger to forestall her. "I would have done so anyway, of course."

Arrogant asshole. To think she'd liked him. "Of course."

"I must admit to some curiosity now. Especially since you mention the infamous Mr. Carter. You are perhaps friends of Lady Carnarvon?"

"Would it matter if we were?"

"In terms of pursuing the miscreant, if your friend is in genuine trouble—and hasn't simply done a runner because he could not pay his rent—absolutely not. We may not be British, Madame, but this is a new day in Egypt. Justice will be served. However, rumors abound about Mr. Carter's excavation of this tomb. About how he is keeping the best of the artifacts for himself."

"Mr. Ibrahim! Aubrey would never engage in that kind of shifty behavior." There was the Tolly that Celeste knew. She couldn't help smiling as her partner continued. "He was a scholar, not a thief."

"The British, the French, the Germans, the Italians, they have taken away two-thirds of all the treasures of the pharaohs under the auspices of scholarship, Madame." The polite tone now had an edge to it. "In any case, I will personally escort a couple of men to Mr. Finlayson's accommodations. Where are you staying?"

Tolly pulled herself stiffly upright. "Shepheard's."

"And Mr. Finlayson's address?"

Tolly looked to Celeste. Celeste frowned. "It didn't have one." She pointed at his notes. "But I can draw you a map."

He pushed the pen and paper toward her. "A flat without a street address? What sort of neighborhood did your friend find lodgings in?"

Celeste drew the twists and turns as accurately as she could. "Not a great one."

He took the paper she handed back to him, and his eyebrows rose. "Indeed." He folded the paper crisply and stuffed it in his jacket pocket before standing. He held out his hand. "Thank you for coming in, ladies. I will send word to your hotel the minute we know anything."

Celeste stood and, perforce, shook his hand. "We could go with you. It might be easier to find if—"

He ran a finger under his collar. "I can't imagine how you managed to get in and out of that particular quarter of the city without mishap, and it would be derelict of me to risk taking you there again, even with my men. No, I promise you I will go myself and report to you whatever I may find." He ushered them to the door. "One last question. Are you aware of any other contacts of Mr. Finlayson's in Cairo? Other... scholars perhaps?"

Celeste glared at him. "No. As far as I am aware, he knew no one else in Cairo."

"Thank you." He opened the door, gestured them out into the corridor. "Sergeant Mahmud will show you out. Sergeant, please make sure the ladies get a taxi back to Shepheard's Hotel." Ibrahim gave them a very continental bow. "I will be in touch as soon as I have something to share with you. Please enjoy your stay here in Cairo."

And that was it. They were dismissed.

Once in the taxi, Celeste took Tolly's hand. She'd never seen her partner so withdrawn. "We're going to sort this out, Tolly. I promise."

"I just ... I have this feeling of dread, Celie. Like we've opened up Pandora's box."

"Maybe. Either way, we'll figure it out." With or without the smug Detective Sergeant Ibrahim.

NINE

They were only a couple of blocks from the police station when she felt the sensation of being watched again. This time, however, it was stronger than the vague feeling she'd had back in Cairo, and her bracelet warmed. She forced herself not to turn, instead sending out her magical senses, seeking for the one who meant her harm.

"We're being followed," Celeste murmured.

Tolly sat facing forward, eyes closed. "Yes. I just felt it. A man on a bicycle." She opened her eyes. "A mortal."

"We could get the driver to outrun him. Take us out of town, then circle back."

"And have them attack us out in the middle of nowhere? How do we know the driver isn't part of this?"

Celeste focused on the turbaned man behind the wheel and felt nothing but a general loathing of tourists from him. "I don't think he is." She chewed her lip. "What do we do?"

"Carry on to the hotel. We will have lunch and then figure out how to contact the Council. I cannot believe a mortal would dare to attack us while we are having lunch in the dining room of Shepheard's."

"Well, not without some serious firepower and the willingness for collateral damage." Celeste fought the urge to look at the man on the bicycle. Closing her eyes, she probed the surface of his mind. She didn't read his thoughts. Not only would that be against the rules, but that wasn't an ability she possessed. She could, however, sense his emotions. "Riled up. Angry."

Tolly refined the emotion. "Fervent."

The taxi pulled up in front of the hotel and Tolly let herself out before the driver could do the honors. She counted coins into his hand and hurried up the broad steps into the hotel, leaving Celeste to scurry after her.

Inside the institution that was Shepheard's, staff busied themselves catering to guests and from the dining room came the clink of cutlery. Despite the noise, there was a dignified hush.

And the sensation of being watched vanished.

Tolly strode forward, and the maître d' smiled. "Madame Tollefsen. What a lovely dress you are wearing. It matches the blue in your eyes."

Tolly had made another conquest. "A table please. Georges. Perhaps one with a view?"

The maître d's smile slipped for just an instant. "That may take a moment to arrange. If you would care to wait here, I will not be long."

He hurried into the dining room and Celeste watched in amusement as the man reseated a rather loud young American couple a few tables away, bowing while apologizing for having seated them in the sun at such a warm time of day. Oh, yes, he was good. The Americans assumed they were getting preferential treatment and would sneer at whoever got the table they had vacated.

Bustling back to them, the maître d' swept them a bow. "Please follow me, ladies." He seated them with a flourish, pulling out Tolly's chair first, then Celeste's. "Your waiter will be with you shortly. And as always, should you require anything else, please let me know."

Tolly gave him a beatific smile. "Merci, Georges. *Trés gentil.*"

The view from their table encompassed not only the entire dining room, but some of the street outside as well. No one could approach them without their knowing it.

"You've got him wrapped around your finger. How do you do that? We've been here less than thirty-six hours."

"It's called being civil, Celie. Something you would do well to practice now and again."

"I am civil."

"You were very rude to Detective Sergeant Ibrahim."

"Me? I was rude to *him*? He thought we were chasing Aubrey like... like..."

"Foolish, besotted women?"

"Yes!"

"For all he knows, we are. We appear young and single and unaccompanied. I'm sure Egypt is full of foolish, besotted women chasing after dashing men."

"He's a misogynist."

"Misogynist? What a word. You've been spending too much time with Gertrude." Tolly shook her head. "He's simply a man of his culture and upbringing."

A waiter arrived, forestalling another "discussion." They ordered a light lunch and by the time the native Cairene walked away, Celeste had lost her head of steam. "I still think he's a horrid man."

"I will reserve judgment until we see what he turns up. He can be the most pig-headed woman-hater on the planet as long as he is as smart an investigator as Sherlock Holmes and as dedicated as John Watson."

Celeste sipped at a cool glass of lemonade. "Fine. I hope we get more cooperation from the Council. How are we going to find them?"

"I've been thinking about that. I suppose I will have to telegraph Alistair."

"He won't be pleased with us, haring off after Aubrey without telling him first."

"He will be furious. And no doubt insist we do nothing more until he arrives."

Celeste clenched her teeth. She wanted to be done with this. She wanted to go home. "That will be weeks."

"Quite likely, yes."

She thought for a moment. "Do we need the Council?"

Tolly clunked her glass on the table, her tone sharp. "Weren't you the one who insisted on it this morning?"

"Yes. But maybe I was wrong. What will they do except complicate things? They didn't believe Aubrey earlier about his suspicions, so I doubt they'll believe us. I mean, I'm automatically discounted for being a loose cannon, and they'll paint you black by association." She frowned. "It's happened before."

Celeste found her eyes drawn to the street outside. Though grateful that the feeling of being watched had gone, she still found herself searching the crowd for a tail. Some might call it paranoia. She called it caution. "Whoever was following us is gone."

"For now."

Their server returned with their first course. As he set the soup in front of them, he addressed Tolly in broken English. "Madame, there is gentleman in lobby who have message for you. He want to know if he join you." The young man pulled something from his pocket. "He give me this to you."

Tolly took the calling card with two fingers, as though expecting it to bite and examined the card. "Sir John Seymour, Esquire." She glanced at Celeste. "Do you know him?"

"Never heard of him."

"Is he an English gentleman?" Tolly asked the server.

"*Aiwa, Sitt. Inglise.*"

Celeste felt the hairs on the back of her neck prickle. A frisson of power trickled into the dining room, like the smell of strong cologne preceding its wearer. "Did he ask for Madame Tollefsen by name?"

A vigorous nod.

Tolly shrugged. "Then I suppose we should see him."

With her bracelet remaining quiescent, Celeste nodded. "I guess it can't hurt. I'm not sensing any danger."

The young waiter smiled, visibly relieved. "Very good. I bring him." He gave a brief bow and scurried off.

"Celie, who on earth even knows we're here except Aubrey?"

A very proper, very English gentleman approached their table, smiling like they were old friends. He oozed power. Old, finely tuned magical power. A mortal would have been respectful and maybe a bit in awe, but to a witch, that feeling magnified tenfold.

They didn't need to find the Council's representative. He had found them.

TEN

A man so typically English, he'd blend in any British gentleman's club, Sir John represented the quintessential specimen of British officialdom, with short-cropped hair trimmed in a cut that would be approved by both mother and King. His suit came from Saville Row, a pocket watch tucked in his waistcoat, which strained slightly over the paunch around his middle. Years behind a desk had taken their toll not only on his waistline, but on his eyes, which were bespectacled.

He held out a manicured hand, soft and delicate, that belied the strength of his grip when Celeste shook it. His gentle, friendly smile was as manufactured as his suit as he gestured to an empty chair. "Thank you for seeing me. I'm Sir John Seymour, the region's magister. May I join you?"

Tolly's spine stiffened, always a slave to rules and the authority of the Council. "Of course, Magister."

Magister, or more formally, Magister Res Publicae, was a title within the Council, just one step below the rank of Councilor. They held power over an entire geographical magical region, the area of which varied not by mortal political borders, but by the size of the magical population. Nominally, that authority applied only to witches, but since the signing of the Pact of 10 May a century earlier, groups of other magical beings like dryads, naiads, and selkies could call on the Council to handle disputes and provide protections. Paris had two magisters; London three. Here, in Egypt, Celeste imagined there was only one. How far geographically his auspices stretched, she couldn't guess. The way she figured it, being given a magistracy in a region this far-flung and unknown had either been a plum assignment or some sort of slap on the wrist. The cold, flinty eyes of Sir John Seymour made her hope it was the latter. She neither liked nor trusted him, despite his affable manner.

Relaxing comfortably in his seat, he motioned for the waiter. After requesting tea and a light lunch of potage St. Germain—something not on the luncheon menu, but which given the man's perceived status amongst the hotel employees, he'd get anyway—he turned that snake's smile on them again. Celeste felt like a mouse under the paw of a cat.

"Madame Tollefsen, I am so pleased to finally make your acquaintance. Aubrey has, of course, mentioned his former spouse often. And your success in Toulon against the Black Coven naturally precedes you."

Tolly nodded. "A pleasure to meet you as well, Sir John."

The man's gaze slid from Tolly to Celeste. She kept her breath even, resisted the urge to scratch the sudden itch in the center of her back. He'd probably caused it. "And Mademoiselle Bérenger. Archmagister Gundersdottir speaks of *you* often." An almost predatory look lit his eyes. "I understand you and Magister Corverus have been matched for this Beltane. You must be pleased. Corverus has an impeccable lineage."

She kept her face impassive. "So I've been told." There, that was the truth. Alistair had spent long minutes expounding upon Corverus' magical predecessors. Then went on for another twenty apologizing for being unable to release her from the contract that she herself had signed. She couldn't tell him she'd been blackmailed into it, nor about the deed that Corverus had used as leverage. She'd taken control of a living being's free will. The Council could have sentenced her to death for that or stripped her of her powers. Permanently.

Tolly rescued her before she said something snarky to the magister. "It was lovely of you to look us up, Sir John, but surely you didn't come just to have a cup of tea and congratulate Celeste."

The magister could have taken offense at Tolly's response, but she said it with such respect and dignity that he either believed she was currying favor, or he was hellbent on maintaining civility. His smile oozed unctuousness. "Ah, but it is such a rare delight to have others of our kind visit Egypt." He sat back as the waiter set the soup and his tea before him. "The minute I learned of your arrival, I determined to come welcome you." He poured his own tea from the pot, added milk and three sugars. With a satisfactory smirk, he said, "So here I am!"

How he knew they had come was something Celeste would debate with Tolly later. Council spies skulked everywhere, even in far-flung Egypt. Tolly's response came out smooth as silk. "How very kind of you."

"Will you be here long?" This question, he lobbed at Celeste.

She made a show of tasting her soup, delaying to piss him off. Long enough for Tolly to nudge her foot under the table. Finally, with a bright smile, she said, "In Cairo? Just a few days. Tolly has been longing to see the pyramids for some time."

Tolly, bless her, picked up the ball. "Oh, yes, I'm desperate to see them. And the Sphinx too."

"A long journey for such a short stay."

Celeste glanced at Tolly. She sent a thought to her partner. *Do we really want to tell him about Aubrey?*

Going to the Council was your idea.

Well, I've changed my mind. This guy is a creep.

Tolly kept her expression even. *You think all members of the Council are creeps.*

That's not true. I like Archmagister Gundersdottir.

The exchange only took a second or two. Seymour kept his eyes on Celeste's face, waiting, eyebrows raised, as though he knew she and Tolly were sharing thoughts.

"Oh, well, we plan on renting a dahabeeyah once we're done here, do the complete Nile experience. Tolly, wasn't it Natalie who sent us pictures of her trip down the Nile?"

Tolly nodded, took a sip of her tea. She didn't have to fake waxing poetic. "Oh, those were just amazing. There is something about the quality of the air in Egypt. The sunsets! When I saw those photographs, I knew we had to plan a holiday here."

Seymour wrinkled his nose. "Natalie?"

"Natalie Westmont. She's a coven priestess in Devonshire."

He nodded sagely. "Ah. Yes. Indeed." Celeste had the impression he had no idea who Natalie was. He followed up with, "I assume she came here before my time."

Tolly gave him one of her patented, sure-to-charm laughs. "Oh, it must have been. You would remember Natalie. She's quite the bon vivant." To Celeste, she thought, *What about Aubrey?*

Celeste gave her a mental headshake. She pushed away her soup, trying to look ill. "Oh my. I think I must have gotten too much sun today."

Seymour nodded. "You do look a bit pink. As does Madame Tollefsen. Afternoons here are usually spent indoors, relaxing. Things pick up again in the evening, when it cools off. If you ladies would permit, I could take you on a carriage ride tonight, show you the pyramids by moonlight."

Now her bracelet pinged. Celeste sent an imploring look at her partner. "Oh, I'm not sure I'm up to it. It was such an exhausting day."

"Of course," said Sir John with a cloying smile. "Perhaps

tomorrow morning might be more auspicious. I can arrange access to places that are off-limits to ordinary tourists. A very dear friend of mine works at the Cairo Museum. You will not find a more learned guide."

Celeste put a hand to her forehead, feigning a fit of vapors. "I'm so sorry. Tolly, I really feel as though I must lie down now."

She stood, and politeness forced Seymour to his feet as well. Tolly rose and took her by the arm. She could sense Tolly's genuine concern. "Celie? Are you ill?"

I'm fine, just sick of this smarmy bastard. She shook her head but leaned against Tolly. Convincingly, she hoped. "No, no, I think it's just the heat. And you know I don't travel well."

In her mind, she heard Tolly's voice, dripping with irritation. *That is probably the biggest lie you've ever told. By the stars, Celie!*

Seymour wrinkled his brow in genuine concern. Ironically, his concerned face looked just like his pissed off face. "I'll just call for one of the staff to help you upstairs, then send a doctor round."

"No." Tolly waved him back into his chair. "That won't be necessary, Sir John. But thank you for your concern. Is there a way to reach you in the morning? Your office, perhaps? Then, if Celie is feeling better, we'd be delighted to take you up on your kind offer."

Yeah, when pigs fly.

"Yes, of course." He reached into his suit jacket and retrieved a silver case. The calling card he handed Tolly differed from the one he'd given the waiter earlier. This one read Sir John Seymour, Senior Attaché, Government House, with an address and telephone number printed underneath. "Please, call me in the morning regardless of what you decide. And if you determine later that you require a doctor, I'll leave the name of my personal physician with the front desk." He gave them an abbreviated bow. "Mademoiselle, I hope you feel better soon."

Celeste let Tolly lead her through the maze of tables and up the stairs. Seymour followed at a discrete distance, but she lost sight of him as they passed further down the corridor to their room.

Once inside, Tolly pushed her onto the sofa with a disgusted noise. "You are incorrigible."

"One of the many things you love about me."

"I am not amused, Celie. Aubrey's life could be at stake."

She sucked in a breath. "You felt it too, Tolly. That man cannot be trusted. Remember Aubrey said he'd talked to the Council rep? That's him, and he didn't believe Aubrey. Now he comes sniffing around here? That's not a coincidence. What if 'Sir John' had something to do with what happened to Aubrey?"

"You think everyone on the Council has ulterior motives."

"They do. They all have an agenda. The rest of us are just pawns on the chessboard to them."

"Why would he hurt Aubrey?"

"For that damned ring. It's got power. I don't know what kind, but Aubrey thought it contained an evil spirit, something capable of possessing people. I'll bet Sir John would just love to get his hands on it."

"You're paranoid."

Celeste stood, poured herself a whiskey from the drinks table. "With reason. After the nightmare in Macedonia, I was the target of a literal witch hunt. A witch hunt sponsored by the Council. I should be dead in a sack in the middle of the Rhone."

Tolly collapsed next to her on the sofa. "Give me that."

Celeste handed her the tumbler, now half-drained, and Tolly knocked back the rest. Her hand shook as she set the glass on the floor at her feet. Pulling her knees up, she shrank into herself, burying her face like a child. "I can't think anymore. Goddess, I'm so worried. It feels like my time of sanction all over again. My stomach's churning, no course of action feels right. If I betray Aubrey to the Council, he'll never forgive me. And I do owe him a great deal. But if

I betray the Council...again...Oh goddess. What should I do? Tell me what we should do."

"I don't know. Yet. But trusting Seymour won't be it."

In a small, trembling voice, Tolly asked, "Then who can we trust?"

It felt odd to suddenly be in charge, to be the strong one. Celeste had spent the better part of fifty years leaning on Tolly. Now, Tolly was counting on her. Could she lead them out of this? Hoping she'd made the right choice, Celeste gathered her partner into her arms and, with Tolly's head resting on her shoulder, stroked her hair. "Us, luv. We trust us."

ELEVEN

The heat of the afternoon and the quiet ticking of the clock on the wall had Celeste dozing before too many minutes. A loud rap on the door jolted her awake. Tolly too sat abruptly upright. At least a couple of hours had passed, judging by the sharp angle of the sun.

The knock came again, loud and insistent.

Celeste crossed to the door and held out her hand, magical senses seeking. Her bracelet gave no warning of danger, yet she still called, "Who is it?"

"Detective Sergeant Ibrahim, Mademoiselle. I have some news for you."

Tolly's face paled. "Let him in."

Celeste smoothed her hair and straightened her dress before opening the door. "Please come in."

His dark, hawkish features gave nothing away as he entered, holding his hat before him like a shield. If his trousers had been more sharply creased, they might be considered a lethal weapon. He took a position just to the left of the door, posture stiff, face grim. "I am sorry to disturb you."

Celeste moved to the sofa, where she gently drew Tolly down with her. She had a feeling the woman would need to sit for what followed. "Not at all, Detective. We appreciate your coming. Can I offer you something? We can have the suffragi fetch some tea or coffee."

"No, thank you." His gaze met hers, then moved to Tolly. "I'm afraid I may have some unfortunate news, mesdames. My men pulled a body from the Nile this afternoon. He had no identification, but he appears to be a wealthy European gentleman, and as far as I know, your friend, Mr. Finlayson, is the only European man currently reported missing. We need someone to confirm his identity. Perhaps you have a male relative or friend who might take on that onerous task?"

Celeste spoke first, angered at the implication a woman could not handle seeing a dead body. "Nonsense. We are quite capable of making the identification."

She looked to Tolly for confirmation, saw her partner shrink back. "I..."

Watching the color drain from Tolly's face, the pinched look of pain and horror in her eyes as Tolly's worst fear came home to roost, Celeste hugged her tightly. Tolly buried her face in Celeste's shoulder. What had she been thinking? It would be cruel to put Tolly through this. "Give us a moment, Detective." Uncaring of what the policeman thought of their intimacy, she kissed Tolly's hair. "I'll go luv," she murmured, "You stay here."

Tolly sniffed, then pulled away and used the sofa to steady herself. "No. No, I'm fine. I'll go."

"We'll go," Celeste corrected. While Tolly sat shell-shocked, Celeste fetched her partner's hat and a light shawl; it would be cooler once the sun set. "Are you sure?"

Tolly blinked then seemed to get hold of herself. She went to the mirror and pinned on her hat. In a stronger voice, she said, "I'm sure."

Amazed at her partner's resilience and determined to provide all the support she could, Celeste collected her own hat and followed the Egyptian detective downstairs to a waiting carriage.

Ten minutes later, they descended a set of tiled stairs into what amounted to a whitewashed cellar that served as the city morgue. Cooled both naturally and artificially, Celeste found it a blessed relief.

Cabinets lined white-tiled walls—easy to clean, no doubt—and a ceramic table occupied the center. An anemic fan spun lazily overhead, barely disturbing the sheet draped over the body. Near where the hand might be, and at the feet, rusty stains marred the white covering.

A European gentleman dressed in doctor's whites stood solemnly at the head of the table.

Celeste could sense Tolly's resolve wavering again and moved forward. "Let's get this over with. Please, if you would, just show us his face."

The doctor grimaced. "I'm afraid the gentleman was rather badly beaten. It is not a pretty sight. Perhaps one of the ladies' husbands might be better suited for such a grim task." He glared at Ibrahim, chastisement for bringing women to the morgue.

Celeste stepped up to the autopsy table, took hold of the sheet covering the face of the body. With a quick twitch, she pulled it back. Despite having only met the man briefly, and the severe swelling and bruising that covered his face, a glance was enough. She replaced the sheet, gave a nod. "It's him. That's Aubrey Finlayson."

Silence stuffed the white-tiled room. All eyes focused on Tolly, whose hand clenched at her side, whether to stifle an effort to cover her face, or some other gesture that might betray emotion. Celeste felt a veil drop between them as her partner closed off her innermost thoughts from Celeste. And possibly Tolly herself.

Tolly stepped up to the autopsy table and cleared her throat before she said, "I must see him."

"Tolly, no." Celeste put out a hand to stop her.

Tolly slapped it aside, startling Celeste, and lifted the sheet. Everyone in the room seemed to hold their breath. The men assumed she would collapse in a heap. They didn't know Tolly. She gazed down at the bloated, battered face of the father of her two children, then calmly covered him. "Yes. That's Aubrey. What happened to his hand?" Unflinching, she met the eyes of the doctor.

His bushy eyebrows rose. "He was in the river some time. His hand was, ah, taken by a Nile crocodile."

Ibrahim hovered solicitously, ready, Celeste supposed, to offer an arm. Instead, Tolly walked to the other end of the table and lifted the sheet again. "His foot as well?"

The doctor swallowed. "Yes."

"Cause of death?"

The doctor frowned, glanced at Ibrahim.

The detective cleared his throat and ran a finger under his collar. At least he didn't prevaricate. "A knife wound to the heart."

"He didn't drown? It was not accidental? When did it happen?"

The doctor blustered. "I hardly think this is a conversation to be had with ladies present."

Ibrahim lifted his chin. "Best estimate is after midnight, based on rigor mortis and other factors."

Only Celeste saw the pain that flashed in Tolly's eyes, now a misty blue. If they were home, they'd arrange a crossing ceremony for him. That couldn't be done here. Yet Tolly would need closure and Aubrey deserved to have his passage eased into the Summerland. Before the doctor could hurry them along, she said, "Could we have a few moments in private to say a prayer for him?"

They could hardly object to that, but instead of leaving the room as she'd hoped, they moved off to a corner.

There would be no circle of friends gathered around Aubrey's body. No oil to anoint the brow, hands, feet and heart to aid in the spirit's journey. No singing or drumming. No candles to light his way. But she was determined to do what she could, for Tolly's sake. Taking Tolly's hand in hers, she quietly intoned a prayer her old mentor Marguerite had taught her.

"Though you travel the path of darkness to the glorious light beyond, let your steps be easy. Take with you our love and return to us when the veil is thin with your blessings. You have only stepped away and over the hill and we will see you anon as the wheel of life turns. Blessed be, Aubrey Finlayson."

The cool façade cracked, and Tolly's eyes brimmed with tears. She squeezed Celeste's hand and the barrier between them evaporated. Celeste could have drowned in those swirling emotions. After a moment, Tolly murmured a choked "Blessed be."

They stood for a moment in silence and Celeste felt a stirring of energy, a shifting as Aubrey's spirit translated from this plane to the next.

An eternity ticked by before Tolly released Celeste's hand. "Thank you, *elskling*."

"You're welcome."

Surreptitiously wiping her tears on a handkerchief, Tolly turned to face Ibrahim and the doctor. "Thank you, gentlemen, for your patience." She cleared the emotion from her throat and resumed in a brisk tone. "I assume you have his personal effects? It seems unlikely he was tossed into the Nile sans clothing."

Ibrahim motioned to the doctor, who fetched a paper sack from the counter. Ibrahim passed the bag to Celeste. "This is everything. A wallet with approximately £200, a Swiss watch, a twenty-four-karat gold signet ring, a black silk handkerchief. The clothes, I'm afraid, are in no state to be returned."

He paused, looking even more uncomfortable. "Given that his personal effects were on the body, it is unlikely to have been a robbery." His eyes settled on Celeste. "I must ask, officially, where both of you were last night between ten p.m. and two a.m."

Celeste spun to face him. "You cannot possibly believe we had anything to do with this."

He spread his hands open. "You were acquainted with the dead man. You visited him, by your own account, yesterday evening, and may have been the last people to see him alive."

"You bastard!" Celeste's anger boiled up.

Tolly grabbed her hand, squeezed painfully. "Stop. It is a reasonable question." Her voice was calm. Too calm. "We were at our hotel. In bed, asleep. I am sure the front desk will be happy to tell you when we returned after seeing Aubrey and that we did not go out again."

Ibrahim inclined his head. "I will be happy to hear them confirm this. Although you still might have been able to sneak out another way."

Tolly's hand continued to grip Celeste's arm, restraining her from shouting exactly what she thought of this idiocy. And yet, in his place, might she not have thought the same thing?

"And why would we have killed him? And then report him missing?"

"I do not know, Madame, but it is my job to investigate all possibilities."

Tolly actually smiled. "I appreciate your thoroughness."

The doctor, who had been watching this volley of words like a man at a tennis match, snorted. "Really, Detective."

Ibrahim ignored the medical man. He inclined his head respectfully at Tolly, and his gaze softened. "Would you be so kind as to examine the contents of the bag? Perhaps you can determine if something is missing?"

Celeste still clutched the paper sack. Stalking to a counter, she pushed aside medical tools and withdrew the contents, one by one.

The ring, which she'd noticed on Aubrey's pinky the night before, bore Aubrey's initials on the flat bezel, with two rampant lions supporting it. The wristwatch was indeed an expensive piece, though the face was now clouded with condensation. The leather wallet was empty, the cash separate in a soggy mass. Last was the partial black handkerchief with a corner ripped off, and which pulsed with power from contact with the object previously wrapped inside.

With her back still turned, she palmed the handkerchief. Replacing the rest of the sack's contents, she folded it closed before she met Tolly's questing gaze with a slight shake of her head. The thing that should have been there was not. The scarab ring Aubrey had shown them, the one stolen from Tut's tomb, was missing.

TWELVE

D etective Sergeant Ibrahim insisted on escorting them back to their hotel. Celeste requested a visit to the site where they'd discovered Aubrey's body, but the police officer refused. He stayed with them, playing the part of a proper British gentleman, providing the sort of well-bred masculine solace he'd been trained to offer. It took nearly forty minutes to convince him they were just fine, thank you, and wave him on his way. From the window, Celeste watched him stride off down the street, keeping her eyes on him until he disappeared into the crowd several blocks away. She suspected that once out of sight, he would slip into a doorway to spy on them or at the very least have someone assigned to do so.

Which meant she and Tolly needed to keep their magical senses open for observers. No, call them what they were. Spies.

"He cannot possibly consider us suspects."

"Why wouldn't he? We knew Aubrey. We reported him missing. I would think you'd be happy he considers us capable of action instead fainting violets too addle-pated to commit such a crime." When Celeste scowled at that, she finished with, "You can't have it both ways. Emancipation is a double-edged sword."

"Hmph." Celeste scanned the scene below their window, but so many local men hung about the entrance to the hotel in their galabeyas and turbans, attempting to sell their services as guides or their genuine ancient relics to gullible tourists, that determining who might be an undercover policeman was impossible. She turned away and stripped out of her sweaty clothes. "Well, we should slip out the back when we go." She rummaged through their wardrobe and pulled out a yellow sundress and a straw cloche with a matching ribbon.

Tolly dropped listlessly on the divan, her mood deflated. "Go where?"

Celeste slipped into her dress and fastened the hook of the halter top behind her neck. "To the riverbank, of course."

"Whatever for? So you can be chewed on by a crocodile as well?"

"No. I have no wish to become an offering to Sobek," she said, referencing the ancient Egyptian god with the head of a crocodile. At least some of Tolly's lectures about Egypt had stuck. "We have to find the ring. It's the key to what happened to Aubrey. He talked of possession. If we can get our hands on it, we can figure out what to do with it." She paced. "And it won't be to turn it over to that stuffed shirt, Sir John." She paused, stared down at the street, her mind racing. "Maybe the ring fell out of Aubrey's pocket when he was attacked. We have to at least look."

Tolly massaged her forehead. "No. Far more likely, the men who killed Aubrey took it from his lifeless body." Her voice caught. "Goddess, I don't want any more to do with this. They killed him for the damn ring, let them have. If they see us snooping around, we might be next. I just keep wondering what he must have gone through. How he must have suffered?"

Celeste dropped onto the couch and pulled Tolly into her arms. "Oh, luv, I'm so sorry." Tolly leaned into her, sniffling, exhausted. When she pulled back, wiping her face with a gauzy sleeve, she looked away in embarrassment.

"I'm the one who's sorry. I should be stronger than this. It's not like I've lost you." She squeezed Celeste's hand.

"He's the father of your children." Celeste tried to tamp down more irrational jealousy.

"He was a good man. We didn't always see eye to eye, but we were comfortable enough together until we could go our separate ways." She straightened, took a breath, and shook off the uncharacteristic melancholy. "Do you really want to go to the river? You can't possibly think the ring is just sitting there in the mud."

"It might be. And even if it isn't, I have an idea how we can find it."

"Why do I think I won't like this?"

"You may not appreciate my methods, but you cannot deny my results."

"You mean like nearly toppling the Tour d'Eiffel with a cyclone?"

"That wasn't me! That was the Red Witch. She was the one who called down the air elemental."

The corners of Tolly's mouth twitched upward. "You are impossible, Celie." She stood and smoothed the skirt of her floral organza dress. "I suppose I could stand to have a little wash. One perspires greatly in this climate. And then change into something a little more casual. Unzip me?"

Celeste grinned and complied.

After a brief interlude, Celeste wrote a note a quick note to Byron, and while Tolly bathed, slipped out, using the excuse that she needed to request additional towels from the front desk. It was true she would visit the lobby, but only as she passed through to find a quiet corner to contact Pyp. Byron would be ill-pleased to be her dogsbody, but she couldn't reasonably trot over to the Council and ask for their archives on djinns and ifrits without explaining why she wanted the information. Nor, for that matter, would she have Byron go through Council-monitored channels. Yet she needed to know more about what Aubrey claimed to have encountered and perhaps even bound into that ring. And Byron had contacts everywhere.

There was no place appropriate inside, but in the gardens at the back of the hotel she found a bench in a discreet arbor, no doubt used by British officers and young women for a spot of privacy. There she pulled out the special coin she had enchanted with a psychic link that would act as a sort of front desk bell for Pyp. She'd written the note upstairs. Now she just needed Pyp to deliver it.

Minutes ticked past, and she wondered if her enchantment worked only to help him find her. After a few more anxious minutes, she heard the pop that heralded his arrival.

He wasn't in his telegram delivery uniform this time. Instead, he sported a brand-new tweed jacket, a white shirt with a jabot at the neck, and a pair of gently worn riding breeches. Brown riding boots completed the outfit. She bit back a laugh. He looked as though he'd stepped out of a painting from the 1880s depicting a young lord ready to mount his horse for a fox hunt.

"That's quite the outfit."

He ducked his head shyly at first. "Thanks. Makes me look more grown-up, right? Like a regular toff."

She nodded. "It does indeed." As long as he kept himself to the Magical Quarter, no one would bat an eyelash. Fashion there reflected a wide variety of cultures and time periods, depending on a creature's life span and predilections.

She handed him the envelope. "I need Byron to read this immediately. So don't dally, and make sure that as soon as he's done what I've asked, you bring me his reply. Tell him I need every scrap of information. Nothing is too small."

"Gotcha."

She almost didn't want the young man to go. She missed home, and he was her only connection to it right now. Of course, she missed Byron too, though she was loathe to admit it, damn the smug, annoying bastard.

"Anything else, miss?"

She rubbed her eyes. They burned from heat and exhaustion. Not from tears. She was *not* crying. "No. Take care. I hope to see you soon."

He snapped a salute. It would have looked more impressive if he'd had a riding crop in his hand. Then he vanished with a pop.

Swallowing her melancholy, she headed back to their rooms, remembering to ask the front desk for additional towels to be delivered on her way.

Around five, Celeste fetched Tolly and flagged down a cab to take them to the approximate location along the Nile where the police discovered Aubrey's body. Another twenty minutes of walking up and down the muddy banks and chatting to local fishermen turned up nothing. In the meantime, they'd acquired an entourage of a dozen curious Egyptian children. One enterprising lad led them to the spot they'd fished Aubrey from the water. The proof lay in the boot prints of the constabulary and the remains of the scholar's round eyeglasses, crushed under someone's shoes.

Celeste awarded the boy a few coins, then sent the kids scurrying off to their supper. Alone at last, they scoured the muddy riverbank fruitlessly, as the sun began to sink behind the cliffs. There was no sign of the ring.

Walking to the river's edge, Tolly twisted Aubrey's broken tortoise shell frames in her hands and stared at the brown swirling waters as though it could provide not only answers but solace. "I told you there would be nothing."

Celeste felt that sense of being on the outside again. Desperate to bridge the gap that widened between them, she pulled the black handkerchief she'd taken from the morgue from her straw handbag and brandished it. "There's more than one way to skin a cat."

"Celie! Where did you get that?"

Celeste shrugged. "I must have accidentally stuck it up my sleeve at the morgue."

"You...you have no shame." She paused, then said, "You know, Nico would object to that idiom about skinning a cat." She referred to the stray cat they sometimes allowed in.

It felt good to hear even the small hint of playful energy in her partner's voice. "Good thing he's not here." She entwined her fingers with Tolly's. "Come on. Let's follow the trail."

Tolly sighed. "What trail?"

Celeste held up the square of black silk. "The energy trail of the ring. I can use this handkerchief like I used the Red Witch's scarf."

"Won't it just lead us back to the morgue?"

"If this ring is possessed, or can cause possession, it is an incredibly powerful artefact. That black handkerchief spent a lot more time absorbing the ring's energy than Aubrey's. I'm sure of it." She tilted her chin up in determination and relinquished Tolly's hand. "I'm going to do this. You are free to come, or you can go back to the hotel and rest, and I'll join you once I've found it."

Tolly's spiky attitude faded. Her shoulders sagged, yet she made a carry-on gesture. "Where you lead, I will follow. But daylight is fading. Let's not tempt fate twice by wandering unpleasant sections of Cairo in the dark again."

Celeste closed her eyes in concentration. She eased her awareness onto the astral plane, an energetic mirror of the physical world, where energy flowed like currents in a stream, and viewed the handkerchief in her hand. A braided thread of brown, spring green, and teal strung off into the distance from the square of silk, a thread of power that throbbed intensely. That had to be the ring. Or whatever magic the ring contained. Aubrey thought it held a malicious spirit, but she sensed no evil, which usually appeared as red or black. The energy signature also tickled her sense of smell, reminiscent of a grassy meadow filled with apple-scented chamomile and spicy yarrow.

With a mental finger on the energetic pulse of the ring, Celeste opened her eyes. "It's that way."

To Celeste's relief, Tolly took her hand, and they headed off down the bank of the Nile together.

THIRTEEN

The gentle breeze from the water cooled Celeste as she made her way along the river's edge. Despite the sleeveless yellow sundress, she dripped with sweat, the wetness soaking her brassiere, her hair, and the back of her neck. Mosquitoes swarmed her, calling "free food" to all their blood-sucking friends. She ignored them while Tolly swatted futilely and grumbled under her breath. She needed to stay focused on the wisp of magical signature she followed. It wavered and kept moving in a sinuous pattern somewhere ahead and to the left as though it were in the water, swimming. Or on the water. A boat perhaps? Could one of Aubrey's killers be a fisherman? Had local footpads killed and robbed him?

Yet they hadn't taken his signet ring. Maybe it had been too tight on his finger to remove. Or they'd been disturbed. She remembered the stump of his arm, his missing hand and foot. Maybe a larger predator in the form of a hungry crocodile had interrupted their search and scared them off.

She nervously eyed the gently lapping water a meter or so distant. This was not a pleasant country brook that burbled over weathered rocks, speckled trout sporting in its clear, cool water. No, the Nile was a muddy green soup that smelled of slimy mud, human waste, and decay. That effluvium had kept the population of the narrow, fertile strip of land on either side of the mighty river fed for millennia, but did not make for a romantic walk, despite what more poetical visitors before her had written.

She thought briefly of Byron. He might have had something lyrical to say about moonlight on the Nile.

She returned her attention to the magical thread of energy, found it drawing closer. Shading her eyes against the red glare of the setting sun, she examined the river for a skiff, or even a swimmer, headed her way. A small ripple indicated movement under the water, and two little round heads popped up above the lapping waves. Turtles, she thought. She'd read about turtles that liked to live in the mud along the banks.

But no boat. No swimmer splashing along wearing Aubrey's ancient, stolen scarab ring. And even though the slums of Cairo carried on their noisome life less than twenty meters away, on the other side of the blank mud brick walls of the crowded houses, she felt alone. Isolated.

As if to pound this notion home, her charmed bracelet singed her wrist, a warning of dire danger.

Nearby, Tolly stiffened. "Celie. I feel something."

The sensation of being watched returned and her scalp rippled. It came from two directions at once, behind them and from the water. The swimming thief and his land-bound accomplice?

She stepped back, looked behind her. Once again, she saw the blank mudbrick walls that stood between them and the winding and claustrophobic streets beyond. She could hear voices, women arguing with children, men arguing with each other in the typical way of all village men acquainted for a lifetime. Muted by walls and distance, donkeys brayed, carts rattled, tableware clunked on wood. Supper smells perfumed the air, lentils, onions, fish, and aromatic rice with both familiar and foreign spices.

Closer, almost directly behind them, the scraping, squeaking sound of a man operating a foot-powered whetstone competed with the incessant drone of mosquitoes. The familiar domestic activity drew Celeste's gaze, and she recognized the timbre of a dry stone. Her youngest brother, Tangi, to whom had fallen the chore of sharpening axes and knives, had never used enough water. Twice she'd had to douse a stray spark in the barn's straw from his stupidity. That distinctive screech still raised both panic and ire.

Yet, none of what she heard or smelled or sensed seemed threatening.

Until the huge shape of a gigantic Nile crocodile surged out of the water, all armored scales and gaping jaws and sharp, gleaming teeth.

Celeste stumbled backward. She slipped in the viscous mud and landed hard on her ass. Tolly raised her hand and, with a word, triggered a rooting spell. Grass and river weed twined around the creature's feet but only slowed its furious high-legged trot up the bank toward them. It had to be twenty feet long, half of that tail.

Celeste scrambled to her feet. She'd thought reptiles were torpid by nature, but this thing moved like a racehorse.

"Celie!" Tolly turned her back on the beast and ran toward Celeste, hand outstretched, the two ends of her long chiffon scarf trailing elegantly behind her.

The crocodile barreled up the muddy slope like a freight train. Its jaws opened wide, then snapped shut—on the ends of Tolly's scarf.

Celeste grabbed Tolly's hand, then felt it yanked violently away as the crocodile shook its head and began scrambling backward toward the water, dragging Tolly with it. The scarf, wrapped securely around her neck, grew taut. Tolly gurgled, one hand clutching the strangling cord, the other groping for purchase in the grass and weeds along the muddy bank.

Celeste knew little about crocodiles but realized if the reptile got Tolly in the water, there would be no way to save her. Nothing she had hung on her bracelet was helpful. Elementally, she could use water, but swamping a crocodile wouldn't hurt it, and would likely drown Tolly. No convenient fires crackled nearby, nor were there any clouds overhead. Just a deepening lapis sky, tinged with carnelian and gold. So, no lightning from a storm. By all the Gods, what could she use to draw power?

Tolly's eyes sought hers, wide, frightened, bulging. 'Do something,' they screamed as her partner's hands clutched reeds to slow her progress toward the water's edge.

The scraping of the whetstone bled through Celeste's panic. The dry whetstone. She sent her mind onto the astral plane, searching for a spark, thinking of her idiot brother, Tangi.

There. A tiny glowing ember in the dust by the man's feet, next to a piece of straw. Not yet caught, not big enough even to catch without some help, it snuffed out. The straw was too damp. But where there was one spark, there would be more.

She focused on the whetstone, trying to block out Tolly's gasping, the sloppy noises of the creature's inexorable path back towards the river.

A spark flew off the wheel.

Celeste caught it, caught the energy of it, fed it. Drew the electrical charge towards her, coaxing it, feeding it with her own power until it formed a spiky spitting, fiery ball between her hands. When she'd given it all she could, grown it as big as a small round loaf of bread, she took careful aim, and she flung the crackling sphere at the crocodile.

A hit! Fire exploded, sparks flying and sizzling as the ball landed right on the creature's schnoz. The monstrous beast's jaws opened.

Tolly rolled and scrambled up the bank. Celeste stood her ground.

The fireball created a nimbus of sizzling orange energy around the crocodile, but it did not dim the thread of teal blue and brown of the thing they'd come for. The ring.

That thread ended in the center of the reptile.

"Tolly, it's in crocodile."

"Run!"

"No. The ring is inside that damned monster. It must have been on Aubrey's hand and the croc ate it."

"No ring is worth your life."

The crackling light faded. The crocodile shivered, half in, half out of the water. Its jaws gaped, and it made a horrible noise somewhere between a croak and a roar.

She knew—or she hoped she knew—what would happen next. She might not have memorized every magical creature from her lessons, but she'd seen snakes retch their live meals when threatened.

The crocodile heaved and lurched, and with a revolting noise, spewed a gushing stream of putrid sludge from its maw.

It stilled for a moment, hissed at them, then flung its massive head toward the water and splashed back into the river. With a powerful sweep of its tail, it submerged and disappeared, leaving only a V-shaped ripple in its wake.

Behind her, Tolly swore in Norwegian using words Celeste knew would irritate her if she understood them. She'd always chosen not to learn. It gave them both some linguistic privacy. Tolly didn't know Breton either. The lack of understanding had the added benefit of avoiding adding fuel to the fire of their occasional fights, since neither knew what nasty things the other was saying in their mother tongues.

Celeste ignored the spate of invectives. The teal and brown energy signature hadn't disappeared with the crocodile into the vast murk of the Nile. It now buzzed like an angry bee in the pile of reptilian vomit.

She approached cautiously, keeping her eyes on the dark water for movement. Her bracelet grew quiescent again, so she allowed herself to relax enough to peer down at the steaming goo and gizzard stones.

Ugh. A pale hand-shaped lump lay in the mess, along with another lump out of which stuck a white shaft. A leg bone. Aubrey's hand and foot. She felt bile rise in her throat, more from the wretched smell than the sight of it. She desperately wished for a stick or a pair of tongs, but with nothing nearby, she'd have to pick up the decaying hand with her fingers.

"Celie, what in the names of all the gods are you doing?"

"I'm rescuing the ring."

"You are the most idiotic woman ever to walk the face of the earth." Tolly drew closer, her voice hoarse.

Celeste smiled to herself. Curiosity killed the cat. Even sensible rule-following cats with elegant hats. Steeling herself, she used thumb and forefinger to grip a slimy, algae-covered finger and flung the dissolving appendage up the shore into the grass. Trotting quickly after it, she squatted down and reached up. "May I have your scarf?"

Tolly had unwound the thing from her bruised throat. "Why not? It's already ruined." She pooled the eight-foot length of wet, punctured chiffon into Celeste's waiting hand.

Using the scarf like a glove, she examined the hand in the growing gloom. Yes. There it was. A ring on the finger. Amazing it hadn't fallen off.

Holding her breath, she worked the ring off the squishy flesh, wrapped it up, then hurried away from the stinking reptile vomit, and the crocodile-filled Nile the dozen or so yards to the row of mud brick dwellings. There, braced against the wall, she allowed herself to be sick.

Tolly held her hair from her face until the heaving stopped.

"That was the most disgusting thing I've ever done."

"I agree." She peered at the bundle in Celeste's hands. "Is it really the ring?"

"Yes. It's the same energy signature I sensed that night at Aubrey's apartment. It's different from Aubrey's energy."

Tolly glanced away, that dark sadness returning. Celeste thought she preferred the outrage and Norwegian cursing to this unusual and deeply melancholic mood.

The sun dipped below the horizon and twilight engulfed them. "I don't suppose you have a light?"

Tolly snorted, spoke a word, snapped her fingers. A small glow of light emanated from her hand, dim but sufficient to show them what lay in the folds of the scarf. Celeste used the material to wipe off some of the gunk, revealing glowing gold and the familiar scarab shape of the ring Aubrey had shown them.

There was a shimmer, then a ripple, visible both on the physical and astral plane.

Celeste felt a shock run through her, and the ring fell to the ground. She bent to pick it up, heard Tolly gasp, and noticed the sudden appearance of tooled leather boots on the sand in front of her.

She straightened and found herself face-to-face with a man. Or rather face-to-chest. Tall, built like a Norwegian god, he would have turned heads wherever he went, even those who didn't go in for men. His mossy green eyes sparkled with flecks of gold, and long chestnut hair flowed to his shoulders like a horse's mane, framing a striking, strong-featured face. Several thin braids were threaded with silver, and a series of delicate finely worked trinkets wove through his locks, an acorn, a pinecone, and a holly leaf. A circlet crossed his brow, reminding her of the old legends of Manannan Mac Lir. He wore a cambric shirt beneath a teal and brown sleeveless doublet, and plaid breeches tucked into his boots.

This must be the ifrit Aubrey imprisoned in the ring.

The creature brushed water and river weeds from his clothes, his patrician nose wrinkled in disgust. Speaking in a language that sounded like a long-lost Celtic tongue, he leveled an infuriated look at both of them, hands on hips.

While her ears didn't understand the words that came out of his mouth, her mind had no trouble comprehending him when he said, "By Mother Epona, it's about time. I've been stuck in there for three thousand years."

Fourteen

The man stretched his arms wide and rolled his neck. "It is good to see the night sky again, even if I can't as yet savor the smell of evening flowers and good earth. You've broken the first seal. Just a little more work and I will be free at last." As if in response to his words, moonlight flashed on a sinuous ripple on the water, and in the dimness, Celeste made out the ridges of an enormous tail. Another crocodile, or perhaps the same one, drawn to the commotion. She took Tolly's hand.

"We have company." She pointed. "Can we take this conversation elsewhere, sir?"

Those mossy green eyes took in the approaching crocodile, and he nodded toward the row of mud-brick houses. "Agreed. Lead on. If I am swallowed again by one of those toothy devils, I may never get out of this cursed prison."

Cleaning the ring hadn't released him, at least not fully. She examined the djinn or ifrit or whatever he was on the astral, saw that red ropes of energy connected him to the scarab ring in her pocket. Then again, she'd lay big odds he wasn't even a djinn. His appearance and language were Celtic, and he'd mentioned Epona, an ancient Celtic goddess.

She'd half expected him to balk or make some imperious request, but he followed as she and Tolly wound their way through the maze of narrow streets toward the Muski. When they reached an area where Europeans equaled the number of Egyptians, their new acquaintance veered away and wandered toward a coffee house. "I am parched. Come, they have food and drink here."

She looked at Tolly, who pursed her lips. It was not proper for a woman to take coffee in an Egyptian coffeehouse. Would they permit them to enter? While their companion towered over the locals, a dark-haired man, outlander or no, would be accepted inside. Indeed, only a few heads turned as he entered. Celeste could smell the glamour he conjured, all grassy with a hint of clover. Many magical creatures had a unique scent, and his was the sweet smell of hay.

She felt the red cords that bound him stretch as he moved farther from her—or rather the ring—and into the coffeehouse. The binding wasn't Aubrey's work. Whatever Aubrey thought he'd done, it wasn't the unfamiliar magic, like nothing she'd ever experienced, that had imprisoned this creature in the ring. The scent and feel of it convinced Celeste of that.

As a result of the glamour the being cast, the mundanes perceived him as a fellow Egyptian, but when Celeste stepped across the threshold of the open doorway, there came a collective mental gasp. Every pair of eyes in the darkened, smoky room lay upon her, flaying her with hostile disapprobation.

Let them glare daggers. She'd spent her life flaunting social conventions. She took another step inside but jerked to a stop when Tolly grabbed the back of her mud-spattered sundress.

"Celie, what are you doing? You can't go in there."

"Of course I can. I don't care what kind of woman they think I am. Hell, I'm damned from the start just for being a non-Muslim."

"We cannot afford to draw attention to ourselves."

"What can they do? They don't trust the police."

"They can call the local imam. Our being here is an affront to their god."

She dropped back a step. She had no desire to be disrespectful of anyone's faith. "But what about the djinn?"

"He can get his food while we wait here."

"And if he disappears? Tolly, didn't you feel the power emanating from him? I don't know what he is, but we need to question him. He must know what happened to Aubrey."

Tolly pointed to the pocket of Celeste's sundress. "We have the ring, to which he is still bound. Even now, those bonds strain, and we're a mere twenty feet away. We may have summoned him into the world again, but he is not free from the spell that chains him to it."

Celeste touched her pocket and peered onto the astral, noting the pulsing thread that snaked into the coffeehouse and disappeared into the broad back of the creature. Yes, he was still soul bound to the scarab ring.

Tolly cocked her head. "In fact, we could simply make our way back to the hotel and he'll have to chase after us. Perhaps that would wipe that insufferable, superior smile off his face. He's almost as bad as Byron."

It felt good to see Tolly's fiery confidence return. "It would also be cruel. He's been trapped in that ring for Brigid only knows how long. Let him enjoy a meal after his long confinement." She glanced back inside. Their new companion stared curiously at them from a small, rickety table. He gestured for them to join him, but Celeste shook her head. She could almost see his thoughts as he took in the situation. How strange the modern world must look to him.

What was he? He'd made them stop here. Did that mean he needed to eat? To drink? If so, how had he survived in the ring all this time? So many questions she wanted answers to, questions she'd have to wait to ask, at least until they got back to the hotel.

Joining Tolly on the vacant stone bench, called a mastaba, to the right of the door, she settled in to wait as the midnight blue dome of the sky darkened to black, slipping her hand in Tolly's under cover of darkness.

"Celie..."

"No one will notice. Nor will they care. And look at the moon." She wished she could snuggle close and lay her head on Tolly's shoulder, but society limited what two women, even European woman, could do in public and not arouse censure.

Tolly looked up and sighed. "Wouldn't it be lovely to sit atop the Great Pyramid with the moon shining down upon us and—"

"Have wild, passionate sex? Yes. Let's go now."

Tolly brightened for a moment. "Someday. Someday the world will be a different place."

A melodious baritone said, "The world already is a different place. And if there is going to be an orgy, I'd like to bathe first."

It was the djinn. He grinned lewdly at them before crossing his arms over his chest. "I don't know what they served me in there, but it was a foul concoction, bitter and thick as mud. I would have brought you some as well, as I gather from their outraged conversations that women are not allowed inside, but I thought I would save you from the noxious beverage. One kindness for another." His teeth shone white in the moonlight against tanned skin when he grinned and gave them another up and down look as Celeste and Tolly both rose. "Now that we are no longer in danger of becoming dinner for a crocodile, let me tell you who you have the honor of releasing. I am Hlwengiemorgawniff, Huntaf Wasson of Mother Epona. Well met." He looked from one to the other expectantly.

"Klooen gee... I beg your pardon?" Tolly struggled to repeat the name.

Celeste put a hand on her partner's arm and stepped forward. The name he'd spoken, and what she thought was a title after it, held all the music and sounds that both Welsh and her native Breton did, but was sufficiently different that she struggled a bit to translate.

"Well met, Hlwengiemorgawniff." She pronounced it slowly so Tolly could understand—Klooen-ghee-morgawn-niff. "I am Celeste, and this is Astrid."

Tolly turned to her. "Is that Breton?"

"No, and not Welsh or Cornish either, but it's close enough. Maybe an older version of one of them. He's been in the ring for a long time and languages change."

He wore a bemused expression as they talked about him. "Let me assist you." He pronounced his name again, and then said, "I am First Servant to the great Mother Epona. I assume I do not need to translate *her* name."

Epona again. One of the original mother goddesses who the Romans had co-opted on their rampage through Europe and the British Isles. Also one of the few Celtic goddesses they'd incorporated into their pantheon, primarily because no corresponding deity existed. Of course, being Romans, they'd militarized her, changed her to meet their own needs, all in the service of *Romanitas*—the imposition of the ideals and identity of the Roman people on everyone and everything. There might still be worshippers of the great goddess, but Celeste had never met any.

Celeste matched his posture, arms across her chest. "No, we are both familiar with Epona. You are a long way from home, Hlwengiemorgawniff." She didn't trip over the name, but it was a mouthful. Tolly would mangle it and probably piss off this servant of a goddess. Perhaps even on purpose, as she wasn't even trying to disguise her dislike of him. "Welcome to the twentieth century. While your name is like a fresh breeze from home, it might be faster and more modern to use a shortened version of your name."

He raised an eyebrow. "This is the way of the world now?"

"Indeed." She turned to her partner. "Tolly this is Guy. Guy, this is Tolly."

Tolly's gaze shot heavenward. "Great. Ghee. We've met a creature named after clarified butter. This day just gets better and better."

"No, not ghee. Guy. Like Mssr. De Maupassant, the author."

"Same pronunciation. And this one is certainly slippery like butter."

Celeste scowled at Tolly. "You're not helping."

Tolly subsided but planted her hands on her hips.

Celeste turned back to Guy. She'd never heard of his title, First Servant of Epona, and knew almost nothing about the goddess. What powers did the First Servant have, anyway? Was he a demigod or something else? Clearly, he had some powers because he'd cast a glamour on himself when he entered the coffeehouse. But he couldn't have god-like powers because he'd been unable to break out of the ring. Or sever his bond to it. And according to him, he'd had three thousand years to try. Not to mention the first thought in his head was to order a meal.

Standing over a head taller than her, he peered down at her like she was a curious and mildly vexing child. "It would appear you have questions. I will be happy to answer them and then instruct you in how you are to remove the magic that binds me to the ring, but perhaps the middle of the street is not the place to have this discussion."

She had been about to suggest they go back to the hotel and found herself annoyed at both his condescending tone and patronizing attitude. Yet Tolly needed answers about Aubrey, and this creature had them. She felt sure of that. So she would use the bargaining chip she had in her pocket to best advantage. And hopefully not piss off a powerful creature in the process.

"A splendid idea. I was about to suggest that myself. If you would follow us, we'll head back to Shepheard's. We have rooms there, and we can be comfortable while we do business."

"Business?"

"Oh, yes. Business." Without explaining further, she grabbed Tolly's hand and started down the dark street toward the hotel.

FIFTEEN

The First Servant of Epona lounged on the divan in the sitting room of their suite, sipping a glass of sweet Chenin Blanc that he pronounced acceptable, though it bore little resemblance to the honey mead he typically drank. Tolly leaned against the edge of the mahogany secretary, ankles crossed, arms crossed, just generally cross. Her scowl was thunderous.

"So happy you like it." Tolly's gaze should have seared his skin. "Now, if you please, tell us what happened to Aubrey."

His eyebrows lifted. "Who?"

"The man who wore the ring," she ground out. "The ring you've been stuck in."

"Ah. Was that his name? Aubrey?"

Celeste sat down next to Guy, putting her body between Tolly and the servant of Epona. "Yes. He was a friend of ours. We're trying to figure out what happened to him. You, to our knowledge, are the only witness."

His curious gaze roved the room while he answered. "A friend, you say? Odd choice of friends. I tried multiple times to communicate with him, but he spent inordinate amounts of energy blocking me. He even tried to reinforce my bindings, which, of course, was beyond him. The spell is ancient, known only to priests of Thoth. I could have taught him how to break it, had he but listened." He turned a beatific smile on Celeste. "And this I shall do for you, kinswoman. A witch of your power should be able to manage it. All we need to do is—"

Tolly had been right. He and Byron could be brothers in insufferableness. He might be a powerful being, but right now, she held all the cards if he wanted to be released. "A moment, if you please, Guy. It is imperative we understand who killed Aubrey and how."

"How so? It relates not at all to my situation. And it is critical that I am released immediately. I must," and here he paused, his haughty facade cracking a bit, "contact Epona without delay."

Tolly's spiky frustration felt like a flail against Celeste's back. Celeste raised her hand and continued. "I can understand that, especially after so long an absence. So—" She stopped speaking abruptly as she felt the tendrils of power.

He'd caught her unprepared. Had he been a vampire, she would have been on her guard, but she had not expected him to capture her gaze and hold it. "It is simple, mortal. Release me and I will tell you how your friend Aubrey met his death."

He'd tried to Command, her with a capital C, but either his imprisonment blocked it, or he'd lost too much power over the centuries for it to work. Without the power of the ring, he'd have succeeded—that much she could sense from the weight of his energy.

She slowly crossed her legs and leaned forward with a smile, maintaining eye contact. "No. You tell us how Aubrey died, and how you got trapped in that ring, and then we'll release you."

His gaze intensified. The air shimmered between them. "You will release me now."

Celeste gave him points for trying. She could sense his focus, his will, and the expectation that his efforts would succeed.

"We will. Right after you tell us what we want to know."

He held the stance for a few seconds longer before he collapsed against the divan. Flinging his hand to his forehead, he groaned. Some of his pain was genuine. She could sense that. But much of it was simply drama. She glanced at Tolly's pinched, pale face. "You were wrong, Tolly, he's not as bad as Byron, he's worse."

A spark returned to Tolly's eyes. "You seem to attract these kinds of people, Celie."

The air shimmered again, but this time, the visual effect came from the door of the bedroom and drifted slowly toward them. Or rather, toward Guy. Even Tolly had seen the anomaly, her eyes tracking the rippling effect as it approached and seemed to sink down toward the floor. The hairs on the back of Celeste's neck rose, and she felt again the distinct sense of being watched.

Guy straightened and stared down toward his feet, where the oddness seemed to crouch. "What are *you* doing here, little servant?"

There came the sound of rustling leaves, or the scratch of a pen nib on stationery. Guy leaned forward and reached out a gentle hand as if placing it on someone's head. "Now, now, there is no need to be afraid. Show yourself, let us talk. I would hear your tale and will offer help if I can."

Despite the warning, Celeste startled when the figure of a woman appeared on the floor in front of Guy, kneeling in a posture of obeisance, with her head touching the floor, her lips resting on one of Guy's boots. She never quite gained solidity. Celeste could see the pattern of the carpet through her if she tried, but the ghostly fingers left indentation marks on the soft leather boots the Servant of Epona wore. With her dark black wig, kohl-lined eyes, filmy white linen dress, and beaded pectoral, she could have just walked off a wall mural from a tomb in the Valley of the Kings.

In her mind, Celeste sensed Tolly's silent response of surprise. Celeste spoke aloud. "Who or what is that? Do you know her?"

Guy's expression had softened, and the flippant arrogance faded away. "She is a servant. An ushabti spirit. Who do you serve in Amenti, child?"

Her voice sounded like reeds in the wind. "I serve the Great Lord, Strong Bull, Pleasing at birth, One of perfect laws, Who pacifies the Two Lands and satisfies the Gods, Who has elevated the appearances of his father Ra, Neb-Kheperu-ra, the living image of Amun, Tutankhamun."

Guy smiled. Tolly drew a sharp breath and whispered, "King Tut."

Guy nodded, although whether at Tolly or the girl, Celeste didn't know. He dropped his hand from her head to her shoulder. "How came you here? Why are you not serving your King?"

The spirit shuddered as he raised her chin to look into her liquid dark eyes. "Someone removed me from the resting place of the Great Lord. The Ba could no longer command me. Instead, the priest, Merimre, instructed me to watch these women and report to him their movements and conversations." She glanced first at Celeste, then Tolly, and ducked her head, as if in shame. Her voice, the sound of desert sand pushed by the wind across the dunes, became fainter. "Help me. I do not wish to serve the evil one." Tears pooled in her eyes but didn't smudge the kohl lining them when they slid down her smooth, young cheeks. "I saw what he did. He imprisoned you and murdered the handmaiden of the Great Lord's sister. He is an abomination in the eyes of Maat. My lord Neb-Kheperu-ra would take vengeance on his sister if he could."

Celeste didn't follow the confession completely, but one thing was clear. The feeling that someone had been watching her and Tolly since those men broke into their hotel room in Alexandria and gifted them with the pig heart and little figurine hadn't been her overactive imagination. This spirit, whatever she was, had been with them, watching and listening—and apparently reporting on their activities —since their first day in Egypt to this Merimre. Even more interesting, the spirit knew how Guy became bound to the ring, had been present when it happened.

Before she could ask any of a dozen questions, someone pounded on the door.

Tolly was the first to react. Celeste sensed her cautious sending to see who or what stood in the hallway beyond. A puzzled look crossed Tolly's face and she wasted no time in flinging open the door.

Detective Sergeant Ibrahim tumbled inside and bolted the door behind him before collapsing back against it. He looked like a boxer badly trounced in the ring. Cuts marred his face and arms, one of which bled copiously, soaking his torn shirt sleeve. A red smear on his chin marked where he'd wiped away the blood that had trickled from a split lip and one side of his face was swollen and darkening. Breathing heavily, he closed his eyes for a moment.

Celeste rushed forward, but Guy got there ahead of her, catching the man before he slid to the floor. He scooped up the tall Egyptian and carried him as easily as if he was a child to the divan. Ibrahim roused as the being settled him with surprising gentleness on the cushions.

"No, please," the detective murmured, "there is no time. I bested them, but more will follow. They have eyes everywhere." He struggled to sit up, groaning. "You must go. They know you have the ring and," he pointed at Guy, "that you have freed this creature."

Tolly slid into healer mode. "Let's get that shirt off you, see those wounds."

Ibrahim shook his head. "No, Madame. I am fine. But you must leave immediately. They cannot be far behind."

"Celie, fetch a basin of water, a washcloth and the first aid kit." Tolly nudged Guy aside to kneel beside the injured man. "Do not argue with me, young man. You will submit to medical attention while you tell us what happened."

He was either too cowed by Tolly—and what man wouldn't be
—or more seriously wounded than he would admit. Celeste fetched
the kit and while Tolly tended to his injuries, both with her mundane
first aid kit and her own healing magic, Ibrahim told his tale.

"I am afraid I have deceived you, Madame. I have known who
you were since you arrived in Cairo. I have done what I could to
protect you from certain elements, but I could not prevent my
compatriots from coming after you." He trailed off and shook his
head. "Brief. I must be brief."

Tolly nodded. "You are part of the revolution."

Ibrahim looked surprised. "The revolution is over. We have
won."

Tolly pursed her lips. "You have made a start. The British are still
in control of many things."

"It is a process. Or that is what I tell my compatriots in the
Brotherhood. It will take time to learn to manage our own affairs."
He waved away his own commentary. "If you know all this, then you
know there is a faction who would prefer a more violent solution to
our internal problems. The reformer, Zaghloul, still has much influence, despite his exile, but certain of the more radical men have found
someone new to follow, a shadowy figure who calls himself the Lion
of Justice and claims descent from a priest of the pharaohs. He claims
he knows holy magic and has convinced many men that the path
forward is through controlling even greater power." He stared in
suspicion at Guy. "He says that creature can be controlled by
whoever has the ring to which he is bound."

Guy's mouth tightened at this revelation. Celeste's hand crept to
the pocket of her skirt, assuring herself the ring remained there.

Ibrahim continued. "This man also claims that he can lead us to
an item that will allow us to empower an army so we can evict the
foreigners forever." His hand crept to the gold cross he wore, hidden
under his shirt, but now visible since Tolly had undone the top two
buttons of his blood-stained shirt to dress a knife cut across his collar-

bone. If the knife had not hit bone, Ibrahim might not be sitting here.

Guy crossed his arms across his impressive chest; a gesture Celeste now associated with a need to mask anxiety. "This account is not brief. Get to the meat of the matter."

Ibrahim nodded, casting a nervous look at Guy. "I have tried to keep you safe, have you shadowed. I followed you personally tonight. I watched as you...defeated the crocodile. And saw this person appear." He crossed himself. "I did not quite believe in all this talk of djinns and magic until then. And I am still not sure that God would approve of you or your consorting with the devils that give you your power. But neither would God condone your rape and slaughter. And that is what the followers of this Lion would have done to you tonight, had I not put myself in their way. They want the ring. They killed your friend, Mr. Finlayson, to get it and failed. They will not hesitate to kill you and me too, now that I am branded a traitor."

Tolly finished her ministrations and stood. "How many were there? How many did you kill?"

Ibrahim's large brown eyes widened. "None, I pray! There were three. I left them nursing their wounds. One was unconscious, the other two I left floundering in the Nile." The corners of his lips curled up. "I believe the expression is, 'I gave as good as I got'."

Guy muttered a word that resembled a Welsh epithet. "They are coming. Now. We must go."

"Go where?" Tolly's head swiveled toward Celeste.

We'll figure that out, luv. Trust me. Up to her again to make the plans, was it? She supposed sighing and flinging herself about like Byron in a snit would be neither appreciated nor productive.

Fine. Well, their next move had to be escaping the hotel, if not Cairo entirely. She hurried into the bedroom to throw a few essentials into a bag. After a moment, she heard Tolly's internal comment about remembering their passports, undergarments, and Tolly's straw hat with the pheasant feathers. Celeste refrained from making a snide comment.

"Memphis," Guy announced. "We need to go to Memphis. In order to perform the ceremony to free me, we must be where it all began."

Memphis? Wasn't that in America? As she stuffed toothbrushes and Tolly's hair pins into her bag, Celeste brought up a mental map of Egypt, searching for the city, then realized Guy had been out of commission for three thousand years.

You should know this, my dove. The modern city of Luxor was called Memphis in pharaonic times.

Aloud, Tolly's tone cut like ice. "That is hardly our priority."

Celeste tossed as many of her own sympathetic spell components as would fit in the now stuffed bag and hurried into the sitting room. Even as she did so, the amulet on her bracelet that warned her of danger grew hot on her wrist.

A seeking spell aimed at the hall outside their rooms showed her nothing alarming, but the bracelet didn't lie. She figured that meant a cloaking spell, and one using magic unfamiliar enough that she couldn't detect it.

Tolly, we've got company. Bad company, if my bracelet is any indication.

Ibrahim, watching the expression the two exchanged, pushed to his feet. "There is a train leaving shortly for Luxor." He glanced at his wristwatch. "We may be able to catch it if we hurry."

Sixteen

A brief discussion, if by discussion one meant a bunch of people shouting at once, ensued about how to get past their pursuers. Celeste put her fingers to her lips and let out a sharp whistle. Once everyone's attention fixed on her, she said, "Let's go," and pulled Tolly toward the small balcony.

Ibrahim stuttered a complaint and Tolly balked, but Celeste ignored them. "If you're coming, now's the time." She slung the long strap of the carpet bag cross-body and climbed onto the iron railing, staring into Tolly's eyes. "Do you need help?"

Tolly pinned her hat to her head and hiked up her skirts. "I certainly do not. But Celie, you hate heights."

"I hate getting murdered by cutthroat revolutionaries more." She gripped the railing and lowered herself over the side. "There's a balcony just below us. From there, it's only about ten feet to the ground, onto those bushes. Should break our fall."

Tolly produced a conspiratorial grin. "Just like the old days. Lead on."

Celeste swung down onto the balcony below, then clambered over the railing as well. She landed on her ass in the garden, having broken nothing but the branches of the roses and possibly some gardener's heart. The thorns did a number on her as she wrestled her way onto the gravel path. Taking a moment, she searched their surroundings while Tolly descended as graceful as a cat, followed by Ibrahim, who jumped down in an unexpectedly feline fashion as well.

She didn't wait to see if Guy and the ghostly ushabti followed, knowing his bonds to the ring would force him to do so. Observing no one in the immediate vicinity, she ran down the garden path toward the gate that led to the street. "Which way to the station?"

Ibrahim followed on Tolly's heels. He pointed. "Let me lead. I know a shortcut."

Her instinct was to object. She wasn't sure she trusted him, and he could in fact just be a stalking horse, leading them right into the hands of the gang he said he'd foresworn. But he also knew the streets of Cairo far better than she and if he wasn't lying about the train, or about waylaying his own compatriots earlier, then it made little sense to refuse his help.

She glanced at Tolly. *Do we trust him?*

Tolly paused, then nodded.

Celeste stepped aside and let Ibrahim precede them through the gate. She saw a gleam of teeth as he passed her. "This way, ladies."

He loped away on long legs, and she had to work hard to keep up. Tolly, who had legs that went to there and back, paced him without effort. She should have been a dancer. She'd have made a fortune at the Folies Bergère. The image of Tolly on stage doing the can-can in feathers, sequined pasties, and little else made Celeste grin.

Tolly caught the thought and mentally tsked. *Is that all you ever think of?*

Celeste giggled, then gulped air and chased after them, taking a step and a half for every one of theirs.

A block later, Ibrahim turned and plunged into an inky alley between a photographer's studio and a chemist's shop. She hesitated.

This could be a trap, and she had no desire to die in some fetid alley in Egypt. She had no desire to die at all.

Something bumped up against her back and she heard Guy's voice in her ear. "This is no time to stop. The miscreants are coming out of the front of the hotel now."

Damn it, she'd wanted to buy more time. She pushed herself forward into the blackness, trailing one hand along the brick wall of the chemist's shop, hoping not to fall through some yawning trap door onto a row of punji sticks, or run headfirst into a giant spider web.

If Byron were here, he'd have tickled the back of her neck and made some snide joke about tarantulas. Goddess, but she missed the arrogant bastard.

They moved deeper into the alley. Her eyes adjusted to the dimness, and she could make out starlight from the narrow gap between roofs overhead. Ibrahim jogged, glancing back over his shoulder frequently. He turned several times into ever-contracting passageways, Tolly close behind, graceful and silent as a ghost.

Celeste tried to memorize the route as they went. Left, left, right, left, right. She kept repeating the directions over and over as they went along. It kept her mind off spiders. And assassins.

After an eternity, the blackness in front of them thinned. Ibrahim paused and crouched in silhouette at the exit of the alley, head swiveling back and forth. After a moment, he straightened, shot his cuffs, and smoothed his slicked back hair. Celeste caught up to Tolly and peered at the street beyond. Typical traffic, European tourists and locals alike, with most of the locals either escorting said tourists or trying to sell them something, or both. All in a night's work, she thought. Much as it had been in London the year she'd discovered the big city. 1666.

"It is clear, I think. The station is just a block that way." He pointed to the left. "We have ten minutes. We can buy tickets once we are on board."

They followed him like ducklings onto the street. Trusting little ducklings.

She sensed more than saw the man who flung himself out of a doorway and knocked her to the ground. As she raised her head to spit dirt, she caught a flash of Tolly, as she spun in a roundhouse kick, just before a fist met Celeste's jaw. As she spun to the side, a weight fell on her back, crushing the air out of her lungs.

Wheezing the Breton word for sizzle, she rammed her assailant with her elbow. The spell from a charm shaped like a phoenix went off and a flare of heat exploded from her body, scorching him wherever he touched her skin. He leapt back, cursing in Arabic. Scrambling to her feet, she spun to face him and saw a bright gleam of silver. His fists weren't his only weapon.

He slashed at her with a short, heavy knife, a common weapon like any Allied soldier would have carried during the war. She'd expected something exotic and curved, but any blade could slit her throat. She jumped back, tripped, landed on someone. Whoever it was also swore in Arabic when a modified version of a hot hands spell that she'd cast on her skin burned him, too.

Her new victim shoved her and sent her sprawling. Knife-man tore after her, kicking her in the ribs. She had just enough time to roll onto her back, prevented from going farther by the carpetbag she wore.

The fool hadn't learned. Knife-man dropped to his knees with a brown-toothed grin and straddled her. She grabbed his arm as he swung the knife, and he screamed. She squeezed his forearm, and his hand opened. The knife fell, skittered away. He did too, and she regained her feet, crouching, frantically searching for Tolly.

Her partner had just given her opponent another kick to the solar plexus, sending him sprawling into the glass window of a nearby shop.

Where the hell was Ibrahim? Had he led them into this mess? Run away at the first chance?

People on the street stopped to stare, although many of the locals had scampered off to avoid trouble. She looked around for their other attackers. Tolly's man was out cold, while her own had gotten his feet under him and, cradling his burnt arm, raced away down the street.

The man she'd landed on groaned. She scrambled to her feet, shocked to find that she'd landed on the detective. The hot-hands spell had dissipated, so she gave him a hand up, noting one of their attackers lay unmoving, face down in the dirt behind the policeman, blood staining his turban.

Still scanning for threats, she caught sight of Guy, standing over the last attacker, sucking on his finger. When he saw her looking, he held up his hand. "I've got a splinter."

The pale, translucent form of the ushabti took his hand and made some gesture. A cool, blue light surrounded the injured finger and Guy's smile grew smug.

Tolly snorted. "We need to move, fast. detective, are you all right?"

He stumbled a few steps but stabilized. He glowered at Celeste. "What did you do to me when you fell on me? My whole body was on fire."

She frowned at him. "Did you set this up?"

He gaped. "No!"

Tolly laid a hand on her arm. "We need to go."

Celeste shook her off. "Not until I know for sure the detective didn't lead us into this."

Guy moved between them and laid his hand on Ibrahim's shoulder. Power emanated from that hand and Ibrahim's face went blank for a moment, then returned to normal. "He is telling the truth. He did not lead us into an ambush."

Did she trust Guy any more than she trusted Ibrahim? At this point, she realized she had little choice. A crowd of tourists were converging on them and soon the local constabulary would arrive. If

Ibrahim was telling the truth, at least some of his fellow policemen were part of the rebellion. They had to get out of Cairo. Now. "Fine. Let's go."

As the well-meaning mob gathered, Ibrahim pulled out his badge and parted them. Tolly and Celeste, with apologetic smiles, hurried after him toward the train station.

They'd only just reached the doors to the station when the last call to board the night train to Luxor blared from the loudspeakers. They broke into a run. With the carpet bag bumping painfully against her rump, Celeste kept her eye on Tolly's back. She was going to be black and blue all over later.

Ibrahim led them through the station to the platform. Women with goats on rope leads, a couple of boys carrying live chickens, a handful of Europeans looking either lost or annoyed, and many turbaned, robed Egyptian men crowded around the doors of the cars. Celeste's group wove and dodged toward the front of the train. Finally, Ibrahim approached a carriage with a handful of Europeans in the process of boarding.

Celeste fixed a pleasant smile on her face and hoped they looked merely disheveled from hurrying, not because they'd just fought off a group of thugs. Standing in line and waiting their turn to board made her twitchy. In front of her, Tolly smoothed her hair and glanced at her watch, like any bored, impatient tourist.

Ibrahim smiled broadly at the conductor and for a moment, Celeste thought he might whip out his badge again. Instead, he greeted the other man in Arabic and gestured at Celeste and Tolly. Guy, she discovered, was nowhere to be seen. The conductor nodded and chuckled at whatever Ibrahim was saying. Likely some story about foolish women tourists who couldn't tell time. The detective handed over some cash and gestured them aboard. She saw his dark eyes flicker over the platform, no doubt searching for more trouble. He didn't look long, and said, loudly, "We are in luck. The train is not overly crowded. I have procured a private, first-class cabin for you, Madame, Mademoiselle. Please to follow me."

Moments later, she and Tolly sat across from one another near the windows, catching their breath and checking each other for damage. Once inside, Ibrahim locked the varnished wooden door behind them and pulled down the shade over the window on the door.

The compartment held six seats, three on either side, upholstered in velvet. The dimness of the car disguised years of wear that under ordinary circumstances would have annoyed Tolly. That she flopped, uncaring, into a window seat gave testament to her utter exhaustion. Celeste sat across from her and mopped her brow, watching her partner in worry.

Ibrahim fell into the seat next to Tolly, his cool, composed demeanor shattering. He put his head in his hands. "*Allahu akbar,*" he moaned. "What have I done? I will lose my job. My pension. My home."

Tolly roused and patted his hand. "It is not as bad as you imagine, detective. We will tell your superiors you were protecting us."

His head snapped up. "That will hardly save me from my brothers in the revolution."

Tolly had no ready response to that.

As the train lurched into motion, the air shimmered, and the ushabti wavered into existence. A second later, Guy appeared beside Celeste. "By Epona's shiny mane, this fellow looks close to tears. What have we missed?"

She did what any sensible and exhausted person would have done. She smacked him in the solar plexus. His oof was gratifying.

SEVENTEEN

Celeste didn't even bother to hide a smile as Guy clutched dramatically at his midsection.

"You," he wheezed at her, "are a heartless witch."

She looked over at Tolly, expecting a scowl of disapproval. Instead, her partner only arched a delicate eyebrow, and offered a faintly amused smile, as if to say, really, Celie?

They all settled into an uneasy silence as the train lurched forward and trundled down the track.

Tolly stared out the window at the endless darkness beyond the window, but Celeste couldn't relax. They'd escaped the hotel, but what came next? How did running away from Cairo get them closer to avenging Aubrey? Would the henchmen of the Lion of Justice follow them? Should she let them? Try to set a trap for them? Or should she and Tolly try to follow them back to their leader? But if the man really was a long-dead ancient Egyptian priest, with who knew what kinds of power, did they have the means to stop him?

Her thoughts went round and round an internal track as the train rocketed down its own, and soon the rocking and rhythmic clacking lulled her too into drowsiness. Other than Guy, it had been a long day for everyone.

Celeste wasn't sure how long she dozed, but she awoke with her head on Guy's shoulder. Tolly still slept, head back against the cushions of the seat, and though Celeste would never have said so to her face, snoring faintly.

It made her smile. Until she saw the smirk on Guy's face. "Shut up."

He didn't speak, just shrugged in wordless mirth.

Celeste looked out the window at the midnight blue sky, wondering where they were and how much further to Luxor.

As if she'd spoken aloud, Ibrahim, across from her, with eyes still closed, murmured, "We passed the village of Girga a few minutes ago. Luxor is perhaps an hour away."

That surprised her. She didn't feel as though she'd slept that long. It would be dawn soon.

At that, Tolly stirred and cleared the sleep from her throat. "Did I hear, detective, that we are almost to Luxor?"

He nodded, mouth set in a hard line. "Yes, madame."

The ushabti, who had as little need for sleep as Guy, nestled in the curve of the Servant of Epona's arm. At Ibrahim's assertion, she whispered something in Guy's ear. Guy merely shook his head, perhaps putting off an answer. The smug smile remained fixed on his face.

Irritated, Celeste turned to the ushabti. "You said a priest removed you from the tomb. Could your priest be this mysterious Lion of Justice?"

The ushabti looked at Guy, who nodded. "Tell her what you know." His tone was coaxing and soft, not dictatorial, more like he was giving her permission to share.

The young woman turned coffee-dark eyes to Celeste. "I think yes. When the Great Lord's tomb was opened, the ifrit of the sem priest took control of the body of one of the defilers. And when that vessel died, he took others, searching for one that suited his plans for power and revenge. The vessel he now occupies he has made strong, and with his magic causes lesser men to follow him."

Celeste looked between Guy and Ibrahim, hoping one of them could make sense of this.

Guy briefly enjoyed Celeste's confusion before his expression morphed into a smoldering anger. "What she means is that the sem priest, who is a high-level priest who helps the dead on their way to the afterlife, and in this case, the abomination of a man who bound me to this damned ring three thousand years ago, has been possessing bodies. He clearly took control of some poor worker who entered the tomb when Carter opened it in order to pick up the ring. And now he's found another man's body to possess and has reinvented himself as this so-called Lion of Justice."

"The ifrit." Tolly leaned forward just as the train lurched around a bend. Ibrahim's arm swept out, keeping Tolly from tumbling from her seat. She smiled her thanks at him.

Guy nodded. "The priest is now an ifrit, bent on seeking revenge on the one who killed him."

Ah. The ifrit Aubrey mentioned. "And what does this Lion want from you?" Celeste studied Guy's face, looking for a tell, for some sense of dissembling. "Why did he bind you to the ring in the first place? And who killed him?"

Tolly nodded. "Yes. It is time for the story. The whole of it. We will not help you without it."

Guy glanced at the ushabti, whose gaze was riveted on him. Celeste decided in that moment that whatever the young woman was, she needed a name. But that would have to wait.

Guy flopped back on the upholstered bench seat of their compartment, and being tall, his head clunked faintly against the wall. He made a sound halfway between a growl and a sigh. "You have no idea how humiliating it is to be beholden to mortals." He pinched the bridge of his nose and squeezed his eyes closed as though he had a headache. "I was once a power to be reckoned with. And then ... I fell in love."

Well, that was unexpected. She had a dozen questions, but kept her mouth shut. After a moment, he stared up at the ceiling. The ushabti laid a slim hand on his arm and he sucked in a shuddering breath. Were those tears in his eyes?

"I came to Egypt at the behest of Epona. The assignment was simple, though secret. Keep an assignation with a priest and his charge, a sister of the former pharaoh, and escort her through the Betwixt to my homeland in the north. Her husband, a Greek, would follow later, via ordinary means. My second night in Memphis, a young handmaiden of the princess, a woman called Nefer-rannet, delivered a message to me. I was supposed to meet the priest and the princess in the desert near Tutankhamun's tomb five days hence. Meanwhile, Nefer-rannet would escort me around the city and see to my needs."

"Your needs?"

Guy's lips quirked. "Yes. She would provide food, be a tour guide to the wonders of Egypt, deliver entertainment. The usual." The smile fled, replaced by something more wistful. "She was a clever woman. Well-versed in local traditions and storytelling, she spent many hours over the ensuing days delighting me with the myths and tales and poetry of her people. She understood mathematics, philosophy, astronomy, magic. She was the most enchanting woman I had ever met."

He fiddled with the tassels on a cushion for a moment before looking up.

"On the appointed day, after the sun sank behind the western cliffs, we set out by ferry across the Nile to the Land of the Dead. She told me, in confidence, that her mistress wanted to retrieve something from her dead brother's tomb, an item critical to the success of their family. Once this was accomplished, we would all leave, the three of us, on a ship that had been prepared for our departure.

"I should have noticed that no ship lay moored on that side of the river. But I had eyes only for Nefer-rannet. I should have observed that only one set of footprints led from the dock where we disembarked, but all I knew was the warmth of her hand in mine as we trudged along a path and into the desert. I should have been struck with foreboding at the dim torchlight that illuminated the doorway of the small tomb of the princess's brother, but I could only think of the couch I would share with Nefer-rannet that night aboard her mistress's ship, and the gentle waves that would rock us to sleep, wound in each other's arms. She had become my world. I have had many women, but Nefer-rannet was like no other."

Tears welled in his mossy green eyes and rolled down his cheeks. He swallowed his emotions before continuing his story. "We heard a voice calling us to enter the tomb. Nefer-rannet thought it sounded like her mistress and so we went down the set of stairs to the door and inside." His hands clenched and Celeste felt a wave of anger and grief. She thought she knew what was coming. The young hand-maiden had betrayed Guy, set him up.

"My love's mistress was not there, of course. Only the priest, a wicked smile on his face. He struck Nefer-rannet first, a quick thrust and twist of a knife. She was gone before I even understood what had happened, the light fading from her eyes as she sought mine." His voice cracked. "I expected a physical attack. I had my eye on the bloody knife in his hand. I didn't see the ring he raised, barely noticed he was muttering words in his native tongue."

Guy fell quiet then, head bowed. Celeste leaned forward, needing to know the rest of the story. The silence lengthened. "And then?"

Tolly shot her a reproachful look as the Servant of Epona's tears dripped silently onto the Turkish carpet. Celeste raised shoulders and eyebrows in protest but subsided into frustrated impatience. Even Ibrahim shifted uncomfortably while Guy fought to regain control.

When he looked up again, he forced a smile. "Forgive me." He cleared his throat. "As I said, I did not register the ring until I felt the pull of the spell sucking me into it. I had only seconds to do something. I knew I could not break the ring's spell, but I could use what magic I had to see that the damned priest didn't leave the tomb either. I prayed to Epona, summoned every last grain of power I could muster, and made one of the giant ceiling blocks crash down upon the priest of Thoth's head. With my last act, I killed the man who murdered my love."

Another pause and a crafty smile curved his sculpted mouth. "Squashed him like a roach under my boot."

Ibrahim's eyes widened. Celeste snickered, then quickly sobered. "And this is the spirit of the man who is after you. The one who has possessed bodies."

He nodded.

Ibrahim still looked horrified. "You killed him. He is now an ifrit! It is no wonder he wants revenge."

Guy's expression grew savage. "He stabbed Nefer-rannet. He killed her without a thought, all so he could steal the treasure the pharoah's sister wanted to take with her to her new home. He probably killed her as well. I was entitled to vengeance."

The man—or supernatural being—had a point. If someone killed Tolly, there would be nothing on earth that could stop Celeste from ending whoever had been responsible, the Council be damned. But Ibrahim was a Copt, a Christian, not a Muslim, and there were stringent prohibitions against killing in the Abrahamic faiths, as her friend Father Dom, a Roman Catholic priest, would no doubt have reminded her.

Tolly raised a hand to forestall a potential argument. "You mention a treasure. What was it this priest wanted to steal?"

"It was the source of power of their lineage. An object that swayed the hearts and minds of the people. With it, even a sem priest might become pharoah."

"If this priest died in the tomb, and your Nefer-rannet's mistress died at his hands, then the object must have been sealed in with Tut, just as the priest's body and the ring in which you have been trapped were."

Ibrahim leaned forward. "That is a good thing, yes?"

Guy shook his head. "Now that the priest is inhabiting bodies, there is no reason he cannot enter the tomb and retrieve it."

Tolly broke in. "Ah, but there is a reason. Now that Tut's tomb is the biggest archaeological discovery of the century, access to it is incredibly restricted. Carter has the place guarded, even at night. Unless he wants to give up the body of this 'Lion of Justice', he cannot get in."

Celeste frowned. "He could always suborn someone to get in."

Tolly shook her head. "Not under Carter's watch. Everyone is searched. No one can remove anything without Carter's say so. He's fiercely protective. If he weren't, Lord Carnarvon would sack him."

"So, this Lion of Justice wants to foment a rebellion. And he needs this object. But right now, he seems to be focusing on the ring. Other than wanting revenge on Guy, what does the ring do for him? Why is he so hot for it that he sent men to get it from Aubrey?"

Tolly came up with an answer first. "With the ring, he will have the tiger by the tail. Guy is a powerful creature. And if the Lion of Justice obtains the ring, couldn't he coerce Guy to do his bidding? Like the genie of the lamp?"

Guy pursed his lips. "I know nothing of this genie or why he would be in a lamp, but I do not believe anyone could coerce me to do anything I do not wish to do. I am, as you say, a powerful creature."

Celeste reached into her pocket and fished out the ring. "Let's just see about that. Guy, fetch me a glass of whisky from the dining car."

"Ridiculous." And then he jerked. His eyes widened and his mouth opened. His face suffused with red fury, just before he disappeared.

Tolly smirked. "I was right."

Ibrahim's face blanched. "Mademoiselle, there is no dining car."

Minutes passed and Celeste began to worry while Tolly sat with a smug smile. When Guy returned, about five minutes after Celeste had sent him on his errand, he held a cut crystal glass half-full of whisky. He handed it to her with a dark look.

She took it but resisted apologizing. "Thank you. At least now we know Tolly's theory is correct."

Tolly took the glass from Celeste and took a drink before passing it back. "Where did you find it?"

"I don't want to talk about it." He flung himself down next to the ushabti as though he'd just finished running a marathon. "Dining car, indeed."

Tolly narrowed her eyes in thought. "Getting back to our discussion, if this priest possesses the object he was after from Tut's tomb, and if it can, as you say, control an army, he could use it to cause a great deal of bloodshed in the name of Egyptian independence."

In Celeste's estimation, Ibrahim had a remarkable naivety for a revolutionary. He gasped and crossed himself. "Dear God. It would be a nightmare for my country. My people."

Tolly nodded. "And it might not stop with Egypt. History is littered with bloody killing fields created by men like this. Agincourt, Waterloo, the Somme."

Celeste shivered. The world still struggled to overcome the worst war the world had ever seen. She could not stomach the thought of more bloodshed in the name of power or greed. "We must stop him."

Guy's head swiveled toward her. "Then free me and I will deal with him. My powers are severely curtailed, bound up as they are in the ring."

Celeste was all for it, but she could sense Tolly's reticence. Tolly shifted in her seat to stare out the window into the darkness beyond.

When she turned back, her jaw was set. "Fine. We will help to break the spell that binds you to the ring." Her changeable blue eyes grew as icy cold as the waters her Viking ancestors sailed. "Given that this odious being is responsible for Aubrey's death, I have an ax to grind as well."

The train lurched again, and the wheels squealed. The train ground to a shuddering halt.

Outside the window lay only the velvety blackness of the desert night sky, so they hadn't stopped at a station. On Celeste's wrist, the warning charm on her bracelet grew warm.

"Tolly, we've got trouble."

She nodded. "Hence the sudden stop. Can you sense anything from the energy signatures?"

And use the talent no one really believes I have? Well, no one but Tolly and Alistair. "I'll try. But we need to get out of here."

"We are going to the tomb?"

She glanced at Tolly, who nodded almost imperceptibly. "Yes, we're going to the tomb. But I can't imagine we're anywhere near Luxor—Memphis—yet."

They could hear agitated noises from further up the car. Ibrahim stood and muscled open the window. "Out. I will go first and help you ladies." He crammed himself, feet first, through the narrow aperture. Good thing he was thin to the point of bony.

The noise in the corridor resolved into pounding knocks and shouts in Arabic. Celeste shoved Tolly out through the window into Ibrahim's waiting arms, and, using a bit of twine she now habitually kept in her pocket, cast a binding spell on the door. At the same time, she explored the energy signatures in the train car, seeking for anything that would register as magical.

She found strangeness. A murky greenish thread that led from a ring worn by one of the mortals in the corridor wove through their cabin and out the window to Ibrahim. They were tracking him. Magically. She spent a moment longer trying to identify the flavor of the enchantment. It smelled the same as what she'd sensed from the ring. And from the men in the hallway at the hotel. She considered the enchantment. She might be able to break the spell, she'd become good at such things during their years in the protectorate, but it would take time, something they didn't have right now.

She gestured Guy and the ushabti toward the window next. Guy just laughed. With a fading smile, he dissolved like the Cheshire cat, taking the ushabti with him.

Pounding started on their compartment door. Celeste grabbed their carpet bag full of essentials, leaving the suit coat and its enchanted button on the seat, and dropped feet-first from the aperture into the night.

EIGHTEEN

T he minute Ibrahim set her on her feet, they fled west toward the desert, where the fertile flood pain of the Nile spread out like a green garment. A green garment that ended in a sharp break at the desert, beyond which the ochre sand stretched to infinity.

Why their pursuers had not left guards outside the train defied understanding, but Celeste was grateful they were either foolish or overconfident. No one awaited them, and no one chased them. For now.

They'd gone maybe an eighth of a mile when shouts drifted through the stillness of the night.

"Get down," Ibrahim hissed.

Celeste dropped, her cheek pressed against loamy, damp earth, body crushing whatever grew beneath her. Light played over the field; some bright soul had thought to bring an electric torch. She held her breath, hoping they were well-enough concealed.

A few more shouts, a few more passes over the fields with the torch, and the voices faded, perhaps moving to the other side of the train. That way probably led to whatever small village huddled along the Nile. Fine, let the fools look there until the camels came home. Meanwhile, Celeste and her friends would escape to... where now?

Ibrahim rose in a crouch and helped Tolly to do the same.

"Ibrahim?" Celeste called.

He glared at Celeste, put a finger to his lips for silence, and gestured west. More light might have shown her endless sand and finally the cliffs that rose from the desert floor, but now she saw only black. In a low voice, she asked, "Where, exactly, are we going?"

Tolly slid her hand into Celeste's, her breath tickling her ear. "He doesn't know. Stop talking. We'll figure it out as we go."

That, from the woman who always had to have a plan. Well, Celeste was nothing if not flexible.

She sensed Tolly's mental chuckle as she responded. *Yes, my dove, you certainly are.*

Ibrahim rose slowly, scanning the empty field. Satisfied they were clear, he motioned them up.

Tolly stood, plucked her squashed straw hat from the ground, and with a flourish, pinned the bedraggled thing securely to her head.

Ibrahim motioned in silence and crept forward, still crouched, even though the crops were only knee high. Tolly strode past him, regal and elegant, despite the condition of her headwear. Celeste followed, passing Ibrahim, who after a moment, straightened and hurried to catch up with them.

It took maybe ten minutes to reach the edge of the agricultural zone. Behind them, the train was a dim shape on the lightening horizon. Celeste heard the engine huff and then the slow clacking of the wheels along the track.

"They've released the train. That means they know we aren't on it."

Ibrahim nodded. "As soon as it is light, they will search the fields, the villages."

"Where can we hide?"

Ibrahim looked ready to drop. "I'm trying to think. I wish I knew exactly where we are."

No matter where they went, they would stand out. Ibrahim was at least a native to the country, but his bloodied suit would label him as a figure of unwelcome authority among the rural folk. Tolly, in her stained dress and crushed hat, looked like a daft European tourist who'd refused to listen to the directions of her porters. And Celeste looked no better. Mud smeared her dress, she smelled like river slime and crocodile vomit, and she probably had bags under her eyes like a cocaine junkie. No matter where they went, they would not blend in.

Blending in. Yes, that's what they'd need to do. She looked around for the Servant of Epona. "Guy?" she called quietly.

The smell of freshly mown hay and chamomile enveloped her, and the Servant of Epona appeared out of thin air, the mousy ushabti with him. "Yes?"

His abrupt appearance made her jump. Tolly remained cool and seemingly unaffected, but Ibrahim stumbled backward, nearly losing his footing. Muttering something unintelligible, he frantically crossed himself.

"Brigid's paps, Guy. Next time warn us."

He shrugged. "You called me."

She shook her head in annoyance. "Listen, when you were at the coffee house earlier, you glamoured yourself to look like a local. Can you do that again?"

"Of course. I am blessed with many abilities, thanks be to the Mother, in addition to my own unique powers."

"Can you make us look like locals, too?"

"I suppose. I will need to draw from an energy source, however, as I am unable to connect to mine." He looked at Celeste. "You have more than enough to spare."

Tolly tensed, her concern for Celeste both comforting and annoying. "How much power?"

"Very little. It is not hard to encourage others to see what they expect to see." He stared at Celeste appraisingly. "The loan will not drain you, if that is your worry."

Tolly snorted. "'He only takes a little. When have I heard that before?"

She referred to Celeste's habit of allowing Byron to take blood from her. He could lose control, drain her dry. He could. But she didn't believe he ever would. He was her oldest friend. She trusted him.

Ignoring Tolly's frustration, she nodded. "How long will it last?"

"As long as you want it to." He paused. "As long as the power holds out."

Ah. "Best to use it only when we need it."

Tolly crossed her arms. "We're at least an hour by train from Luxor. You don't expect us to walk 60 or 70 kilometers across the desert to the Valley of the Kings, do you?"

Ibrahim broke in. "I have been studying the cliffs. I believe we are close to the city of Quena. Which means we must be very near a place I know well, a large village called Dishna. I visited there many times when I was young. I have a cousin there who will hide us. We can remain until the search is over, then take the train on to Luxor."

Tolly didn't look impressed. "Can you trust your cousin? If they search the village, and we are found, he could be in big trouble."

Ibrahim nodded vehemently. "Yes. He can be trusted."

A breeze, redolent with the fresh, clean scent of morning, brought a chilling sound. The baying of dogs.

She exchanged glances with Tolly and Ibrahim. "Dishna it is."

Guy broke in. "Don't I get a vote?"

In unison, they all said, "No."

Celeste hadn't expected Egypt's nights to be cool. It wasn't that she didn't have experience with deserts—she and Tolly had spent a good six months in Mongolia early on in their work together. There was no reason to expect the Sahara to be any different, and yet the shivering chill surprised her.

Tolly held Celeste's hand in hers, sharing the warmth. "We should have thought to bring wraps."

Ibrahim walked a few steps ahead of them, hands shoved in his trouser pockets, and led them into the desert.

Celeste's nap on the train hadn't done much to rejuvenate her. She trudged along behind the detective, her feet as heavy as lead bars while the sky lightened in the east. Through the still dim light, she saw dark arable land to their right. Farther to their left, she sensed the weight of the looming cliffs. Other than those features, which Ibrahim must be using to guide him, there was nothing to be seen but endless stretches of sand and rocks. "How much farther to Dishna?"

"Not far. Maybe another hour."

"That means we'll be visible when we get there," Tolly said. "Should we find a place to hide until it's dark again?"

Ibrahim stopped and came back to them, shaking his head. "We have no water, and I do not know for certain how to get to the caves we played in as children. But if, as you say, the one you call Guy can make you look like locals then if we are seen, we will look like workers coming to the fields, or to town. You will see as we get close, there will be many such people."

Celeste waited for Guy to catch up. "Tell me honestly. How long will your spell be powered before I collapse?"

"Celie, I will not let him drain you to that point."

She held her hand up to Tolly and looked at the Servant of Epona, who sighed almost as dramatically as Byron. "An hour, perhaps two, depending on how much energy you are expending." He gestured at the horizon, now turning the mauve of her least favorite of Tolly's hats. "If it gets hot, and you have to trudge through more of this damn sand, likely far less than two."

Celeste looked at Tolly. "That's cutting it close if we start now."

"It will be dangerously light in a matter of minutes. I can't imagine they've stopped searching for us. Even now, we might be suspicious looking silhouettes." She took Celeste's hand. "You must tell me the moment you start to feel weak."

"I will. Promise."

Tolly's eyes held a spark of humor. "And I will be here to make sure you keep that promise. For a change."

Guy crossed his arms over his chest. "Very well. Give me your hand, little witch, and open your mind."

She did so, more nervous about having him in her head than being drained of energy. She hated that slithery sensation of someone entering her thoughts. She'd endured it three times, four if she counted, when her first magical mentor, Marguerite, had slipped in without Celeste knowing to see if she was indeed a witch. That time she'd felt nothing, but every other time felt like a violation, as though she'd been raped.

She tensed for the intrusion—and felt nothing. No, not nothing, she felt a tug that started not in her head, but in her gut. Guy had linked them astrally, soul thread to soul thread.

He took a deep breath and closed his eyes as if in ecstasy. "Ahhhh, to be able to touch real energy again. I feel almost reborn." Then he laughed. "As though I were ever born to begin with."

"Wait, you're done?"

He shrugged. "What were you expecting?"

It wasn't worth getting into, but she was grateful it had been so painless. She could feel that pull in her midsection, although at the moment, no energy flowed through the connection. "So how does this work?"

"You're all ready?"

Ibrahim rubbed the back of his neck. "I am not sure about this. It is fine for you, but perhaps I will remain un...transformed."

"It won't hurt," Celeste assured him. "It doesn't change you, just changes the way others see you."

Tolly nodded. "I understand your true concern, but I do not think your god would mind. You are doing a good thing, helping us. That said, we would never force you to compromise your beliefs. If you choose not to have the glamour, then we will hover around you, as you will stand out dressed in a western business suit amongst a group of locals."

His hand reached for the cross he wore around his neck, now safely tucked inside his shirt, then fell away. A few moments of silence passed before he said, "Very well. Do this thing so that we may be disguised and let us get moving again. Standing here, I feel as though I have a target painted on my back."

Celeste nodded at Guy, who posed, arms across his chest, like a genuine djinn from a story book, and after a moment she felt the shift of energies within her. As a witch, even before her training, she'd intuitively tapped into the energies of the elements. Earth first, as her feet always connected to it, but later, as her awareness grew, air, fire and water. Typically, unless she channeled that energy for a particular purpose, energy flowed into her as natural and automatic as breathing.

Now, the energy traveled away, not toward her, and not under her control. Like water leaking from a cracked jug, not fast, just a steady drip.

Guy winked at her. "See? You'll scarcely notice it." He tipped his head to one side and looked each of them up and down.

"Hm, yes, I think that will do."

She looked at Tolly, then at Ibrahim. Both still looked like themselves. "I don't think it worked."

Guy huffed. "Nonsense. It worked perfectly. You can't see it because you three know each, and as I said, the spell is camouflage. People will see what they expect to see, and here they will expect to see workers heading to the fields and everyday Egyptians going to into town."

Tolly turned to Celeste and muttered, "He better not be lying to us."

Guy snorted. "I can hear you, you know."

Wanting to short-circuit an argument, Celeste made a rolling gesture with her hand. "Let's go. I want to get somewhere safe before too much of the morning has passed."

Through the connection she now shared with Guy, she heard him say, "*At least one of you understands respect.*"

She ignored him, glad that Tolly hadn't been on the receiving end of that remark. She'd have laughed herself silly to hear that Celeste had been accused of having respect for authority. Wearing a grin and trusting Guy enough to protect his own interests by keeping them alive and free, she tromped once more after the detective.

NINETEEN

T he village of Dishna reminded Celeste a bit of the village in
Brittany where she had grown up. A cluster of small houses
in mudbrick instead of wattle and daub huddled together
along a jumble of paths that could masquerade as streets if people
only traveled by foot.

At the bray of a donkey and a grumble in Arabic sounded behind
them, they hugged the wall as a turbaned man led his beast of
burden, plodding along under a pannier of stuffed baskets, past
them.

Okay, she amended, paths big enough to permit both humans
and donkeys—but only single file.

They'd come into the village in the direction of the fields, where
dozens of locals worked to ensure the year's crops, perhaps cotton or
grain. Celeste could not tell one from the other, since they were not
medicinal herbs. No one paid any attention to them, a confirmation
that the glamour worked. A good thing, too, since small communi-
ties tended toward the insular and xenophobic, and everyone knew
everyone else. No one paid any attention to Guy, and the ushabti was
invisible.

She and Tolly kept silent. Speaking in English would no doubt shatter the glamour Guy had cast, and as Ibrahim had explained, accompanied by their men, Egyptian women kept pretty quiet. Celeste chafed under this as a matter of principle, but she would not risk Tolly's life just to make a point about women's emancipation.

By the time they reached a spacious house, surrounded by a stone wall with a wrought iron gate, dust coated every inch of exposed skin. Mixed with sweat, it formed a thin shell, making her itch. Before they left this place, she determined that they'd find themselves local garb, not only for disguise, but to protect them.

A young boy with big, dark eyes and a mop of shining black curls jumped up from his stool by the gate and did his best to stare stonily at them.

Ibrahim flashed the boy a brilliant smile and said something to him in Arabic. The boy nodded and ran into the house, an impressive two-story structure. The only house with more than one floor, its size and ornate decoration indicated unusual wealth and status.

Ibrahim glanced at Celeste and Tolly and put his finger to his lips before turning to face the man with a grizzled beard, wearing European trousers and shirt who strode toward the gate, the young boy on his heels.

When he saw Ibrahim, he shouted a hearty greeting in Arabic, and yellowed teeth showed through the beard as he hurried to unlock the gate. A good deal of hugging, backslapping and rapid-fire words followed. The man had to be Ibrahim's cousin, and she wondered how long it had been since they'd seen one another. Dishna was a far cry from Cairo, and in her experience, people who lived in villages like this never traveled far from home.

She kept quiet as the older man escorted them inside.

Whatever Celeste had expected, it was nothing like what she saw. A modern, comfortable divan held center place in the large living area. On a gorgeous, hand-carved low coffee table, a shiny brass hookah burbled. From it wafted the sickly-sweet smell of cherry-scented tobacco.

Another chair sat nearby, occupied by the most shriveled, tiny, elderly woman Celeste had ever seen. She wore a voluminous black garment, belted at the waist, and a traditional head covering. All that black fabric seemed to devour what was left of her.

Ibrahim addressed the old woman reverently with a little bow. He gestured toward Celeste and Tolly and the woman rose from her chair with more alacrity than she looked capable of. She fixed shining black eyes on Tolly and made a following motion. Celeste's skin prickled. Something about the creature made her uncomfortable. Nothing magical popped on the astral that indicated a spell or a charm, but the sensation of danger still tickled her hind brain.

Tolly obediently followed, but Celeste grabbed her arm. She was not about to let them be separated from Ibrahim, their only ally here. "detective?"

Some of the man's gloom dissipated, and he looked more comfortable in his skin than he had since the first time she'd met him. "It is good. This is my grandmother, a revered elder in Dishna. She will take you both to a room where you can refresh yourselves and rest."

"And then what?" She would not be relegated to some modern form of a harem, no matter how luxurious.

"I will have a private conversation with my cousin, explain our current situation. It is best done between the two of us. For all he is a modern man, women here are not...not as unfettered as women in Cairo or Paris. After we have talked, I will have someone fetch you and we can discuss what our best course of action is."

"I will not be shut up—"

Tolly placed a cautioning hand on her arm and interrupted. "A wise suggestion. I look forward to examining our options over a meal."

Ibrahim's face wrinkled. There were rules about strange women sharing meals with the menfolk, and certainly an open conversation would be an anomaly, but Celeste didn't care. Let the old woman's head explode.

With a "we'll talk about this later" look at Tolly, she followed Ibrahim's grandmother up a set of narrow stairs and down a long hall into a guest room furnished with a comfortable bed and a small dresser on which sat a washbasin and a modern table lamp. Nice, except for a lattice screen covered the wide window, affixed to the outside.

The old woman said something sharp in Arabic then backed out, closing the door. Celeste waited to hear a key in the lock, then relaxed when nothing happened.

After the woman's retreating footsteps faded, Celeste turned to Tolly. "I don't like this. Something feels off."

Tolly dropped onto the narrow bed and took off her crushed hat. "I agree. But we are strangers here, and certain social proprieties, no matter how they irritate us, must be followed."

"You and your damn rules." She paced, frustrated. "And I don't like the cousin either. We didn't even get introduced. We're just women, not worthy of even names, apparently."

"I saw nothing on the astral to indicate any kind of magic, but you're right, I did feel that something was not quite right. I mean, look at this place. It's a palace compared to the homes of the other villagers."

"So where did his wealth come from?"

"I don't know. But it's something to consider. I wish we spoke the language, maybe we could winkle some information from some of the household staff."

"You think they have servants?"

"In a house like this? And with that infirm, old matriarch? Someone has to be responsible for cooking and cleaning and doing laundry, and I guarantee it's not her."

Celeste paused in her frantic pacing. "Do you suppose the cousin understands English?"

"It's possible. We should watch our step around him. If you think something is off about it, then there probably is. I trust your instincts about such things."

A timid knock sounded. Tolly bade their unknown visitor to enter, and a young girl, wrapped up in an outfit like the old woman, but in white, entered carrying a large basin of water, and a few towels slung over her arms. Another young woman followed her, with white garments for the two of them, including the wimple-like hijab. Without meeting their eyes, the first girl placed the basin on a dresser with the towels, then both young women bowed and ducked out of the room again.

"Thank Freya. I have sand in places sand should never be." Tolly began stripping off her clothes. "Stop your fretting and get those clothes off. They're practically ruined. Coco will be so unhappy."

Celeste consented, happy to be out of the gritty garments, but not happy about the clothes that awaited her. When she'd left her home at 16, the blaze of the fire still hot on her skin, she swore she'd never be subservient to another man again. Now here she was, deliberately enslaving herself.

Tolly took a towel and washed Celeste's back with comforting strokes, the cool water raising goosebumps on her skin and making her think of other, more amorous uses of cool water. She sighed. That sort of thing would not be happening here.

"Naughty girl," Tolly whispered. She continued aloud. "In any case, you are not enslaving yourself. You're disguising yourself. And some day you really must tell me the story of your escape from Brittany."

Maybe, she thought. It was a story she'd never revealed, a story from an ugly chapter of her life. Maybe one day. But not now.

They had just about figured out how the clothing worked when she heard a familiar pop. Oh, no. Not here, not now.

She turned toward the sound and groaned. Sure enough, it was Pyp.

Pyp bowed and winked at her with a saucy grin. Today he'd dressed nattily in a 20-year-old formal suit with a waistcoat and morning jacket. He wore a top hat on his head and white spats covered his black patent shoes. A cane and a monocle completed the look.

Tolly gasped and fell back, raising her hands to cast a spell.

Celeste put herself between them. "Tolly, no. It's just Pyp."

"What on earth is he doing here?"

Celeste turned back to her messenger. "Do you time your visits deliberately to discommode us?"

Pyp blanched, realizing he'd been targeted with a nasty spell. He took off his hat, and the monocle fell from his eye. "Sorry, Miss. His lordship said I was to come right away."

She threw up her hands. "Stop calling him that. You're just feeding his already bloated ego."

"Celie, what is going on?"

Time to fess up, especially if the changeling was going to appear at random and inconvenient times. "I arranged for Pyp to carry messages from home."

"Actually, Miss, it was his lordship's idea to—" He broke off at Celeste's slight shake of her head.

Tolly stood, hands on hips. If a scale for glares existed, hers exceeded the top mark. "I cannot believe you agreed to that."

Celeste sat down on the narrow bed and clutched at her hair. She sucked in a breath for a count of four, held it, let it out again. "Tolly, please, can we have this conversation later? When we're alone? In the meantime, I get the sense that Bryon has important information for us. I asked him to look into djinns and ifrits." She reached out to Pyp. "Just give me the letter and toddle on back to His Arrogance."

Pyp's brows drew together, and he shifted his weight from one foot to the other. "Those wasn't my instructions, Miss. I was to read you the letter like last time, then wait for a response."

"Weren't," she corrected. "Weren't your instructions." She gave up. "Fine. Tolly, maybe you should sit down."

She did, back straight, aggravation oozing from her. "We will talk about this later." The words were quiet, but potent.

Celeste braced her hands on her knees. "Okay. Go ahead."

Pyp pulled the letter from the inside of his morning jacket and flapped it open, as he'd done before. Clearing his throat, he began.

"My dearest Celeste,

Hope you are well, and all the usual flummery. I have been your dogsbody here and dug up some information for you, although I'll wager a significant sum that you'll be utterly gobsmacked, to use a vulgarism from the lower classes, by what I've found."

Pyp's tone and inflection mirrored Byron's so closely, Celeste once again felt like he was in the room. When Pyp began to pace, one hand behind his back, he even imitated Byron's limp. The result was uncanny, and she wondered if Pyp's innate fae powers fueled the illusion or if he was just a natural mimic.

"First, the information available to my sources on djinns and ifrits is probably nothing a student of magical creatures such as yourself doesn't already know. Djinns are creatures who predate the current Islamic faith popular in the region through which you travel. They are supernatural creatures who can make themselves invisible. Not immortal,"

and here Pyp's voice dropped to a sotto voce, indicating one of the parentheticals that littered Byron's missives, "pity for them, as it's such a lovely thing," before returning to his normal speaking voice and continuing.

"They can be both benevolent and evil. They also are thought to have their own society, a sort of tribal arrangement, and feud with one another over perceived grievances. It is said that a sufficiently clever and

strong individual can do battle with one and potentially kill it. They, in turn, are believed to marry, kidnap, and kill mortals. One supposes which behavior depends upon their mood.

"Ifrits are many and varied, but one type, at least in Egypt, which I assume is the focus of your request, is thought to be a member of the vengeful dead. And not just any dead, but those who have been killed violently. They seek revenge on their murderer and can kill the living and cause great unpleasantness to their quarry. Some believe they can possess the living. Quite nasty creatures."

Pyp paused in his pacing and in his own voice asked, "Don't suppose you've anything to drink?"

No one had provided anything, which was a shame, as Celeste was thirsty too. "Sorry, no."

The young changeling shrugged slim shoulders. "S'alright." He returned his gaze to the letter and leaned against the wall, his or rather Byron's 'bad' foot crossed over the other in a perfectly Byronic pose.

"That's really about all I could find. My source—and no, I shan't tell you his name—says there isn't a lot of information about the magical community in that part of the world. All very hush-hush. So, what he gave me, he says, might not be all that accurate. He suspects they feed the West fairy tales to keep the truth a secret.

"However, and I pause here for dramatic effect, La Tollefsen's former spouse has quite the reputation. I expected the old chap would be dull as dirt, and as much a stick-in-the-mud as his ex-wife—and if she's listening, I apologize, but she knows how I feel."

Beside her, Tolly snorted. "I am not a stick-in-the mud." But her lips twitched up.

Pyp, apparently tired of standing, moved to the bed and lay cross-ways behind them, propped up on his elbow, making his audience shift around to face him.

"Your friend Aubrey is in a bit of hot water with the Witch's Council, as I've been given to understand."

"What? Impossible." Tolly leapt to her feet. "Aubrey has never done anything to incur the displeasure of the Council."

Celeste reached for her hand. "I suggest we let Pyp finish, and we can discuss the validity of what he's found later." She glanced meaningfully at Pyp. "In private."

Tolly scowled but allowed Celeste to pull her back down on the bed. A winter storm over the North Sea brewed in her eyes.

Pyp flipped a page over and continued.

"Apparently, he's become involved with a mortal woman some years his junior. That in itself doesn't appear shocking to moi. The annals of literature are filled with older men lusting after younger women. I don't believe that your council objects to his involvement with a mortal, although I've been told that for a witch to have children with one is a violation of some sort. Must not want you witches squandering certain magical, procreative emissions."

His voice changed, indicating yet another set of parentheses.

"Which brings to mind an image of a man spending himself into a container during a romantic interlude to prevent himself from inseminating a mere mortal, and that implicit ability to control one's natural urges is highly entertaining.

"Then again, Finlayson—and did you know he's a member of the peerage? So your amour is really Lady Astrid, unless he stripped her of her title when they parted ways—is a Scot and we are known for our stoicism and self-control. Well, some of us are. I'm sure Mad Jack's contribution to my make-up explains this apparent deviance from my mother's people's tendencies in this matter."

Tolly said a bad word in Norwegian. "He goes on and on and never says anything! Get to the point, you insipid bastard."

Pyp chuckled and continued.

"But back to Finlayson's crimes, even spreading one's seed in forbidden ground isn't the worst. My source tells me he is under investigation for researching a formula that grants a mortal, if not immortality, a long enough life as to be almost such. And that, my sweet, is

just not done. Can't be giving those lowly mortal fools the gift of long life. That is allegedly what he was really doing in Egypt, searching for eastern secrets that would grant his beloved the ability to stay young and with him forever."

Celeste placed her hand on Tolly's shoulder. The woman seemed about to explode. Grief, anger, and embarrassment fought for expression on those fine porcelain features, and she made a wordless noise before turning away, her shoulders shaking with silent tears.

Celeste rubbed tired eyes. Poor Tolly, it was just one hit after another. "Is that all, Pyp?"

"Pretty much. Some news from home, but nothing more about what you asked him."

"Then give me the letter and I can read the rest later. I think it's time you went home."

"But he told me to wait for your letter back."

She shook her head. Tolly needed her. Byron would just have to wait. "I'll call you when I've had a chance to write it. Tell him he needs to be patient for once in his life."

Pyp pulled a few sheets of Byron's monogrammed stationery from his coat, along with a pen. "I'll leave these here. He wanted to make sure you couldn't use that as an excuse. Er, I mean, he wanted you to be well-supplied."

"Nice save. Now, go back. I'll respond as soon as I'm able."

"He won't like it."

Meaning he might fly into one of his rages and break things. She wondered if Pyp had seen one of those temper tantrums yet, though Byron had them less frequently than in the past. It had only taken a little over ninety years for him to mature. "I know. But I need you to go now."

"Right-o. I bid you adieu, ladies. I will see you anon."

With a wink and a bow, he disappeared with a pop.

. . .

After Pyp had gone, Celeste fortified them both with a brandy from their large satchel, then sat next to Tolly and took her partner into her arms, stroking her hair and murmuring words of comfort. At first, Tolly remained rigid and unyielding. It wasn't until Celeste said, "I realize the man you knew then was a good man," that she finally broke down, sobbing into Celeste's shoulder. When the torrent of tears ebbed to sniffles, she nestled into the embrace, spent.

"He *was* a good man. I cannot believe he would do this. It has to be some awful smear campaign."

Celeste knew she was on tricky ground. But Tolly would sense any disingenuousness if she outright lied. "Well, all I know is that if you were mortal, I wouldn't be able to face life without you. I'd do anything to keep you by my side."

"But the gift of immortality? You know how the Council feels about that kind of magic."

Celeste grumped. "Oh, I know. Goddess forbid anyone but the three big factions be allowed to live extraordinarily long lives. Gotta keep all that power for themselves."

"That's not—"

"Of course it is. Who are the movers and shakers in the magical world?" She ticked off the answers on her fingers. "The fae, the Vampire Conclave, and the Witch's Council. Who gets to be practically immortal? The fae, the vamps, and us witches. That's no coincidence, Tolly. And for someone deeply in love, to have to live with the knowledge day in and day out that the person who means the most to them is doomed to age and die in what feels like a heartbeat has to be agonizing. Grief is hard enough. You shouldn't have to see it coming."

She thought of Martin and the secrets she'd read in his journals last year. The agony of his losses and his vow to never fall in love again. A vow he'd broken when he'd met Byron. She had no desire to live that way, suffering endless cyclcs of pain.

Tolly clasped Celeste's hand. "And that is why the Council forbids congress with mortals, my dove."

Celeste gave Tolly's hand a squeeze. "No one can help who they fall in love with."

Her partner was silent for a moment. "So you think what Byron wrote in his letter is true? That Aubrey fell in love with a mortal woman and broke all the rules to keep her with him?"

"I don't know what to believe. All I'm saying is that it's possible. No matter how much of a rule follower you are, no matter how wed to the Council, love changes everything." She squeezed Tolly's hand. "I know it certainly did for me."

Tolly pulled away, but there was no anger in the action. "He did like to dabble in thaumaturgy. He was always researching formulae for the Council, ostensibly to find ways to combat that kind of magic." She brought Celeste's hand to her lips and kissed it tenderly. "And yes, love does change everything. I never knew real love until I met you."

"We should try to find her. She deserves to know what happened."

Tolly nodded. "A task for Alistair, I think. If it's true, it is heartbreakingly ironic." She met Celeste's gaze and kissed her palm.

The gesture stoked Celeste's already pent-up desire. She pulled Tolly down onto the bed and pressed her lips to Tolly's, softly, slowly, tasting soap, salt from the sand, and two days without a toothbrush, and it was still the most wonderful thing.

Tolly twined her fingers in Celeste's hair and pulling her closer, deepened the kiss. Even after over fifty years together, that fluttering of joy and excitement she felt at Tolly's touch never abated.

Celeste's fingers fumbled with the voluminous folds of Tolly's skirt. She'd just found the hem and was inching it, and her hand, up Tolly's leg when someone rapped on the door.

"Kac'h." Breton was such an expressive language to swear in.

"Pokker," was Tolly's response in Norwegian, which Celeste was pretty sure meant the same thing.

Damn it, why now?

They scrambled to their feet and adjusted their clothing before Celeste went to the door. "Yes?"

The old prune, with her ferocious scowl, hovered at the door like a vulture. She looked them up and down, then jabbed a finger at the hijabs still laying on the bed. Without another word, she stalked off toward the stairs, her message clear. Put on the headgear.

When Celeste was sure the matriarch was gone, she swept Tolly into her arms for one more lingering kiss. "I guess we'd better go make some plans."

"Why are we doing this again? We know now some evil ifrit killed Aubrey."

"We're doing it because it's the right thing to do. To avenge Aubrey's murder, to solve the problem he sent for us to fix, and to free Guy. Not to mention save Egypt from a megalomaniac who can body hop like a flea on a dog." Did that cover it all? "Oh, and to emancipate that poor ushabti. The girl needs a name, damn it. I can't keep calling her ushabti."

Tolly's tired features brightened. "Leave it to you to want to emancipate a creature whose entire existence is to serve. You are impossible, my dove." She stroked Celeste's cheek, raising goosebumps, and fueling the inner fire she *would* quench properly later.

They broke apart and helped one another with the hijabs. Thus cloaked, she figured that even with Tolly's blue eyes, they might pass as locals. As they headed for the stairs, Celeste said, "What about Berenice?"

"Who is that? Oh, you mean a name for the ushabti. After your first Council teacher? That's a lovely thought. Although, you know, she's not an actual person. She was created to be an object that functions as a servant."

"That's nonsense. Maybe that was her original status, but she's

just as feeling and human as you or I now. Didn't you see her unhap-
piness at having to do the will of 'the evil one'?"

Tolly gave her a sad smile. "Oh, my dove. You have such an enormous heart." After stroking Celeste's cheek, she carried on down the
stairs.

They reached the ground floor and found Ibrahim and his cousin
sitting on the divan. Two hard-backed, unpadded chairs had been
provided for the women. The air was redolent with cherry tobacco,
and the men now sat drinking thick, steaming Turkish coffee from
small cups.

Celeste sat and leaned forward, arms on her knees. "Good afternoon, gentlemen. Is there more where that came from?" She gestured
at the cup in Ibrahim's hand.

Out of Cairo, Ibrahim had subtly changed. Gone was the more
tolerant urbanite, and the deference to European women he had
shown them. At home with his country cousin, he'd lost some of the
British shine he'd exhibited in the city. The frown he turned on her
was both cautionary and unfriendly.

Tolly, too, laid a hand on her arm, another kind of caution. "Perhaps some water to drink, detective?"

Ibrahim addressed his cousin, using the name Faisal, the only
word in the string of Arabic that Celeste could understand.

Faisal snapped his fingers and one of the young girls who had
delivered their new clothing appeared as if out of thin air. Moments
later, she returned with two modern glasses filled with water.

Celeste smiled and said the only word she'd learned in Arabic.
"Shukran."

The cousin nodded curtly at her thanks and, with a sharp
gesture, sent the girl back to wherever she came from. The blatant
misogyny made Celeste's blood boil. She hadn't witnessed much of it
in their time here, but now the prejudice couldn't be ignored, and a
scathing retort burned on her lips. Wisely, she kept them shut.

Guy and the ushabti appeared in a corner of the room. As no one else paid them any mind, she assumed Guy had cloaked them in some fashion. Sure enough, she felt a pull in her midsection as Guy drew a small amount of power from her.

Ibrahim took his time finishing his coffee. He set the cup on the table next to the hookah and cleared his throat. "Faisal has agreed to allow us to stay here overnight, but recommends we leave in the morning. There is an early train to Luxor. He has sent one of his sons to buy tickets, to save us time and exposure at the station. If we time it right, we should be able to board immediately. He has even been thoughtful enough to provide us with first-class accommodations."

Tolly nodded. "Please express our gratitude for your cousin's kindness and generosity, alhammdullila."

The detective raised his eyebrows. "I did not know you spoke Arabic."

"I have picked up a few phrases. An effort to be respectful."

Was that a ghost of a smile on Ibrahim's face? If it was, it soon vanished. "As women generally do not dine with men in this house, you are welcome to join Faisal's wives and daughters, as well as our esteemed grandmother, for the evening meal. Or, if you'd rather, Layla will bring dinner to your room."

With Tolly's hand still on her arm, Celeste let her do the talking.

"Thank you, detective. Unless it would be rude not to dine with the other women, I think we would prefer to stay in our room. We're both exhausted and will likely retire early."

Ibrahim spoke rapidly in his own language, and after a moment, the cousin nodded in approval. "Faisal says that would probably be for the best. I tend to agree. Modern western women might tax my grandmother's patience with foreign ways."

Celeste seethed. She wanted to get Layla and her sister alone for an hour and teach them what it meant to be an independent woman, to teach them self-reliance and fortitude, to make them abhor the servitude in which they were kept and show them how to thrive on their own. But of course, they'd be beaten or worse for even attempting to liberate themselves.

Tolly spoke, mind to mind. *That would be like trying to teach a wolf to be a lamb. A waste of breath.*

Ibrahim stood and called to the eldest of Faisal's two daughters. Celeste understood nothing he said, but hoped all he told them was that the two strange women would eat in their room. Her suspicions of him flared again. What if this was all some elaborate trap?

Tolly again caught her thought. *What would be the point? What would he gain? He's risked himself coming here, hiding us. You're jumping at shadows.*

I hate it when you make sense.

Ibrahim turned back to them. "Faisal and I are going to have a good fadl, so I can catch up on family gossip. I've not been here for many years. We'll leave for the train station just after dawn. One of the girls will come to wake you and bring bread, cheese and fuhl - a paste made from fava beans."

Celeste couldn't stop herself. "And coffee. I need coffee."

Ibrahim grinned, his old self for a moment. "And coffee."

Tolly stood, and Celeste followed suit. "We will retire to our room then. Please thank your cousin for his hospitality and I hope you have a pleasant evening."

Coming from her lips, it didn't sound insincere at all. Celeste knew she would never master that particular skill. Following Tolly up the stairs, she cursed Faisal, then Ibrahim, then all men in general. Except for Byron. And Martin. And Eddie. And Alistair.

Beside her, Tolly laughed, privy to her thoughts. "You may as well stop while you're ahead. Not all men are evil, not all women, good. And a curse, even made in jest, is never a wise idea."

Celeste blew out a frustrated breath, and the moment Tolly shut the door, ripped off her hijab. "I hope dinner is soon. I'm starving."

"You are always starving."

Flopping back on the bed, she adopted a mocking tone. "Blah blah blah blah blah."

Tolly laughed, used to her tantrums.

Lying there, staring up at the plastered ceiling, she almost wished some new calamity would occur. She was bored, frustrated, and damn it, she missed Byron. Hell, she even missed Guy and the ushabti. Or rather, Berenice.

It was going to be a long night.

TWENTY

Neither Pyp nor Guy made an appearance all night, despite Celeste having composed her return letter to Byron. But she knew Guy had heard the proposed plan, and since she had the scarab ring to which he was bound, he'd have to follow.

Faisal's daughter, Layla, knocked timidly at the door when the eastern horizon still held more purple than mauve.

Celeste clutched the fine cotton sheets around her while Tolly, annoyingly prepared like all morning people, had already dressed in what Celeste was calling her habit. Tolly opened the door a crack and Celeste could hear the young woman speak softly. Tolly murmured shukran and brought the breakfast tray in herself, closing the door with her foot.

"Such a pleasant young woman. Well, perhaps not woman. I doubt she's more than a year into puberty."

"They marry them off at that age. To old lechers who've already worn out two wives."

"Celie, I'm sure those kinds of men are the exception, not the rule."

"And I'm sure it's the opposite." The tantalizing aroma of the coffee drew her out from under the covers.

"Ah, ah, ah." Tolly held the cup out of her reach. "Dress first and pack all our belongings. Especially the ring."

Celeste reached under her pillow for the ruined stocking she'd hidden the ring in the night before, climbed out of bed and threw on her borrowed clothes. Then, while her partner sat cross-legged on the floor and drank coffee, Celeste double checked their belongings were safely stuffed into their bag. Which left the question of how to carry the ring. Remembering all the running and chasing and narrow escapes of recent days, she took the satin tie of the sailor suit Coco had made her and slid the ring onto it.

"Good idea, *elskling*."

Celeste held up her hair while Tolly knotted the tie at the back of her neck with a kiss and Celeste received the compliment and the reward of coffee with delight. "Thanks. Now what's to eat?"

They polished off every scrap of food on the tray: flat bread and fuhl, redolent with garlic, oregano, and onion; a boiled egg apiece; and a soft, salty cheese. Filling, but Celeste wished there was more coffee. She supposed asking would be perceived as rude or ungrateful.

Tolly did a final sweep of the room, finishing just as someone knocked again, much louder.

The miniature elderly despot in black scowled at them as they threw on their hijabs, then shooed them down the stairs. The woman looked happy to see the backs of her unwanted guests.

Ibrahim waited for them in the main room, dressed in a more traditional, but finely made white robe trimmed in embroidered gold ribbon.

The crotchety woman shoved a basket into her grandson's hands and flapped her arms at him too, hurrying him out the door. Such a loving old thing. If Celeste's mother had lived, she'd probably have been an old harridan as well.

They set a brisk pace toward the village's tiny train station in the pre-dawn dimness, trusting Ibrahim to know the way. After the third or fourth turn, and the house was no longer in sight, Ibrahim sighed. "My God, it is exactly as I remember from childhood. That house, this place. Faisal's father was a wealthy businessman by country standards, and Faisal now runs the family concerns. I feel like I have just left a museum."

"You seem almost relieved to be leaving," Tolly commented softly.

"It was lovely seeing my cousin and grandmother again, but to be honest, it will be a long time before I return. I am sorry if I appeared rude last night, but what do the English say? When in Rome, do as they do? I could not arouse any suspicion. I did not tell him why we needed shelter, only that I am protecting you from criminals."

Celeste wondered if he hadn't enjoyed playing the role a little too much. He'd been a right arse.

Tolly nodded. "Very wise. Ah, and here is Guy and...my dear, we have decided that you need a name. Celeste has dubbed you Berenice, in honor of her first official teacher. May you grow as wise as she."

The ushabti stared, blinking. Finally, she looked at Guy. "Master?"

He broke into a hearty laugh. "Wonderful! It had not occurred to me, but that is indeed an excellent idea. If you are going to work with me, it will be easier if you have a name."

Celeste sputtered. "Master? She's now your servant?"

"Nonsense. Not a servant, although that is why she was created. No, she will be my, erm, helper."

Celeste snorted. "And what will she be helping you with? If you lay one finger on her, I'll take your ring and throw it into the nearest forge."

Tolly restrained her. "Calm yourself."

"But what if he turns her into some sort of sex toy?"

Tolly gave Guy one of those looks that made courageous men shake in their boots. "Is that what you have in mind?"

"Of course not!" That could have been a lie. Then he continued. "If I want erotic entertainment, there are countless actual women who would be happy to lie with me. I assure you; I have never had to coerce or force anyone in my entire existence."

That at least sounded believable and further reminded her of Byron. The poet had to beat women off even at the heights of his debauchery. She put her hands on her hips. "If I learn different—and trust me, I will learn of it—I will find a way to end you."

Bemused, he raised his eyebrows. "I believe you would try. Very well. I give my word as First Servant of Epona that I will not ask... what was it? Ah, yes, Berenice. I will not ask Berenice to do anything she objects to, and that I will not lie with her." He paused and Celeste tried to reach his mind to see if he spoke the truth, but she couldn't, despite the energetic link that still connected them.

"Fine."

Ibrahim shifted from foot to foot. "If we're quite done? We have a train to catch."

Tolly eyed the group. "Do you think we need the glamour? I'd like to cut the power connection until we absolutely need it."

Ibrahim examined them. "If you keep your heads bowed, and don't look anyone in the eye, it should suffice, particularly since we will be in a private compartment."

Guy shrugged. "If you are quite sure."

Tolly gave a brusque nod. "Quite."

Butterflies tickled Celeste's stomach, and the energetic link broke, thank the Goddess. Though she had to admit he'd been a gentleman about it, not trying to pull too much power from her. Nor had he attempted to invade her thoughts. Well, that she was aware of.

Ibrahim scanned the surrounding streets, where early risers made their way to the fields or the market. "We need to go. And remember, mesdames, to walk behind me. In Egypt, it is *not* ladies first. Now, shall we?"

Tolly gave her hand a comforting squeeze, then followed Ibrahim at a careful distance. Celeste had no choice but to follow suit.

Tired of getting wound up over things she knew she could not change, Celeste said nothing. The sooner they got to Luxor and helped break Guy's bonds to the ring so he could go deal with the sem priest, the sooner they could get out of this benighted country.

The train pulled into Luxor several hours later. Ibrahim chivvied them from the station into a carriage. Tolly wanted to go to the Winter Palace, where they had reservations, but they'd be advertising their location to their enemies.

The detective settled the debate by giving the driver instructions in Arabic and the carriage rattled off down the street, raising a cloud of dust.

They passed through the tourist district and turned into an area of narrower streets and less opulent homes, then into an even less salubrious neighborhood. The sun cast long shadows when they pulled up in front of an unprepossessing three-story mudbrick building. A sign over the door, in both English and French, read simply, "Hotel".

Dripping with sweat and caked with road dust, Celeste sagged. She'd have bet a million francs there would be no luxurious bath in this establishment.

Cracks in the exterior plaster radiated from the wood-framed front door, and a handful of cloudy windows on the second and third stories broke the monotonous dun facade. At least the rooms on the third floor sported wrought iron two-foot-deep balconies, and each had a window box with a handful of bright flowers. Next to her, Tolly sighed.

"I realize it is not up to your standards." Ibrahim's voice held a note of apology. "But I can almost guarantee no one will look for ladies of quality here. And it is clean."

They entered, and Ibrahim greeted the man behind the desk like an old friend. After a bit of back and forth, broad smiles and hugging, Ibrahim arranged for two rooms on the third floor. Guy and Berenice were nowhere to be seen, but Celeste was sure they hovered nearby, observing. The ring lay warm against her chest, tucked into her camisole and she wondered if that's where Guy disappeared to and if he had some sort of living arrangement inside the ring. She'd have to ask him.

They climbed the stairs, and she thanked the Goddess they had no luggage, although they would need to purchase some clothes before returning home if they could not retrieve their own things from Shepheard's. She imagined returning to Marseilles on some tramp steamer, dressed in Egyptian clothing, enduring weeks or months on crew rations and weak beer. She shuddered.

Tolly caught her thought and said, "Uff da."

Ibrahim unlocked the door to the room and ushered them inside but refused for propriety's sake to enter. "I am in the room across the hall. Please do not hesitate to knock should you need anything. I propose we slip out after dark for a meal; there is a place I know nearby that serves excellent food and is frequented by both Europeans and by locals."

Tolly anticipated Celeste's next problem. "We will need to purchase clothing and toiletries as well. And is there any place to bathe?"

Ibrahim smiled. "There is a full bath at the end of the hall. A shared one, but I know the manager and he keeps things scrupulously clean. He will never likely attract the clientele Shepheard's does, but more middle-class tourists come every year, and now, with the opening of Tutankhamun's tomb, the famous hotels are always booked. A perfect opportunity for Khaled to grow his business."

Tolly smiled politely, then asked, "And towels? Soap?"

"I will ask for those to be delivered."

Tolly thanked him and urged Celeste inside. After shutting the door, she drew the drapes over their window and the balcony beyond and collapsed on the brass and iron bed. The springs underneath squeaked, but from the sigh of contentment, Celeste figured the mattress was at least comfortable. Sitting on the edge, she slipped off Tolly's shoes and rubbed her feet, which elicited a moan of pleasure from her partner.

"You are always so good to me. I know I've been rather shrewish lately. I'm sorry."

"Don't be ridiculous. First, you're dealing with Aubrey's death. And then all this on top of it?" She gestured vaguely around her. "You've been pushed to the brink." Pressing her lips to Tolly's damp forehead, she said, "Why don't you wait here for the towels, and I'll go run the bath, so it will be all ready for you."

"You are a treasure."

"I suppose it would be scandalous for me to join you..." She let the invitation linger on the air, always hopeful.

"You suppose correctly. I'm sorry."

At least they'd had a couple of nice days on this trip. "You wait here. I'll be back in a few minutes."

By the time she'd returned from filling the huge, claw-foot tub—a perfect size for two, damn it—a youngster was just leaving after delivering the towels and a lovely bar of lilac-scented, French-milled soap.

She escorted Tolly to the bathroom and, playing maid, helped her to strip, ripping off the black garment. She had to get her fun in somehow. "This bathroom really is nice. Not the Ritz, but the fixtures look new and well maintained, and there was certainly no problem with hot water. This Khaled fellow seems to know what he's doing."

Tolly relaxed, tense shoulders falling. She even smiled. "He does indeed." Testing the steaming water with her finger, she climbed in and sighed. "Oh my stars, that feels good."

It took all of Celeste's willpower to hand over the soap and towels and go back to their room. At home, they enjoyed sharing a bath, and it saved on hot water. Although now with reliable indoor plumbing, no one had to bring up buckets of hot water to fill the tub.

Still, they were both so grimy that it would require the tub to be refilled after Tolly washed off the sweat and dust, so sharing was impractical. She tried to think of a way to get her partner to stay while she herself bathed, but no excuse would satisfy Tolly's rule-following sensibility or quell the raised eyebrows of anyone who might notice.

So she waited for Tolly to return, occupying the time by reading Byron's letter again, especially the part Pyp had not recited aloud, with pen and paper beside her on the bed ready for her response.

She skimmed through what she'd already heard, the info about djinns and ifrits and the dirt on Aubrey, just to make sure Pyp hadn't censured more, and perhaps salacious news of Aubrey's misdeeds, and being disappointed, moved on to the next section.

I hope you're enjoying yourself. Desmond has left for Egypt.

Well, that was unexpected. What was the psychopathic and sole other member of Byron's vampiric family doing here?

She read on, a little ball of anxiety over that news tangling in her stomach.

I understand he spent time there after the Crimea, on his way to a post in India. Before he left or your part of the world, he did as I told you he would. He created a familiar without permission, which, at his young age as a vampire, is strictly forbidden. But there's no stopping a man with an ego of such oversized proportions.

She snickered at that. Who was calling who an egotist? She read on.

At any rate, he's gone, leaving this apartment that much emptier.

Fortunately, Martin and I have reached a detente. I will be sharing his lodgings for some undetermined amount of time, although I am not particularly enamored by the idea of spending my days, insensate and vulnerable, in the company of Faulkner. I think it is perhaps wise to retire to my crypt come morning to woo my respite in Lethe's arms there. Martin says Faulkner is utterly reliable, but I've seen the way the fellow looks at me, as though I were some sort of parasite that crawled out of the sewers and attached myself, leech-like, to his precious charge.

Not much else to report. Eddie and Father Dominic ask after you. Please, I implore you, write back with all possible haste. I languish without you.

Byron

She thought again of Desmond. What was he doing in Egypt? Finding someone to bring over? Or spying on her? She did not trust the bloodsucker for an instant.

Still, Desmond's departure had triggered Byron to reconcile with Martin, so that was good.

The onion skin paper Byron had provided was his own stationery, and the pen was a dream, the nib smooth. It glided over the page without ever feeling scratchy, and she considered keeping it in payment for being at his beck and call. But then Tolly would want to know where she got it and then they'd have another conversation about how Byron was going to get them both in trouble with the Council and blah blah blah. Best just to give it back when Pyp came to retrieve her letter, a task she'd need to arrange soon, before Tolly finished her ablutions.

Next, she told him about Aubrey's death, Guy, the ushabti, the ring, and their escape from Shepheard's. She complained about the plight of women, the horrible black garment, detective Ibrahim's odious grandmother, and the oppressive heat, sweat, and dust.

She ended by expressing her happiness that he and Martin had settled their differences, and told him to relay her best wishes to Martin, Eddie, and Father Dom.

Then she pulled out the enchanted coin and summoned Pyp. He arrived with the usual pop, this time dressed in his ordinary clothes: a pair of hounds tooth knickers and a loden green jumper. His red curls were a mess, and his eyes bloodshot and bleary.

"Late night?"

"Aye. His Lordship had me helping cart his stuff over to Martin's flat. Don't understand how a man can have so many things when everything he owned burned down not three months ago."

"Honeymoon over, is it?"

"No, no, we're mates, Byron and me. But you'da thought that old stick up his arse Faulkner could have helped a bit." He yawned, then held out his hand. "You got a letter for me?"

"I do, thanks. And sorry to drag you out of bed." She handed over the sealed envelope.

Pyp looked around, curled his lips. "Thought you only stayed in fancy places."

Celeste just shrugged. "The bed is comfortable."

He sat down on it and bounced up and down a few times, making it squeak. He waggled his eyebrows. "Hope you don't have neighbors. Byron says you and Madame Tollefsen can be rather noisy and with those springs…" He petered out when he saw her expression.

"What Madame Tollefsen and I do is none of your business. Nor is it any of Byron's, either. You be sure to tell him that."

Pyp flushed, making his swath of freckles disappear. The impudent grin, however, did not. "Yes, Miss." He tugged a forelock since he had no hat to tip and vanished with that telltale pop, leaving her both irritated and amused. Byron needed to learn to keep his mouth shut. And how did he know about that in the first place? Something else to talk to him about when they got home. Shaking her head, she returned to waiting—what was Tolly doing in there all this time?— for her own turn in the tub.

TWENTY-ONE

After her bath, Tolly fell into a doze on the bed. Celeste took her time with her own ablutions, luxuriating in the sudsy water. She washed off a pound of dust and sand, and afterward, donned the wrinkled clothes she'd stuffed in the bag before they'd fled Shepheard's. The enchanted coin for summoning Pyp went into the pocket of her cardigan.

Moving to the window, she watched the dwindling sliver of the setting sun turn the sky a rainbow of pastel colors as it slipped below the horizon, and the monochromatic gloom of twilight settled over the neighborhood.

Residents trickled onto the streets, now that the heat of the day had passed. Mothers strolled, gaggles of children trailing along behind them like ducklings. Two shopkeeps, a chemist, and a coffee shop owner, sat on a stone bench in front of their respective venues, gossiping like fishwives. Even a few Europeans, lost or unable to afford one of the more luxurious hotels, searched for a place to eat.

The traffic, the smiling faces, and the laughter that drifted up made the neighborhood feel a little bit like home. She missed Paris, missed the Magical Quarter, missed the cafes and the chansons and, to be honest, the croissants. After a vagabond life, the strange realization hit her that she never wanted to live anywhere else. She'd become settled. She had a home.

The bed squeaked and Tolly, in the rumpled sundress she'd pulled out of the traveling bag, came from behind to wrap her in an embrace. "Penny for your thoughts."

"Just thinking about home." No, she would not cry.

"Mm. Yes, even I feel homesick. This trip did not turn out as I'd imagined."

"I really am sorry about Aubrey."

Tolly rested her head on Celeste's shoulder. "I still can't quite believe it."

"Love makes people do strange things." She thought about the night on the Eiffel Tower in November, when she'd believed the Red Witch had killed Tolly. Rage and grief had transformed her into a beast. Yes, love, and the potential loss of it, made one do uncharacteristic things.

The gentle rap on the door startled them. They broke apart and Celeste triggered a seeking from her bracelet to see who stood outside.

Ibrahim.

She opened the door only far enough to admit him. He tumbled in, arms piled high with shopping bags and string-wrapped parcels, which he dumped on the bed.

Tolly raised her eyebrows, and Celeste recognized the emblem of several fashion houses Tolly frequented. "You've been shopping?" Celeste raised her eyebrows in surprise and inquiry.

"I cannot take you to dine in a local restaurant with you dressed as two Coptic ladies. It's not done. So, I purchased some western clothing items. I hope they fit."

Celeste could have kissed him. It would be so wonderful to feel like a real woman again, not some dirt-encrusted farm hand after a day in the fields. "That was so thoughtful."

"There are also some toiletries and..." He snagged a familiar type of circular box tied with a ribbon and presented it to Tolly. "I think this is at least close to the one that was ruined."

Celeste groaned. Another bloody hat.

Tolly untied the ribbon and opened the box. Pulling out a straw sun hat with pheasant feathers that looked remarkably like the one trampled during their flight from the train, she beamed at him. "I don't know what to say."

She put it on, admiring it in the mirror. "It's perfect. Thank you so much, detective."

He cleared his throat, shifted from foot to foot. "I felt it was the least I could do. You could easily have turned me over to the thugs or abandoned me."

"Nonsense," Tolly said. "We would never do that."

"Tolly's right. Not to mention they are now after us, too." Celeste gestured at the packages on the bed. "We'd best change. Should we knock on your door when we're ready?"

He nodded. "I too purchased a few things for myself."

Tolly pulled some money out of her purse. "I insist on reimbursing you. Until it is safe for you to resume your life, you will need money. Living is expensive on the run, as Celie and I know all too well."

"No, no, I couldn't. These things, they are gifts."

She pressed the wad of bills into his hand, using the voice that no one ever argued with. "I insist." She folded his fingers over the cash.

He looked so distraught, Celeste figured he'd throw the money and flee. But reason trumped pride. "I thank you."

Celeste held the door open for him. "We'll see you in just a few minutes. I promise I won't let Tolly primp too long."

With a bashful smile, he crossed to his own room and disappeared inside.

"I hope you didn't give him all our money. We're going to need some, too."

"Ah, but we have a way of getting more. Byron can replenish our funds courtesy of young Pyp. He knows we're good for it."

Celeste's eyebrows rose in surprise. "I hadn't thought of that."

"You're not the only one who can be crafty, my dove." And with that, she started opening boxes and bags with glee.

Not more than twenty minutes later, dressed in a simple drop-waist frock of pale blue, matching pumps, and a white cloche, Celeste knocked on Ibrahim's door. Tolly, still adjusting her hat, promised she'd join them in a minute. Ibrahim exited his room in a pinstripe suit with a fedora and...by the stars, he was wearing a false mustache. And it looked remarkably real.

"You look very dapper, detective."

He stroked his mustache. "Thank you, Mademoiselle Berenger."

Tolly came into the hallway and echoed her sentiment. "How very dashing you look, detective. Like that Rudolph Valentino fellow in *The Four Horsemen of the Apocalypse*, though he did not have a mustache. I approve."

He flashed a brilliant smile. "Merci, Madame." He glanced up and down the hall and lowered his voice. "For tonight, I propose we should go by given names, in case anyone is listening who might report back to the people who search for us."

It made sense, Celeste thought. Using "detective" could be dangerous—the Brotherhood no doubt had members and thus potential spies everywhere. "Perhaps you could call me Marie. That's my middle name. I'm afraid Celeste is a little too unusual here."

"And I am Rami."

Celeste winked. "A romantic sort of name. Goes with the mustache."

His eyes twinkled, lighting up his angular features. Even with the fake mustache, he'd no doubt make the women swoon, especially if he smiled. "Thank you. I do not think I have ever shared my given name with a Western woman."

Turning to Tolly, he bowed over her hand in a very continental manner. Apparently her partner had acquired another admirer.

Tolly laughed. "I suppose Astrid is not very common either. How about Anna? That's *my* middle name."

Celeste's head snapped around. "That's your middle name? Why don't I know that?"

Tolly linked arms with Ibrahim. "Because, my dove, you never asked."

Celeste hurried to catch up as they headed down the stairs and out into the growing crowds in the street. As Ibrahim led them through the throng, the charm on Celeste's bracelet that warned of danger grew hot. She scanned her surroundings but saw nothing. A moment later, the charm settled down.

Tolly shot her a questioning look.

"Probably nothing. The bracelet went off, but it's stopped now."

Ibrahim, sensing only their concern, increased his pace. "We should hurry. It is not much farther, just around the corner."

A few minutes later, under the light of a gibbous moon, they rounded a corner. About ten meters away, a group of people milled in front of an open door. Given the small bistro tables in the forecourt, it had to be the restaurant. Locals sat both outside at small tables, and inside as well. Even a few tourists in western garb gathered, waiting for a table.

Ibrahim halted them both. "Wait here. I will make sure it's safe." He trotted ahead and slipped inside.

"What does your charm say? And why, by all the gods, is everyone in France named Marie or Jean? Can you people not think of other names?"

The charm on her wrist was warm, but not any warmer than the others on the bracelet. Still, the range was short. "I should get a little clos—"

Ibrahim bolted out of the doorway. He paused long enough to shout, "Run!" before pelting the opposite way down the narrow street. Two men barreled through the hovering patrons and chased after him. Celeste started to race forward, but Tolly caught her arm. "No!"

She struggled to free herself. "We have to help him."

Even as the words left her lips, the sharp report of a pistol echoed off the walls of the buildings that lined the street. One shot. Two. Three.

She saw Ibrahim falter, stumble a few more steps, then fall face-first onto the sidewalk. "No!"

Tolly dragged her around the corner, clutching her arm so tightly her fingernails dug into Celeste's skin. She hissed in her ear. "We must hide. Now."

"The hotel?"

Tolly, still gripping Celeste's arm, walked them quickly but casually down the street. "No. They might have followed us from there. It's not safe to go back." She was smiling as she spoke, in sharp contrast to their grim discussion.

"But those men were inside already. Waiting."

"Perhaps they discovered where Ibrahim was staying and posted someone there in case he showed up. He said he knew the place. And he had been out shopping, so someone could have spotted him and followed him back there."

"He's dead, isn't he?" Celeste hadn't realized how much she liked him. And relied on him. Did he have a wife? Children? A mother to cry over his bullet-ridden body?

"Very likely. And we certainly can do nothing to save him without getting shot ourselves."

A figure stepped out of a doorway in front of them. "Please, ladies. Follow me."

Celeste threw her arm in front of Tolly. "Who are you?" Her charm hadn't heated up in warning, but something about the man made the hairs on the back of her neck stand up.

"I am friend of Rami. He spoke to me yesterday, told me to watch out for you. So, I follow when you leave hotel."

He was a tall man, taller even than Ibrahim, with eyes like obsidian, cold and black. He had a neatly trimmed VanDyke that made him both handsome and dangerous looking.

His eyes kept flicking left and right, and he was almost crouched, as though hiding. "Please. There is no time. We must go."

Celeste glanced behind them, saw the two gunmen enter the street and pause, searching the crowd. Darkness had fallen now, but two western women, especially one who was tall and wearing a straw hat with feathers, would soon be spotted. She glanced at Tolly, who pressed her lips together and nodded.

The man opened the narrow door behind him and shooed them inside. He gestured them up the stairs. And up. And up. On the fourth floor, he guided them down a hallway and through a door mottled with peeling green paint.

Celeste entered first. She had just enough time to notice the room's lack of furniture, and to feel the bracelet on her wrist become fiery hot before a rooting spell trapped her and she stumbled to her knees. She tried to use a spell from her charm bracelet, but before she could say the trigger word, a hand clamped a sickly sweet-smelling cloth over her nose and mouth. The last thing she heard before the world swam away was a swear word in Norwegian.

TWENTY-TWO

S he awoke in a dark place that smelled of odd spices and stale
air. A blindfold covered her eyes, and her hands had been tied
behind her back, making her shoulders ache. Her head
pounded and her stomach roiled, likely the aftereffects of the chloro-
form. Even in the absence of being able to see anything, she felt the
space spinning around her.

She became aware of a presence beside her and heard a groan.
"Tolly?"

"Oh, Freya, my head. I think I'm going—" Tolly retched, adding
a new smell to the place's already pungent menu of odors.

A shuffling sound captured her attention, then a voice boomed
and echoed. "I am so sorry to have made you sick, Madame Tollefsen,
but it was a necessary evil. And do not try to use your foreign
magicks here. I had the djinn," and there was a mocking emphasis on
the appellation, "create a field of annulment around you both. It
won't last for long, but long enough."

"I'm sorry, my friends." Celeste recognized Guy's voice. "I had
no choice."

The other speaker laughed. "No, you didn't. Now that I have the ring, you are mine to command."

Celeste could no longer sense the ring. Seething, she faced the direction of the speakers. "What do you want? Where are we?"

"Where? Oh, you shall soon find out. As for what I want, I already have what it. The ring, and of course, the ushabti you stole from me. Everything back in its proper place. Soon the whole of Waset will be under my control as well."

Celeste tried a spell off her bracelet again, but nothing happened.

The man chuckled. "I told you."

Gathering her legs under her, she lunged toward the voice. She stubbed her toe and shin—by the stars, he'd taken their shoes!—on something hard as stone and fell forward into a shallow puddle of water with a splash. The landing knocked the wind out of her and the pool smelled rank. She spat out the noxious fluid.

"I advise you to wait until you have removed your blindfolds before stumbling about in here. You could hurt yourselves rather badly, perhaps even perish. And I have use for you later, once the ritual is complete."

"Where are we?" Tolly asked. "What ritual?"

"Oh, that would be telling. And it is, as you Westerners say, on a need-to-know basis."

She heard Guy mutter something unintelligible.

"Get down on your knees, servant, and kiss my shoes. You are lucky I have not already destroyed you. Abase yourself."

Guy ground out the words. "Yes, Master."

A rustle of fabric came before a dull thud, like a blow. Maybe Guy getting kicked? Oh, how the mighty have fallen. Celeste's anger rose by the second. She chafed against the rope that bound her wrists but found no wiggle room, ending up only abrading her skin.

The voice came again. "And now we leave you. Enjoy your temporary home. I promise future accommodations will be much less...dank."

She heard snapping fingers and then silence.

"Tolly?"

"I'm here. I've almost got the blindfold off." Some noise ensued, along with a few Norwegian epithets. "There. Oh, thank God, he left us with some sort of magical light—like one of our glow spheres. But where on earth are we?"

"Well, if you'd get over here and help me, we could figure it out together."

"Patience, *elskling*, I'm coming. Try to stand, but don't move a foot farther, or you'll hurt yourself."

Celeste obeyed, teetering a bit in order not to shift too far in any direction. When Tolly reached her, she worked the blindfold up and over her head with her teeth, pulling Celeste's hair in the process. "Ouch!"

Celeste blinked and gazed around her. They were in a large chamber, with plastered walls painted with scenes like ones she had seen in Tolly's books on ancient Egypt, although the plaster had flaked away in places. The container they'd awakened in was a stone sarcophagus, resting on a platform in the middle of the space. Around them, planks rested on piles of rubble over pools of water, like the board in the storeroom in Saint-Denys that allowed Byron to get out without walking on holy ground.

She'd read in one of Tolly's blasted books that underground tombs flooded during the infrequent but fierce spring thunderstorms. The water, and the chill of being far underground, made the tomb chilly and dank.

A pile of planks lay in front of her, studded with rusty nails. If she'd fallen on one of those, the injury might not have been deadly, but certainly painful. Not to mention the threat of tetanus or infection.

At the far end of the chamber, a set of stairs led upward into a rectangle of yawning blackness.

Her bonds chafed. Stepping gingerly across the debris-littered floor to the tomb, she rubbed the ropes against the jagged, broken edge of the stone until she was able to snap the bindings. Then she assisted Tolly with hers.

Tolly pecked her cheek in thanks and rubbed her wrists while Celeste made her way toward the steps. She'd gotten halfway when she ducked reflexively at a sound like a Howitzer shell exploding in the no-man's-land between trenches. The floor shook and dust rained down. Tolly toppled over and Celeste fell to her knees.

The rumble faded away, succeeded by the whisper of sand sifting from the ceiling and the slither of loosened plaster sloughing off the walls. Cracks had appeared on the chamber's plaster facade, and in the curved vault of the ceiling.

Worse yet, that yawning black rectangle, the only exit, was now filled floor to ceiling with rubble.

Celeste crawled to Tolly, who lay still. No, not again. She couldn't lose her again.

"Tolly? Come on, wake up. Please wake up."

Fear gnawed in her already upset stomach, and her hands trembled as she felt for a pulse. Her partner groaned and pushed her chilly hand away.

"I'm fine, I'm fine. Just a bit rattled."

Celeste blinked back tears. "I thought you'd hit your head and..." She couldn't say it. Giving voice to such things made them happen, gave them power to manifest.

Tolly climbed to her feet and brushed off her new dress. Having heard the frightened thought, she said, "That's stuff and nonsense. You're acting like a superstitious villager." Walking over to the stone sarcophagus, she pulled out the new hat Ibrahim had bought her, now mashed flat, with the feathers crumpled. She brushed this off too and tried to reshape the crown. With a disgusted noise, she affixed it to her head. "Egypt is very hard on hats."

Celeste burst into laughter. "You are the most amazing woman."

"Of course, I am. How else would I be able to keep up with

you?" She took Celeste's hand, and their fingers entwined. "Now. You're the clever one. How do we get out of this?"

Celeste's knees felt weak. Her head was still muzzy, and the jittering fear from moments ago buzzed in her brain like angry hornets. "I need a moment."

The stone lip of the sarcophagus made a perfect perch. Tolly hopped up beside her and they leaned against one another, shoulder to shoulder.

"You're thinking about the detective," Tolly said.

She couldn't get the image of Ibrahim's bullet-ridden body jerking and collapsing onto the street out of her head. "Goddess bless him, he was just trying to help us."

"He was involved with some very dangerous people. And he crossed them."

"To protect us!" Celeste squeezed her eyes and blinked away the tears that wet her lashes. "How did they find us? We were disguised and we've only been in the city a few hours."

"He must have been spotted on his shopping trip."

Logical, but somehow that didn't feel right. "I suppose. But what about that cousin of his? He was a creep and I'm betting his 'business' wasn't legal. Antiquities theft perhaps, or something even more nefarious. I mean, what could he possibly do in that dusty little village to earn the kind of money he clearly has?"

"The detective trusted him. He wouldn't have taken us there if he didn't. You just didn't like him because he offended your suffragette sensibilities."

Celeste shrugged. "And another thing. Why didn't my charm warn me about that odious man who kidnapped us?"

Tolly put an arm around her shoulder. "That is a good question. If he was the Lion of Justice, your bracelet should have been shrieking. He must have magic of his own."

"He's possessed by the spirit of the priest Guy killed in the tomb. He's magical by nature."

"By nature, yes, but to block your charm, he must be able to cast a blocking spell. And as far as I am aware, ifrits are avenging spirits with only one goal: to kill the person responsible for their deaths. They have no spell-casting abilities. Frankly, I find it hard to believe an ifrit could even possess someone."

Celeste thought about that, trying to recall Guy's story. "Guy said that the ifrit had been some kind of priest in ancient times. Maybe their priests had magic. Didn't the ancient Egyptians work magic spells?"

Tolly nodded. "Yes, they had an interesting mix of magic and science. And you're right, Guy did say the man was a priest. So that makes sense."

"Let's look around." Celeste hopped down and by the light of the glow lamp the so-called Lion of Justice left them, walked the perimeter of the room, hoping for an exit they'd overlooked. Meanwhile, Tolly picked through the debris surrounding the sarcophagus. Bits of gesso-covered wood from the remnants of an anthropoid shaped coffin, scraps she thought might be from mummy wrappings, and shattered bits of pottery that might once have been offering vessels lay among piles of rock fall from the unstable ceiling.

Celeste examined a vertical crack in the flaking, moldy plaster, but if a secret door existed, it remained so. "Did you learn anything about Egyptian magic when you were training?"

"What, you don't remember that entire class on world magic systems? Celie, really."

Ignoring the comment, Celeste continued her circuit. She wished she had a brighter light source. A few sections of the paintings on the tomb walls were spectacular. She could make out vivid colors: Blue, red, green, yellow. In its prime, the frescoes would have been magnificent. Now all this art lay hidden in a chamber no one would ever see. "Incredible art, appreciated by no one."

Tolly chuckled, the sound echoing off the high vaulted ceiling. "I'm sure the tomb's occupant appreciated it."

Celeste continued her walk, not finding any kind of tunnel or shaft. "You didn't answer my question."

"Which question?"

"About Egyptian magic."

"Ah. Actually, though I'm loathe to give him credit, Byron had the right of it. Not much is known about the magical system of ancient Egypt. And any information about modern day practices is a closely guarded secret."

Celeste completed her circuit, having discovered no other way out. Was it her imagination, or was the air growing stale?

Tolly still examined the bits and bobs tomb raiders over the millennia had left behind.

"What are you looking for?"

"I was hoping to find an ushabti figurine. The coffin is empty. Perhaps with their master, the owner of the tomb gone, it might have no one to serve, like Berenice. Perhaps we could convince it to help us."

"That's...inspired!"

Tolly came back to the sarcophagus and sat down next to her. "Unfortunately, I cannot find one." She sighed. "I suppose you would have shouted if you'd found another exit?"

Celeste nodded. "Sorry."

Tolly reached over and squeezed her hand. "We'll figure something out."

"Your hand is freezing." It was. And Tolly had been walking around in the puddles on the floor, too. "Here, swing up here and tuck your feet under my legs."

"You're hardly warmer than I am."

"Still. Give me your hands to warm."

Tolly submitted gratefully. Despite being from Norway, or perhaps because of it, she despised the cold, whereas Celeste hated the heat. Well, excessive heat, anyway.

"Perhaps we could remove the rubble," Celeste suggested. "Work in shifts. Is the glow light moveable?"

"Ours are. Not sure about his, whatever his name is. What on earth do we call him?"

"Rat? Boil on my arse? Plague bubo? Perhaps, PB for short."

"I don't suppose you remember what Guy called him?"

Celeste shook her head. "Let's call him PB. Fitting, I think. He comes out of nowhere and sentences us to death, and he probably smells too."

Tolly looked at the rubble filling the entrance. "It would take us weeks to clear that, even supposing we could lift all those stones."

And would require a lot of heavy breathing. The air grew increasingly stale, but she wouldn't be the first to mention it. How long would it be until they suffocated?

Tolly swung her legs down again. "Your turn."

They switched positions so that Tolly could now warm Celeste's hands and feet. "Damn it, there has to be a way out of here."

"He did say he had a use for us later. Let's just hope he comes back before the air runs out."

So she'd noticed it too. Celeste blew out a breath and tried to pull in energy from the earth but couldn't reach it. Like being enthralled by a vampire. "I can't pull in any power. Can you?"

Tolly sat still, her eyes closed. After a long pause, she shook her head.

Celeste snorted and jumped off the stone lip. She refused to accept that this would be the way they died, waiting to fall into an oxygen-deprived sleep from which they'd never awaken. She had a beef to pick with PB, not only for putting them through this, but for shooting Ibrahim and turning Guy into a slave. If she was going to die, let it be while attempting to save them, not huddled in acceptance.

She crossed to the pile of rubble and started to toss aside stones. She wanted to clear a path to the top of the doorway. Perhaps they only needed to move enough stone at the top of the passage for them to wriggle through to the entrance.

After a few moments, Tolly joined her, bussing Celeste's cheek. "I love you, *elskling*. There's no one on earth I'd rather escape from a tomb with."

Celeste returned the kiss. "I love you, too."

They rolled, carried, tossed, and levered rocks ceaselessly until both panted and ached, yet when they stopped to take a rest, they'd barely made a dent. They'd need a team of workers to shift all the fill.

Tolly leaned against Celeste, exhausted and gasping. "This isn't going to work."

Celeste agreed but didn't say so. They needed hope—and a new strategy. She put her arms around Tolly and tried again to pull in power. Nothing.

A loud echoing pop broke the silence, and a high-pitched voice with a Hibernian lilt said, "What in the name of Manannan mac Lir would you be doin' here?"

Pyp.

TWENTY-THREE

Surprise and relief flooded Celeste as she stared at the fae changeling. "How did you get here? There's supposed to be some sort of magic-blocking spell surrounding us."

Pyp shrugged. "Don't know nothin' 'bout that. I just followed the coin and Bob's your uncle." He'd lost some of his polish, and his brogue wound its way into his voice in his surprise. "And where exactly might here be, then?"

Celeste hopped off the ledge of the sarcophagus. "Trapped in an underground tomb in the Valley of the Kings."

"That's still in Egypt, right?"

Celeste and Tolly both said "yes" with varying degrees of annoyance.

"Oi, Miss, don't shoot the messenger. I'm just here at his nib's request."

Celeste grabbed Tolly's hand. "He got in, maybe he can get us out."

Pyp backed out of the puddle soaking his shoes and shook the water off. "Cold in here. I thought deserts were hot."

Celeste felt hope, real hope. "Pyp, can you take us with you into the Betwixt?"

He frowned, and after a moment's consideration, shook his head.

"Well, what other magic can you do?"

"I'm not empowered. All that I could have been got snuffed out when they traded me for that human brat." The saucy street kid she knew vanished, and the hurt from his own kind's betrayal showed in his green eyes.

"Damn it." She stared at the blocked stairs that led to the surface. "Wait, maybe you could ask Byron to help."

Tolly waved away her thought. "To do what? He's 3,000 miles away."

"Well, maybe he could talk to Alistair, who could call Sir John, and he could, I don't know, have a bunch of men clear the tunnel." She knew the plan wouldn't work. It would take too much time. By then, they'd have suffocated. Or the self-styled Lion of Justice would have returned to collect them.

When Celeste's face fell, Tolly nodded in agreement.

Pyp wrinkled his nose, a look between annoyance and concern. "So, do you want me to go back to his lordship after I read his letter? I can't go back this time without a response. He was very clear about that."

Celeste threw her hands up. "Pyp, we're running out of air. I don't have time to write a bloody letter. We need to get out. Now." She felt Tolly's hand on her shoulder and the touch provided such comfort. Whatever happened, they'd face it together.

"So I guess that's a no?"

"Go back. Tell him we're trapped in a tomb, and running out of air and options. If we survive, I'll send for you and give him the story of our daring escape."

Pyp grew serious. "That don't sound too hopeful."

Tolly took Celeste's hand and squeezed it. "It isn't. But we've gotten through—"

A scrabbling noise started by the stairs, and the mound of rocky debris began to tumble into the tomb.

Pyp backpedaled, eyes wide. "What's going on?"

The noise grew, as though a huge mole clawed his way through the rocks. More rubble fell into the room, some pieces big enough to crush a person. Tolly hopped up on the sarcophagus and pulled Celeste up with her. Pyp scrambled up too and they took refuge inside the stone container. The rockfall avalanched and the tomb vibrated like the skin of a bodhran.

When the clatter of rocks slowed to a stop, a shape loomed through the settling dust. "Who dares to trespass on holy ground?"

The booming voice echoed, causing fragile flakes of plaster to sift down from the ceiling and slough off the walls. Celeste's eyes watered and she blinked to clear her vision. The dust in the air made it difficult to see the speaker, but a portion of its bulk nearly filled the chamber. It rumbled, a low sound like a growl.

Celeste cleared her throat. "Who are you?"

A cool breeze caressed her sweat-damp cheeks, and the air cleared, revealing the outline of an enormous bulky head with slitted amber eyes, tawny fur covering massive shoulders and forepaws, and finally, a disturbing, and fully human face, shrouded with the famous Nemes headdress familiar from images of King Tut. Beside her, Tolly gasped, and Pyp muttered something in the fae tongue.

The continuous low growl made her teeth ache, and the creature's eyes narrowed. "Answer me," it snarled, "or I shall tear you limb from limb and crush your bones between my teeth." Those enormous paws, each almost as big as the sarcophagus, flexed wicked claws. The back side of the creature—surely, a sphinx—disappeared up the stairs to the outside, with the front half poking through the tomb entrance like a cat with its head in a mouse hole. Celeste could imagine a long tail twitching back and forth.

Tolly, always the diplomat, climbed out of the sarcophagus to address the beast while Celeste goggled. Sphinxes must have both stone and living forms, like gargoyles. Alistair would be delighted with all the new magical knowledge they'd be bringing back. If they made it.

"I am Astrid Tollefsen and this is my friend, Celeste Berenger. We are visiting here from France. The young man is named Pyp, he is our message carrier who works for," and here she cleared her throat, "a great lord in our homeland. Pyp is a magical servant, although not ours to command."

The sphinx squinted at them. "You are sorcerers and your magic smells alien. Why are you here, in this holy place? You are foreign interlopers, unbelievers. I will not allow you to disturb the king."

Since interlopers in antiquity had already desecrated the tomb, Celeste wanted to tell the sphinx he'd done a poor job of protecting it, but she kept her mouth shut.

"We travel here to learn about the magic of Waset. We had accommodations in the city of Thebes." Tolly's language became formal and archaic in construction. "An evil priest, one who murdered a royal princess and others, coveted our unfamiliar magical. He ordered his servants to capture us, and smiting us upon our heads, placed us in the coffin of the king, to seal us away for his further abuse. It was he who he caused the entrance to collapse and fill with rubble."

And this was why Celeste let Tolly do the talking. First, she'd been doing her research—who else would know whatever the word Waset meant.

The creature peered through cat-slit eyes at Tolly, tilting its head. The low growl quieted, the claws retracted, and those eerie amber eyes opened wider.

Tolly bowed her head respectfully, and the sphinx shifted a bit as it considered what she had said. Pyp, meanwhile, crouched in the tomb behind Celeste, utterly still.

"The rules still apply," rumbled the sphinx. "You have entered the tomb of the king and by your presence you defile it."

Tolly shushed Celeste before she could object. "This was not our intention. We are here involuntarily. Surely mitigation of some kind is possible."

The sphinx sniffed the air. "Hm. I must consider. Meanwhile, your companions must remove themselves from the sarcophagus. It is a great offense to disturb the body of the king."

Celeste grabbed Pyp's hand and dragged him onto the rock-strewn floor of the chamber, although she stayed well behind Tolly.

The sphinx remained silent for a time. At long last the creature nodded and bared preternaturally white teeth in a ferocious smile. "Very well. Our kind have cousins far to the north across the sea who possess a ritual for preventing the *xenoi* entry to the cities they protect."

Celeste knew *that* word at least. It was Greek for a range of individuals, from enemy strangers to ritual friends. Her tutoring of the ten-year-old Byron in Greek and French still paid dividends. The sphinx's cousins were in Greece and she now knew what ritual the sphinx had in mind.

The sphinx continued. "I will put to you three riddles. If you can answer them all, I will let you live."

Tolly frowned. "I would counter that arrangement. Not only will you let us live, but you'll see us freed from our imprisonment."

The sphinx's smile broadened. "A lively and intelligent interchange. I have not had such discourse in centuries. Very well, I will let you live and assist in freeing you, but you must teach me something of your magic."

Tolly's eyes lit, and her lips quirked up; an expression Celeste knew from their trips to the market that meant Tolly had the upper hand on a deal. "I will accept those terms, however the lessons in our magic must wait until we have concluded our business in Egypt. We will return here when we have completed our tour and spend a day with you."

"And how do I ensure you will comply?" He paused, considering.

"I will keep hostage your friend, the creature of darkness, whom I found above, near the entrance."

Tolly looked at Celeste, and her internal comment was strident. *Creature of darkness? By Odin's balls, it better not be Byron.*

It can't be, came Tolly's response.

Then who else?

Tolly turned a puzzled expression on the sphinx. "I don't know who you mean. We have no friends here, and certainly no one who matches your description."

"The pale, undead foreign man with the colorless hair. He speaks like you."

Pale. Undead. Oh hell. Byron had written that Desmond had business in Egypt. What was he really doing here, at this particular tomb? Was he hunting them, looking for a taste of witch's blood outside of Byron's purview?

Celeste shivered. "Oh, damn."

Tolly opened her eyes wide. *No. Surely not that psychopath.*

Celeste shrugged. *Who else could it be?* She dared to speak. "Did the man say he was a friend of ours?"

"He said, after I coerced him to speak, that he was waiting for you. And although he was with you, he had not yet entered the tomb. I pinned him beneath a block of stone so heavy even his kind could not move it and came down to confront you. He is not harmed, merely rests in a pit of sand."

If it was Desmond, it must be well past sunset. He must have been following them.

"Tolly, Pyp needs to return to the great lord Byron with news of the newcomer."

Tolly bit her lip and addressed the sphinx. "This undead creature may be known to us but is not one of our party. Still, we would see him unharmed, as he is an important, er, courtier to the great Lord Byron."

"I see. That explains his continued existence as an undead—made a servant in punishment for crimes he committed in life. And you wish this one to return to your lord?" The sphinx gestured with a scimitar-like talon at Pyp, who stood blanched and motionless. "He, too, is not human. He is like...an ushabti."

Tolly nodded. "He came to us only moments before you entered, with a message from Lord Byron." Somehow, she kept the disdain from voice when she said the poet's name. "He must return immediately to his master."

"You wish me to release him?"

"We would consider that a great boon."

"I give no boons. You will teach me more of your world and your magic to pay for his departure. Three days you will stay with me."

"If you guarantee we can return home unharmed, exactly as we are, including the undead man, then you have a bargain."

The sphinx smiled, revealing the sharp canines of a large feline. "I accept these terms. Send away this messenger spirit and then prepare to answer my riddles."

Celeste nodded at Pyp and murmured, "Tell Byron about Desmond. And that he's lucky we saved the creep."

Pyp grinned, relieved to be released. "Absolutely, Miss." Then, in a whisper, "Thanks." He vanished with a pop.

The sphinx watched the departure curiously, as if trying to figure out how it was done. Then he rested one paw on top of another. "Now. Let us begin."

TWENTY-FOUR

The sphinx's eyes narrowed again, and in a smug voice, he said, "You are prepared?"

Celeste heard Tolly's voice in her head. *This one's on you, my dove. You're far better at puzzles than I am.* Tolly stepped back, leaving Celeste center stage.

Grateful that life had made her an adept liar and a consummate poker player, Celeste didn't let her anxiety show on her face. She fixed her attention on the sphinx's amber, cat-like eyes and spoke in an equable and confident tone. "Ready."

"Very well. Here is your first riddle. What always runs yet doesn't walk; often murmurs but doesn't talk; has a bed but doesn't sleep; has a mouth but never eats."

Celeste's jaw relaxed. That was easy. "A river."

Tolly patted her back, her relief palpable through their mental link.

The sphinx's eyebrows rose. "Very good. A nice simple one to warm up." The creature paused for a moment, as if choosing from a long list of riddles in his head. "Ah, yes. Ready for the next one?"

Celeste nodded.

"I have no mouth but eat many things. I fear water, but I love wind. What am I?"

She repeated the words in her head, mind riffling through possibilities. None of them fit. Sweat trickled down her back, despite the chilly draft wafting down the passage from the outside.

The sphinx smiled. "Do you admit defeat?"

"No. I just need a minute."

Tolly queried her through their link. *Elskling?*

I'm thinking, I'm thinking.

"You are running out of time, witch."

So, he had figured out what they were. Since she didn't think they had witches in ancient Egypt, that meant the creature had contacts in the world beyond the Valley of the Kings. She ignored that and ran through the riddle again. What ate many things and liked wind but not water? Ate. Consumed? She remembered that night in November in the funeral home that Byron's vampire friends called home, and the fire elemental she'd tapped to burn the place down. Fire consumed. Fire loved air. And hated water.

She didn't smile but relaxed her shoulders. "Fire."

The sphinx frowned. The only sound for the next few seconds was the clicking of its claws against the stone as it did the lion equivalent of drumming its fingers. A rumble started in its throat again, grating against nerves, vibrating in her ears. It had counted on her failing.

"You were slow to answer. I will not allow as much time for the third and final riddle."

"That is not fair. I should get the same amount of time for each one."

The sphinx sneered. "This game is not about being fair. If you want fair, go play Sennet. This is *my* game, and I make the rules."

Don't aggravate him, Celie.

She ignored Tolly and crossed her arms over her chest. "Are you ready with the next one? I grow weary of this."

He harumphed but took at least a minute before he spoke. He must have had nothing in mind for riddle number three, assuming they would have forfeited already.

Celeste tapped her bare foot, though the effect would have been better had she been wearing shoes. "I should get at least as much time to answer as you take to pose the riddle."

"That is not—"

"How the game works? So you have said. Are you ready yet?"

Be careful.

Can you access your magic yet?

A fraction of a second later, she felt Tolly's triumphant mental shout.

A smile bloomed on Celeste's face. *Don't tap in yet. Just be ready. I'd rather win by his rules.*

The claws stilled. "Do not bait me, witch. Answer this. I am as large as a pyramid, yet lighter than air. A thousand strong men cannot move me. What am I?"

Large, weighing nothing but can't be moved. She needed to buy time. Clearing her throat, she asked, "Can you repeat that, please?"

"You are stalling. But I will be gracious." He repeated the riddle, then said, "Do witches taste like priests, I wonder? I became fond of priests who tried to defile the tombs."

She blocked out his words, knowing he meant to derail her. Focus on the riddle. Lighter than air...vaporous? Which went with can't be moved, so perhaps insubstantial? Large as a pyramid. Hm. She recalled the Great Pyramid of Giza, with the evening sun behind it. And how it cast an enormous pyramid-shaped shadow on the sand.

She stared directly into those amber eyes. "The pyramid's shadow."

The creature let out something between a growl and a roar, although it sounded less bestial coming from a human-shaped mouth. A paw whapped at a pile of stones, sending them scattering like shrapnel. Celeste held her ground, ignoring the pelting. Show no fear. Do not back down.

Tolly moved to stand beside her and clasped her hand before addressing the infuriated sphinx. "We have successfully passed your test. Now release us so we may be about our affairs. When we have completed them, we will return here and fulfill the rest of our bargain."

A ripple of irritation twitched along its shoulder. It spoke in a voice stiffened with cold iron. "Very well." It retreated from the rubble-strewn tunnel that had once been a set of stone steps methodically cleared by modern archaeologists.

Celeste scrambled up the scree and out into a night as cold and clear as any December evening in Paris. The Milky Way arched over them, illuminating the pale sand that ran to the dark horizon like the sea. Tolly followed her out, and for a moment they both stood, hand in hand, staring up in wonder.

The twitching of the sphinx's tail brought Celeste back to the moment. The creature crouched next to a massive stone block, likely a remnant from a ruined temple. "Your undead friend can rest in the tomb you have violated as we await your return. It will take time to find a priest to sanctify it again." A muffled noise emanated from under the block and the sphinx chuckled. "He was quite loud when I came upon him, but once I buried him in the sand, he wisely closed his mouth."

Celeste envisioned Desmond stuttering mad and being vile. She'd never seen Desmond fully transformed, but he was frightening enough in his charming, psychopathic human form. "Are you sure he can't dig his way out?"

The sphinx arched his eyebrows. "Do you doubt my ability to control such a small, fragile being? How do you think I got him into his sandy grave to begin with?"

Celeste decided she didn't want to know. Still, Byron would be in a political pickle if something happened to Desmond.

Tolly must have sensed her agitation and put a quelling hand on her arm. "We will go now."

"When will you be back?"

"I am not sure. Celie and I have some small business matters which could take a few days to arrange satisfactorily."

"I will give you three days to return. After that, your friend's life is forfeit, as is our bargain. I will hunt you down and consume both you and your powers."

Tolly's grip tightened on Celeste's hand, the only sign of her anxiety. She'd have made a hell of a poker player too, had she any desire to play cards. "Three days is perhaps too short a span."

The sphinx made the equivalent of a shrug. "Then I suggest you leave quickly and be about your task, because that is all the time you have."

Celeste's scalp tightened, and blood heated her cheeks. "That's—"

Tolly trod on her foot and gave the imperious creature a slight bow. "Until then. Adieu." Keeping a firm grip on Celeste's hand, she marched off across the sands.

When they had walked far enough that Celeste could no longer see the sphinx or the giant slab of rock that formed a lid on Desmond's ersatz tomb, she halted. "Tolly, wait."

"If you say you're tired or cold, I shall stab you with a hatpin."

For the first time in what felt like days, Celeste felt a moment of joy and comfort. Only Tolly could express care by offering to stab her with something. "What I was going to say is that we're headed in the wrong direction." She jabbed a thumb to the left. "The Nile, and therefore Luxor, is that way."

"And what is in Luxor for us to go back to?"

"Fresh clothes? Footwear? Someplace warm?"

"We have no money."

"True, but I have a way to get some."

"Oh. So you still have the coin with which to summon Pyp?" Tolly asked hopefully, recalling the plan to hit up Byron for money.

"Well, no, actually." The summoning device had been in her purse, which their abductors either now possessed or had disposed of. Byron was going to be pissed. "But," she said, wiggling her fingers, "I have skills. I haven't spent my *whole* life as a member of the bourgeoisie."

"You mean pickpocketing? Celie, really, you have no shame." The words were harsh, but the tone was mild.

Celeste shot her partner a cold look. "When you are homeless, hungry, cold, and not willing to sell your body, it becomes the only option. I won't apologize for wanting to survive."

Tolly squeezed her hand. "And I'm not asking you to. You are right about Luxor. We need to regroup, figure out what our next steps are."

"The next step is helping Guy. He's—"

"Right here. And how thoughtful of you to think of me."

Celeste spun to face Epona's lap pony, ready to slap the smirk off his face, but stopped at the sight of him. Gone were his elegant garments, replaced with filthy rags. Soot and something that looked like mud but smelled like excrement painted his face, arms, and hands in streaks. "What the hell happened to you?"

"More importantly," Tolly added, "how are you here? I thought that maniac has your ring."

"He does. My oh so beneficent master has sent me to spy on you in your cold and nasty prison. I'm to report, in juicy detail, on your state of misery and assure him of your continued incarceration." He looked and sounded miserable.

Celeste reached out a hand to offer comfort, but Guy waved her off. "I wouldn't do that unless you want to smell like this, too. As for what happened, I have merely been performing whatever odiferous and humiliating tasks he's been able to devise." He clenched his fists.

"I must comply, as I am under the control of he who wears the ring. But if that weren't enough, he has threatened to crush Berenice's figurine if I do not. And I have grown somewhat attached to the creature."

"The bastard!"

"Celie, language. So, you must go back and tell him we are free."

"Don't be ridiculous. I will phrase my report in such a way that is truthful but will not harm you. You are, in truth, still in the Valley of the Kings. And you are cold, tired and miserable. Hungry and thirsty. On the point of collapse." He pointed at them. "All completely accurate."

Celeste grinned. "Thank you for not betraying us."

The smirk was back. "Well, you are the only ones who can free me."

A sly response, but she would bet her life he harbored deeper and more genuine feelings underneath that flippant exterior. "What now?"

He shrugged. "My main purpose here is to provide you with information. The fool neglected to order me not to reveal his current activities, and if you are going to free me and Berenice, then you need to know what his plans are."

He paused and Celeste heard Tolly mutter, "Wonderful, more drama."

She gently elbowed her partner.

Guy paused a beat. "What, no gasp of horror or surprise? Does no one now appreciate a well-told tale?"

In a flat tone, Tolly said, "Of course we do. We are merely waiting politely for one."

Guy's lips flattened in disapproval. "Then listen carefully. The priest, one Merimre, is no longer satisfied with revenge upon the being who caused his death." He pointed to himself. "He plans on using a ritual to bind his soul to his current body and entreat Thoth to acknowledge him as rightful ruler of the Two Lands. Once that is done, he will force me to find the amulet that Nefer-rannut's mistress went to collect from her brother's tomb and use it to raise an undefeatable army with which he will conquer all of Egypt."

Tolly's eyes widened. "He wants to become pharaoh?"

"Clever girl. In essence, yes. His plan on that night so long ago was to kill us, steal the amulet, and make a grab for the throne. He has convinced himself that rulership was rightfully his, and that he's been cheated."

"That explains his interest in gathering Ibrahim's fellow revolutionaries to his banner." Celeste thought of Byron and his quest to free the Greeks from foreign rule. A banner he died defending. She wondered, and not for the first time, how on earth Byron's vampire sire had turned him, whoever he was, as closely monitored as Byron was in the fraught days preceding his death.

Guy was still talking. "He has moved to a temple in the desert for his ritual. Once that is done and he is mortal again, he plans to take one of the local girls as his first wife, in order to ensure an heir."

Celeste balled her hands into fists. "By Brigid of the Forge, if I wasn't moved to do away with him before, now I swear I—"

"Stop." Tolly placed just enough power in the word that it came close to being a Command.

Celeste closed her lips. She hated to admit it, but Tolly had been right to silence her. Spoken aloud, sworn intentions had power, especially those that invoked a goddess. Announcing the desire to kill someone, even in jest, created consequences. The Universe was always listening.

"Sorry."

Tolly stroked her shoulder, mitigating the action, before addressing Guy. "When is this ceremony supposed to take place?"

"He must wait for a propitious day. I am tasked with finding an existing copy of the ancient calendar, so he may forecast such a thing. But if I am not quick, knowing the way the desire burns within him, he will move ahead regardless."

"Have you found one?"

"I know where one is located. I have not been there and 'found' the item in question. Yet."

Tolly chuckled. "I approve of the way you think."

"What does this ritual entail? And how long do you think we have?"

Guy's shoulders lifted. "I am unsure, but he has been scribbling on pieces of paper in his ancient script, and from the buzz of energy, I believe they are spells. He mumbles about smiting his enemies, poisoning their food, and something about a sandstorm. He was not happy when he discovered me listening."

Guy shifted from one foot to another, wincing, although from what injury, Celeste couldn't tell. "As for how long? A few days, maybe less. He demands almost instant results for the tasks he sets. His punishments are swift and terrible." He turned, revealing the unmistakable wounds from a flail on his back.

Celeste winced. "Oh, Guy! Those gashes need to be disinfected, bandaged."

He backed away, waving his hands. "No. He cannot know I have seen you and would notice immediately if anyone did anything to tend to them. He wants me to suffer." Vengeance smoldered in his eyes. "He will find it is very hard to kill a demigod."

"Tolly, we can't let him go back."

Her partner took her hand and kissed it. "We must, my dove. Or Berenice will cease to exist. Not to mention, the fiend still has the ring. He could call Guy back in a trice and inflict even worse on him."

Oh, this priest was going to pay. "How do we stop him from completing this ceremony?"

Guy opened his hands. "That is up to you. My magic is useless to thwart his will as long as he possesses that ring. I will contact you once I know when he is ready. Bring powerful magic, prepare in whatever way you witches do, because he grows stronger by the day."

Celeste grimaced. "We will need to plan and gather spell components. Which means we need to get to Luxor fast." Hopefully, she gazed up at Guy, but he shook his head.

"As I mentioned, my powers are severely curtailed. He can sense when I use them. In any case, my magic does not include whisking you somewhere else, or I'd have used it that night in the tomb to get Nefer-rannut to help."

Celeste laid her hand on his arm now. She could say nothing to ease the grief. When she thought she'd lost Tolly in November, no words would have lessened the awful ache in her chest or the emptiness that consumed her. "Please be careful and tell Berenice we're coming. Once we have what we need, where should we meet you?"

"There is a wadi about ten forrach from here." He pointed toward the east.

Tolly looked skyward. Celeste chuckled and did her best to translate. "Forrach. That's based on old Gaelic, right?"

"I have no idea. You asked how far—"

She held up her hand. Gaelic was not as familiar to her as other ancient Celtic languages, but Marguerite had spoken what passed for Gaelic in the 17th century and a forrach was something like 40 modern meters. While math was not her forte, even she could multiply 40 and 10 in her head.

Her partner's eyes bored into hers, frustration simmering. "I've got it, Tolly. It's about a half of kilometer."

Guy jerked and spun around, controlled by an invisible hand. "Merimre calls, I must go." He vanished in a blink.

Left alone, the night felt chilly and threatening. She turned to Tolly.

Bright moonlight revealed lines of exhaustion and worry on Tolly's face. The frustration from moments before seemed to amplify, and the normally controlled woman let out a sort of growling shriek before sinking to her knees in the sand.

Celeste felt a wave of utter grief from Tolly, one the tightly controlled woman had been holding in since they'd viewed Aubrey's body. Celeste knelt and caught Tolly in her arms. Stroking that silken, honey-blond hair, she waited until Tolly's bunched muscles relaxed and her slim shoulders shook in silent tears.

"I'm sorry, *elskling*." Tolly tried to push away, but Celeste held her in place.

"No apologies. You've been wrung dry; you're entitled to shed some tears. I'm here, I love you, and we'll get through this."

After a moment, Tolly straightened, sniffling. "You're right." The words had no confidence behind them, but they were a start. "It's just so awful. Aubrey dead? We've been estranged for a long time. I never imagined how hard his death would hit me. Not to mention, what on earth has he been doing? What do I tell Alistair about his father? Could I have stopped it? If we'd been faster, went back to find him sooner? Should I have forced him to go to the Council that very night?"

"Tolly, no, this isn't your fault."

"Logically, perhaps not. But it feels like it is. What if Alistair blames me for this, the way Dagmar blamed me for my years of sanction for, as she insists, ruining her life? I cannot lose them both. And I would not hurt Alistair's career. He's come so far."

"Alistair is a sensible man. He cannot possibly blame you. As for Dagmar..." She shrugged. She'd never met the girl. Hell, had never even known her name until recently. "She's an idiot if she blames you."

"You don't know. You don't know what I did."

That was true enough. "No, and one day, I want to hear the story. When you're ready. But I know *you*. And whatever happened, I love you and I believe in who you are. You'd only break a rule in order to save someone else."

Tolly finally met her gaze. Something like hope sparked in her eyes. "By Freya, I love you. Thank you." She lifted her chin, threw back her shoulders. "And I will tell you. But now is perhaps not the time." She shivered a little from the cold and wiped tears from her face.

"Agreed." Celeste climbed to her feet and drew Tolly to hers. "Feeling up for a hike?"

Tolly nodded.

Celeste kissed Tolly's damp cheek and took her hand. "Then let's go. That way, this time." She pointed.

Tolly surprised her with a laugh. "Lay on, MacDuff."

Twenty-Five

T hey reached the Nile during that brief window of time where the brightest stars still shone in the deep blue overhead, but the pastel shades of dawn shimmered, opalescent as mother-of-pearl, on the horizon. They squatted in the dimness a safe distance from a sandy bank where local fellahin who lived on this side of the river had parked a handful of small boats used to ferry tourists and archaeologists across the Nile from their lodgings in Luxor. As they waited for those ferrymen to arrive for their day's work, Celeste watched the river and wondered aloud if crocodiles lay submerged beneath the rippling current, and if those rickety ferry boats could get them across in one piece.

"Don't be silly, *elskling*." Tolly murmured, but the gentle bite of her admonition meant she had her emotions under check once more. "Hundreds of tourists travel from the city to the Valley of the Kings every day, and I've never read one article about someone being eaten by a crocodile."

"And you read the Luxor newspaper often, do you?"

Tolly huffed. "It would be in *Le Figaro* if some poor French tourist lost her life to a crocodile."

"Hmm." Celeste had her doubts, but it wasn't worth arguing over. Being in a long-term relationship had taught her that being right wasn't always important.

In a reversal of their usual roles, she put an arm around Tolly's shoulders and pulled her close. They'd warmed up while walking, but now sitting motionless on the cool sand, the breeze off the river ruffling their hair and clothes, Tolly's body felt as cold as Byron's usually did.

Tolly rested her head on Celeste's shoulders and snuggled close. After a time, she began snoring in Celeste's ear. When a couple of men arrived on the muddy bank, Celeste hated to wake her exhausted partner, but better to enlist these first boatmen before more of their fellows showed up. The fewer witnesses to two French women wanting a ride *back* to Luxor at this hour of the day, the better.

She cleared her throat, and Tolly awoke with a start. "We've got company. Can you stand?"

Tolly climbed to her feet and raised her chin, pride overriding any debility. "Of course I can."

Hand in hand, they limped over to beg a ride.

In the early morning hours, a mist floated above the waters of the Nile. Once ashore, they thanked their rescuers, telling them to come to the Winter Palace the following afternoon to receive their reward. Celeste hoped she and Tolly would be alive to keep that appointment.

Running across the road called the Corniche, Celeste led Tolly through a maze of narrow streets filled with local dwellings whose inhabitants were just coming awake. In a side alley, Celeste snagged a couple of galabeyas and headscarves from a laundry line and they pulled the robes over their own clothing and helped each other with the head coverings.

Promising herself and Tolly that she'd replace the borrowed

garments with new ones, she led Tolly back toward the Corniche and the Winter Palace.

Acquiring some fast cash meant they needed a crowd. And what better place than in the middle of the swirl in front of the best hotel in Luxor, where wealthy tourists mingled with the fellahin hawking wares and services?

She parked Tolly on a low stone wall and slipped into the throng, scoping out her prospects. A bellicose Englishman and his haughty wife stood surrounded by vendors displaying a variety of wares and young children begging for baksheesh. Celeste, head lowered, and shuffling along like a dutiful wife behind a local man, closed in. She felt a thrill, a flush of anticipation. While happy she no longer had to pickpocket to feed herself, she missed the exhilaration of the hunt and the score.

Nearing the British couple, all it took was a stumble. She pitched forward, knocking into the startled gentleman. He released a string of appalling epithets and jumped back as though she had the plague. She apologized in broken English, groveling on the ground before him as he shouted at her clumsiness. His wife, wrinkling her nose in disgust, plucked at his sleeve and the man had the audacity to shove Celeste aside with his foot as they tried to continue down the Corniche with the gaggle of peddlers following.

One young Egyptian, a skinny lad with doe-like eyes and long lashes, hung behind, grinning at her. He nodded at the wallet she held close to her body and, with a wink, held out his hand. He'd seen through her charade, and possibly even her disguise.

She knew the drill. She opened the wallet, pulled out a ten-pound note, and passed it to him. A cut of the proceeds and payment for keeping mum.

He winked at her, then scampered away to find another mark.

The encounter made her grin. Even with the handout, plenty of cash remained for her and Tolly and whatever magical supplies they decided they'd need to fight their opponent—and maybe enough left over for some decent clothes, too. Clothes shopping always improved Tolly's mood. But no hats, she determined. She was drawing the line at more hats.

The Suq in Luxor was a glorious madhouse of shops and merchandise of all kinds. Vendors stood or sat outside their storefronts or stalls, where their goods spilled out into the narrow passageways in a riot of color. Brass, textiles, spices, perfumes, as well as an abundance of postcards, cheap faience baubles, and miniature carvings of Nefertiti's bust, the Sphinx, and the Great Pyramid at Giza. The visitors gobbled up those tchotchkes like starving dogs, providing a nice income for the shop owners. Celeste figured the tourists were fair game. They had to pay somehow for stealing all the ancient Egyptian treasures to hide away in their musty, old country estates.

She snorted at a tour group of loud Americans, handing sheaves of bills to a smiling, elderly local man missing more teeth than he had left. The fools were convinced they were buying genuine antiquities, but the creation and selling of fakes was a primary income source for the locals. Then the rich buyers would complain loudly about having been cheated. But if the British, and the French before them, hadn't built their fortunes by holding back the native people, there'd be no need for these poor locals to resort to foisting off replicas to greedy tourists. She gestured at one corpulent, particularly loud gentleman in a sharply pressed pinstripe suit. "That toff just got taken for three hundred U.S. dollars. Serves him—"

Tolly raised her hand when Celeste opened her mouth. "Do not say it. I do not need another lecture on class struggles and colonialism."

"But—"

"No. Enough. Where is the list you made of supplies? You did remember it?" She raised her eyebrows.

Celeste dug in the pocket of her borrowed garment and pulled out the folded slip of paper with relief. "Of course, I remembered it." She waved the piece of paper at Tolly.

"Thank you. Now keep your voice down. We're supposed to be locals and neither of us speaks Arabic."

Celeste laughed and crooked her arm through Tolly's. Together, they strolled deeper into the Suq.

Earlier, while waiting for the crowd to gather in front of the Winter Palace, they'd brainstormed a handful of spells to fight Merimre, based on the information Guy had provided. Now they just needed to find the symbolic or physical components to help focus the effects.

They stopped first at a booth that sold little brass incense bowls. They'd use that to mix the herbs and spices Tolly would need for both a rooting spelling and a hot hands spell. They'd also need cotton wool for a silence spell, a couple of feathers since they were versatile for off-the-cuff effects, and if Merimre meant to call down a sandstorm, they'd need a globe with a hole in the bottom to create a bubble for them to take shelter in, similar to the wine goblet she'd once used to create a force shield.

All they could find by way of a glass bubble was a little hand-blown glass ornament with holes in the bottom and top. Several herbs and supplies they normally used had to be substituted; a candle, melted down and formed into pellets instead of cotton wool for the silence spell, mandrake root instead of dandelion root for the rooting spell.

A few other odds and ends completed their list; a roll of twine, a bag of chicken feathers, a chunk of amethyst for protection, and a circular tin of lard—from what animal Celeste hadn't asked—which Tolly wanted but refused to disclose what she planned to use it for.

In the end, it was all about intent, not particular ingredients, nor did they have all day to wander the market. Celeste wanted to rescue Guy from his torturer as soon as possible. Not to mention, get

Desmond out of his grave. Oh, and incidentally, prevent a lunatic evil spirit from raising an army to conquer Egypt.

Ah, it was good to have goals again.

They'd spent little on their ingredients, leaving them with money to spare. Enough for food and then some. Celeste's stomach grumbled louder than the goat who'd just tried to chew the sleeve of her robe.

"I saw a stall selling some sort of kabobs and rice a while ago," she suggested to her partner.

Tolly screwed up her face. "I know haste is of the essence, but we have time to get a decent meal. At a real restaurant. We need to fortify ourselves if we're to go up against this Merimre."

"We can't exactly go there looking like this."

"No, we can't." A glint came into Tolly's eyes. "We'll need proper clothes. Have we enough money left?"

The woman wanted to go shopping. Celeste grinned. Did she know her partner or what?

She scratched at an itch, and hoped the robe she wore wasn't harboring insect life. "Excellent idea. Clothes and a meal. Then we go."

Tolly nodded. "Yes. Then we go."

The happy smile on Tolly's face melted Celeste's heart.

Tolly, of course, knew just the spot for clothes—she could smell a fashionable boutique from miles away. The thought of shopping for a new outfit brightened her up. She hummed discordantly—the woman couldn't carry a tune in a bucket—as she led them back toward the Corniche, the street where most of the European community shopped, and just down the road from the Winter Palace.

There they found several high-end European shops and Tolly, being Tolly, picked the most expensive one. Though she preferred couture fashion, they had no time for a seamstress to produce a dress, so the extravagant venue made the prêt-à-porter line, which she normally shunned, more palatable to her.

The store clerk looked appalled when they entered until Tolly gave her a sob story about having been mugged the previous evening during a nighttime visit to Hatshepsut's temple and stripped of their own clothing. Then the iron-haired woman was all tea and sympathy.

After trying on, and requesting feedback on a dozen outfits, Tolly settled on a simple pair of heather gray trousers and a lilac blouse. Celeste found a pair of pajama pants in navy blue, almost a twin to the now-ruined ones Coco had made for her, a yellow silk blouse with a jaunty bow, and a yellow straw cloche. They bundled their stolen local robes into a bag the store clerk provided.

As Celeste stood at the mirror, admiring the rather bold look, Tolly came up behind her, flourishing a blue ribbon, which she wove into the hat. It tied the ensemble together. Stepping back, Tolly gave a low whistle of appreciation.

Celeste preened and spun around to strike a pose. "You like?"

"Oh, yes, I like. Although," and she gestured at her own choices, "Probably not the thing to wear for a battle with an evil, body-snatching revenant in the middle of the desert."

She snorted. "I'm not sure there's a dress code for that. We should be fine." She glanced at Tolly's bare head and relented on the promise she'd made herself earlier about no more hats. "What, no jaunty chapeau? I'm shocked."

A grin. "I have selected two and cannot decide between them. Come help me."

When they left the shop to have tea at the Winter Palace, Tolly was beaming.

TWENTY-SIX

An hour later, seated in the elegant dining salon, taking time over their meal that made Celeste chafe, she swirled the tea leaves in the bottom of her porcelain. She knew they needed a little recovery time, not only physically, but energetically. They were busy storing up reserves of elemental energy, even as they ate. While Tolly munched on a chicken salad sandwich and watched a tennis match being held on the lawn of the hotel through the broad windows, the lines of strain in her elegant face began to smooth out.

Concentrating on the bits at the bottom of her teacup, Celeste let her gaze soften, encouraging a vision. Scrying had always been one of her strengths and it took no time for an image to appear.

What she saw filled her with foreboding.

Tolly, unmoving, face first in the sand under the moonlight. A strange man attacking Celeste with a knife that already dripped blood. And Guy, kneeling, forehead to the ground in obeisance, his body shuddering as though from wrenching sobs.

When the vision cleared, she flung the dregs of the tea into a nearby potted plant. The future was not immutable. Visions were perfidious, only showing you part of the truth, often out of context. And yet.

"Oh, well done," Tolly said, as the current match ended. "When we get back to Paris, we should take up tennis."

Celeste hadn't the heart to break the mood. She squeezed Tolly's hand and forced a smile to hide her own trepidations. "I think that would be wonderful."

And it would be. If they ever made it home.

Tolly suggested a walk in the gardens after tea and would not be budged. They had time, she insisted. And to be fair, this little respite of civility acted as a balm to the frantic running and fear of the last few days. For these few hours, Celeste could simply enjoy Tolly's company, forgetting about crocodile-mutilated corpses, strange, tortured demigods, and megalomaniac ifrits.

Staying too long in the dining salon at the Winter Palace, where all the western world congregated and where the men who killed Ibrahim could assume Tolly and Celeste might logically go, could be dangerous. The garden, with its secluded corners, provided an agreeable, safe space. Tolly settled on a bench screened from the hotel by trellises covered by prolific climbing roses and lifted her face to the sun.

After a moment, Celeste said, "You're going to get sunburned."

Tolly's eyes were closed, her response relaxed. "We've been walking in the desert for days. I already look like a strawberry."

"I'm just trying to look out for you."

Tolly scowled. "I do *not* need looking after."

Celeste thought about Tolly's several breakdowns but pressed her lips together. Instead of provoking an argument, she said, "I had a thought about our plans."

"And?"

"And...if the spirit of the priest inhabits other people's bodies, and those bodies die after he moves to another, if we kill the body he's inhabiting to stop the ritual, won't he just move into one of us?"

"Kill? We cannot kill anyone. The Council strictly forbids taking a life."

"A pox on the Council. I don't see another way of stopping him."

"We could render him unconscious."

"You think he's going to just let us walk up behind him and cosh him over the head with a frying pan? He'll just tell Guy to protect him."

"I understand that. But there must be another way."

"Well, what do you suggest?"

Tolly gazed out over the gardens, fragrant with roses, and raised steepled fingers to her lips as she considered. "It seems to me the way around this is to get the ring from him." Inspiration lit up her face. "I know you say it's almost impossible to slip the ring off his finger, but surely he must take it off sometime."

"I wouldn't."

"Naturally. You only own one pair of shoes."

"And what has that got to do with anything?"

"It means if you didn't have to take them off to get into bed, you'd never do so."

Celeste gave a low growl. "This is getting us nowhere. And I do too own more than one pair of shoes. I have walking boots and that pair of patent black evening pumps you bought me."

"And you wouldn't have those if I hadn't given them to you." There was a teasing sparkle in Tolly's eyes.

Celeste giggled. "This coming from a woman with enough shoes for a centipede." She took a breath, attempting to refocus. "We need more information about this ritual. About whatever it is priests do. And I still say we need information about how to exorcise a spirit from a body."

"Hmm. And how do you propose we get that?"

"I don't know, maybe from Guy. Or we could go spy on him."

"And get captured in the process? Absolutely not."

Celeste ruminated in silence while Tolly stared into the middle distance. This was how they worked best. Two minds focused on one goal. She'd missed this type of collaboration since being relegated by the Council to training young witches; a punishment for Celeste for a mission gone horribly awry in Greece.

Celeste finally said, "I propose I go to scout, and you can stay here. We must know what we're dealing with, and I don't imagine we'll hear from Guy or Berenice until it's time to act. We cannot go into this blind. That's what we did when we confronted the black witch near Calais, and you nearly had your brains bashed in, as a result."

"We won that battle, if you'll recall."

"Out of luck."

"Luck and skill." Tolly pursed her lips. "No, it's too dangerous."

"It's too dangerous not to." She tried a smile. "Besides. You love planning, and as you are always telling me, you cannot effectively plan in an information vacuum."

The corners of Tolly's mouth twitched up. "Throwing my own words at me, are you?"

Celeste drew Tolly's hand to her lips. "Did it work?"

"Hmm."

Turning Tolly's wrist over, Celeste began planting delicate kisses on the soft skin. "What about now?"

Tolly smiled. "Better."

Celeste scooted so they were thigh against thigh. Tolly's lips were soft and warm, and for just a moment, she yielded to the kiss.

A pair of voices on the path behind them forced them to break apart. Tolly checked her coiffure and Celeste slid to the other side of the bench. She only hoped that the flush on her cheeks appeared to be sunburn.

The couple, a young English serviceman and his companion

dressed in the latest mode, strolled past, eyes fixed on one another. Celeste figured they wouldn't have noticed if she'd been nude and straddling Tolly's lap, so enraptured were they with one another.

When the couple passed out of earshot, Celeste shot Tolly a wicked grin. "I bet we could find a more secluded corner and finish what we started."

Laughter bubbled up, even as Tolly shook her head. "You are incorrigible."

"So, you keep saying. And yet you keep coming back for more."

"Indeed, I do." Tolly lowered her voice. "You are determined now to spy on this miscreant, I suppose."

"In the old days, before the Council relegated us to teaching baby witches how to whittle willow wands, that's what we would have done." No way Tolly could refute that.

With a sigh, her partner shrugged. "This is true." She smoothed her skirt, fidgeted with her hatpins. "Then I am going with you."

That surprised Celeste. "Are you sure?"

Worry and frustration shadowed Tolly's features. "Yes, my dove." She took Celeste's hand. "I know I have been less than helpful since we...since Aubrey...met his end."

"I'm so sorry, Tolly."

"I would have suggested we return home immediately after his body was discovered, but despite our frequent marital struggles, I do still feel as though I owe him some sort of justice. He didn't deserve to die like that."

Celeste felt that twinge of jealousy again, even more ridiculous now since the man could hardly be a threat to their relationship from the grave. "I promise you we'll avenge him."

Tolly patted her knee. "I know we will."

"I don't mean to pry, but you have mentioned a couple of times about strife in your marriage. Was it over physical intimacy? He didn't hurt you, did he?"

Tolly dismissed the notion with a shake of her head and a sad smile. "No, no, nothing like that. He was old-fashioned to be sure, and wives, even ones who were fellow witches, had certain roles, certain obligations." Her eyes closed and, in that moment, she felt so far away from Celeste and the present, that it hurt Celeste's heart.

"It brought back so many memories," Tolly continued. "So many regrets, so many emotions. When I was released from my time of Sanction, the Council determined I needed to be re-indoctrinated. My union with Aubrey was arranged, not just to combine our lineages, but to make sure Aubrey kept me in my place. It wasn't always a pleasant situation."

Celeste had heard none of this. She knew if it had been her, she would have said to hell with the Council and run far and fast. But she wasn't Tolly. The Council meant everything to her.

Tolly shook herself. "But all of that is in the past. And you, you are my life now. My present and my future. Whatever we do, we do together."

Celeste wrapped her arms around her partner and hugged her tightly, watchers be damned. "I'm so sorry. It must have been awful. All of it."

"It was," came the surprising answer. "I've never talked about it," she whispered in Celeste's ear, "but it was excruciating. And doubly so, as my crime lay in trying to do the right thing."

"I suppose now is not the time for that tale?"

Tolly waved off the question. "No. We've got to get ourselves across the river and deal with this miscreant whose lieutenants murdered an honorable man."

Celeste pressed her. "But you will tell me, *non*?"

After a brief pause, Tolly nodded. "Yes, *elskling*, I will tell you the story. The whole story, I promise."

"Including the part with Eddie?"

A grimace. "Yes, even that."

Celeste stood and pulled Tolly to her feet. "I love you. You know that, right?"

"Of course I do. Now, stop being mawkish and—"

The telltale pop made Celeste's stomach drop. Damn it, this was not the time.

Pyp materialized on the bench they had just vacated, a cheeky grin on his freckled face. "Good afternoon, ladies. Boy, are you in trouble."

TWENTY-SEVEN

The changeling carried on talking. "His nibs is in a right state, he is. Pacing and shouting and tossing things about. Never seen him in such a temper. I scarpered just as soon as he flung his letter at me. Even Old Sour Puss looked a mite frightened."

When he paused to take the letter out of the pocket of his elaborate but decades outdated morning jacket, Celeste broke in.

"Old Sour Puss?"

"You know. Stone Face."

"You mean Martin?"

"That's the one. Anyway." He cleared his throat and lounged on the stone bench, one knee up, elbow bent, and his head cushioned by his hand. A pose oh so familiar to Celeste.

Pyp cleared his throat and Celeste stepped forward and cuffed the back of his head, knocking off his black slouch hat. Both the coat and the hat had to be courtesy of Byron. Next, he'd be wearing Byron's old opera cloak.

"Oi!" Pyp rubbed the spot where she'd whacked him.

"We don't have time for a Byronic performance, Pyp. This will have to wait."

"Oh no. Not a chance. You didn't see him. He was spitting mad. Literally. I thought he might have a fit and take ill. If I don't come back with some kind answer from you, I may lose my position."

Celeste looked at Tolly, who mouthed "diva" at her.

But was he? She'd seen him in a violent temper. It was frightening and, at least in life, she had worried about him having a brain bleed.

Tolly saw her wavering and tapped her wrist where a watch might be worn.

Celeste faced Pyp. "Sit up. Make it fast. Skip the acting."

Pyp grumped as he unfolded the cream-colored, monogrammed stationery.

"Celeste - where in the hell are you? Are you even alive? Why won't you reply to me? What is going on or have you simply deserted me?"

Pyp eschewed the postures and gestures, but his tone and cadence were so much like Byron's, Celeste had no trouble imagining the state her friend was in.

Pyp looked up. "He goes on a bit like this. Do you want me to continue, or do you just want to read the rest yourself?"

The kid looked deflated at not being able to deliver the message in dramatic style. Celeste took the letter from him and folded it again. "I'll give you a verbal message to take back. Tell him we're safe again for now but leaving immediately to destroy a lunatic ghost who has possessed a mortal and wants to take down the Egyptian government and become Pharoah." She paused. "Do you have that?"

Pyp nodded. "As you know, I have a remarkable memory."

Remarkable? Even Byron's vocabulary was rubbing off on his young protégé. "Repeat it back."

He did, word for word, including her own inflections. She nodded, satisfied. "Now, when you deliver it, I want you to also ask Martin a question and then bring me his answer. Right away."

"Got it, Miss."

She glanced at Tolly, who looked amusedly resigned, which was far better than the annoyed expression Celeste had expected. Perhaps the rest had done her good. "Ask Martin if he knows a way to evict an evil spirit from a living human. A sort of exorcism. I need as many details as he can provide."

Pyp repeated that back as well. "And you want me t0 come right back with the answer?"

"As fast as you can. If Martin is unavailable, don't hang around waiting. Come back here and let me know that too. I need the info now, or not at all." It wouldn't do to have Pyp pop up at some inopportune moment—like in the middle of a magical battle with the sem priest.

"Right-io, Miss. Might take me ten minutes to get there and back with an answer. The Betwixt has been behaving odd-like of late. But I'll be back fast."

Celeste nodded. "Good. And tell Byron I'm sorry. I haven't deserted him. But this is life or death, and there is no time for chitchat. I'll tell him the whole story when I'm home."

Pyp raised copper eyebrows. "When? Or if?"

"When, you little guttersnipe," said Tolly in motherly tones.

Pyp stood and doffed his hat. "Toodle pips." Another pop and he vanished.

Feeling worried and out of sorts, Celeste returned to the bench and patted the stone beside her. "You may as well make yourself comfortable while we wait."

"You've sent him on a fool's errand." Tolly sat primly beside Celeste.

"I'll take any help we can get right now."

"Hmph." Despite her gruff tone, Tolly entwined her fingers with Celeste's. "Do you really think Martin will help? He's not overly fond of you."

"Maybe not, but he saved you back in November. That's got to mean something." The sun beat down and her hair grew damp under her cloche. "Why does he despise me so much?"

"Isn't it obvious?"

Celeste shook her head and Tolly continued. "My dove, he's jealous. You and Byron...well, anybody on the outside would consider you a couple. You share a certain intimacy that some could misinterpret."

"We share nothing of the sort!"

"Not that kind of intimacy. But a closeness. And as the world discourages close friendships between members of the opposite sex, the only relationship they can imagine you share is that of lovers."

"And what does that have to do with Martin?"

"Only that he sees that closeness, too. Martin and Byron might be lovers, but you have known Byron for over a century. And a physical relationship does not necessarily equate with love. He looks at what you and Byron share and wishes it was he whom Byron holds in such regard."

"Balderdash. Byron adores him. Loves him."

"As much as he's capable of that emotion."

They were both silent for a moment. "So, you really think he's jealous?"

"Celie, everyone thinks that. I can't believe you haven't seen it yourself."

Well, that explained a lot.

But before she could ponder any further, Pyp appeared again. He'd forgotten to create the dramatic sound effect this time. His hair was tousled, his jacket askew, and the hat had disappeared.

He arrived and placed hands on thighs, gasping and looking green.

Celeste jumped up and put her arm around him. "Are you hurt?"

"Nah. Just a wee queasy."

When he straightened, Celeste noticed a red mark on his cheek. "You *are* hurt."

A flush reddened his fair cheeks. "'Tis nothing. Just didn't duck fast enough."

"Did that conceited ass throw something at you?" She knew Byron's rages. If he lost control of himself, he'd been known to even injure his friends. The abject remorse would come later once he was himself again. She hadn't seen many of these since he re-entered her life, but he was under extraordinary strain right now, a known trigger.

"Of which conceited ass do you speak?" The grin was particularly impish.

"Byron," she ground out. "I'll kill him."

The brogue from his early youth on the Emerald Isle grew thick. "Nae, t'was not he."

"Martin?" Her ire rose. Pyp was little more than a child by fae standards. Neither he nor Byron had any right to abuse him.

"Neither, Miss. Something whipped through the Betwixt as I entered. Caught the motion from the corner of my eye, but I wasn't quick enough to dodge it complete."

Celeste felt blood throbbing in her temples as she gripped his arm. "Don't lie to me, Pyp."

"'Tis truth. I swear. Now leave off." He shook his arm free. "I got your answer, but if you're going to manhandle me, I can go back where I came from."

Tolly's hand was cool on her arm. "Why don't you sit down, young man, and tell us what Martin has to say?"

To Celeste, he said, "I told you there was queer things happening in the Betwixt." He sat down and abruptly shifted his posture and manner. Back straight, shoulders back, one leg crossed precisely over the other, Celeste could imagine Pyp in Martin's white dinner suit. He pulled another piece of stationery out of his jacket. When he spoke, it was in Martin's quiet, arrogant tones.

"Celeste. I am given to understand from your message to Bryon that you are dealing with some kind of spirit possession and are looking

to exorcise said spirit. I know little about exorcisms but am willing to share what I can."

Pyp paused and made an aside. "He's only helping because Byron pitched a fit about it." He adjusted his posture again, smoothly mimicking Martin perfectly.

"In my limited experience, the way to evict a demon from a mortal is to chant certain prayers, which I have written down for Pyp to carry to you. As you are not dealing with a Christian demon, those prayers may have little to no effect, but if you call upon St. Peter, you may receive some assistance. I do not mean the Peter who became the first pope, but a later saint. In fact, I knew him for a short time while he was in a Roman prison. A kind and wise man, even to those who jailed him and ultimately brutally executed for that kindness."

Good Goddess, Martin had become just as verbose as Byron. She made a rolling motion with her hand to speed up the recitation.

Pyp broke character and flashed a grin. "He goes on almost as much as His nibs, don't he?"

"Doesn't he," she corrected automatically.

Pyp continued.

"The ceremony may need to be performed many times, and it is usually advisable to restrain the sufferer, as the demon can cause them to be violent and attack the person performing the exorcism. The most important element is, of course, faith."

She could almost hear the unvoiced comment, "which you clearly lack." She had plenty of faith, thank you very much—in her own goddess. By Brigid's paps, what did Byron see in this arrogant, self-righteous prig? He might once have been an angel, but he was one of the Fallen now, the bastard.

Through their mental link, Tolly sent her an image of Martin, imaginatively unclothed in all his beauty, posing like Praxiteles' statue, Eros, which, in fact, he'd actually been the model for. Although Celeste's sexual preferences had never included men, she could appreciate beauty in the male form, and Martin had it in spades. She snorted. Yes, Byron had a weakness for beautiful young men.

As if he could see the image in her head, Pyp snickered before continuing in Martin's acerbic tones.

"That is all I know in this regard. Would that I could talk with my old friend, but the Host is no longer taking my messages. Byron and I wish you luck."

The changeling held up the letter so that Celeste could see it. There was a bit of script that had been scratched out and in Byron's hand, and she read, even as Pyp voiced the words in Byron's voice:

"You'd better succeed. If you do not come back, I shall never forgive you. Either of you."

Tolly snorted.

Finished, Pyp handed her the letter and slouched on the bench in a typical teen-age pose, long legs stretched out in front of him. "Lord B would have gone on, but I told him you were in a hurry."

Byron could never be hurried. Pyp must have crawled pretty damn far under Byron's skin to make an impact.

In a positively desiccated tone, Tolly remarked, "Not much help."

What Tolly had meant was, "I told you so."

"I had to ask. He used to be an angel. Surely, he would know about exorcisms."

The slanting rays of the late afternoon sun shone on Pyp's face, and he sighed. "Nice place for a vacation. I'm tired of the damp chill at home." His eyes gleamed. "Maybe I could travel with you, be your errand boy and porter."

Tolly bestowed a fond smile on the boy. "We very rarely travel, young man, so it would be a poor living. Have you grown tired of working for your current patron?"

"Oh no, not at all. His nibs is very good to me and I'm learning all kinds of things. But I'm dragged back now and then to Tír na nÓg to do dirty work for my betters, and it's so lovely there. Warm sun, pleasant breezes. Don't even need so much as a coat or a jumper to ward off the cold."

"I'm sure it is," Celeste agreed. "Right now, however, we need to get moving. Give our regards to 'his nibs' and Martin."

Taking his cue, Pyp stood and gave them an abbreviated salute. "Adieu, Madame et Mademoiselle."

He popped out of existence, the sound almost painful, as though to make up for the absence of it on his arrival.

Tolly took her hand and began to pull her along the garden path toward the hotel, then stopped abruptly. The hairs on Celeste's arms stood on end as the air in front of them shimmered like a heat mirage.

"Berenice?"

The ushabti's form didn't coalesce, but her voice came through, like wind rattling autumn leaves. "Tomorrow, when the barque of the sun is high." A scrap of yellowed linen swirled down onto the paving stones, and the shimmer evaporated, leaving behind an echo of the of the last word she had spoken.

Goosebumps rose on Celeste's arms as she picked up the bit of cloth. It bore a sort of map on it, with the starting point being the Temple of Hatshepsut on the west bank. As she stared at it, the visions she'd seen earlier in her teacup played like a silent film in her mind.

Tolly's face also reflected trepidation. "Leaving early to do a little reconnaissance was a good plan, Celie. If we hurry, we can still arrive in time for that."

Celeste just shook her head. Why had she even bothered? She and plans never got along. She could only hope that her instincts and improvisational skills served her as well tonight as they had in the past.

If not, at least she and Tolly would face their fate together.

Twenty-Eight

T hey joined a long line of tourists boarding a boat for a night excursion to Hatshepsut's temple at Deir el-Bahari. Sitting at the back of the boat with their bag of spell components between them, Celeste and Tolly watched the scenery, jittery but determined. Tolly studied the surrounding tourists, listening in on their vapid conversations and shaking her head with a tolerant smile at their lack of knowledge about all things Egyptian. Celeste, on the other hand, scanned the gently rippling surface of the water for signs of crocodiles.

On the quick trip across the Nile, the brief Egyptian dusk came and went; one moment the sun was a swollen, ruddy orb and the next a faint glow in the darkening sky. Even as they reached the shore, multitudes of stars glinted overhead. More stars, she thought, than she'd seen in Paris since the seventeenth century. The sight should have awed her but worries and half-formed plans crowded out every-thing else.

They disembarked with the other tourists and followed the guide toward the temple, but they lagged farther and farther behind until they could veer off the path unnoticed and slip into the darkness.

The map on the scrap of linen left much to be desired. No distances were marked. The route into the desert could have been two miles or fifty. Guy, who had to have drawn the map, had scribbled a few land-marks along a trail winding through the canyons, or wadis, as they were known here.

Given what she'd already seen of the rocky, ankle-turning terrain, and the way the wadis dead-ended and meandered, she had doubts about them finding their way in time to stop Merimre.

Tolly, always in tune with her thoughts, broke her ruminations. "We *will* get there, by Freya, and in time."

In a burst of foresight, Celeste had purchased an electric torch and a compass on the Corniche on the way to the tourist boat. When they'd tromped through the sand and rocks for a sufficient distance, Celeste turned on the torch. The light didn't extend far but it would prevent them from running into the wall of a cliff. Or trip over a sleeping crocodile.

Beside her, Tolly chuckled. "There are no crocodiles in the desert, my dove. Here, give me the map. I may have no innate sense of direc-tion, but you're hopeless at trail finding."

"I'm a city girl," she groused as she handed Tolly the piece of fabric.

"You certainly didn't start out that way. You were born in a tiny village in Brittany."

"Yes, but I've spent the majority of my life in cities. London, Paris, Venice."

Tolly halted her and directed the beam of the flashlight on the map. "The first landmark is a rock formation that looks like a hawk. As far as I can tell, it should be fairly close. But what are these little figures beside it?"

Celeste squinted at the squiggles. "Ants?"

Tolly snorted. "They have four legs, not six."

"Well, what do you think they are, then?"

"Dogs?"

"Dogs don't have tails like that."

There came a distant braying ahead of them, the noise echoing like a trumpet in the stillness.

They looked at each other, their faces harsh and angular in the torchlight. In a single voice, they said, "Donkeys."

Though they rushed toward the noise, it took them some time to reach the entrance to a narrow wadi that snaked off into the darkness. Just inside, tails swishing, stood a pair of donkeys. They stood placidly as if there was no place else they'd rather be, though there was no sign of food or water for them.

Tolly wrinkled her nose at the pungent smell. "Horses would have been nicer, but I'll take what I can get."

The smaller of the two beasts, a sweet little jenny, trotted over to Celeste and snuffled at her hand. Poor girl wanted a treat. Reaching into their bag of supplies, Celeste pulled out two of their six apples—a rare commodity in Egypt, but a fruit she knew wouldn't spoil as fast as others—and tossed one to Tolly. "Make friends."

The donkey grabbed the apple with its lips far more gently than she'd expected. She crooned and patted it before she attempted to mount. No one had supplied blankets or any sort of tack, but she found a long length of cloth tied around the donkey's neck. When she picked it up, energy jolted through her. The cloth pulsed with magic, and though she'd only been in Merimre's presence once, the magical aura smelled like the tracking spell she'd encountered on the train.

"Tolly."

Her partner mounted her own donkey, and using a little pressure on the animal's neck, turned it toward Celeste. "What is it?"

She held up the cloth. "Guy left us a guide. This turban cloth belongs to the man whose body Merimre is inhabiting. I feel the priest's magic on it." She grinned. "And you know what that means."

"Is it strong enough to follow?"

Celeste nodded, then leaned forward and whispered in the donkey's ear. "And I bet you even know the best way to go, don't you?"

The donkey turned its head to look at her, and the keen intelligence in its eye impressed her. It ducked its head as though saying yes.

And then the donkeys made sense. Guy was a Servant of Epona. A horse goddess. These animals were clearly under his control.

With a glance over her shoulder at Tolly, Celeste urged the little jenny deeper into the wadi, holding on to the headcloth. Donkey travel wasn't fast, but it would be faster than walking. Guy had said ten forrachs, but they weren't traveling a straight line, so they needed to pick up their pace.

Slipping onto the astral, she observed a muddy green-gray line, the energy of the sem priest she'd seen on the train. It wound off into the distance, and she began to feel better about their chances. They had magic, they had Guy, and most of all, they had each other.

Her confidence grew over the next few minutes as they rode deeper into the wadi, her donkey picking her way through the rocky scree, with a determination that assured Celeste the jenny knew where she was going. If things went their way, in less than three weeks, they could be back home in Paris, nibbling croissants and sipping smooth, rich Parisian coffee at the Café de Flore on the Boulevard Saint-Germain.

Tolly picked up on her thoughts. "It's always about the pastry, isn't it?" But her tone held no bite.

The blast of a rifle shot drowned Celeste's response, echoing through the wadi like a mortar shell.

Beneath the booming echo, she heard Tolly swear in Norwegian. *"Hva i helvete?"*

. . .

Another shot ricocheted off the steep cliffs of the wadi. The jenny, instead of bolting like a horse might have, turned to face the danger. Brave, Celeste thought, but not the smartest move. She slid off her short mount and pushed the donkey towards a tumble of boulders, Tolly hard on her heels.

The donkeys stubbornly refused to take shelter against the cliff wall. They stood sentinel-like, perpendicular to the sheer rock face. While donkeys were known to be protective of humans they liked, Guy must have been imbued these with some special orders.

Tolly reached out through their mental link. *Merimre must have sent gunmen to stop us. Did you see how many? Or where they are?*

Celeste shook her head. *Too dark, no time. We need to flush them out.*

Followed by a rooting spell?

A bullet struck the rock above them, showering them with sharp stone chips.

Celeste rifled through their bag. "It won't hold them for long," she whispered. She found the ingredients and handed them to Tolly, before pulling the head scarf from around the neck of the donkey. "Be ready."

"Celie. What are you thinking of?"

Dodging the arm Tolly shot out to stop her, Celeste wound the long strip of fine cotton cloth around her neck, leaving the ends to trail behind her. Dashing out from behind the outcrop, she ran down the wadi in a zig zag pattern she'd learned in her years as a street thief, hoping to draw out their pursuers, but also hoping to look sort of ifrit-like with the flowing white fabric wafting out as she ran.

She sensed three mortal energy signatures and something magical, probably an amulet. She didn't have much time to examine it on the astral, she was too busy trying to be a difficult target, but it felt more like protective magic than an offensive spell. Guns worked just fine for that.

A bullet whizzed past her ear and struck the rocky ground a few meters ahead. Another shot, this time from something with a sharper, less booming report. That meant at least one rifle and one pistol.

In her and Tolly's past adventures, back when they had worked for the Council's Protectorate branch, they'd been in many firefights, but the ammunition had been spells, not bullets. They had nothing to stop a bullet, no shield spell powered by two witches that would protect them from nonmagical projectiles. If they had the coven with them, perhaps.

Two more bullets hit the sand.

Sand. A flash of memory, a spell that her first mentor, Marguerite, had taught her, but it involved blood magic, which the Council strictly forbade. It was a capital offense.

Another shot, closer this time. Their aim was improving. She didn't dare look back, but she threw herself sideways and rolled toward the rock face.

Shards from the tumulus that sloped down from the cliff sliced and jabbed her. She came to her knees, dripping blood from myriad small wounds. Her shoulder, the one she'd dislocated escaping a vampire's lair, throbbed at the fresh abuse.

None of that mattered. Adrenaline flooded through her and she doubled back, head ducked, toward Tolly and the donkeys again. If she could reach them before their pursuers reached the outcrop, Tolly could hit them with the root spell.

Tolly caught the thought. *We have only one shot, Celie. We have to save most of the components for Merimre.*

It won't matter if we die before we get there.

A volley of gunshots sounded, not from the direction of their pursuers, but from farther down the wadi, in the direction they'd been headed. The hope that they were rescuers, and were firing at the other men, vanished when bullets started to pepper the ground just steps behind Celeste. A classic pincer movement. They were trapped.

She reached Tolly and for a moment the shooting stopped. Men from both ends of the wadi were converging on them.

Tolly's eyes widened. She held out her hands as if to say now what, her usually quick mind devoid of options. *Rooting spell?*

Too little, too late. It would only stop a couple of their adversaries.

Despite the darkness, she sought Tolly's gaze. *I have a plan. You're not going to like it.*

Will we live?

Like as not.

Then do it.

Celeste hated to use the donkeys as shields, but hoping they were somehow protected from the bullets by Guy, she dove behind one to scrabble through their bag for the two tin cups they'd brought. She filled one with sand, accompanied by a few chips of stone she didn't have time to remove. The spell should still work. She hoped.

Setting the cups down, she found a stone chip with a sharp edge. Clenching her teeth, she slashed a jagged wound in her palm, gasping at the pain. Every sound she made echoed like a clarion.

Tolly drew in a sharp breath as Celeste dripped blood from her hand into the empty cup. "Oh, Celie, no."

Celeste ignored her. They only had seconds. Holding the cup filled with sand a foot above the other, she began to chant the words Marguerite had taught her all those centuries ago. She stood, and as she tipped the full cup to let the sand trickle into the empty one, Tolly whispered to the donkeys, then mounted her own.

An unnatural stillness settled over them. No more wind, no more sounds of footsteps, no flapping of garments. Time itself had stopped for as long as Celeste kept the sand pouring from one cup to another. When the sand ran out, or if the flow halted, the spell would be broken.

Which meant she couldn't mount her own donkey, something she hadn't thought through when she'd cast the spell.

She approached the line of four men in galabeyas who stood frozen in place, gaze glued to the two cups to ensure the sand trickled from one to the other in a thin but steady. Tolly followed on her donkey.

"Tolly, go ahead. I'll follow as quickly as I can."

"You cannot run and pour the sand."

They closed the gap between themselves and the gunmen. Two-thirds of a cup of sand remained in the top vessel. If they could just reach what appeared to be a turning in the wadi, they'd be out of sight at least long enough for Celeste to mount her donkey and goose the little animal into a fast trot. Not much chance of outrunning the enemy, but the best they had.

"I won't leave you behind, Celie."

"Better one of us escapes than both of us die. Someone has to avenge Aubrey and free Guy."

"I will not leave you."

Fear, love and gratitude fought for dominance. "Then let's move faster. I'll do the best I can not to spill, but we'll have less time."

The jenny, who walked beside her gave a soft snort of what felt like agreement and ever-so-gently tucked her head under Celeste's upraised arm, which was starting to tremble from strain.

"You're a lovely creature, Genevieve."

Tolly snorted too, in derision. "You've named your donkey?"

"It seems the right thing to do."

Though Celeste couldn't see it, she knew when Tolly's stern expression evaporated. "Then I shall have to name mine as well. As the creature is male, I will call him Halvar, which means guardian."

Nervous laughter threatened to break Celeste's concentration. Why did they have such inane conversations while in the middle of a crisis?

The turn in the wadi lay only a short distance away, but the cup had less than a finger's width of sand left. "Tolly, please. Run. Get as far away as you can. We're almost out of sand."

Her partner said nothing. Stubborn woman.

Beyond the turning, the wadi opened out onto the rocky, barren landscape of the western desert, which spread out like a valley, bordered in the distance by more cliffs. They'd be sitting ducks out there.

Halvar suddenly veered to the right. That must be the way they were supposed to go.

Genevieve removed her nose from underneath Celeste's arm just as the last of the sand trickled out of the upper cup. The jenny tossed her head and fixed Celeste with a dark-eyed stare, as if saying "mount up, you silly human."

Gunfire shattered the stillness. Celeste could imagine the men's confusion as they realized their quarry had vanished between one moment and the next.

Some distance away, she saw the dark, lumpy shape of Halvar, with Tolly astride, trotting across the desert floor, ignoring his rider's efforts to get him to stop. With a grim smile, Celeste urged Genevieve forward, an unnecessary action. The little donkey took off as fast as a Breton horse.

Whether it would be fast enough remained to be seen.

TWENTY-NINE

Crouched low over neck of a donkey racing at top donkey speed across a rocky landscape at night became Celeste's most despised mode of travel. Even worse than riding a horse, an activity she'd never been fond of, despite it having been the primary means of long-distance transport for most of her existence. She'd never really gotten on with horses. Bumping along a road, being bounced up and down on the back of a beast determined to throw you off or smack you in the face with every branch that hung out over the path, didn't predispose one toward them.

Now, as they raced along at high speed, she almost longed for those hip-jarring rides. The uneven ground went by in a nauseating blur. When their mounts suddenly jumped, a mad thought that maybe Guy had given them the ability to fly entered her head.

The landing rattled her teeth and Tolly was nearly launched ass over teakettle, saving herself only by wrapping her arms tightly around Halvar's neck.

The donkeys dove under a concave section rock and snugged into the back, making room for Tolly and Celeste to dismount. From a distance, especially at night, Celeste imagined the overhang would be invisible against the sameness of the desert floor.

She slid her aching body off Genevieve's back and rubbed the animal's chin, whispering in her flicking ear. "Such a smart girl, aren't you? And brave too." She offered the same affection to Halvar, after which Tolly also murmured some Norwegian in his twitching ear.

"That better have been a compliment."

Tolly spoke directly to Celeste's mind. *Be quiet. Voices carry long distances in the desert.*

Sweat and inaction drove the chill of the night into Celeste's bones. She shivered and Genevieve pressed up against her. Despite the unpleasant aroma of the animal's filthy coat, Celeste was grateful for both the warmth and the comfort.

The night air soon filled with the shouts of men, though the voices came from a distance. Celeste wasn't sure how long they stood huddled against their stalwart steeds, silent and unmoving, before the searcher's cries grew fainter and they were left with only the whisper of windblown sand.

Stepping out from under the overhang, Tolly smoothed her lavender blouse and motioned for Halvar to join her. She mounted and stared back at Celeste. "I don't know if Merimre sent his men to delay us or if they spotted us in Luxor, but we've lost a great deal of time. As our American cousins would say, let's get this show on the road." Not waiting for Celeste, she urged her donkey into a gentle trot.

Tolly using American argot? That was new. Celeste mounted and caught up with her, and they let the donkeys have their heads. She hoped they knew where they were going.

As she came even with Tolly, her partner said, "Thank you for saving us. I would never have thought of that."

Celeste shrugged. "Marguerite taught me."

"It appears she taught you a great deal that would not have been sanctioned by the Council. Someday you'll have to tell me more about her and how you came to be with her."

Was there a hint of jealousy in Tolly's tone? "It wasn't like that, Tolly. She was ancient when I first met her, nor had she any interest in me that way. But even if she had, that was several hundred years ago."

"You were jealous of Aubrey."

True. But he was or had been still alive. And Tolly had been married to him. Though darkness obscured Tolly's expression, she sensed the smirk. Damn the woman, she was poking fun at her. "You can be a right arse, Astrid Anna Tollefsen."

A chuckle. "So can you, my dove. We were made for each other."

The donkeys' pace accelerated the nearer they got to the cliff face that loomed like a castle's curtain wall in front of them. For a moment, it seemed they were going to run straight into the rock face, but a narrow, black crevice appeared, an abyssal void against an already towering darkness.

The donkeys plunged, single file, into the inky space and then slowed to a stop after a few meters. Beneath her, Genvieve gave a shake, and Celeste had the distinct impression the little jenny wanted her to dismount.

Was this what it felt like to be blind? The blackness felt oppressive, claustrophobic. Her ears picked up a scuttling noise, and something squeaked overhead, but she couldn't see what made the sounds. The stench, however, was the worst part, a pungent smell like ammonia and decay. She could be standing next to a gruesome, decomposing body. Except, no. She knew that odor. She shuddered.

"Guano. Ugh. Bats." Her skin rippled in panic. She scrabbled in their bag, trying to find their electric torch but couldn't. Had they lost it during the trip through the wadi? She couldn't remember the last time she'd had it. Damn it, she needed light. Needed to see. Long-buried fears clawed their way to the surface, and her heart pounded.

Tolly murmured "lux," and a pale blue globe sprang to life in her upturned palm. "I don't understand why you cannot remember to refresh the spells on the charm bracelet I gave you. Those new-fangled torches never work when you want them to."

Celeste's voice shook, but sarcasm had always been her emotional shield. "New-fangled? They've been around since before the turn of the century. One day, you're going to have to join the rest of us in the modern world." Then, after a breath short-circuited by a coughing fit brought on from potent fumes, she added, "Thank you."

In reaction to the light, things rustled and squeaked overhead. She looked up and saw she'd been right about both the noise. And the stench. "I hate bats."

Tolly ignored her and the bats, who began to quiet, and turning in a slow circle, illuminated their surroundings with the magical glowlight she'd cast.

Faded paintings on plaster decorated the walls of a squared off chamber. The most complete frescos decorated the back wall, a bizarre scene of strange men with the heads of animals posed as though walking. One of them, with a dog's head, was doing something to the mummy of a man laid out on a table. In another vignette, a dog-like creature with the snout of a crocodile sat under one side of a large scale with a kneeling figure on the other side, though the head and shoulders of whomever had sloughed off the wall. Even after all these centuries, the vivid hues of yellow, blue, red, and green still surprised Celeste, looking like the artist had just laid down his brushes and strolled off for a coffee break.

In a reverent tone, Tolly said, "It's a rock-cut tomb." She shone the light around again, "Although I see no coffin."

Celeste examined the floor, littered with bits of painted plaster, sand, and chips of rock that might have blown or washed in from outside. "No signs of a mummy." Thank Brigid. The thought of crushing bits of mummy under her feet made her twitch.

"I've never known you to show such irrational aversions, Celie. First, the panic about crocodiles, then bats, now mummified remains. Considering all the dangerous places we've been, and all the nightmarish things we've dealt with, I cannot imagine why you're so afraid."

Memory washed over her. "When I was little, my older brothers used to stir up the bats in a nearby cave and toss me inside." She didn't mention that they'd wrap her in a wet winding sheet before they threw her in, telling her they were going to leave her there until the bats sucked all the blood out of her. Bastards. How was a child supposed to know that bats didn't actually drink blood? Well, most bats. She shook off the memory and continued. "As for crocodiles and mummies..." She shrugged. "Crocodiles can eat you. And mummies. I mean, would you be happy if someone was tramping all over bits of your body?"

"Bah. Now you sound like Aubrey and his talk of curses."

Better not to respond to that.

She startled as Genevieve nudged Celeste's back with her nose. "Want another apple, do you?"

The donkey shook her head and pushed Celeste harder toward the back of the tomb.

Celeste glanced at Tolly. "I think she, or perhaps Guy, wants us to go over there."

"But why? It's just a wall." Tolly stared at the painting. "Perhaps a message within the artwork?" She crossed the small chamber and began examining the images and the hieroglyphics with her glow light.

"You can read those?" Celeste joined her, not wanting to stand in the dark.

"I have been studying the beginner books on hieroglyphics by Mr. Wallis Budge of the British Museum, but it is very difficult."

So, that was a no. Celeste stepped away and began feeling the wall for cracks or seams. Maybe a hidden compartment had been chiseled into the rock, one that Guy had stuffed something into?

After a bit of time searching, Celeste swore. "We're wasting time. There is nothing in here. Maybe the donkeys just wanted a rest."

From behind her, Halvar snorted in an almost human fashion. He nudged Genevieve aside and moved to a shadowy corner of the back wall where a three-foot-tall mountain of detritus and plaster flakes had created a midden heap of the past. He pawed at the pile, danced sideways, and leveled an annoyed look at the humans he obviously considered idiots.

Celeste had to laugh. She'd never been shamed by a donkey before. She picked her way to the corner and called for Tolly to bring the light.

"You could create one yourself, you know." She crouched down and held the glow light low to the floor.

"I could have, but since you've already cast one, why waste the energy?" She dug through the debris, sending up a cloud of fine particles. Coughing, eyes burning not only from the bat guano, but from the dust, she kept pawing, looking for some bit of gold amongst the dross and hoping nothing with fangs or stingers had a nest within.

The air grew thick now and Tolly, coughing, backed away. Celeste sat back on her heels with the crook of her arm across her face and waited for the powdery mess to settle before resuming. As the air cleared, she thought she could see the top of an opening. "Bring the light!"

"What do you see?"

"It looks like there might be some kind of hole. Maybe Guy hid something in there." She pulled off Merimre's head cloth from around her neck and, using a sharp piece of stone, ripped it into two pieces. "Put this around your nose and mouth."

Both now somewhat protected from inhaling flying mouse feces, Celeste made room for Tolly, who knelt and dug into the pile herself, scooping handfuls of chips and plaster bits and dried guano and depositing them bchind her.

"I suppose," Tolly choked out, "this is what archaeologists must do all day. I am glad not to be one."

It took longer than expected to clear the small hill of debris from the corner. Wheezing, eyes streaming, they stood back and looked at the small opening in the wall. Celeste had stuck her hand inside, feeling for some hidden object, but found nothing. In fact, a lot of nothing. Though she stretched her arm as far as she could, there didn't seem to be a back wall.

"What now?" Tolly brushed her hands, a pointless action, on her once lovely heather trousers.

"Give me the glow light. I'm going to take a better look."

"Oh no you don't. You were a fool to put your hand in that hole. You are not sticking your head in there. There could be snakes. Scorpions. Booby traps."

"Give me the light."

With a scowl, Tolly transferred the magical light, releasing her own connection to it and binding it to Celeste.

With a glance up at the bat-infested ceiling to reassure herself the little rats with wings weren't yet stirring, Celeste got down on the ground and, arms outstretched, stuck her head and shoulders through the opening.

THIRTY

If the glowlight had been a candle, Celeste was pretty sure it would have gone out. The air was stale and thin in the space beyond. She grew light-headed in seconds.

The space stretched farther than the light could reach so not a secret hiding place but a tunnel. She crawled in, hoping it led to another chamber of the tomb. Sweat dripped down her face, making tracks in the dust and burning her eyes. She blinked and kept squirming forward, like a soldier crossing no-man's-land on his belly, acutely aware of the weight of the mountain overhead. She wondered when the memories of the recent war would fade.

About two body lengths in, the glow light picked out what might be a ladder ahead.

"Celie! Celie, are you all right? What do you see?"

The tunnel expanded gradually in height as she went. Rising to her hands and knees, she crawled another meter to better shine the light on the object ahead.

"Celie!" Tolly's voice grew more frantic. "Say something!"

"I'm fine," she shouted. Or tried to shout. The air grew thicker and though she kept gulping air, her lungs burned, and her head pounded. "There's a ladder."

The light flickered. No, not the light. She'd closed her eyes. It burned to keep them open, and her eyelids were so heavy.

Something grabbed her ankles, and she screamed as she was dragged back along the rough stone of the tunnel and out into the chamber.

"What in Helheim did you think you were doing?" Tolly held a cup of water to Celeste's lips. "You could have died in there. And you wouldn't talk to me or tell me what you were seeing. I ought to..."

Celeste sat propped up against the side wall of the tomb with her half of the headcloth, now cool with water from their canteen, pressed against the back of her neck. She searched for a snappy come-back, but her brain had overheated. "I *did* respond to you."

"You most certainly did not." Elegant, long-fingered hands pushed Celeste's new pajama pants up above her knees and dabbed with the other half of the headcloth at the blood oozing from her skinned knees.

"My face hurts."

"You scraped your cheek and chin as I was pulling you out."

When the wet cloth touched those abrasions, Celeste swore. "Stop that. It hurts."

"You're such a child, sometimes. Don't make me smack your hands. Leave them in your lap until I'm finished."

"I am not a child." That came out petulantly. Well, she was feeling petulant.

Tolly continued her ministrations. "You act like one. A very naughty one."

Celeste's brain, and other parts of her, fired up again. In a sultry voice, she asked, "If I'm very naughty, does that mean I deserve a spanking?"

Tolly sat back on her heels, glared at Celeste for a long moment, then burst out laughing. "How can you even think of that at a time like this?"

Celeste grinned. "I think of that all the time."

Tolly tossed the wet cloth at her with a shake of her head and a suppressed grin. Putting her hands on her knees, she pushed herself up. "As you are clearly recovered, tell me what is in there, what you saw."

After drinking more water, Celeste cleared her throat and began. "It's a tunnel. It goes for some meters. At first, I couldn't see the end, so I crawled farther. It opens up a bit, so I could rise on my hands and knees, and I suspect from what I saw, that you can stand upright at the end."

"And it just ends there?"

"No. There is a wooden ladder at the end, going up."

"Does it lead outside?"

"I don't know, since someone dragged me from the tunnel."

Tolly pressed her lips together. It didn't take a mind link to know what she was thinking.

With a chastised look, Celeste reached out her hand. "Thank you for rescuing me. I did pass out. The air was bad, and I know I shouldn't have gone on."

"Damn right." Tolly looked at her wrist for a watch that was no longer there. "We've lost so much time already. Perhaps we should just get back on the donkeys and try to follow the map. We'll have no time to reconnoiter Merimre's camp if we dilly dally here."

The donkeys. Celeste peered around the tomb for Genevieve and Halvar. They were nowhere to be seen. "Tolly, where are the donkeys?"

"They're right..." She scanned the tomb as well. "They were right here. Or I thought they were. Halvar showed us where to dig and then..."

"Then nothing. I can't recall seeing them since then." She forced aching limbs to stand and went to look out the mouth of the tomb. Not a donkey in sight.

Tolly scowled. "Those little cowards. They've abandoned us."

Celeste came back inside, took Tolly's hand, and kissed it. "No, not abandoned us. They led us here for a reason. Once the job was done, they were free to go back to wherever they came from."

"But we're not at the temple where Guy said the ritual would take place."

Celeste glanced toward the opening. "I propose I go back in to explore the ladder and where it leads. If it looks like an exit, I'll holler for you to come ahead. If it's not, I'll come back here."

"I don't like this plan."

Celeste stood on tiptoes and kissed Tolly's cheek. "You never like any of my plans. It'll be okay."

"If I let you do this, you have to promise me you'll keep talking to me. Every inch of the way."

"I promise."

"And if the air hasn't gotten better, you'll come back immediately."

Celeste nodded and started back toward the passageway.

"Celie, what about your knees? Could we fashion a pad or something?"

Already on the ground, she looked back at her partner as she cast a glow light spell, using the little lantern charm on her bracelet as the sympathetic component. "I'll be fine," she said softly.

Before Tolly could object, Celeste plunged back into the tunnel.

The rickety ladder, made of sticks lashed together with some fibrous plant, leaned up against what proved to be a vertical shaft. That it hadn't crumbled to dust amazed Celeste, but perhaps modern-day tomb robbers brought it in more recent times. After all, someone had cleared the tomb of valuables and the tunnel of rubble. Still, Celeste wouldn't have let a pixie climb it. Straightening, she held her light high. The shaft led to another opening, which appeared to be the only other way to go except out through the front of the tomb.

She called to Tolly. "The ladder leads to an entrance or exit. The air isn't great, but it's better, so come ahead. As you get close to the end of the tunnel, you can stand up."

A whispered epithet, *faen*, echoed in the tunnel behind her as Tolly began crawling. Norwegian for something like damn, or that's what Tolly told her. "This better be a way out, my dove, or I shall force you to eat lutefisk and lømer for a month."

"Rotting fish and those revolting little flat bread things? Unfair! And pointless since I'm the one who does the cooking."

"I'll make the effort, just to punish you." Tolly reached her, and after attempting to brush the dirt off her sweat-stained garments, examined the shaft with a doleful expression. "You realize we could just leave the arrogant creature there."

Celeste put her hands on her hips. "No, we can't. Regardless of Guy, to whom I've made a promise, we cannot let Merimre complete his ritual. That would mean allowing him to take control of an entire country. And you couldn't avenge Aubry."

"So now you're keeping promises?" It could have been the start of another of their 'little discussions', as Byron called them, but Tolly's tone was teasing.

The tension eased, and Celeste smiled. "I've learned my lesson."

"So Guy means for us to climb that?" Tolly waved a slim, long-fingered hand toward the less than sturdy ladder.

"Apparently. I don't see another way up. There is an opening in the wall up there. See?"

"That's a good four meters, and I'm not sure that thing will hold either of us."

"At this point, I'll believe anything is possible." She leaned against the wall, not sure if she was more exhausted, hungry, or frustrated.

"Brigid's paps, I feel like we've been running around Egypt for days and not accomplishing a thing."

"That is why I like plans, *elskling*."

"But our plans keep going awry." Which is why Celeste hated plans.

Tolly tested the ladder, pulling on the rungs, examining the sticks. "Then it's a providential you are a master of improvisation. We make a good team." She stepped on the bottom rung and climbed to the next without ill effect. "Now pull yourself together and let us get to it. Up and out, I hope."

"Up and out," Celeste grumbled as she watched Tolly ascend with appreciation. How did the woman climb a rickety ladder elegantly? Still, the view was pleasant.

Minutes later, they stood upright in a tunnel carved out of the sandstone that formed the cliffs in Upper Egypt. Well, Celeste was standing straight. Tolly had to stoop just a bit. "Ancient Egyptians must have been shorter than you Vikings."

Tolly made a point of looking down at her. "Yes, short. Like you Celts." She wiped perspiration from her face in the stifling warmth. Tolly had reignited the glow light while Celeste climbed and shone it down the tunnel.

They both peered into the darkness.

"Is that a faint light down there?"

Tolly scoffed. "If there's any justice, yes." She took Celeste's hand. "Let's go."

Chips of stone crunched underfoot as they crept forward, the darkness pressing in on their small circle of magical light. Celeste wondered who had created this apparent back door to the rock-cut tomb and why. The tunnel's builders had dressed the stone with plaster, and from what she'd read, tomb robbers were more the smash and grab type, not Raffles the Gentleman Thief, so she felt sure it had been the tomb's original construction crew.

Without warning, a waft of cool air tickled Celeste's skin. "Did you feel that?"

"Yes, but where's it coming from? If there were an exit ahead of us, we'd surely be seeing daylight by now." A frown. "The air could just be coming from a fissure."

Celeste stopped after a few more meters and held out the glow light while turning in a circle.

Damn.

Tolly sighed. "It's a dead end. The passageway just stops."

Guy would not have led them to a dead end. "There has to be an exit here."

"All I see is rock walls."

Celeste took a second to ground and center herself before opening her senses, reaching beyond the plastered stone they saw on the physical plane. She slid on to the astral, aware now of a scent she'd earlier ascribed to the smell of mummies.

As she stood in the river of existence, the side walls of the tunnel appeared as a sort of smudgy energy on either side of her. The river swirled in fog-like fashion around her ankles. In front of her, however, shafts of multi-hued light broke through from outside, prism-like, shimmering on the mists like sun through the rose stained-glass window on the floor of Notre Dame Cathedral. If she focused her intention, she could see a vague representation of the real world behind this magical veil, a photographic negative of the sand-covered desert and a vast expanse of sky, lit by the black orb of a low-hanging morning sun.

Dawn had broken. They were running out of time.

She groped for Tolly's hand. "Can you see this?"

A warm hand grasped hers. "See what?"

"Slip onto the astral."

A moment passed and Tolly gasped. "What kind of magic is this? I've never seen anything like it."

"Probably ancient Egyptian magic. Hiding the back entrance of the tomb from without and within."

"But the tomb robbers clearly found the tomb. The only thing left of its original inhabitant are scraps of mummy cloth and desiccated bits of tomb offerings."

Celeste shrugged. "I don't understand either, but frankly, I don't much care. Right now, all I care about is getting out of here." She took a step forward, tugging on Tolly's hand.

Tolly held her ground. "How do we know if it's safe to pass through that?"

"We don't. But it's better than dying in here, or letting those gunmen pick us off like ducks on a pond."

Even her ever-cautious partner couldn't argue with that. Still, Tolly had a point. And if anyone was going to die from doing something foolish, that fate should be Celeste's, not Tolly's. Besides, she'd made a life out of doing rash and foolish things which, so far, had mostly worked out.

"I'll go first." Before Tolly could react, she focused on the kaleidoscopic lights and plunged ahead.

Thirty-One

Fractured shafts of bright blue, ruby red, sunlit green, and royal purple enveloped her, and the air tinkled like bamboo chimes. She raised her foot to take a step, and it took hours, maybe days, to complete the action. She became fascinated watching it inched forward, as though it was some magical creature and no longer a part of her body.

Some unknowable time later, when someone grabbed the back of her shirt, she shrugged them off. Her only desire was to remain enraptured by the play of light on her shoe as it descended in infinite slowness.

Fragments of color floated around her like shards of a stained-glass window. A blue shard in the shape of a trapezoid—or was that a house, or square with a pyramidal hat—captured her attention and she followed its lazy path around her.

When the hand attached to her blouse kept her from turning to follow the path of the glowing shard, an emotion bubbled up that might have been anger if she hadn't felt so peaceful, then faded away. Other slivers of shimmering color swam around, calling for her attention.

Sound buzzed in her ears like a persistent mosquito, drowning out the irregular plashing of a fountain that had replaced the tink-tink of the chimes. She tried to wave away the annoyance, but the discordant blatting grew louder and more persistent.

Peace ebbed away. The buzzing became a voice. Frantic. Strident.

Celeste! Snap out of it.

Her foot thudded onto the ground. She lost her balance and would have toppled over save for Tolly's grip on her shirt.

Take my hand and go through to the other side. Drag me out if you have to.

Awareness of a reality other than the colors and the sounds came back. Time sped up. Grabbing Tolly's hand, Celeste pushed her body forward, though a part of her mind fought to stay in the peace and beauty that enfolded her.

She burst forth into bright sunlight. Unable to see, she took several rapid steps forward, hoping she wasn't standing on the edge of a cliff. Still gripping Tolly's hand, she pulled her partner forward. It felt like dragging one of her father's ditch goats somewhere it didn't want to go, but a decisive tug did the job. Tolly tumbled out into the sunshine, and it was Celeste's turn to prevent a fall.

She dropped to the hard-packed desert floor and Tolly followed suit, still shielding her eyes against the glare of the morning sun. A lapis blue sky domed over a rusty red landscape of sand and rocks.

"Where are we, *elskling*?"

"I'd guess on the other side of the wadi. Not sure where to go from here, though."

"Where is the map Berenice gave us?"

Celeste rummaged into her bag of magical supplies and pulled out the small scrap of parchment Berenice had supplied. They both peered down at the map, squinting against the sun, and Tolly traced her finger along the meandering line that ran from what they now knew was a rock cut tomb (so that squiggle was a mummy?) to an oasis, indicated by a pool of water and two palm trees.

Celeste snorted. "Goddess, it's like trying to follow one of Mary Read's fake treasure maps."

"You sailed with Read?" Incredulity warred with curiosity on Tolly's face, and maybe a little awe.

Celeste bit her lip. "Well, not so much sailed with her. But I did drink with her. Briefly."

Tolly's eyebrows rose. "And she created fake treasure maps?"

"It was a lark. Someone suggested it to her, and she thought the idea hilarious."

"Hmm. I wonder who that was." With a smile she tried to hide, Tolly returned to the map. "It looks we should travel that way. Can you use the scarf to help us?"

Celeste pulled out the remnants of the headcloth that they'd torn in half and concentrated.

And got nothing.

"I can't sense anything. Either tearing it broke the link, or he's blocking us in some fashion."

"Damn." Tolly looked down at the map. "Back to a more practical method. Is that picture there a lion?"

"I'm sorry." She felt like she'd failed.

"Oh, *elskling*, no." Tolly squeezed her hand. "You did not fail. Much as people want to believe, magic is not a solution to all problems."

Celeste took a breath, pushed past her frustration, and looked at the squiggle on the map Tolly had pointed to. "Not a lion. Probably a sphinx. I don't think there are lions in Egypt." Celeste glanced at Tolly nervously. "Are there?" First crocodiles and now lions. Even after all their travels and all the strange and uncomfortable places they'd been, Egypt had become her least favorite. "Are there?"

"Not live ones, not anymore. But perhaps it is a statue, in which case it's likely to be, as you say, a sphinx."

"I hope it doesn't come to life like the one who trapped Desmond in its litter box." She blew hair from her face, which glowed with a sheen of sweat, and gestured with her chin toward the map. "Be nice if there was some kind of scale to that thing."

Tolly snorted. "If wishes were horses." She climbed to her feet. "Come. As Shakespeare might have said, we're burning daylight."

"Shakespeare said that? Sounds very modern."

"Do you not read? Mercutio from Romeo and Juliet, Act 1, Scene 4." Tolly walked away, shaking her head.

Brushing the sand from her clothes, Celeste trudged after her partner into the desert wastes.

An hour of walking brought them to a tumbled down building. Mud bricks littered the area in which stood an incomplete foundation. There was no way to know if it was an ancient structure or something newer, but given the lack of water here now, and no signs of any other structures, Celeste put her money on ancient. She lay odds there had been a village here in the distant past.

Tolly asked for their canteen of water, took a few sips, then encouraged Celeste to drink a bit as well. They had to ration it, yet collapsing of heat prostration would ruin their chances to free Guy and take down Merimre.

"We must be getting close," Tolly said. "This could be some kind of municipal building or the house of one of the lower class unable to afford something closer to the oasis." She marched forward.

Probably heading in the wrong direction. The woman could follow a map but possessed no internal compass. Were they even on the right path? There'd been no sign of anything resembling a sphinx or a lion.

She tugged on Tolly's sleeve. "Hang on. We need to know we're going the right way."

"And how do you propose to do that? There's no compass rose on the paper to indicate direction."

"I'm going to see if I can use the headcloth to track Merimre's location. If we're close enough, that might work."

Celeste focused her awareness on the torn cloth, now grimy with dust and sweat. For a moment, she saw a muddy green thread, but the mists of the astral abruptly washed over it, and the connection vanished.

She tried twice more, but no matter how she concentrated, the aura did not reappear. "I think he's blocking me on the astral."

"Blast. I kept hoping his magic was mostly smoke and mirrors, but apparently not." Tolly took Celeste's hand, gave it an encouraging squeeze. "Well, we've dealt with worse." Then she tugged. "But we need to hurry. Berenice said, 'when the barque of the sun is high.'"

Celeste shielded her eyes to scan the empty waste ahead of them. "What is a barque, anyway? And where's the cursed lion? I'd feel better if we'd found it by now."

Behind them, a waterfall of sand hissed from a growing height, followed by a low, rumbling growl. A growl that became a menacing chuckle.

"And find it you have. Or rather, I have found you. Again."

Celeste turned, recognizing that voice. "Sphinx," she said to Tolly. "Not lion. Not sure which of us was right."

Like the Cheshire Cat, the sphinx grinned at them, baring its large, sharp canines. "Doesn't matter. I decide who is right. Or have you forgotten?"

Celeste started to reply but quieted when Tolly put a hand on her arm. The sphinx just kept talking.

"Have you completed your mission? Time is running out."

"Not yet," Tolly said. "What are you doing here?"

A good question. How had Guy known this creature would be here, now?

"You are not the one who asks the questions." The creature's tail twitched back and forth, raising dust clouds.

Tolly crossed her arms and stared cooly at the sphinx. "Do you want to end our bargain?"

Amber eyes narrowed. And relaxed. "If you must know, the spirits whispered through the sands, telling me I could find you here. I desired to learn if you were attempting to escape across the eastern desert. I am hungry."

"What spir—"

Tolly shushed Celeste and ignored the sphinx's implied threat. "We are not attempting to escape. Our errand takes us here, to a temple beside an oasis."

"Good. It is very close, so you may finish your business quickly."

Celeste cleared her throat, and two sets of eyes fixed on her with varying degrees of irritation. "How is Desmond? Is he still alive?"

"He was never alive in the time I have known him. But if you mean to ask if he still exists, I assure you he does. Although his undead state is unchanged, his anger has increased a hundredfold." Again, the toothy grin. "This amuses me."

Tolly stepped in again. "If you know the oasis we seek is near, then you can direct us there."

"I could."

Tolly used her fiercest "instructor" scowl. "If you want us to teach you, then it is in your best interests to do so."

"I will not help you do whatever you plan on doing there."

"We do not ask that you do. But we can dispatch our task more quickly if we do not waste time wandering aimlessly through the desert."

A long pause ensued. Eventually the creature's eyebrows lifted. With a tilt of its head, it said, "I think I am beginning to like you. Very well. Your oasis is perhaps two hours walk that way." It pointed with a paw and Celeste was relieved to know they had been roughly on the correct bearing.

Tolly nodded curtly. "That is most helpful. When we are finished and ready to complete our bargain, we will meet you at the previously agreed upon location."

"You have only two days left before our assignation. If you are not there, I will end your undead pet and arrange your own demise. Which would be a pity, as you are an interesting and intelligent specimen."

Tolly neither flinched nor preened. "We will see you at the appointed hour. Good day." At which point, she grabbed Celeste's hand and hauled her in the confirmed direction.

In her head, she heard Tolly's voice, felt the vibrating, fear-tinged tension. *Do. Not. Speak.*

Hard as it was, Celeste kept her mouth shut. When she looked behind them a few moments later, no trace of the sphinx remained.

During the next four hours, with little ability to steer an accurate course, they crossed their own path three times. When the tops of the palm trees appeared above a low rise, Celeste nearly kissed the sand.

Tolly's hair was disheveled, her clothes wrinkled and sweat ran in tracks down her sand-coated face. The scowl on her face would have sent the bravest of war veterans running in the other direction.

Celeste started up the scree-covered rise, dropping onto her belly as she neared the top. She had expected the site to look something like Hatshepsut's colossal mortuary temple at Dier el-Bahri, but all that remained of this one consisted of a couple of pylons, the lower half of the statue of a god, broken at the knees, and the remnants of walls that outlined the structure's size and shape. As Egyptian monuments went, this one barely deserved a footnote.

In a hushed voice, Tolly echoed her thoughts. "Rather unimpressive."

Some little distance west of the ruined temple lay an encampment. Celeste and Tolly lay silently, side by side on the hill, watching the place while sand hissed around the dun-colored rocks that littered the slope. Three small tents, and one larger one—maybe four meters on a side—clustered around a spring fed pool, amid a profusion of reeds and several date palms.

No squads of armed guards patrolled the camp, as she'd expected. Where were the men who followed the Lion of Justice today?

Instead, she saw a handful of women and two bald, brawny spearmen dressed in the kind of ancient garb she'd seen on tomb walls and in Tolly's books. Must be Merimre's attendants. The young women jingled as they scurried in and out of the large tent, earrings, beaded necklaces and bracelets glinting in the sun. The men had on those skirts—kilts, Tolly's internal voice reminded her—Celeste had seen on tomb paintings, and broad turquoise and red beaded collars covered their bare chests. At the moment, they stood at attention, like Beefeaters, on either side of the large tent's entrance.

Although too far away to make out faces, Celeste would have bet twenty francs that all of Merimre's attendants wore kohl around their eyes and rouge on their cheeks. Another reminder of her time in the court of Louis, where she'd sniggered behind her fan at the men in their powdered and pink faces like Punch and Judy puppets.

And then there was Guy. Standing ramrod straight between the two spearmen, he wore one of the traditional white linen kilts too, covering him from waist to mid-thigh, showing off impressive thews. Like the other men, his broad shoulders and muscular torso were bare to the late morning sun, but unlike them, he hadn't shaved off his mane of red-gold hair. Even Celeste found the demigod an impressive sight.

A roar of anger came from the tent. Merimre. "Do not spill another drop, you wasteful idiots, or shall whip you within an inch of your life!"

Two girls hurried out of the tent toward the pool, carrying big tubs. They filled them and carried them back to the large tent, struggling under the weight of the water. Celeste's back and arms ached in sympathy. She well remembered the exhausting job of carrying water for baths.

Tolly leaned close. "Must be for a ritual bath. Priests would do that before ceremonies, to purify themselves."

A bath, huh? "And he'll be naked?"

Tolly stared at her. "One usually is."

"And if it's a ritual bath, he'll remove everything. Right?"

"Is the sun getting to you, *elskling*? You are not unfamiliar with baths, this I know. You keep me in ours until my fingers get pruny."

She winked. "That's a different kind of bath." She wished they were in a large soaking tub right now, with lavender scented water steaming up, their arms and legs twined around each other. "My point is that if he strips off everything, including Guy's ring, then I have a chance to snatch it."

Tolly frowned but her eyes sparkled. "You know I would never condone theft, my dove, but it would be a shame to pass up an opportunity like this for you to, er, polish a useful skill. Keeping up with old talents is always a good thing. How do you propose to get in unnoticed?"

Celeste rummaged through their bag and pulled out a small knife. Perfect for cutting through tent canvas. "A disguise. If I'm not successful, you'll have to think of something else."

She didn't give Tolly time to argue. Bending low, she fast-walked down the side of the hill, toward the smaller tents. Using the reeds and trees of the oasis as cover, she slipped behind the first of them.

No sounds came from inside the tent and, sending a quick seeking, she sensed no presence, mortal or otherwise. Kneeling, she cut a two-foot-long slit in the canvas and wriggled through.

In her mind's eye, she'd envisioned a rack of costumes from some silent film like The Sheik with Rudolph Valentino, or a chest with filmy ancient Egyptian gowns spilling out of it. Instead, she found only a rickety camp cot and a burlap sack stuffed with a long, loose-fitting garment and a head scarf.

Disappointed, she moved on to the next small tent. This one was occupied by a young woman, either asleep or possibly drugged. Celeste wanted it to be Berenice, but no. Spirits, or whatever Berenice was, didn't sleep.

A quick but quiet survey revealed the same meager furnishings, the camp cot, the burlap sack filled with ordinary clothes, and a few new items. A small washbasin on which sat a wooden palette, the divots filled with black and pink goo, and turquoise powder. Paint? No. Make-up. The rouge and the eyeshadow could be applied with fingers, and the kohl with a thin, modern eyeliner brush that lay across the palette. A hand mirror, dusty with the ever-present sand, lay on the ground nearby.

At a small noise, she turned to the cot. The young girl couldn't be much past puberty. She wore a translucent gown and a fearful expression. As she sat up, she crossed her arms over her chest in hope-less modesty.

Celeste knelt and whispered, trying to match Tolly's soothing tones. "It's okay. I'm not here to hurt you. Do you understand?"

The girl's eyes widened, and she swallowed hard.

Okay, so not a French speaker. On to pantomime now. She pointed to the slit she had cut in the tent and made a shooing motion. "Go. Run home. Now."

At Celeste's tone, the young woman huddled into the corner, her knuckles clenched and white.

Celeste moderated her tone again and opened the slit. Sunlight streamed in, and beyond the grass and other greenery, they could both see the sand dunes. She gestured the girl again toward the opening and pleaded softly. "Go. Go home. I'm going to get rid of the bad man, but there's not much time." Now she pointed toward the big tent then mimed slitting her throat.

The girl gasped in terror and shrank back when Celeste tried to pat her soothingly on the arm. Where was Tolly when she needed her? Giving up, she simply shooed the girl toward the slit in the tent.

Fear or self-preservation finally won, and the girl bolted like a doe through the opening, vanishing into the greenery like a ghost.

Guy had said something about Merimre wanting a bride. If this child was Merimre's choice, Celeste loathed him even more.

She searched for whatever finery the girl was supposed to change into—surely, he wouldn't wed her in that barely-there nightgown she wore—but nothing else came to hand. That meant no subterfuge. It was to be a straightforward sneak attack then.

With a sigh, she exited the tent and crept clockwise around the oasis. Merimre's tent had been situated under the meager shade of two date palms. From behind the structure, she watched the two serving women bring two more tubs of water, then scurry away.

From inside, Merimre shouted for Guy to attend him. As Guy turned to obey, he peeked his head around the side of the tent, grinned, and gave Celeste a wink.

Needing him to help her, to provide a distraction, she sent a mental message to him through the remnants of the link he had created with her. She had no idea if he received it. Hoping he had, she positioned herself at the back corner of the tent, ready to slit the ties that kept the flaps closed and listened, waiting for an opportunity.

THIRTY-TWO

The moment Guy entered the tent, Merimre started sneering orders at him in what must be ancient Egyptian. Guy understood but replied back in antique Gaelic. She had no idea what Merimre said, but if she concentrated, Celeste could understand some of what Guy was saying.

"Yes, Master, I shall be happy to prepare you for the [meeting? summoning? Did he mean ritual?] Please hold out your arms and I will help to remove your garments and jewels."

Merimre groused and muttered something else.

Guy was smiling; Celeste could hear it in his voice. A sly smile. "Would you not prefer one of your female servants to anoint you with the [flowers? smells? animal fat? Maybe that meant perfumes and oils?] after your bath? A little game of [smiting? skin touching? Oh, good Goddess, did he just say slap and tickle?] would certainly raise your energy for the coming ritual, eh?"

Merimre must have understood the suggestion because she heard a loud smack, then an oof and the sound of a body slamming to the ground.

Guy began to moan and carry on as though he were dying. For a second, she thought he really was, then realized this was her moment. Merimre's attention would be on his pain-in-the-ass djinn.

She cut through the ties and slipped in.

From her vantage, she watched Guy writhe dramatically on the packed sand of the tent between a gauzy drapery that curtained off a luxurious bed and an extra-large cast-iron claw-foot bathtub raised on a small wooden dais. Three adults could have occupied that tub. She saw lotus flowers floating atop the water.

Assured Guy hadn't actually been harmed, she scanned the rest of the tent. Beyond the glorified tub sat the chest of clothes she'd hoped for in the smaller tent. Next to it, someone, likely Guy, had laid out the get up that Merimre would wear for his ritual on a very modern plush, slipper chair. Martin's man, Faulkner, could not have done a better job.

Merimre growled and kicked Guy in the ribs, causing a real yelp of pain before the priest shouted something at him.

Guy groaned and pulled himself to his feet. A red wheal marked his cheek from Merimre's blow, and another showed on his abdomen from the kick that sent the demigod to the ground.

The demigod had to be seething. The minute Celeste could release Guy from the ring, Merimre would wish he'd never re-entered the mortal world. She just needed to find the bloody thing to make that happen.

Guy gathered up the clothing items he'd assisted Merimre to remove, and fetched a wide, gold, beaded breast plate or collar and a couple of rings and bracelets from another chest. But the ring Celeste was after wasn't part of that cache. That ring still adorned Merimre's hand. Damn it.

The priest, now naked, took his sleek, muscular body to the dais, where he snarled something and pointed to the ground. Guy hobbled over and scrunched down like a turtle to become a footstool for his master to step on to get into the enormous tub.

Fury burned in her. She wanted to drown the priest in that tub.

Standing in the steaming water, the priest dismissed Guy with a curt gesture. When the servant of Epona had exited the tent, Merimre finally slipped the ring off his finger. It clinked against the small, tessellated tile-topped table next to the tub. Aha! Perfect. She *knew* he would take it off.

From outside, she heard something like a tambourine banging out a rhythmic rattle, accompanied by women chanting. Merimre clapped twice and the two lanterns that lit the tent snuffed out, leaving only a single candle for illumination.

Celeste snorted inwardly. Mood lighting.

A brass ewer sat on the small table next to the tub, along with fancy glass vials that must contain the oils and perfumes Guy had mentioned. Picking up the ewer, Merimre bent over and filled it, then sluiced himself down with the water, murmuring a chant of his own in a sing-song voice. Celeste crept forward during the splashing and chanting, hoping the noise would cover her approach. She skirted the perimeter of the tent, staying in the shadows, moving behind Merimre. Her plan involved slipping the ring off the table and dashing out of the tent before Merimre noticed. She'd been a damn fine street thief, and she'd only been caught once.

While Merimre continued to chant and pour water over his muscular physique, she eased her way out of the shadows and toward the table. Only meters away, a hidden rock pierced her knee. She clamped her lips together to hold back a cry, wobbling. Trying not to topple over, she sent a prayer to Brigid. When Merimre continued his sacred ablutions without pause, she sighed a silent thanks.

She centered herself, willing her heart to stop pounding, then crept up behind the table. Millimeter by millimeter, she eased her hand up and over the tabletop, then froze again as Merimre stopped.

Her injured knee, now bleeding again, stung from the sand she'd ground into it. She balanced, unmoving, one arm outstretched. Her fatigued muscles trembled as she strained to hold the pose.

The trick to not being noticed was to be just another piece of furniture, solid, expected, still as only inanimate things—and servants—are. During her life before Tolly, she'd had plenty of practice being a still, invisible servant. And like all servants, she watched and waited, hoping she remained invisible, but fully expecting him to turn and grab her.

Instead, he raised arms and eyes heavenward and intoned a long prayer, probably beseeching some god or other to bless his efforts. His voice boomed but did not echo off the smothering canvas of the tent.

Hoping the chanting fully absorbed his attention, she took a breath through her mouth, closed her fingers around the ring, and crabbed backward into the shadows toward her exit.

The chant ended with an ululating cry. He clapped his hands again and the lanterns flared to life. While the women outside continued singing, the two spearmen hurried in, followed by Guy.

The time for subterfuge had passed. She scrambled on hands and knees toward the slit in the tent.

One of the spearmen caught the movement. Shouting, he bolted toward her.

Blessed Brigid, my favorite goddess, what have I done to piss you off? And then, to Tolly, she sent, *Run!*

She made it to the exit and squirmed out. Merimre was shrieking and shouting orders in Arabic. Sandals slapped on sand as the spearmen raced toward her, grunting as they squatted to pursue her through the slit in the tent.

Someone grabbed her ankle. She kicked hard, dislodged the man. Free, she ran toward the desert beyond the greenery of the oasis and to the hill behind which Tolly waited. Hopefully, where she *had* waited, but now had run away from.

Hope flamed to cinders when she saw Tolly's head pop up from behind the hill.

Still, she ran, and the sensible shoes she'd purchased at the boutique in the Corniche hit soft sand.

A spear knocked her sideways. She hit the ground face-first. One of the spearmen knelt astride her back and whacked his weapon onto her wrist. Her fingers opened involuntarily, and the spearman prized Guy's ring from her throbbing hand.

Somewhere ahead of her, she heard a whoosh, like one of Tolly's air burst spells going off, followed by Tolly's scream of pain. Whatever happened next disappeared into a ringing agony as the man sitting on her back boxed her ears, and the world momentarily went away.

When the ringing stopped and the world swam back into view, it was Merimre, not one of the spearmen, who hauled Celeste up by the collar of her sweat-stained yellow silk blouse and held her, facing away, against his chest. A sharp knife bit into her throat, and she felt blood mixed with sweat trickle down her neck.

Tolly, one arm twisted painfully behind her back, raised her free hand to cast a spell but never got the chance. Another of the bald men hit her in the midsection with the shaft of his spear and she collapsed forward with a grunt.

"Tolly!"

The knife at her throat sliced deeper. "Djinn," Merimre snarled, "Block their magic."

Guy sagged, and with a horrified look at Celeste, he waved a hand. Her magical senses shut off like a light switch.

The pressure of the blade eased a bit. Merimre pointed his chin at Tolly. "Ahmed, grab that creature and take her to the temple. I must finish my preparations." To Celeste he said, "Walk," then frog marched her toward his tent.

Guy hurried ahead of his master in order to hold the tent flap up, and they all entered, one of the spearmen at the tail end of the little procession.

The tent still smelled of incense and perfumed oil. Merimre shoved Celeste toward the spearman. "Hold her."

The large man's hands caught her, spun her to face the room, and gripped her arms with hands that could have snapped her bones. Still, she fought him, squirming and thrashing. She had to get to Tolly. What was happening to her? Had that blow from the spear hurt her badly?

She'd almost managed to break the guard's grip by prying at his fingers, when Merimre shouted, and Guy sucker punched her in the gut.

She fell forward, gasping. Bastard.

When she could look up again, awful remorse filled his gaze. He'd had no choice but to obey, yet the act still felt like a betrayal.

Merimre ignored her wheezing. Still naked, he resumed his place in the bath and ordered Guy to wash off the sand that coated his skin. Celeste straightened, trying to maintain what little dignity she had left. After a moment, the priest exited the tub and stood, arms held out. Guy dutifully dressed the priest in an almost see-through white linen kilt and an animal skin—a leopard, she thought—which draped across one shoulder and around the hip on the opposite side. The head and a front paw of the pelt hung down over his shoulder and Merimre grasped the tail with his opposite hand. She didn't think leopards lived in Egypt, at least not now, so she could only imagine where he'd acquired it. Probably Guy.

With his task completed, Guy stepped back and bowed in obeisance with compressed lips.

Merimre nodded in satisfaction before turning to Celeste. "You will bear witness as the god Thoth gives his blessing and recognizes my right to rule as king. The Two Lands shall be made great again by my hands."

Celeste lifted her chin in defiance. "There is no pharaoh in Egypt anymore. There is no throne to claim."

He stepped close and backhanded her, the scarab on the ring he'd taken back from her scoring her cheek as her head jerked to the side.

"Once I have the situation under control, I will teach you not only who is in charge, but the proper way to behave as you serve your king. You will learn, or you will die." He looked her up and down. "And I will enjoy the process either way."

Turning on the heels of his sandals, he snapped his fingers. "Djinn, give me my staff. Guard, bring her. Do not let her escape."

Escape. Yes, that was her first priority. She reached out to Tolly. *Are you all right?*

I'll live. I knew your plan was dangerous.

I had the ring! It worked.

Until it didn't. Tolly's tone was matter of fact, not scolding. *What now, elskling?*

Celeste didn't have an answer. She could only trust that an opportunity would appear. There would come a moment, and they'd take it.

Just be ready.

The guard's grip tightened, and he forced Celeste to follow the others. Outside the tent, the two young women who had been chanting earlier fell into line behind Guy, singing joylessly and playing their rattle-like instruments as they processed toward the remains of the temple.

THIRTY-THREE

The ruins of the Temple of Thoth comprised a few square meters of dressed stone paving slabs, one intact column minus its decorative capital, the stubs of two others, the broken statue Celeste had noticed earlier, and a tumble of stones that outlined the walls. Merimre had found a cracked wooden, gesso and gold leaf-covered statuette to replace the image of the god.

Two spearmen held Tolly and Celeste and a third stood between them, ready for whatever Merimre needed him for. The singing girls stayed behind the makeshift perimeter, looking glum and cowed.

Tolly stood tall, uninjured as far as Celeste could see. Celeste shot a glance at her partner a glance. *Any idea what he's going to do?*

Tolly, arms pinned by the spearman, couldn't move enough to shrug, nor did she shake her head, but her eyes widened, and her brows rose and fell in an 'I have no idea' way.

Merimre began to chant a litany in his ancient tongue, raising his arms and gesticulating. The hairs on the back of Celeste's arms rose as Merimre conjured the first stirrings of power. Overhead, wisps of clouds gathered like strands of cotton candy and the sands whispered in the burgeoning breeze.

In her mind, she heard Guy translating the chants. "All good things come from you, O Mighty Thoth," it started, followed by a long litany of praises and an even longer speech about Merimre's qualifications as the legitimate heir to the throne. Minutes later, he finished with the aggrandizement and got down to business. "As your good and faithful servant, I beg you to give me the power to turn away the enemies of the Two Lands and take their place as rightful ruler of the people. I would break the bonds of their servitude to foreigners and restore a true son of Khemet to the throne of the God-King. I am that true son. Grant me your blessing to take the double crown, and release to the god's faithful servant all good spells and powers so that I may return the land to its rightful place in ma'at."

Guy mentally crowed in glee. "Release all good spells? Why, of course, Master."

Celeste felt the barrier that blocked her magic crumble. Suddenly the astral plane was again accessible, and she reveled in the elemental power that flooded back.

She also sensed a stirring from the little wooden statuette as the god it represented woke from its millennia-old sleep to Merimre's propitiations.

It was now or never. *Tolly, can you do hot hands? And I'll do a rooting spell?*

Tolly's chapped lips curved in a smile. In the time it took Celeste to focus her concentration on her own spell, Merimre faltered in his chanting, then stopped, gazing at his hands in perplexity.

He shook them, rubbed them together, trying to rid himself of the growing burning sensation. As he turned to face Celeste, fury contorting his features, she loosed her own spell with the whispered word for root in Breton. "*Gwrizienn.*"

With a howl of rage, Merimre took a step forward before the magical and invisible roots Celeste had summoned twined around his ankles and calves, holding him in place. She'd seen the spell used in battle so that only the feet were affected, in the hope that the target would topple over from their own momentum and break their ankles, but she had vowed not to break the First Rule of Do No Harm, if she could help it, if only for Tolly's sake.

Merimre screamed. "Djinn! Break these spells!"

Celeste couldn't turn enough to see Guy's face, but she heard the smug tone and could imagine the nasty smile on the demigod's handsome face. "I cannot negate another's spells, Master. That is not one of my abilities."

The sand beneath Merimre's feet liquefied into a viscous puddle. Celeste glanced at Tolly, whose face was clenched in concentration. What had she cast?

The stench of rancid lard and candle wax wafted across the sand. Somehow Tolly had combined the hot hands spells and the lard she'd insisted on purchasing in some hybrid spell. She mentally grinned at Tolly. Just like in their days with the Council's Protectorate branch, her partner had created something on the fly that was both brilliant and effective.

The molten quicksand covered Merimre's still rooted feet, and he flailed, making him sink into the mire. He screamed at the spearmen. "Help me! Pull me out!"

The three guards looked at one another, wasting precious time. The liquefied sand was now up to Merimre's knees.

Celeste spoke to the one who held her. "Now's your chance. He can't stop you from leaving. And if you don't help him, then we can take care of him once and for all."

He pursed his lips, muttered, "Inshallah," and looked again at his compatriots. As one, they turned and ran.

Merimre raised his arms over his head, scrabbling for purchase beyond the quicksand while shrieking threats at the guards. "Worms! I'll kill you all!" Panic laced his voice. "Djinn, get me out of here!"

Guy cursed in his native Gaelic tongue and sent Celeste one

more mental message. "He'll be inside the ring with me. Unbind me!"

Suddenly, Merimre's struggles ceased and his body went limp. Celeste raced toward him, determined to get the ring off his hand but by the time she reached him, the quicksand had swallowed him up.

Lying flat, careful not to fall in herself, she plunged her hand into the muck. She felt around, found his hand, grabbed hold of the ring and yanked. Molten sand burned her skin. When she pulled free of the boiling slurry, she had not only the ring, but the finger too. The rest of the body of the man Merimre's spirit had inhabited sank beyond reach.

"Celie, you idiot!" Tolly grabbed Celeste's ankle and dragged her away from the edge of the quicksand. "It's too late. Let him go."

"I don't give a fig about him. I had to get the ring."

"The ring? Oh. The ring." She knelt next to Celeste, her eyes still on the spot where Merimre's body had disappeared. She looked stricken and it took Celeste a moment to realize why. Tolly thought she had just consigned someone to death. A mortal sin in the witching world.

"Oh, Tolly."

Tolly raised her chin. "I didn't mean for the spell to do what it did. I only meant to trap him. Not kill him."

Celeste squeezed her partner's hand. "You didn't kill him. Merimre did. That body was just a host for the priest's spirit. The man whose body he stole was dead the minute Merimre evicted his spirit and took him over."

"How can you know that for sure?"

"Marguerite told me."

Tolly tore her gaze away from the sand, which had begun to resemble regular sand again, as the effects of Tolly's hybrid spell faded. "Your old teacher? What would she know about ifrits?"

"She knew nothing about ifrits, but she knew about malevolent spirits occupying the bodies of the living." She waited for Tolly to scoff and accuse her mentor of practicing folk magic, but instead Tolly nodded. "From all you've said, she was a wise old hedge witch. I still wish I could be certain. The Council—"

"Need never know, one way or the other." She reached over to brush Tolly's hair from her face with her other hand and winced.

Tolly stood and gathered herself. Celeste knew her partner would agonize over all this later, but for now, her common sense reasserted itself. She glanced around the little oasis. "We need something to take care of that burn. And if I'm not mistaken..." She crossed to a cluster of low-growing plants with long, thin spear-like appendages. Tearing off several of the spears from the base of the plant, she brought them back.

"Aloe vera. The ancient Egyptians thought the plant held the secret of immortality." She squeezed a gooey, clear substance from the leaves and began to smear it on Celeste's hand and arm. The burning sensation ebbed almost instantaneously. "There, that will help and gives me a component through which to work healing magic. Now, sit still for a moment."

"There's not time. We need to rescue Guy somehow."

"Rescue him from what? Where has he gone, anyway?"

Clearly, Tolly hadn't been on the receiving end of Guy's mental commentary. "In the ring. With Merimre." She relayed Guy's final message.

Tolly frowned. "I assume Guy was the one who released our magic?"

"Yes. He was translating what Merimre was chanting. The fool asked..." She thought for a moment, trying to remember the exact words. "...to release to the god's faithful servant all good spells and powers so that I may return the land to its rightful place in ma'at."

Tolly smiled. "Literalism has its uses. Very clever. And the ring?"

"I'm guessing, really, but when Merimre asked Guy to get him out of here, Guy used that as a command to transport them both into the ring."

"I'm gaining a grudging respect for the fellow." She held Celeste's burned arm by the elbow and closed her eyes.

Celeste felt more than saw the cooling blue healing energy emanate from Tolly's hand to encase her entire forearm, following the sticky, gooey coating of aloe.

After a few moments, Tolly said, "How does that feel?"

"Much better."

"Good. If we're going to rescue Guy, you'll need two working hands." She sat back on her heels. "How do you propose to do this?"

Celeste rolled her shoulders and stood. "Guy said the unbinding had to be done at the place where he was bound, so we have no choice but to go to the tomb of Tutankhamen. After that..." She shrugged. "I wish there had been time to extract something specific from Guy. I assume we focus our energy on the ring and unwork the spell cast on it."

"That's not much of a plan. And you're the expert in unworking spells. What can I do?"

"What you always do. Provide the energy." She tried to smile reassuringly, while her whole arm throbbed from the burn. "It will be fine. You'll see."

With a sigh, Tolly stood and offered Celeste her hand. "You insist on doing this, then. As far as I'm concerned, Aubrey has been avenged, and Egypt is saved."

"But Guy is still bound to the ring, and that evil priest is now in there with him."

"I could rightly say that's not my problem."

Celeste frowned. "But you wouldn't." She paused, searching Tolly's face. "Would you?"

The moment stretched. Tolly sighed. "No. So let's go get it done. It's a long walk to the Valley of the Kings."

She turned and strode off. Grinning, Celeste hurried after her and gently turned her partner in the proper direction. "I love you. I'll make this up to you somehow. I promise."

Tolly chuckled. "Oh, you will, *elskling*. I guarantee it."

THIRTY-FOUR

The trek back to the Valley of the Kings was hot and exhausting, but no one chased them or shot at them or tried to kill them in any other inventive ways. The sun dropped behind the western cliffs as they entered the Valley, and the air cooled refreshingly.

Celeste parked herself on a slope of detritus built up from a tomb excavation and dumped the sand from her shoes. She'd have the smoothest feet in France after her many blisters healed.

Tolly dropped down beside her with a groan and emptied her own shoes.

Celeste could sense Tolly's exhaustion too, but the weight her partner had been carrying since they'd first met with Aubrey had lifted.

"You feel better now."

"A bit, yes. I know it's ridiculous. The man whose body Merimre inhabited didn't drive a knife into Aubrey's heart. His thugs did, and we've no way of knowing which one. Yet I do feel this thing is complete."

Celeste gave her a quick side hug. "I'm glad for that."

Tolly leaned over and kissed Celeste. Not some peck on the cheek, either. When they broke apart, Tolly clambered to her feet. "Thank you. For everything. You didn't have to come with me, you didn't have to help me. And I appreciate it."

"Of course, I did. I love you. We're a team."

"Oh, that we are." She tugged on her shoes again. "So. Let's finish this tonight. I don't want to perform an unbinding tomorrow in the daylight surrounded by a bunch of idiot tourists, dragomen, and donkeys."

"We need to be at the tomb."

"I know. It's that way."

Celeste had little faith, given Tolly's previous directional errors. "Are you sure?"

"Yes. I memorized the map in Mr. Baedeker's guide. This is the tomb of Ramses VII that we're sitting beside. Carter's excavation should be roughly that way." She pointed. "But we should be as quiet as possible. I read that Carter hired local men to guard the tomb at night."

Celeste stood, stretched. When she reached down to slip on her shoe, her fingers brushed something buried in the sand. Pulling it out, she discovered an archaeologist's wide horsehair excavation brush. She almost tossed it aside, then changed her mind. One never knew what might come in handy. Worse came to worst, she could use the handle of the brush as a wand to cast a circle when the time came for the unbinding.

The moon had risen, silvering the dusky landscape. In the stillness—and the lack of people trying to kill her—she sensed for the first time the energy of the desert. Beneath her feet she felt the somnolent dead and the heavy, ponderous antiquity of the subterranean structures that housed them. Beyond that, the hardpacked, barren earth hummed low and sonorous, unchangeable and ageless despite the busy buzz of the modern world.

The moon had reached its zenith in the sky and began its journey to the west when they began to encounter wooden signs announcing this or that tomb lay down a beaten track. Tolly slowed her steps and pulled out some of the candle wax they had melted into pellets and, drawing a bit of energy from the earth, cast a silence spell on them. She handed one to Celeste before continuing along the path.

Starlight had joined the light from the rising moon when Tolly paused and pulled Celeste behind a mound of excavation fill. Ahead, the main track veered to the right. Peeking around the pile of rubble and sand, Celeste made out the shape of a large canvas tent next to a low mudbrick, three-sided enclosure. Although darkness had fallen and the entrance to the enclosure was on the far side, she saw no guard, either in front of the enclosure or the tent. Perhaps luck was finally on their side.

Still under the protection of the silence spell, they crept past the tent and around the enclosure. On the open side, a set of stone steps led down into the earth, ending at a door. A wooden door behind a padlocked iron grate.

She glanced at Tolly. *Now what?*

Do we have to be inside? Surely, this is close enough.

Celeste wasn't sure, but whatever guard slept in the tent prohibited them from even trying to get past the grate and the door to enter the tomb. With a shrug, she pulled out the ring and cut a piece of thread from the hem of her filthy pajama pants, which now resembled beggar's rags.

They'd argued on their walk whether to invoke a goddess's blessing on the work. Celeste had insisted on it. She knew they needed all the help they could get, particularly since this was foreign magic and they were winging it, adapting an existing spell to a situation it wasn't meant for. After what had happened earlier with the quicksand, Tolly harbored even more fear about doing something on the fly.

Then the discussion had turned to *which* goddess. Celeste wanted Brigid, since that was the divinity she worked with almost exclusively. Tolly made a case for Freya, her personal divinity since she would be the one channeling the energy to Celeste's spell. They had bickered back and forth as they trudged through the sand until Celeste halted in the path, smacked motionless by the hand of inspiration.

"We're idiots," she'd said. "The goddess we need to invoke is Epona."

Tolly froze, hand raised to object, then grabbed Celeste and danced them around in a circle. "You are brilliant, my dove! I love you and your twisty brain."

All the fear and jealousy Celeste harbored about Aubrey finally drained away. Whatever Aubrey had meant to Tolly, that was in the past. The warm, pink, glowing love she'd felt in that moment settled into her bones like a perpetual hug.

Now, as they stood outside the tomb, Celeste grounded herself, sending imaginary roots into the earth and reaching her arms skyward to connect with the energy of the moon. She had no wand or athame with which to cast a circle, so she gathered power into her hand...then remembered the excavation brush. A brush with horse-hair bristles. And horses were special to Epona.

She grinned and held the brush out in front of her as she paced a wide circle three times round, intoning the circle chant while envisioning a sphere build up around them, above and below the ground.

She felt the air still when she finished. The circle kept out the weather, as well as a host of malicious entities.

Next, she set about calling the Quarters, one element per direction, Air, Fire, Water, and Earth, asking the energies of each quarter to lend their support and protect the circle. Finally, she called on Epona. Using the horsehair brush as a focal point, she bid Epona to enter the circle and assist in breaking Guy's binding, using the most antiquated version of Welsh she could muster.

When she could feel the thrumming of the energy from the four elements and the Horse goddess, she retrieved the ring from her pocket and slid onto the astral plane to magically examine the structure of the binding spell.

She reared back a bit when she got a look at it. A writhing ball of snakes confronted her. Two black, slithering asps with eyes like onyx, and red, flicking tongues. The ball-shape of twisting, twining snake bodies was hollow, and inside whirled a glowing teal globe—Guy's spiritual essence.

Were those squiggles she saw actual words written on the asps' scaled bodies? She leaned in to get a closer look. Yes, glowing symbols, but they weren't written in any alphabet she knew. They were hieroglyphs, running up and down the length of each of the two creatures.

One lunged at her, hissing, fangs at the ready. She yanked back her energy-self to avoid the attack. She had no doubt a bite from one of the snakes would not only hurt her energetically but physically as well. The asps continued to writhe hypnotically, and the lines of hieroglyphs whirled by in a kaleidoscopic blur.

She recalled what Byron had relayed to her about Egyptian magic or heka, as it was called. Words, imagery, and intent, united in one concept. Not so different from the magic she wielded. The last major binding spell she'd unwound had looked like a pile of spaghetti, a hopeless tangle, but that had been a ruse. A subtle pattern revealed itself once she realized that most of the spell threads were camouflage. Examining the undulating snake bodies, she could discern no such pattern. And she couldn't read the hieroglyphs, even if she could determine where to start.

She reached out to Tolly via their mental link and relayed what she was seeing. *How do we know what the hieroglyphs say?*

Tolly gave the astral equivalent of a shrug. *Focus on the snakes first. Can you see a tail? Maybe if you were to take hold of a tail and pull, it would unravel.*

She tried to see past the astral illusion of a pair of snakes to the energy beneath. Where had the caster started? Where was the beginning of the spell?

As Celeste narrowed her attention on the glossy, glowing snake bodies, one of the hissing heads reared, flaring its hood, and struck out again. Damn, that had been close. And the thing had grown longer to accomplish its attack, while not unwinding from the roiling ball at all.

Celie? I saw an energy flare. Are you all right?

Yes, fine. The snake heads attack. I managed to jump out of the way. But they're fast and they seem to be able to stretch to reach me.

Be careful.

Celeste studied the glowing magical threads again, trying to merge herself with the flow to discern the pattern. Ah, she thought, as she mentally rode along with the whirling construct. There it was.

The two snakes moved independently of one another, but in a carefully choreographed dance, and they mirrored each other. Like an intricate Celtic double knot. Yet each snake—or the energy each represented—was unique. The energy signature of most spells usually reflected the caster, so how could there be two?

The answer came, deceptively simple. Two casters. Two magic users had created the binding on the ring.

Tolly, I'm going to need your help.

Tolly balked when Celeste briefed her on the spell. "I don't do unbindings."

"Not normally, but you *can* do them. And we're going to have to go after this together."

"I don't know that I can manage the energy flow and work on a complicated reversal."

Tolly's uncertainty surprised Celeste. "We'll just split the load."

Celeste felt a flare of emotion from her partner. Abject fear.

When Tolly spoke again, mind to mind, she was close to panic. *I can't. I can only focus on one thing, Celie. I'm not you.*

It had been so long since they'd done battle together. Over twenty years. She'd almost forgotten their roles, their rhythm, the way they'd always strategized their plan of attack. Tolly managed the power, managed the elemental energy. Celeste handled the spell work, particularly any kind of sympathetic magic. Celeste had always assumed that was how Tolly liked to work. Never in her wildest dreams had she imagined Tolly didn't feel adept at something.

Which meant that Celeste would have to deal with deconstructing one spellcaster's half of the binding while fending off the attack of the other.

How did one cut off the head of an astral spell snake?

Tolly, I need something I can use symbolically as a weapon, something with an edge. This brush isn't going to work.

"What are you going to do?"

"What do you usually do to a snake? Cut its damn head off."

The writhing snakes hissed louder now as they wound sinuously around one another in their proscribed spherical fashion, faster and more agitated. While Tolly hunted for an ersatz weapon, Celeste studied the movements of the spell's guardians, hoping to find a moment in their pattern where the two heads were in close proximity. If she could cut both heads off in the same blow, that would be ideal.

She sensed Tolly cut open the circle to step outside it, then seal it shut again. Celeste kept her attention fixed on the asps—also called Egyptian cobras, and the creatures allegedly responsible for Cleopatra's demise. Their movements mesmerized her, and her attention became fixed on the faint, dry, susurration of scales sliding along scales. The sound lulled her. If Tolly hadn't cut her way back into the circle, disturbing the buzzing energy of their casting, she might have taken another involuntary step too close to the whirling ball. She hadn't even realized she'd moved.

Clever spell. Damned clever.

She blinked to clear the cobwebs from her mind.

Here.

Tolly pressed something into her left hand. The wooden handle was smooth and her thumb found the sharp metallic triangle past the haft.

It's a trowel. Flat-bladed, unlike a garden trowel. Will that do?

Far better than the horsehair brush she'd used to cast the circle. Keeping her movements nonthreatening, she exchanged the tools so that the trowel, with its edged blade, was in her right hand. On the physical plane, it probably wouldn't have done the job, but here on the astral the object was symbolic, so the relative sharpness meant nothing.

In her left hand, she gripped the horsehair brush, stroking the bristles with her fingers, creating a mental connection to the horse from whom the hair had come. Then, through that horse—a mare, she discovered, an old chestnut girl who'd born six foals before her mane had been used for the brush—to the goddess Epona, patroness of horses. When she could feel a thrum of unfamiliar feminine power, she called out to Tolly through their mental link. *I need energy now. I'm going to do the unbinding.*

Tolly lightly clasped her unburned wrist. A trickle of energy warmed both her physical hand and her astral one, building until it zinged her skin. Sizzling, sparking energy danced at her fingertips. Not painful—Tolly kept the energy carefully gated—but powerful.

Underneath the tingling magic, she could smell the cool desert air, feel the tugging ripple of waves on the Nile, grounded herself on the sun-baked floor of the Valley, drawing in all the surrounding elements that would fuel her spell work.

Dropping deeper onto the astral, she became subsumed by the fragrance of apples and hay and the warmth of the summer sun on her flanks as she galloped, unfettered, across a metaphorical meadow.

Epona's energy, flowing through her.

Her awareness narrowed to the task at hand. She'd need to cut the heads off those astral asps, then figure out what came next. She assumed there would be another layer, though she couldn't sense it, and it had to have something to do with the hieroglyphs she couldn't read.

But. One step at a time.

Energy flowed in a steady stream. Directing it to her right and dominant hand, she pushed power to the edge of the trowel. When it glowed lightning blue, she thrust at the head of the first serpent.

The blade sizzled as it sliced through the astral body of the asp. She'd timed the blow well, making sure the two heads were as far apart as possible on their proscribed looping journey around the heart of the sphere.

But distances on the astral were subjective. What appeared to be enough space between the heads was not.

The strike on her nondominant hand burned when the snake's fangs drove the venom into her flesh. She stumbled back, dropped the brush, and clutched her hand to her chest. The veins began to pulse red, and she watched in fascinated horror as the astral venom crawled slowly up her flesh.

Celie? What's going on?

One of the damned snakes bit me.

Tolly's aura flashed anxiously, then steadied. That famous Norwegian pragmatism came to the fore. *I'm coming. Stay very still.* Tolly's astral form appeared beside her, quelling Celeste's own incipient panic.

Her partner tied a tourniquet made of the blue satin ribbon from her hat around Celeste's forearm, above the glowing red road map of the venom.

Celeste's hand alternately burned and froze, like she was sticking it into a cooking fire and then plunging it into a winter pond. She tried to turn to look at Tolly but found her neck wouldn't move more than a centimeter and her heartbeat, thudding in her ears, slowed.

Tolly? I can't move my arm. My neck.

Tolly moved into view, but so slowly it might have been comical. *Loki's balls. Too slow.*

Exactly. Everything is slow.

No, I meant I was too slow with the tourniquet. Some of the poison must have gone farther up.

The words in Celeste's head distorted into strange sounds. She clenched the trowel in her right hand, the left side of her body now frozen and useless.

One cobra had disappeared with the strike, but the hieroglyphs on its body continued to whirl around, as though the snake was still there. The remaining cobra reared its head and flared its hood with a hiss. Celeste knew she had to cut off its head too. And since she'd already been bitten, the risk now was moot.

She focused on her own words, needing to communicate, and to understand Tolly's response. *Do you have another ribbon? Or something like it?*

Tolly's reply still sounded slow and garbled. *What are you thinking?*

That if you give me a tourniquet on my right arm, I can block the venom and finish what I started.

It could kill you!

It might be doing that already. I gave my word. I'm keeping it from now on. I promised you that.

Stubborn, foolish witch was Tolly's reply even as she ripped the sleeve from her blouse and tied it so tight around Celeste's arm, her hand began to grow numb.

Gripping the trowel, needing to move fast before she lost all feeling, she fixed her gaze on the snake as it swayed, hood flared in front of her.

I need power.

She couldn't see Tolly's expression. Had no way even to move her left leg outside of dragging it. Gathering the power Tolly provided, the aroma of apples and hay and horse flooded her. She embraced it, drew it in...then pushed it to the edge of the trowel's blade. Relying on will and her body weight, she flung herself toward the snake and slashed, counting on the creature to extend itself in a strike.

Powered by the energy, she timed the strike perfectly. The head of the snake parted ways with its undulating body and the slinky, black-scaled construct fell away, leaving only the glowing hieroglyphs behind as though printed on air, still writhing in the complicated pattern.

Celeste pitched forward and collapsed as well. Though no real ground existed on the astral, she nevertheless dropped to one knee. The other leg splayed out to the side, useless. Burning cold spread to her shoulder, into her collarbone, and down her side to her left leg as the poison trickled inexorably through her veins.

Her focus dissolved like morning mist. The astral plane faded.

Tolly knelt on the hard-packed earth beside her and took her hand. Cool blue light flooded into her, easing the pain and returning some control to Celeste's muscles. After a moment, she said, "I can't eliminate all of the venom, not without more time. But I have stopped the spread, and I collected it into your left arm."

Celeste flexed the bitten hand. Now back on the physical plane, she spoke aloud. "At least I can move it."

The fingers felt like they'd been frostbitten. The joints crunched when she opened and closed her hand. No pain, but no fluidity or fine motor control.

Tolly clambered to her feet and pulled Celeste up. "Can you stand on your own?"

"As long as I don't have to dance a jig." She steadied herself, adopted a wide stance to improve her balance. Her left leg was almost entirely numb. When she felt steady, she slid back onto the astral again. Tolly followed, and they both examined the remaining part of the binding spell.

Long strips of glowing hieroglyphs spun round and round, like symbols on ticker tape, with the glowing orb that was Guy still imprisoned inside the spherical construct. Tolly blew out a breath. *Thank Freya, at least the asps are gone. I half expected them to sprout additional heads.*

Thank Epona, actually. Celeste stared at the glowing figures as the strips of text sped through the complicated looping pattern. Now what?

Tolly pursed her lips. *Guy said something about words of power that night on the train. Maybe...what about names? Names are the most powerful words.*

Do you suppose Merimre knew Guy's name?

It's worth a try. She touched the tourniquet. *But we need to hurry.*

Celeste rolled her shoulders, flexed her hands. *I need more power. Give me a moment to center.*

While Tolly gathered power again, Celeste marshaled her own, pulling in non-specific energy through her feet from the earth below before directing her magical attention to the binding spell.

Guy's name was a long series of syllables, and she took the time to rehearse them in her head to get the pronunciation correct. When she could rattle off the name perfectly, she took three cleansing breaths.

I'm ready, Tolly announced.

On the physical plane, Celeste groped for Tolly's hand and twined their fingers together. *Me too. Let's get this done.* Before I collapse and pass out.

You know, when it is, we'll still have to deal with Merimre.

I know.

Do you have a plan for that?

Blast him with the power of Epona?

Blast him? Tolly laughed. *You sound like a novice.*

Power thrummed through Tolly's hand into hers. Her senses flooded with impressions, the salty taste of the desert sand, the cool, moist, pre-dawn air blowing across her skin, the fishy scent of the Nile. The element of fire remained muted, as the sun, the only nearby source of fire, was still hours from rising.

Could Tolly channel enough energy for Celeste to use in a frontal assault on Merimre's spirit? Doubtful. But it might be their only option.

Magical energy couldn't be stored, at least not for long. The human body, magical or no, made a poor battery. Pent-up energy demanded release, and Celeste's track record with control was notoriously inadequate.

Her whole body vibrated with the energy Tolly channeled to her.

Ready, my dove?

Yes. Celeste concentrated on the spiraling glyphs. It wasn't actually possible to speak aloud on the astral, but she could certainly use her voice on the physical.

She started by humming a neutral, mid-level tone. When she was certain she could both speak on the physical plane and maintain her focus on the astral, she directed her will on the binding spell, and slowly, exactingly, enunciated Guy's full name. "Hlwengiemorgawniff."

She pressed her lips shut, not uttering another sound. Watching. Waiting.

The hieroglyphs continued their circuit, unaffected. If the snakes had still been there, they'd have been mocking her with hisses.

She looked at Tolly.

Did you pronounce it correctly?

Yes. Well. I think I did.

Try again.

She did so, pouring power at the binding as she pronounced the name again.

Still, nothing happened. Although...was that a faint response from the binding? A sense of something yielding, then rising, like poking dough that bounced back.

We must be wrong, Celie.

No. I don't think so. I felt something shift, so we're on the right track. But there's something we're missing.

She thought back to all her interactions with Guy. How had he first introduced himself? He'd given his name. And then...Ah. His title.

Titles littered Egyptian inscriptions. Tut had half a dozen of them. So had Merimre. And Guy did as well.

She refocused on the binding spell, pulling in power, then started again, this time finishing with the titles Guy had rattled off. "Hlwengiemorgawniff, Huntaf Wasson of Mother Epona."

As she spoke the last word, the strips of glowing hieroglyphs exploded into a shower of signs and sparks before fluttering away like ashes in the wind.

The scent of apples, hay, and singed horsehair filled the air. The green, glowing sphere held captive in the center of the binding swelled and burst apart like a Guy Fawkes firework, sparks flaring and winking out as they fell to earth.

Celeste's concentration faltered, and she slammed back onto the physical plane, falling with a thud on her ass. Even as she hit the rocky sand, she sucked in power through Tolly and their surroundings. She couldn't reach Fire, but the breeze that presaged dawn ruffled her hair, so she reached for Air, coaxing it to her.

The imposing figure of Guy coalesced before her. Tall, regal, his long hair bound into a braid, those imperious green eyes burning with hauteur and fury.

Something else flitted around them in a widening circle. Oily and blue-black, it resembled the cloud of exhaust from a motor car.

Merimre

In a blink, the essence of the priest shot off into the darkness and for a brief moment, Celeste thought perhaps the spirit wouldn't come back.

Well, a girl could hope.

Guy reached down and pulled Celeste up and into his arms. "You did it, you delightful little witch! I'm free!"

An angry shout broke the celebratory moment.

A rumpled man staggered out of the tent next to the tomb. In a clipped British accent, he said, "Who are you people? And what in the bloody hell is going on out here?"

Celeste started forward then froze as the man, no doubt the estimable Howard Carter, aimed a pistol at them.

Tolly spoke up in her reasonable, cool fashion. "Our apologies, Mr. Carter. Please don't fire, we're just tourists. Our dragoman—"

A whirlwind of black smoke arrowed from the dark pit of stairs that led to the tomb straight toward Carter. He spun as the dark mist swirled around him, forcing itself into the archaeologist's nose and mouth. The fellow fell, jerking and spasming, booted heels pounding into the ground.

Tolly grabbed Celeste's arm and pulled her away. "Come! Now!"

Celeste balked, and not only because the poison still flooding her body impeded her progress. Tolly meant for them to leave Guy to fight alone. "No. We can't go. Not yet."

"Celie, you've freed him. You owe him nothing now."

Guy stood, feet apart, and Celeste felt him draw energy from the earth. "Your mate is right. This is my fight now."

Carter leapt to his feet, although it was no longer Carter in control. He raised his hands to the sky and uttered a command in ancient Egyptian before he lowered the muzzle of his pistol at Guy's chest and fired.

THIRTY-FIVE

L ight exploded.

The boom of the shot echoed like cannon fire in the Valley of the Kings.

When the smoke cleared, Guy was on his knees, a startled expression on his face. In the stillness, everyone stood frozen in tableau, like a scene at Madame Toussaud's Wax Museum. Time seemed to stop, except for the growing bloom of blood on Guy's shirt.

Celeste stumbled toward Guy, pushing past the stiffness of her poisoned muscles. As if to make things harder, the ground rumbled beneath her, loose stones rattling and grains of sand jumping like a million fleas.

Merimre's lips stretched into a wicked smile. Was he causing the shaking?

His voice held a different tenor now, lower than before, and the cadence more musical than Carter's blustery tone. "And now we'll deal with you." Shifting his aim, he fired again, not at Celeste, but at Tolly.

Another flash, another explosion. Then came a sound like the roar of a train, distant but growing. Celeste only had time to face her partner and shout the trigger word of the shield spell they'd prepared before the sandstorm Merimre had cast hit them.

The invisible barrier, a bubble about three feet in diameter, sprang up around Tolly just as the tsunami of wind-blown sand scoured them. It parted around and over the shield like a river around a rock. Inside, Tolly still stood, blue eyes wide in shock. Slowly, her brows drew down and Celeste saw her lips moving as those change-able eyes grew storm-gray and fierce.

The sandstorm hit Celeste like the train it sounded like, knocking her off her feet again. As the trembling intensified, the earth shook so much she expected a fault line to form beneath her. Had Merimre also released an Earth elemental?

The sem priest toppled over, his grin vanishing.

If he had called an elemental, it wasn't planned.

Guy crumpled onto his side, gasping guppy-like, clutching his chest. The ushabti, transparent as a ghost and unperturbed by either the sandstorm that raged or the quaking of the ground, appeared beside him, tears dripping down her cheeks as she cradled his head on her lap.

Celeste buried her face in the crook of her arm against the sand and tapped into the power of the gale. The storm was just that—Merimre hadn't endowed it with enough energy to elevate it to an elemental. Gathering the power to her, she flung it at the priest in a raw, uncontrolled burst.

The priest flew back, slamming into the flapping corners of the tent, ripping one side loose from its mooring stakes. The canvas collapsed around him, and he flailed like a drowning man to escape.

She struggled to her knees against the wind, and drew in more power, shaping it into a cannonball. She had no desire to kill Carter, and doing so would once again release Merimre's spirit, causing him to seek a new host body. It could very well be her or Tolly this time.

Tolly.

She risked a glance at her partner as the sandstorm ebbed.

Merimre had shot her, and she'd seen Tolly stagger back before the storm had hit full force, but she'd been on her feet just before the gale hit.

Thank the Goddess. Her beautiful partner still stood tall, arms raised in invocation. Her expression, however, wasn't dutiful or worshipful, but murderous. Her mouth moved, but the shield contained the sound.

Sand scoured Celeste's skin. She covered her face against the onslaught and crawled toward Carter's collapsed tent, trying to remember what Martin had written about exorcising and banishing a spirit.

Something heavy thudded into the sand a few feet away. Several somethings, accompanied by the smell of horse and hay and summer flowers. She shaded her eyes and peeked between her fingers.

The enormous hocks of a powerful white mare filled her vision, the animal stamping its hooves only a meter away. It whinnied, and a keening wail erupted from its rider, a raven-haired Amazon in a belted tunic, plaid pantaloons, and a long vest embroidered with flowers and animals. Brilliant golden light limned both rider and horse.

Epona. In all her glory.

The goddess raised her hand and Howard Carter's body rose, recumbent but twisting and flailing, into the air. A tortured scream tore from his lips, grating against Celeste's soul.

The wind died, like someone shut off an electric fan. The screaming did not. Celeste watched the black smoke roil out of Carter's mouth and nose. It formed the shape of a cobra. Lengthening itself in mid-air, it struck at the goddess.

Epona's mare reared up, its hooves striking the spirit snake.

Carter's body slammed into the ground.

The cobra solidified, dropped to the earth as well, and the horse fell upon it, trampling it under foot until nothing but black scales and a wet, red mess remained.

. . .

Celeste coughed and spat out sand. Her eyes burned, tears streamed down her cheeks, and she blinked away grit.

The pre-dawn air lay cool on skin scoured raw by the sand, like a balm. She felt her shield spell dissipate as its power ran out and she got to her knees to look for Tolly.

"I'm right here, *elskling*," came a voice at her side.

Celeste fell into Tolly's arms, and they knelt there, locked together for a time.

"He shot you. I worried I'd find you dead again," Celeste murmured into Tolly's ruined blouse.

Tolly pulled away, patted her chest over a tear in the fabric. With a grin, she reached under her clothes and pulled out a tin she'd tucked in her brassiere. The tin the lard had come in.

The bullet had struck it, deformed and dimpled it.

"We're lucky Carter didn't use a bigger caliber." Her eyes turned summer sky blue. "Planning, my dove. It's everything."

A gentle cough had them both standing to face Epona. Tolly bowed her head in gratitude. "My thanks, Lady, for heeding my prayer."

The goddess slid off her steed and nodded at Tolly. "I thank you for calling me." She crossed to Guy, who lay pale and unmoving, his head still in Berenice's lap.

She toed her recumbent servant's side. "Oh, get up, you dramatic idiot. You are not dead. A bullet cannot kill you."

Guy's mossy green eyes flickered open. "My lady." His voice sounded weak, breathy. "Your humble servant begs your forgiveness." He coughed wetly.

Epona grabbed the front of Guy's blood-soaked shirt and yanked him to his feet. With her other hand, she slapped him on the back and something small and hard zinged onto the rocky sand.

The bullet.

Guy yelped in pain and drew in a deep breath, followed by a bit more coughing.

Epona rolled her eyes heavenward. "Where have you been, you lazy, insolent boy? I sent you here eons ago to fetch the princess and her magic tonic." She smacked him on the back of his head.

"Thank you, Lady, for removing the bullet," he said, talking fast. "It was most kind and generous of you. As you are, always." The speech started ingratiatingly yet retained a note of smirking insouciance that surprised Celeste. She would never speak to Brigid that way, were she ever given the chance.

The goddess took him by the shoulders, gave him a little shake, then patted his cheek like a fond but exasperated mother. "You silly boy. I don't know why I put up with you. Now," she said, turning to Celeste and Tolly. "You are uninjured?"

Celeste brushed off her tattered outfit and addressed the goddess with as much dignity as she could muster. "Except for the poison, yes."

Epona touched her hand, and Celeste felt a coolness wash through her. The burning pain vanished, the stiffness eased, and the red glow faded away. After a moment, the goddess removed the tourniquets. "Good idea, this. Saved your life."

Celeste shot Tolly a grateful look. "She's full of good ideas."

Epona nodded at Tolly. "And you? You are also unhurt?"

Tolly put her arm around Celeste. "We're fine now, thank you. But Mr. Carter is most assuredly not." She gestured at the still form of the Egyptologist lying amid the ruin of his tent like a broken doll.

"Ah. Yes. The evil one evicted his spirit when he took control."

Tolly raised her chin. "We have no right to ask, but the man was an innocent in all this. Please, Lady, would you deign to save him and rejoin his spirit with his earthly form?"

Epona waved a hand in a negligent fashion. "There is no need to ask or for me to acquiesce. His spirit lingered, driven by an unusually strong will to complete his mission here. I will merely assist in the reintegration..." She gave a nod at Carter. "Behold, already he recovers."

Carter moaned, shifted.

Epona continued. "He'll have a monstrous headache when he wakes, and no doubt suffer aches and pains. But he will live to see his work here finished."

Tolly bowed, poked Celeste to do the same. "Thank you."

Epona pinched Guy's ear. "You have some explaining to do, foolish servant. Let us go home."

Guy dug his feet in, literally. "Yes, of course, Lady, but I would bring this creature with me." He took Berenice's hand.

Epona looked the ushabti spirit up and down. "Nay, boy. Her place is here, with her king. Put her representation back into the tomb so she may join him in Amenti. And while you're down there, fetch what I sent you for to begin with."

"But—"

"Hlwengiemorgawniff, she is not a toy for you to play with. Return her to the place she belongs."

Guy consulted the ushabti. "This is what you desire?"

Berenice smiled and, standing on tiptoes, bussed Guy's cheek. "Please. And thank you." She ducked her head as she turned to Celeste and Tolly. "Thank all of you. The great lord will know of your kindness."

Celeste frowned at Tolly, who gave her a fond smile. This enforced servitude rankled against what Tolly would call her suffragette sensibilities. But if it was what the creature wished, she could hardly argue. Everyone had the right to free will.

Berenice dissolved into smoke and the figurine she had once been dropped into the sand with a plop.

"As you wish." Guy snatched up the ushabti, and with a snap of his fingers, vanished.

Moments later, the servant of Epona reappeared at the bottom of the stone steps of the tomb and labored up toward them, holding his chest as though his wound bothered him. Fishing for sympathy. When he reached his mistress, he held up a small, stoppered glass vial with the image of a kneeling Isis, golden wings spread wide, on it.

Epona peered at it but didn't take it. "Yes. That's it. The elixir." Not touching the vial, the goddess mounted her mare. "Give it to them." She gestured at Celeste and Tolly. "They will safe-keep it. The world has changed, and we are no longer the ones to hold that responsibility. Come along now."

Guy nodded and pressed the little bottle into Celeste's hand. "I cannot think of two better caretakers."

He swept them an elegant bow and then abruptly pulled Celeste into an embrace and kissed her thoroughly. With tongue. Almost as cheeky as Byron. "Ladies, it has been a pleasure. I owe you my freedom. I hope one day we will meet again."

Celeste staggered back as he released her. Before she could form a reply, Guy transformed into a roan stallion and, following his mistress, galloped westward toward the Land of the Dead, away from the glow of dawn.

"Impudent creature. How dare he kiss you like that?"

Celeste laughed. "Are you jealous?"

"Certainly not. You have better taste. And I am a better kisser."

From the ruins of the tent, Carter groaned again.

Tolly took Celeste's hand. "We should go too, before he fully awakens."

Dazed, still trying to process what had happened, Celeste let Tolly lead her down the path—for once, in the correct direction. "We're sure Merimre is gone?"

"Yes. Epona saw to that."

"And what do we do with this?" She held up the delicate little vial.

"We give that to Alistair," her partner said firmly. "Let him lock it away in the vault."

"So the Council can use it? We don't even know what it does."

Tolly frowned. "The vault is the safest place. Whether the Council gets its hands on it or not will depend on my son's good judgment."

While Celeste liked Alistair, and had even come to respect him, she didn't have the faith in him that Tolly did. He was, after all, a high-ranking member of the Council.

But sufficient unto the day was the evil thereof. They'd deal with Alistair and the fate of the vial when the time came. She tried to brush sand from the bodice of her dress. "I want a bath."

Tolly brought Celeste's hand to her lips. "As do I. And breakfast. With coffee."

"Loads of coffee. Bathtubs of coffee." She imagined the two of them, naked in a fragrant bath, sipping coffee and feeding each other pastry.

"Oh, Celie, is pastry all you ever think about?"

Celeste let the scenario in her head continue to the activities that came after the eating of pastry. "No. Not all."

THIRTY-SIX

The warm lights from the crystal chandeliers in the lobby of Winter Palace might have been the sparkling sunbeams of the Summerland, so enticing were they. Celeste and Tolly dragged themselves through the front doors and approached the desk. The small moue of disapproval, the wrinkling of the nose and the raised eyebrows of the desk clerk told Celeste how disreputable they looked.

Tolly straightened her shoulders and looked down her nose at the slight, middle-aged Egyptian. Radiating an aura of irreproachability that Celeste could never match, Tolly tapped her fingernail on the highly polished wood of the counter. "We are checking in. The last name is Tollefsen. We've been through a dreadful ordeal getting here. This country is full of shameless criminals who take advantage of women travelers, and I demand a hot bath and a meal immediately."

Celeste knew her part. She let her lip quiver and tears form in her eyes. They weren't even crocodile tears, she was exhausted, both physically and emotionally, and the idea of a comfortable room and real food made her want to weep. "Please. If you would be so kind.

We were waylaid by bounders on our trip from Cairo and trekked through the desert for days to get here."

The clerk looked both terrified by Tolly's hauteur and appalled at the implied story. He grabbed a book that presumably held reservation information, flipped pages, glancing up at Tolly as he searched the oversized tome. "Ah, yes, Tollefsen. You were to have arrived several days ago. I'm afraid—"

"If you tell me you have given away our reservation, I shall—"

"No!" The clerk ran nervous fingers through his oiled, black hair. "No, madame, of course not. I, uh, I'll just go find the manager so that we can make sure your rooms are ready." Which meant they had given away their rooms. Of course they had. But the clerk, knowing that aggravating an apparently wealthy aristocratic tourist, which is what Tolly appeared to be, meant he had to make it right in order to keep his job. "Please wait here, I will be right back."

He scurried off and Tolly sagged against the counter. Celeste put an arm around her. "You laid on the command aura a bit heavy."

"It had to work the first time. I have very little magical energy left." A thin smile curved her pale, cracked lips. "Besides. It felt good."

Celeste rested her head against Tolly's shoulder. "You're damn good at it. You probably didn't even have to magic him."

"I didn't even have to break one of the Rules. He wanted to help us. I just encouraged his normal inclinations."

Celeste chuckled. "I love it when you're sneaky."

Tolly raised her chin. "I am not sneaky. I am clever."

As they waited, they heard the staff scurrying and chattering behind the scenes, readying for their day dealing with pushy European tourists. Outside, the sky blushed in pinks and corals, and waiters in the dining room clinked and rumbled, preparing breakfast for guests leaving for early excursions to the Valley of the Kings.

Only fifteen minutes later they were escorted up to a suite of rooms on the fourth floor. As the bellhop ushered them in, he bowed and said, "I have had your luggage brought here. It arrived on the train many days ago and I made sure that it was stored for you."

Luggage. Fresh clothes. Toiletries. Mana from heaven.

Tolly pressed a few coins into the young man's hand. It was unlikely he, personally, had made sure their luggage hadn't been discarded or sold off, but neither of them cared. "Thank you. What time will breakfast be served?"

"Seven o'clock, Madame." He flashed a brilliant smile. "I am Daoud. My cousin, Sayyid, works in the dining room. I will have him save for you a wonderful table."

Celeste exchanged a knowing glance with Tolly. This act would require another generous tip, no doubt. Still, these people had to make money somehow and Celeste thought the expense worth it. It was about time they actually got to enjoy themselves.

Tolly returned the young man's smile. "Thank you, Daoud. That would be very nice." She gestured at the door and encouraged him out.

"Seven o'clock? That's only...two hours from now." She collapsed onto the divan. "I want a bath and then a nap."

"The bath you can have. But there can be no dillydallying if you want a lie-down. We have many things to do before this day is over."

"What more needs to be done? We stopped an evil undead priest from taking over Egypt, freed Guy from bondage, saved Berenice, and got justice for Aubrey. What more can you possibly want?"

"For starters, we have to save your pet vampire's pack mate from death at the hands of a sphinx. Even if that worm of a sociopath wasn't involved, I do not renege on promises made to creatures who can track me down and kill me."

Celeste groaned. She'd forgotten about Desmond and the sphinx. "Can't it wait until tomorrow?"

"Starting our lessons with him can. But we need to contact him."

She plopped down on the divan next to Celeste. "Second, we need to find out what happened to Detective Sergeant Ibrahim. Perhaps contribute to his family. Burial costs are likely not any cheaper here than anywhere else."

It shocked Celeste to realize she'd forgotten about Ibrahim as well. She shifted and rested her head on Tolly's shoulder, blinking back sudden tears. "Damn."

"Indeed." Tolly settled back with a sigh. "Finally, we need to contact Alistair and let him know everything that's happened."

"He's going to be pissed."

"Likely. But like you, I don't trust the Honorable Mr. Smythe, and someone needs to know about Aubry."

"That sounds exhausting."

"Best get it done. The sooner we can settle things here, the sooner we can catch a train to Cairo and book passage home."

Home. Oh yes, home sounded wonderful. She didn't think she ever wanted to leave again.

After a moment, Tolly pushed herself to her feet and reached for Celeste's hand. "Come along, *elskling*. Time for that bath."

Morning sun poured through the windows of the hotel dining room and glittered on the silver place settings and crystal stemware as they came down for breakfast the next day.

Tolly wore a lilac lawn day dress. A bit outdated, but it suited her tall, slender frame, and the color brought out violet highlights in her eyes and complimented her honey blonde hair. Celeste had thrown on a wrinkled blue cotton sundress and refused all entreaties to find something better. The dress was comfortable and cool and other than brushing out her short curls, Celeste had no desire to fuss further.

The crowd in the dining room had thinned. They had both over-slept their nap, and it was nearly nine by the time they'd made it downstairs. Most of the tourists had already left for their day trips, though three sets of couples occupied separate tables at some distance from them, and a small group gathered at another of the "good" tables, which meant by the windows.

The middle-aged, well-built gentleman of that group wore what in Egypt had to be called "working clothes," a pair of khaki trousers and a white shirt, quintessential archaeologist's garb. A woman of the same middle age sat beside him, and to Tolly's clear dismay, was similarly attired, with a short canvas skirt and a tool belt that jangled every time the woman moved. With them sat a younger couple, a fellow so dark in complexion he could have been an Egyptian and a girl with the loveliest red-gold hair Celeste had ever seen. Celeste watched their dynamic in fascination. The older gentleman was loud to the point of being bombastic, complaining vociferously about someone named Lacau. His wife let him carry on for a bit, then silenced him with a comment. At this, the younger couple exchanged amused looks. Clearly, this was not a novel occurrence.

The waiter approached, interrupting Celeste's people-watching. The young man introduced himself as Sayyid, Daoud's cousin, and flashed a smile as bright and shiny as the flatware. "A very good morning to you, ladies," he announced in delightfully accented English. "I have many specials this morning. You will find many delicious dishes. We even have the kippers. Would you care to start with tea?"

Tolly sent him away with their order of coffee and croissants and absolutely no kippers. Celeste tucked in as soon as the food arrived, even going so far as to order a rasher of bacon, a predilection she'd picked up during her decades in London. Tolly gave her an indulgent smile.

Celeste had just poured a second cup when a rumpled man burst through the doors to the dining room and hurried to the table occupied by the archaeologist and his family.

The older woman stood as her husband belted out, "What the devil, Carter!"

"Calm yourself, dear. Howard, what's happened?"

Howard Carter, looking much as he had the night before, flopped into a chair. "I swear to you, someone was at the tomb last night. I had the strangest dream where I became possessed by some evil spirit and I shot a woman, and when I awoke, I was sprawled outside my tent, covered in sand. There were tracks all around the tomb entrance." He ran a hand over his face.

"Did they get through the locks on the gate? Was anything taken?" the loud archaeologist demanded.

Carter shook his head. "I don't believe so. The chains were still in place and the door locked. But I swear someone had been there. Given the number of footprints, I can't believe I slept through it."

The older woman patted Carter's hand. "It's a lucky thing you weren't injured. You're sure it wasn't just part of the dream?"

Their voices dropped and Celeste grinned at Tolly. "What an interesting dream Mr. Carter had."

Tolly laughed, the first genuine expression of joy Celeste had seen in her since New Year's Eve. The outburst drew stares from others in the quiet dining room. Not caring who was watching, Celeste bussed Tolly's cheek.

"Celeste!"

"Let them be scandalized. We leave in a few days, anyway." She pointed to the English language newspaper Tolly leafed through. "Anything interesting?"

"Just the usual governmental woes. Zaghlul is causing trouble."

"At least he's just a mortal rebel. Merimre would have been so much worse. I still think the Council should give us some kind of medal."

Tolly, still engrossed in the newspaper, sucked in a breath.

"What?"

Tolly took a moment to finish reading whatever had caught her attention before quoting, "Egyptian police detective Rami Ibrahim, found shot three times on the street three days ago, is now reported to be in stable condition at Luxor Hospital. No new leads have been generated regarding the culprits responsible for the shooting, but the Commissioner of Police says the case is still active and open."

"He's alive! Oh, thank Brigid!"

"Thank Brigid and Freya, both." Tolly's blue eyes grew misty. "We must go see him before we leave Luxor."

Celeste stuffed the last piece of bacon in her mouth and nodded in agreement. "Do you think he'll get his job back?"

She heard the dreaded "pop", and the air shimmered just behind Tolly's head. Pyp appeared, dressed in a paisley satin smoking jacket, a navy ascot and a pipe dangling from the corner of his mouth. Celeste nearly spit her coffee. "Good gad. Where on earth did you find that get up?"

His face lit up, and he tucked his thumbs behind the black lapels and puffed out his chest. "It's wizard, ain't it?"

Wizard. Magical quarter slang for excellent. She and Byron really needed to talk when they got home. She shook her head but didn't have the heart to tell him how ridiculous he looked. He was so proud of himself. "It's certainly striking. I assume you're here with another missive from Byron?"

"Why else? His nibs is in a right snit, you know. Practically frothing at the mouth. Wearin' a hole in the carpet pacing. Throwing things. The demon what works for Stone Face glares daggers at the both of us constantly."

Pyp's sudden appearance had caused a bit of a stir. No one had seen him enter, of course, and his choice of clothing caught everyone's attention. Even Howard Carter's friends were staring.

Tolly stood and set her serviette on the table. "For pity's sake. Let us take this conversation elsewhere. Now."

As they left the dining room, all Celeste could think was that at least they'd been breakfasting instead of engaged in some other, more private activity.

Pyp dropped onto the divan in their sitting room, draped an arm over the back, and crossed his ankles in a perfect imitation of Byron. This time, he didn't even pretend to read the letter he no doubt had in his possession. He just began speaking as though he were the poet himself, his gaze drifting out the window in studied ennui.

"My dear Celeste,"

he drawled in a long-suffering manner.

"You have been gone far too long. Martin is still away most evenings to attend to certain Fallen business as penance for his saving your darling Tolly's life, I am languishing alone in this coffin-sized apartment too small for even a family of mice with the ever-present and odious Faulkner, and Desmond has not sent a telegram in days. I insist you come home immediately."

Tolly snorted. "Insist, does he? He's lucky I don't report him to the Council."

Celeste shot her partner a look. "You wouldn't."

Tolly pressed her lips together, then threw her hands in the air. "I'm going to fix my hair. Make sure this young man is gone when I return."

Pyp, as himself, grinned. "Tolly and Byron must be in love, the way they insult each other. In Shakespeare—"

She raised a hand to squelch a lecture and stared in wonderment. Byron had Pyp reading the Bard? He must really care for the lad. "I don't think I'd use the verb "love". In any case, would you just give me a summary of Byron's complaints? Is there any meat to this missive?"

"Well, he's lonely, ain't—isn't he? Especially with Desmond out of touch. Much as the two of them shout at one another like fish-wives, snotty mean company is better'n none."

She had forgotten about Desmond again. "Desmond will be coming home soon. While he's currently occupied, he should be free to sail home in a few days."

"What's he doing here?"

"A very good question, but as I have no interest in his affairs, I will likely never know. Is that all?"

"Not quite." He resumed his Byron impression.

"Alistair is in quite the temper. He can't get hold of you either and while he senses that you are alive, he's furious you won't respond to his many messages. I share his sentiments. Quite rude. Says that as soon as I have word from you (I had to tell him about Pyp - thought the old boy was going to blow a gasket, as Desmond might say), I'm to tell you that you are to return to Paris immediately because there is some odd goings on in Brittany - two old women have apparently come down with a mysterious magical illness - and he wants old pinch face's help in researching a treatment."

"A magical illness?" Those were rare. And the fear of the plague returning, despite it having been stamped out centuries earlier, always remained. Still, she wouldn't question Pyp about it. No point in starting a panic. Besides, Alistair would never have said anything to Byron if it were the plague.

Pyp shrugged. "Probably nothing. His nibs says some witch probably cursed another one and gave her magical boils."

Celeste blew a breath out her nose. Her oldest friend could be a right arse. "Anything else?"

Pyp slumped out of his Byronic pose. "That's it. But you better reply, or I may be looking for a new job."

Celeste found a piece of stationery in the little secretary and scribbled a quick note, telling Byron they'd be here in Luxor three more days, then sailing home from Alexandria at the end of the week. And to tell Alistair the same. Further, if he learned any additional information about the illness, to send a telegram to Cairo and they'd pick it up en route. She added a few placating words, told him Desmond was in Egypt on some undisclosed errand but would also be home soon, and that what Byron needed to do was find a way to make friends with Faulkner, because if he and Martin were going to stay together, that would be a necessity. She signed off with Your older and wiser friend, Celeste.

Folding the paper, she handed it to Pyp. "No need to come back. Tell his nibs we'll be home soon enough. Got it?"

Pyp laughed. "I can tell 'im but can't guarantee he'll listen." He stood and gestured toward the closed bedroom door. "She okay? Byron said her old husband died."

Aubrey. There'd be no getting his body back to return it to Scotland for a proper burial or cremation, not in this climate. Still, she'd need to arrange something once they got home. He needed a proper ritual, even though he'd already made his crossing. "Give me that back for a minute."

Scribbling a postscript at the bottom of the page, she gave Byron a few instructions, things he could arrange in their absence, so even without Aubrey's physical form, she could give Tolly more closure. And for Alistair as well. Alistair, who didn't even know about Aubrey's death. She cautioned Byron to secrecy, then added a few more ideas.

"There. I guess if he has questions, you can pop back over." She glanced at the bedroom door, too. "And yes, she'll be alright, in time. It's sweet of you to think of her."

Pyp's energy ebbed a bit and his natural joie de vivre faded. "I had a brother once. Not blood kin, but close as. He came over with me. Didn't make it past the first year. All I had was this gimpy leg, but he had something wrong inside him." The boy wouldn't cry, or at least not in front of Celeste, but he came close. "I held him while he died. I was there for him. I hope her husband had someone with him."

Celeste bit her lip. "You are a good friend, Pyp. A good brother." She laid her hand on his cheek. "I'm proud to know you."

He allowed the touch for a moment, then tucked the letter in his smoking jacket and when he looked up, the bright, saucy glint in his eye was back. "You'd best not dawdle coming home. I can only control his nibs so long."

His laughter rang in the air even after he disappeared.

THIRTY-SEVEN

4 February 1923
Rue de Belleville, 19th Arrondissement, Paris

Celeste couldn't decide which part of their Egyptian adventure had been worse. In the retelling to Byron, and the debriefing with Alistair, she waffled between the three days they spent being grilled by the sphinx, during which she regurgitated more knowledge from her Council training than she thought she'd internalized, and the ten dreadful days spent at sea, regurgitating not information but every damn thing she put in her mouth, including the stupid ginger chews Tolly kept force feeding her.

At least the sphinx had been entertaining in a self-aggrandizing and arrogant fashion. Having been close friends with Byron for the better part of a century, she knew how to deal with that. In the end, they'd actually learned a few tricks from it, most of which they'd even shared with Alistair. Most. Celeste kept a couple of spells to herself. You never knew when you'd need something tucked up your sleeve in their line of work.

Two weeks after their return, late in the afternoon on a freakishly bitter-cold day, Madame Fournier's baby decided to arrive. It was Celeste's turn for midwifery, so she bundled up in coat, scarf, hat, and mittens, and quick-stepped it into the heart of the magical quarter. Sometime after midnight, following a great deal of sweating, screaming, and blood, tiny little Vincent Fournier entered the world, healthy, happy, and emitting tiny blips of magic. She recorded his name, birth date, and the color of his aura in her notebook for Council records, and after donning her winter wear again, headed back out into negative temperatures.

The streets in the center of the quarter bustled, but as she neared their home on the outskirts, a hush settled over the gas-lit streets.

Her scalp rippled. Darker, she thought, than it ought to have been. Flinging up a ward from a charm on her recently recharged bracelet, she detected an oily aura, and the scent of loam and pine tickled her nostrils despite the muffling of her scarf.

A shadow stepped out from a doorway just in front of her, pulsing with the red aura of a vampire. She stopped, heart thudding. It was not Byron.

Hair the color of summer straw and silky as corn tassels peeked out from under a natty bowler hat that in no way kept the fellow's ears from frostbite, and his lips parted in a charming forgery of a smile. "Celeste, my dear, I'm so glad I ran into you."

"Desmond. What do you want?" She answered him in the English he'd addressed her in.

"Want? Why, I desire many things. Are you feeling obliging tonight? We could start with you accompanying me home where you'll let me have my wicked way with you and end with you sharing that lovely elixir in your veins."

"No." She didn't meet his eyes, her gaze fixed over his left shoulder. "You've clearly been waiting for me. Why?"

"Is it too much to think I might sway you? I cannot fathom what you see in our errant poet. I'm a far more dapper gent and I'm the bally son of an earl. I hardly ever drink myself into dissipation. Not to mention the old boy's gone to seed. Always did carry a bit too much weight and now he's positively pudgy. I say, Celeste, what does he have that I don't?"

His smart set patois grated on her nerves. She crossed her arms over her chest, a trick given how bundled up she was, doing her best to radiate power and confidence. "A conscience."

Desmond snorted. "So you believe." He turned to face the direction she traveled in and crooked his arm. "Allow me to escort you safely home."

Refusing his arm, she continued forward, brushing past him and forcing him to follow. Home, yes. The sooner she got there, the safer she'd be.

"I will admit, the longer I know you, the more impressed I am. Your performance in Egypt was nothing short of brilliant. All that fire, passion and power. I do adore a feisty girl." He pronounced girl like 'gell', annoying her further. Which was his goal. He was baiting her.

She debated increasing her pace but was afraid it would look like fear. Never run from a predator. They only chase you. She bit back a snide remark, refusing to engage with him.

"You know, you'd make the most amazing familiar. Only think how much your powers would increase. I don't think there's ever been a witch familiar before. We'd be bloody unstoppable."

She had to respond to that. "No."

"So you're saving yourself for that pederast?"

"No."

When he reached for her elbow, the action set off her ward and he jumped back with a yelp. "You little witch!"

She smiled like Little Red Riding Hood's grandmother. "I wouldn't do that again if I were you."

He stopped. "Can you please just give me one moment of your attention?"

She turned to face him. "I'm listening."

He clenched his jaw. Adjusted his fur-collared ulster coat. Shoved his gloveless hands in the pockets. "I just wanted to say, er, thank you. You didn't have to do what you did. I imagine you'd have preferred to leave me there under the sands of that benighted country." He wound down, looked away, and shivered, more likely from memory than the cold.

"I didn't do it for you. I did it for Byron."

He cleared his throat. "Regardless, I thank you. And I am duty-bound to say that I am now in your debt."

Why didn't that make her feel good? She didn't want any business with this creature, no matter who was on the receiving end. She stared over his shoulder. "You're welcome. But you owe me nothing."

"Ah, that's where you're wrong, my girl. I have a great many stellar traits, but I value my honor above all. Should you ever need my help, it is yours." His snake-like smile returned. "Despite your fondness for my ersatz brother."

He gestured with his chin up the street. "I am happy to escort you the rest of the way home."

It would be a favor then. Accepting his offer, she'd discharge the debt. Tempting to do so now, but who knew when the help of a vampire would come in handy? "It's not far." Don't even say thank you. That might acknowledge he'd done something. Why were vampires so damn cagey?

He shrugged. "Well, I'm off then. I leave you to your chilly walk." Another crocodile smile. "Toodles."

He shot upward, black upon black, and disappeared before she could blink.

Exhausted by the exchange, not to mention the birthing, she hurried home, hoping to Brigid she'd never have to call in that favor, no matter what the future held.

———

The story continues in That Old Plague of Mine.
Keep reading for a preview!

That Old Plague of Mine: Chapter 1

Celeste Berenger sat at a small bistro table on the patio of the Cafe de Marronniers in the Tuileries Gardens, inhaling the intoxicating scent of spring in Paris while she waited for her companion and host to join her. The offer of lunch here, in one of her favorite spots in Paris, had been an excellent bribe. Corverus, the sneaky bastard, had done his research. From whom he'd received his intelligence, she didn't know but would make it a point to find out.

He arrived too soon, long before she'd had her fill of the soothing ambience of the place. She'd promised herself a lovely ramble through the gardens after enduring the requisite hour with the odious warlock, plus a short trip to the Louvre as it was Sunday and therefore free.

Corverus, better known in the mortal world as Doctor Alexandru Petrescu, dressed in mundane street clothes instead of the ancient mantle and suit he garbed himself in when at home in the Magical Quarter. The navy, double-breasted jacket and sharply creased pants had a red pinstripe in them, accentuated by the deep red tie that dripped down his starched white shirt and into his waistcoat.

With his dark, slicked back hair, and lean features, she imagined most women found him handsome. The Romanian accent, which she had reason to know was not manufactured, probably also made him charming and exotic. But the only man Celeste had ever found even remotely desirable in a romantic fashion was her old friend Lord Byron, and it would take more charm than even that infamous lothario possessed to convince Celeste to lie with a man.

If her partner in both business and all other things, the lovely and elegant Astrid 'Tolly' Tollefsen, had been here, she'd have scolded Celeste mentally to pay attention and be polite—no matter that Celeste despised the warlock who now bent over her hand and pressed his wet lips against her skin. Goosebumps of revulsion prickled her arms.

"My dear Celeste. Thank you for meeting me on such short notice. You look lovely, as always."

The once over he gave her wasn't quite a leer, but it still made her squirm. The idea that he would have his hands all over her in a little over two weeks' time, on Beltane Eve, as part of the Great Rite, soured her stomach and made her sweat.

He sat, either oblivious or uncaring. After motioning to a waiter, he said, "I hear the salmon here is excellent."

The thought of eating anything now repelled her. "I'm not really hungry."

"Nonsense. I know of your penchant for delectable food."

Pastry. I like pastry, you arrogant jackanape. His intelligence source had gotten that wrong.

The waiter brought menus, but Corverus handed them back. "We'll have the salmon and a bottle of Pouilly-Fuisse."

Her face heated, and she clenched her fists. Making eye contact with the waiter, she ground out, "I will have the mushroom tarte and a cup of coffee, thank you."

The waiter looked from her to Corverus, who nodded. She

wanted to wipe the indulgent smile he produced. "Very well. The salmon for me and the tarte for the lady." He turned the smile on her. "But I insist you join me in a glass of wine. At least a sip for a toast to our impending joining."

If she'd had breakfast, it would have made a reappearance. Instead, bile rose in her throat. While she mastered the burning sensation, Corverus chattered on. He could not be ignorant of how she felt. He had magical senses too, after all. Clearly, he chose to ignore her feelings.

"I will, of course, be wearing my Count's sash, with my medals and orders. The sash is a deep burgundy. Do you have a gown in this color? If not, I will arrange for a seamstress to stop by and make one for you."

Jets of steam should be spraying from her head, like in all those political cartoons with furious heads of state during the talks in Versailles after the war. "We are not being wed, Magister. You've blackmailed me into this despicable charade of a pairing. I have agreed to it because I have no choice. But do not for one minute think I will be doing anything special or acknowledging it in any way. I'll show up. That's it."

He made a moue of disappointment. "I do not think it is too much to ask that you present yourself with some decorum."

Which made her want to come dressed in rags smeared with filth. She wouldn't. Tolly wouldn't let her disrespect the ceremony in such a way. But she refused to honor him by dolling herself up for his salacious entertainment. The dress would be coming off in short order in any case. Unless he just wanted to lift her skirts and gain access to her womb without all the fuss. In fact, that might be best. The less contact he had with her body, the better.

The waiter brought the coffee and the wine, and she didn't even bother to stir cream and sugar into her cup before taking a gulp. The flavor was bold and stimulating, exactly what she needed to weather this conversation. Thank whichever goddess was in charge of coffee beans. "Don't worry about my dress. It will be appropriate." Another sip. "Is that all you wanted of me? I have a busy afternoon."

He leaned across the table and laid a cool hand on her wrist, pinning her arm in place. She could yank it back if she needed to, but not without risking knocking over her cup or causing a scene. The protective warning charm on her bracelet grew a little warm, signaling danger from someone or something around and she had the unmistakable sense that someone was watching her. Someone other than Corverus.

The danger, of course, came from her lunch companion. The sense of being watched could be easily explained as well. She'd hired the young changeling Pyp to keep watch over her during her meeting. If anything went awry, he was supposed to run back to Tolly and let her know. She didn't really believe Corverus would harm her or even kidnap her. After all, he was getting his way. But she didn't trust him in the slightest and he was a wolf when it came to women, so she'd made sure she hadn't come alone. After last fall, and the fiasco following Eddie the gargoyle's kidnapping, she'd vowed to be prepared.

Smiling pleasantly, she leaned forward too and spoke through her teeth. "If you don't let go of my arm, I'll kick you in the crotch so hard you'll be walking funny into next week."

He didn't release her and replied in a terse whisper. "And I'll tell you why you won't." He kept his head still but shifted his eyes to the bench on their right, just beyond the patio. A woman sat there in a drop-waist pink dress with white trim with a matching frilly parasol sitting beside her. She appeared to be absorbed in the book resting in her lap but glanced up and met Celeste's eyes before returning her attention to whatever she was reading.

Lizbet Montgomery. A leading member of the Witch's Council and a woman whose greatest desire in life was finding cause to remove Celeste's powers or see her drowned in a sack in the middle of the nearest river.

Celeste forced herself to relax and lean back in her chair, but her throat had closed, and her heart hammered in her chest.

Corverus followed suit after gently patting her hand. "What time should I send the seamstress, my dear?"

She swallowed, fixed the smile back on her face. "We close the shop after nine."

"Excellent. I'll make the arrangements after lunch. Unless you'd like to stroll with me through the gardens?"

"Thank you, no. I do honestly have things to do." That those things were strolling through the gardens and visiting her favorite paintings, he didn't need to know.

The waiter brought their food, and she picked at her tarte, wishing she could take it home for later. When he raised his glass to toast their impending sexual union and the progeny that was the goal of such a pairing, she followed suit and hoped against hope that she turned out to be infertile. Or that he was. The thought of carrying his child filled her with loathing. Actually, that applied to the notion of carrying any man's child.

He chattered on, filling the silence, telling her of his excitement in planning a post-ceremony trip for them to his home village of Arefu in Romania, a thing she determined to squirm out of.

"You will love it there. Very quaint by modern standards, but full of color. Many people still dress in traditional costumes and perform the old dances. And, oh, the music! Some of my relatives sing and play the flute and violin. I am anxious for you to meet them. One of my cousins is like your friend Byron. He comes from a very prestigious Family and can trace his lineage back to our most famous strigoi."

He winked, expecting her to get the joke. She didn't.

"Our national hero? Vlad Țepeș?"

"I'm sorry. I really don't know much about Romania."

She could see genuine disappointment in his eyes. "Vlad Dracul? The inspiration for Mr. Stoker's novel 'Dracula'?"

Now it clicked. "I had no idea that he was a real person."

Corverus' smile shifted, becoming sly. "Oh, he is real. Very real."

Is? Her eyebrows rose. "I see."

"Perhaps you will even meet him." He finished off his wine. "But that is for summer. Now, we must focus on Beltane."

Ever aware of Lizbet Montgomery's presence not ten yards away, Celeste tried to remain pleasant, or at least neutral, for the rest of the meal while suppressing the urge to run screaming down to the Seine and throw herself in to wash off the whole lurid affair. The pong of the filthy river had to be better than Eau de Sleazy Warlock.

At long last, Corverus rose, a bit unsteady after polishing off nearly a whole bottle of wine solo and offered to escort her home.

She declined, saying she had errands to run for Tolly while she was in the heart of the city, envisioning herself at the bookstore Tolly liked in order to pick up a stack of tomes, and visiting a butcher for a rabbit for supper. She couldn't feel any attempt by him or even Lizbet to sense her thoughts, but better to create the mental image of her alleged itinerary just in case.

Finally, he swayed off, not quite staggering, and she spent a few minutes pushing around flakes of pastry from the barely touched tarte and finishing her coffee. A crowd of tourists came along the path, obscuring Lizbet, and by the time they had sorted themselves out and moved along, the woman had vanished, book, parasol, and all.

She waited even longer before making her own departure. As she headed toward her favorite section of the gardens, Pyp appeared beside her, footfalls silent as a wraith.

"Your date's a creep."

"Yes, he is."

"I thought you were with Tolly."

Her smile now was genuine. "I am. This is...a business arrangement."

"Ah. And you can't trust him, eh?"

"Exactly."

She paused, pulled a couple of centimes from her purse and placed them in his hand. "Thanks, Pyp. Don't spend it all at the Gateau Magique."

Grinning, he gave her a salute. "Always at your service. You know where to find me." With a wave, he bounced happily away. Gods, to have the energy and optimism of youth again.

Relaxing her shoulders, she tried to soothe herself in the beauty of the gardens, but like a cloud covering the sun, the feeling of being watched lingered. Scanning the area, she could sense no other witches in the area. Either she was still spooked by the presence of Lizbet Montgomery, or she was imagining things. After about ten minutes, she gave up and headed toward the Louvre.

———

The Mona Lisa usually inspired both wonder and curiosity in Celeste. Such a small painting but so evocative, and she couldn't help wondering who the woman had been and what she'd meant to da Vinci. Perhaps just another commission, but the romantic in her wanted her to have played an important role in his life. A lover, perhaps, or even a dear friend.

It occurred to her she now possibly had a means to find out. Martin, Byron's current *amant*, had known da Vinci and in fact had been there when the great man died. She could ask him, although she'd have to admit she'd learned about his connection to the artist by secretly reading his journals the previous fall. That admission, however, would do nothing to endear her to him and they had a rocky relationship as it was. Best, perhaps, to remain ignorant.

As she stood there, staring into the subject's enigmatic eyes, her scalp prickled, an unmistakable sign of being watched. The halls thronged with tourists and locals taking advantage of the free admission. The Louvre had been free to all before the start of 1922. Now art was being reserved for the paying public except on Sundays. It seemed to Celeste a travesty to force people to cough up their hard-earned money to experience beauty.

She grounded herself and slipped onto the astral plane, keeping her eyes on the painting, as though deep in study. Scanning her surroundings, she discovered several magical energy signatures nearby, two that read as spellcasters of some sort and likely witches from either outside of Paris or one of the small start-up covens, and one that glowed like a ruby in firelight. One of the Fallen, and as she focused on it, she could sense the black oiliness that meant vampire. A zing of fear hit her. It wasn't that long ago she'd been in danger of being targeted by the vampire community. As she zeroed in on the energy, her shoulders sagged in relief. She knew this particular bloodsucker.

She spun, relief morphing into indignation, and hot-footed it toward the figure doing his best to appear like an innocuous tourist in a pinstriped, three-piece suit similar in cut and color to what Corverus had worn. The outfit was topped by a bowler, and the bastard had even hung an umbrella over his arm, like some damned British toff.

Which, as the sixth Baron Byron, he was.

He saw her coming, probably sensed her scrutiny with vampiric senses as well, and his features recorded the brief moment he considered vanishing into the crowd with the unnatural speed displayed by his kind, as well as the decision to stay and face her with an insouciant smile.

"Why, Celeste, my sweet! Fancy meeting you here."

She grabbed him by the sleeve of his bespoke suit and pulled him away from the milling crowd. "What the hell are you doing here?"

"Why, taking in some of the greatest art in the world. Whatever one says about Parisians, you cannot deny they are unparalleled geniuses at making away with masterpieces that rightfully belong to the cultures that created them."

She smacked his arm, and he winced dramatically, clutching the spot. "Zounds, you hellcat, you wound me!"

She hit him again, harder. "*This* is why you wanted a taste of my blood yesterday, isn't it? Not to feel the spring sun on your bloody fool head, but to follow me today. Damn you for a sneaky, lying bastard, George."

One of the greatest poets the world had ever produced, dead now nearly a hundred years, turned his most charming smile on her, full, cupid lips and sparkling blue-gray eyes full of mischief and mirth. "Sneaky I may be, but I am neither a liar nor a bastard. In fact, my reputation for speaking unpalatable truths earned me both respect for my work and the disapprobation of my personal life. No, I meant what I said. It is spring, and the sun feels like a benediction. You know it is one of the things I miss most about being mortal."

"You still tricked me." Her anger was fading, as it always did. Even as a boy, when she'd tutored him in Greek and Latin, he'd had a way of defusing her irritation at his boyish pranks like tossing spiders at her, his ten-year-old way of paying her tender attentions. "Why are you here?"

"Oh, come now, even a dolt should be able to figure that out."

"I'm not a child. Even Tolly didn't feel the need to have me followed. I met the man in a public venue in broad daylight. And I'm perfectly capable of taking care of myself."

His smile was cryptic. "He is a snake, and I trust him about as far as I do Desmond."

Something about that smile bothered her. He was keeping some bit of information from her. Another lie of omission. Had Tolly trusted her to come without an escort? Or had she instead gone behind Celeste's back and enlisted Byron?

"Well, the danger has long since passed, if there were any. So, you can go away, sit in the sun now, and leave me in peace."

"He could come back. Sneak up on you, and you, all unawares."

She put her hands on her hips and glared up into those oh-so-innocent baby blues. Vampires were hard to intimidate, and her five-foot two stature compared to his nearly six feet didn't help. But she'd known him when he was just a boy and some of that stern student-teacher bond still remained. "Go. Away."

He took on a hurt expression and raised his hands in capitulation. "Very well. Spurn me again. Stab me in the heart, as is your wont." His lips twitched as he fought a smile. "Just know that I am always but a heart-beat distant, awaiting word that you have need of me."

Now when she smacked him across the front of his double-breasted suit, it was with a groan of amusement. "Oh, stop. Thank you for your concern, but I'm fine."

He sobered. "He did follow you here. Or at least, he entered the museum shortly after you did."

That raised her hackles. *Had* Corverus been following her? Had he maybe drugged her wine and even now lay in wait for her to collapse? No, that was impossible, and she was being paranoid. The man had what he wanted; her guarantee, a signed contract registered with the Council, that she would join with him at Beltane during the Great Rite. There was no need to kidnap her, or even wine and dine her, as he had been trying to do since she and Tolly returned from their trip to Egypt a couple of months ago. "We met in the Tuileries. It's natural that he would come here while he was on the grounds."

"Still. If you're quite done staring at this portrait of an incredibly plain and ugly woman, I would be happy to escort you home."

"Not necessary. Besides, I have a couple of errands to run yet, when I'm done here."

"Then I could help carry your packages, like the good little lap dog that I am."

She snorted a laugh. "You only want in my lap for one reason, George. Besides, I thought you had a new lap to bury your head in. What about Martin?"

The expression in his eyes softened and his smile lost its usual cynical edge. The poet was beyond smitten. "Martin is like rain to the desert of my heart."

She felt a flush of warmth, of genuine happiness to hear him say that. He'd been miserable for so much of his life, mortal and other-wise, and to see him giddy with love for his unlikely paramour, a gargoyle who'd once been an angel but was now one of the Fallen, filled her with joy. "Then go back home. Make him a nice meal for when he comes down off his perch."

He waggled his eyebrows. "Have no fear, I'm quite capable of satisfying his hunger."

She clapped her hands over her ears in faux shock. "Enough! I say again, fie, fie! Away with you."

"Careful now, my sweet, your age is showing. No one says fie anymore."

She turned and walked away, calling over her shoulder. "And no one says zounds anymore either, smart ass. À bientôt."

———

The afternoon sun cast golden slanted rays through the trees as she strolled toward the Pont des Arts. She decided she'd make good on the imagined errands she'd created while talking to Corverus and check in with the booksellers, Mssrs. Allouard and Arsenault, as well as visit the butcher for a rabbit to cook for dinner. And maybe on the way home, she'd treat herself to a cup of coffee and a croissant at Cafe de Flore. After all, she'd visited the Louvre on a free day, and Corverus had paid for lunch, so she'd spent nothing so far. Plus, she'd walked everywhere, to save taxi fare. Just look at all the money she hadn't spent. Surely, Tolly couldn't object to one croissant.

She'd nearly reached the bridge when she heard the sound of running feet behind her.

"Mademoiselle! S'il vous plait!

A man jogging alongside a bicycle waved frantically at her. She paused, allowing him to catch up.

"Oh, thank you, merci." Gasping and perspiring, the young man, perhaps in his twenties, spoke in strangely accented English. He smelled faintly of healing magic, a floral fragrance underlaid by woody notes, characteristic of folk spells and backcountry belief systems. Probably an herbalist of some sort.

"Can I help you?"

"Please, yes, thank you." He reached into a knapsack in the basket of his bicycle and pulled out a rough, hand-drawn map. "I am looking for this place. A shop on the Rue de Visconti. I have been told they may have work for me there. I have been searching all the morning long, and I am lost." He ducked his head and smiled ruefully. "I am not so good with maps."

She took the cheap piece of paper he shoved at her, his hand lingering just for a moment on hers. His touch made her shiver, and he yanked back his hand, looking embarrassed.

"Pardon, Mademoiselle. Desolé."

He wasn't a pervert; she'd encountered plenty of lechers over her many centuries. It had likely just been an inadvertent touch, but she felt the zing of his natural magic, which he hadn't shielded. He might not even know he had it, since most trained spellcasters were taught from the first day of lessons to create barriers both to keep other's energies out and to keep their own in.

She made a note of the address written on the map so she could find him later. If he was untrained, it was her and Tolly's job to bring him into the coven, so he could be. She gave him a reassuring look. "You are not too terribly far." She pulled a fountain pen from her bag and, using a nearby bench as a desk, extended his map and added a few details to get him to the proper neighborhood. "You want to follow this street to the Pont des Arts. Once you are across, go right until you reach Rue Bonaparte, then left some distance and Rue Visconti will be on your left." She pointed at the original part of his map again. "It's a few blocks down from there."

"Oh, grand merci, Mademoiselle. I cannot thank you enough. Paris is … much bigger than I could ever have imagined. So many people. And so few who have the time to help a poor stranger from the country."

She smiled as he reclaimed the map and held it to his breast like it was the holy grail. "Of course. I was new to the city once, too. Welcome, and I hope the promise of employment works out for you."

He bowed and turned his bicycle toward the bridge. In moments, he vanished in the bustle of a golden Parisian spring afternoon. Something about him made her think of her own early years in a small Breton village on the coast, of the boys she had known, of the brothers she had grown up with. He was not so different from them, both in his backward speech and his awkward manners.

Well, he'd either find his place here or he wouldn't. While Paris was her favorite city in the world, it could, like all other cities, be cold and cruel, a fact she had learned the hard way in her first days in a metropolis hundreds of miles from home. And though the world was a very different place now, human beings hadn't changed much in the intervening 400 years. All she could do was wish him well.

———

A sign hung on the door to the bookstore of Mssr. Allouard and Arsenault, announcing they had closed early for the day. She stamped her foot in frustration, regretting it instantly as pain radiated up her calf and into her hip. She was tired and her whole body ached from having walked all this way. She'd wanted to do something nice for Tolly, and it had all been for naught. There had also been no rabbits at the butchers, so she'd wound up with an old hen instead, and she was heartily sick of chicken stew. She wanted nothing more than to flop down on a bench and take a nap.

She trudged toward home, too tired now even to enjoy a cup of coffee at the Cafe de Flore. Her head pounded, a pain increased by the sun, now glaring in her eyes as it dipped lower in the sky. She stripped off her pale blue cardigan as she trudged up along the Seine toward Le Boulevard de Sébastopol, suddenly sweating.

A block later, the sweats became chills. She stumbled to a bench, her legs shaking. She needed to sit, close her eyes against the stabbing pain in her head. Had the wine been too strong? Had the mushroom tart been off? Or had Corverus drugged her? If he had, she wished he'd come snatch her and take her somewhere she could lie down.

She could remember feeling this wretched only once before. London, 1665. A plague year for mortals, and the year she'd first come to that crowded, complicated city. But it wasn't just an illness for mortals that locked down the metropolis. Some magic user, no one had ever discovered who, had engineered a magical plague, one that only affected magical beings. It mimicked the pneumonic plague in every hideous respect. She'd entered the city on a Tuesday morning in August and had collapsed shortly after lunch, feeling just like this. If Chrisos hadn't found her, she'd have died.

Brigid help her, she couldn't have the plague now. If she'd had it since morning, she could have already infected Tolly. Or half the Magical Quarter.

The Seine, just a few dozen feet away, made a horrendous gurgling noise, and the crowds hurrying past her spun dizzily when she tried to open her eyes.

Someone bent over her. "Mademoiselle? Vous allez bien? Mademoiselle?"

The words echoed in her throbbing head. She squeezed her eyes shut against the slanting rays of the sun, and the world faded away for a moment. A blaring siren woke her from a doze, and men in white coats were lifting her onto a stretcher and strapping her down. She tried to protest, tried to make them go away, but they wouldn't listen. The doors of the ambulance slammed shut, and blessed darkness and quiet reigned. In that dim peace, thanking the Goddess that at least they'd be taking her to a mortal hospital where no one magical worked, she slid helplessly into a fevered sleep.

———

Thank you

Thank you so much for reading A Djinn and Tonic, the second book in the Magical Underground series.

If you enjoyed the book, I hope you will consider leaving a review. Reviews help readers find the next book to light their fire, and helps authors find readers who will love their books. Thanks in advance!

———

Excited to see what happens next to Celeste, Tolly, Lord B, and the rest of the folks in the Magical Quarter?
Turn the page for a sneak peek at the next book, That Old Plague of Mine, coming soon!

Books by Nan Sampson

Tales of the Magical Underground

Your Goyle and Mine

A Djinn and Tonic

That Old Plague of Mine (coming soon)

The Coffee & Crime Cozy Mysteries

Restless Natives

Office Heretics

Forest Outings

Fringe Benefits

Love & Larceny Historical Romances

The Christmas Caper

The Bonfire Night Plot

The Valentine's Day Deal

The New Year's Eve Assignment

The Harrogate Chronicles Steampunk Adventures

(Written with Susan Wachowski)

Atahualpa's Mummy

Teacakes & Kraken Bait (a novella)

Merlin's Tomb (coming December 2025)

Aztalan's Idol (coming spring 2026)

ABOUT THE AUTHOR

Nan Sampson has been creating new worlds and peopling them with quirky characters since she was old enough to hold a crayon. Convinced she was an alien, she spent her adolescence reading SF/F, watching Star Trek, and waiting for her real family to arrive in a spaceship to take her home. Since that didn't happen, she now happily lives through her fiction, where she can time travel, pilot spaceships, cast powerful spells, ride clockwork horses, and find magical macguffins, always finding love along the way. When forced to exist in the mundane modern world, she is an avid history nut, a terrible but earnest gardener, and consumer of many cups of tea and coffee. She likes to imagine she lives in Roger Zelazny's Amber, but it looks remarkably like the suburbs of Chicago. Who knew?

Sign up for her newsletter for info regarding new releases, fun historical facts, and the occasional scone recipe at www.nansampsonauthor.com . Or chat with her on Facebook www.facebook.com/nansampsonauthor.

www.ingramcontent.com/pod-product-compliance
Lightning Source LLC
Chambersburg PA
CBHW051331250626
47155CB00007B/2546